14

# EXILE'S RETURN

First Book of Elita

# EXILE'S RETURN

## First Book of Elita

## KATE JACOBY

VICTOR GOLLANCZ

LONDON

First published in Great Britain 1998
by Victor Gollancz
An imprint of the Cassell Group
Wellington House, 125 Strand, London WC2R 0BB

A catalogue record for this book is
available from the British Library.

ISBN 0 575 06527 3

Typeset by SetSystems Ltd, Saffron Walden, Essex
Printed in Great Britain by
St Edmundsbury Press Ltd, Bury St Edmunds, Suffolk

98 99   5 4 3 2 1

# Acknowledgements

My thanks to George Ivanoff, who first encouraged me to write this story. To Muther, Father, Michael, Peter and Rachael. They helped a lot. Leslie Gardner from Artellus and her fine judgement were a great help as well. To Ian, Kerri Valkova, Max, Karen Pender-Gunn and Annie. They helped too. Much help was also blessed in the form of Jo Fletcher of Gollancz. And Karen Mitchell who helped much more than she realized.

In the spring of 1341 a fierce and determined army crossed the border of Lusara intent on taking the country by the end of summer. Lusara, savaged by years of internal bloodshed between the Houses, could do little to halt the invaders as they marched east. Gathering their forces together, the loyal magnates fought a great battle on the fields of Nanmoor and while many died, no clear victory was won by either side. Weeks later, as dawn rose over Seluth Common, the armies faced each other again and this time there was no quarter called. By sunset, Lusara, the oldest of the Seven Nations and never before humbled by an invading army, was conquered.

Of her soldiers, many were killed on the field of battle. Some died from treachery while a few survived only to be executed at the hands of the conqueror. Still fewer lived to see the years that followed, and of those that did survive, most were old men or mere boys. With the king dead, the country taken and the greatest lords shackled by the conqueror, Lusara withdrew in upon herself, yearning only to survive. An uncomfortable peace settled on the country under the crushing rule of the conqueror. He, like all such men before him, believed the people were broken, their will destroyed. With no one left to challenge him, his victory was secure.

However, it was to be another man who would decide the true destiny of Lusara, a man who carried within him a terrible secret. But, as these things go at the hands of fate, Lusara's greatest hero was not to rise until many years after that last battle had been fought – and lost.

Excerpt from *The Secret History of Lusara*
Ruel

I know I am
the wanderer of all the ways of all the worlds
to whom the sunshine and the rain are one
and one to stay or hasten because he knows no ending of the way
no home, no goal

CHRISTOPHER BRENNEN

# Prologue

In a tiny cove on the southern coast of Lusara an old man
waited by the rocks for a signal. It was a black, bitter night
plagued by howling winds which drove the rain on to his
back and through his woollen cloak. His hands, wrapped up
against the cold, were thrust under his arms while he shifted
from one foot to the other to keep his blood moving.

The old man kept watch. His eyes darted from the cliffs
opposite to the inky blackness out at sea. But there was
nothing there, only the occasional white cap catching a
splinter of moonlight as the stormclouds tumbled across the
sky.

Though the fishing port of Aaran stood not half a league
away, his little cove was hidden by the wall of cliffs which
sheltered him from the worst of the wind. But while the
cliffs protected him, they could not prevent the coastal
patrol from riding this way – even on a night like this. And
they had been here once already, not long after dark. They'd
not seen the old man then, no – but they would be back.
And if they came when . . .

'Damn you, Dunlorn! By the gods, I hope you're out there
somewhere!' He hissed in a breath, pulled his hood about
his face, then began to chuckle. 'Well, Dalzie Kerr, you old
fool, now you're beginning to talk to yourself as well. Things
are getting bad indeed!'

Once again he squinted up at the cliffs. There was just
enough moonlight to be sure he was completely alone. Not
even the gulls were out tonight. There was no sign of the
patrol.

His eyes then scanned the ocean. It was like looking into
the pits of hell, where only the gods themselves could say
what demons dwelt there. But as he watched, the unbroken

gloom gave up a single, solitary offering. A bleak yellow lantern, almost invisible in the driving rain.

Without thinking, Dalzie started forward, leaving the shelter of the cliff. He stumbled across the sands to the water's edge. Gradually, a blacker, more solid form emerged before him. A boat.

As it came aground he reached forward to grab the bow. There were five or six men in the boat, one of whom jumped out and helped him hold it firm. Then a voice called out to him, shouting over the wind.

'Sorry to get you out in this weather! We would have been here hours ago but I think the ship's captain got lost!'

Dalzie knew that voice. In a moment of panic, he turned again to peer at the ridge. If that patrol were to return now, all would be lost.

Someone landed on the beach beside him and Dalzie caught sight of the young face, the sunny smile. Micah Maclean. He smiled, but Dalzie couldn't voice a welcome. Instead he turned back to the boat as a second figure jumped down. The man's face was shrouded by the hood of a raven-coloured cloak which seemed immune to the wind. Dalzie knew he should turn now and lead them up the beach to the cave. The boat was leaving; he heard the splash of oars and felt the bow lurch away from his hands, but still he could not take his eyes from the second man. Hope and expectation tumbled together inside him, leaving his stomach cold and unsettled. Hope was tainted by apprehension.

Then he heard a voice speak low and clear under the storm, a voice both familiar and forbidding at the same time.

'Come, old friend. Let us move.'

At that moment, the wind changed direction, lifted the side of the cloak hood. For just a brief second, Dalzie glimpsed a lean and weathered face.

He'd come back. After three years of self-imposed exile, Robert Douglas, Earl of Dunlorn had finally returned to Lusara.

Dalzie led them up the beach to the eastern cliff and the

cave he'd used many times over the years. He had food waiting and a brazier lit. Maclean dumped the bags on the floor and warmed his hands by the blaze, but Dunlorn remained outside, his back to the cave, his face towards the heavens.

From the shelter of the cave mouth, Dalzie watched him, not knowing what to do. Then the young Maclean joined him, his curly red hair dripping with rain. As he rubbed his hands and face with a slip of rough linen, Maclean said, 'Don't worry about him. It's just that ... well, he never thought he'd come back.'

Dalzie nodded slowly. 'Then he's not the only one. What will the King say? And the Guilde? The Proctor still wants your master's blood. Does Dunlorn think they will welcome him so easily back to court? Does he believe he can return to his favoured position? If he does, then he's mistaken. The Guilde will hound him to his grave the moment they know of his return. I should warn you too, there is still some talk about the death of his lady wife. By the gods, Micah,' Dalzie turned to the young man beside him, 'Dunlorn challenged the Guilde before the King and lost his seat on the council as a result. But there are still some who say that his hasty departure was more to do with the curious manner in which the lady died. Tell me, my friend, is Dunlorn blind?'

Maclean raised his eyebrows at that. With callused hands he smoothed the hair away from his face and replied with a shrug, 'My master is many things, Dalzie, but he is not blind. He has determined to have nothing more to do with the court or the Guilde. He believes they will be content to leave him be. As to Lady Berenice? You know my master and you know there's no truth in those stories.'

The old man knitted his brows together and only grunted. Caution drew his eyes back to the cliffs outside and the man who stood in full view of them. 'This is ridiculous,' he hissed, then raised his voice in competition with the storm. 'Come inside, my lord! The patrols could return at any minute!'

Dunlorn turned slowly, his face in shadow. Then he was

at the cave mouth, pulling the hood back, removing his cloak.

He had changed, Dalzie noted with little surprise. Dunlorn was still a young man, only twenty-eight, but it was sometimes difficult to remember he was not older. His dark hair was shoulder-length now, tousled by the wind. The straight nose, full mouth and firm jaw were animated by the faintest hint of a smile. That smile, however, did not reach to the cool green eyes which studied Dalzie. Dalzie shifted under such scrutiny, feeling more than a little uncomfortable. He remembered that gaze more precisely than anything else about the legendary Earl.

Dalzie jutted out his jaw and tried hard not to be intimidated. 'You had to choose a night like this, didn't you, my lord. You know how bad the autumn storms get. You could have drowned crossing the gulf. Why couldn't you wait until spring?'

Dunlorn rewarded him with a smile, abruptly changing his whole face. The deep lines which had been there moments ago vanished. In their place was the familiar easy charm, the quiet confidence Dalzie remembered. He moved further into the cave. 'Spring was not suitable. We'll need horses and supplies, Dalzie, if you can help us a bit more. I want to leave tomorrow. We have a long way to go if we're to cross the mountains before the first snow.'

'Of course,' Dalzie nodded absently. He moved closer to the brazier but didn't take his eyes from Dunlorn. 'You must know they won't leave you alone. Hatred is a bitter thing for the likes of Vaughn. And things have changed since you left.'

'How?'

'The Guilde has spread its Halls throughout the country. You cannot help but encounter them on your way back to Dunlorn. Every day their grip tightens on Lusara. The people will expect you to . . .'

'I know, old friend, I know.' Once again, Dunlorn smiled. 'But they'll have to expect help from somewhere else. I have already done all I can. What little I did do only made things worse. Do not fear, Dalzie, you will hear no more stories about me.'

Dalzie was not comforted at all, but as the wind beat across the cave opening, he turned his mind to hot food and wine and tried to forget the shadow around Dunlorn's eyes.

Outside, the rain thundered on to the beach. When the patrol passed by moments later, they were weary and wet and harassed by the storm. They travelled along the top of the cliffs with thoughts only of home and warmth and so did not notice the glow from the cave and never discovered who was hidden inside.

# 1

'Your Grace?'

Rosalind gave no sign that she'd heard, even though the voice had startled her. Other words, sinister and secret, still echoed in her mind. A whispered conversation overheard through the door behind her. A conversation she was never supposed to hear.

Numb with shock, Rosalind kept her eyes on the view from the window. The knotted garden below had paid the price of autumn. Servants swept along the rows of lavender, under the peach trees in the north corner and around the old well. Once teeming with a confusion of summer colour, the garden was now grey, its life sapped away into the cold earth. In a few weeks even the grey would be gone, wiped clean with the first snows of winter.

'I'm sorry to disturb you, Your Grace, but I came to look for you. There are but a few minutes before the reception and you are not yet dressed to meet the ambassador from Mayenne. You must not be late.'

Rosalind turned away from the window and folded her hands together. Years of harsh lessons learned at this unforgiving court kept her hands steady, her face calm. But stern-faced Camilla was waiting, Lady Camilla Murray; gentlewoman to the Queen – and spy for the King.

With an obedient nod Rosalind led Camilla down the passage. She didn't hurry, even though a voice inside her screamed to run before anyone came through that door and found her there. That same voice urged her to warn them, now, before it was too late. Tell someone, do something...

Who? Who could she tell? Who would listen to her?

It was a short walk to her apartments, a walk that gave her too little time to think, to plan. But who was she to trust? Certainly none of her ladies, nor even her Confessor. All those served Selar and her warning would be deemed nothing less than treason.

The fire in her dressing room was built up against the chill wind rattling the window casements. Camilla wasted no time, immediately bringing water for Rosalind to wash, a comb for her hair, the finest clothes for her to wear. She was diligent in the execution of her duties – all of them. If Rosalind gave the slightest sign that something was amiss, she would be lost.

She stood still as Camilla and the other ladies fussed over her. If only she had more time, more help. So much depended on her – and yet she had no one. Of course, Selar had arranged it so. Twelve years as Queen in name only. By the gods, even her friends had deserted her over the years. It didn't matter that she was born of the great House of MacKenna, was mother of the heir to the throne. She was nothing to this court, nothing more than a symbol of unity between Lusara and the man who had raped her country and stolen the crown. She was a traitor Queen, her son a bastard heir.

'Is my sister still with the children?' The words were out before she thought them through. But no matter, her instincts guided her – perhaps Samah could get word to somebody.

'Lady Samah is in the nursery, Your Grace,' Camilla replied with a frown.

'Will you ask her to join me for supper, after this reception?' Yes, that was it. Samah would not leave for her priory until tomorrow. She would have time to help before then. But could Rosalind endanger her with this?

'Certainly, Your Grace.' Finished with her work, Camilla stood back and held up a polished mirror.

Rosalind barely glanced at the mirror at first – then paused to take another careful look. At twenty-seven she was still young enough to be seen as an adornment. Her auburn hair shone with glints of gold, her hazel eyes retained the clarity of her father's gaze. She'd once been pretty, but

Rosalind felt those days were long gone. Now, perhaps, she was merely handsome and soon – soon she would be old and plain. But plain or no, she was still Queen and would hold herself with pride, impress upon this loathsome envoy from Mayenne the dignity which still dwelt within the hearts of all true Lusarans.

Even if it seemed the gods had finally deserted them.

*Sweet Mineah, help me through this. Help me face that man!*

With two of her ladies following, Rosalind descended through the castle until she reached the great hall. It was all but deserted since this first reception was to be a small gathering without the full court as witness. In silence, Rosalind passed under the heraldic banners hanging from the vaulted roof and paused before a carved ebony door. The guards on either side bowed and pushed the door open, then stood aside for her to pass. Respect for the crown she wore and nothing else.

There were a dozen men in the room beyond and all eyes turned to her as she entered. Almost the full council. Chancellor Dai Ingram, a small, mousy man, stood by the window, the Duke of Ayr, Tiege Eachern, at his side. A maternal cousin of Selar's, Eachern had followed him into the first battles of the conquest, distinguishing himself on the field as a ruthless and bloodthirsty warrior. Eachern's courtly clothes were of the finest quality, brutally at odds with his stocky neck and bullish head. With hair cropped close for battle, the Duke would never look anything other than what he was – in direct contrast to the man who stood beside him. George, Earl of Kandar, was Eachern's cousin but, with the exception of his grey eyes, looked nothing like him. Tall, fine and fair-haired, George was every inch the courtier – and the only person at court who treated Rosalind with any respect. But respect or no, Rosalind could never trust him with her secret. His whole career was bound up with Selar, his allegiance devoted.

And what of the two men who stood beyond the table? Duke Donal McGlashen and the young Earl Payne. These two were all that was left of the old order, the last of the great Houses of Lusara still represented on the council. They watched her with a mixture of kindness and wariness; their own positions were too tenuous to afford Rosalind any hope.

A swirl of bright yellow caught her eye and she turned towards the fire. There he was. Proctor Vaughn, resplendent in the formal robes of his beloved Guilde and with him, two of his governors, Osbert and Lewis. Vaughn's long, hawk-like face was creased in a smile but there was no warmth in there, merely the absence of soul. Rosalind felt nothing but repugnance and frantically tried to still the memory of those words he'd uttered behind that door.

Other men, richly attired, stood with Vaughn by the fire, but her attention was caught by Selar, who strode across the room towards her, a smile on his striking face.

'Rosalind, my dear, how kind of you to join us!' He took her hand and led her forward. 'Come, allow me to present my brother's emissary. His Grace, the Duke Ogiers, represents Tirone in these discussions and has travelled long and hard to do his duty.'

Stunned, Rosalind held out her hand to the Duke. He took it, bowed over it, brushed his lips across her fingers – but all the while, Rosalind couldn't take her eyes off Selar. Why had he greeted her so warmly? He'd hardly spoken to her over the last year! What game was he playing? Was she supposed to play along? And why . . .

'My dear,' Selar continued, taking her hand and tucking it in the crook of his arm, 'His Grace tells me he has brought gifts for us, you and my children. They arrive in his baggage train tomorrow. Do you not think that was most gracious of him?'

Yes, she was expected to play along. With a distracted nod, Rosalind produced a smile from somewhere, 'Yes, my lord. Most gracious.'

Selar led her to a seat by the fire but kept hold of her hand. Rosalind wanted to snatch it from him, demand to know what was going on. The others knew, Selar's councillors. Not one of them showed the slightest surprise. They must have been warned what to expect. But why?

It was all a show for Ogiers — for Tirone. Selar was Tirone's younger brother, but had despised him all his life. Blindly ambitious, Selar had made no secret of his desire to displace Tirone from the throne of Mayenne — which was why, when the opportunity came, Tirone had helped Selar to invade Lusara. With a new country to subdue and rule, Selar would stay out of Mayenne and leave Tirone alone. Once the conquest was complete, Tirone had severed all relations with his brother and a stiff silence had existed between them for the last thirteen years.

So why this sudden embassy? Why was Selar trying to impress Ogiers with this façade of a happy and united family? What was he doing? Would Ogiers believe it?

The discussions continued on around her but she couldn't concentrate on their words. Powerless, Rosalind sat there, her skin crawling in Selar's grasp. Now, more than ever, she must find a way to pass on what she'd heard.

Selar's voice intruded on her thoughts. She turned to look at him. His blue eyes were alight, his gestures animated. The cobalt robe he wore suited his blond colouring, his hair fashionably long, his beard neatly trimmed. The tallest man in the room, Selar dominated the conversation as he liked to dominate everything around him. His passion for power was surpassed only by his determination to achieve it.

'And so, my lord, do you have any news for us regarding these raiders?' Selar took the cup of wine Payne offered and raised it in mock salute. 'I must say, I was somewhat dismayed to find a Mayenne sergeant amongst their number. It was a pity the man died with the rest of his band. I had hoped to find out more about him.'

The Envoy's dark eyes glittered but he did not pause in his response. 'I have no concrete information, Sire. Without a name, we are unable to trace his origins. I would suspect he is nothing more than a deserter, seeking his fortune by means of these raids which plague your borders. I assure you my King will do everything within his power to find out all he can.'

'So I am not to believe the rumours I have heard?'

21

'Rumours, Sire?'

Selar took a sip of his wine, 'That these raids are the work of your King.'

Ogiers shook his head in confusion, 'To what end, Sire?'

'That he might bring about instability within my kingdom – in the same way the Troubles affected it fifteen years ago. It was that instability that let me conquer Lusara in the first place. Is it not possible that Tirone wishes to do the same to me now?'

His face frozen, Ogiers bowed stiffly. 'My King has no designs on your crown, Sire. My embassy here is, as I have said, primarily to extinguish all paths of misunderstanding between our countries. This has been his desire for several years but only now has Your Majesty permitted this visit. I assure you, my King wishes only peace between us.'

'An admirable desire,' Selar replied curtly, then softened it with a smile. 'To that end, I have decided to accede to his request on the matter of your embassy. You are indeed welcome to winter with us. When spring comes you may return to Tirone and assure him of our own desire for peace.'

'Your Majesty is most wise . . .'

For the third time that day, Rosalind was stunned into silence – only now desperate denial stung her every thought. It could not be. She must have misread Selar, must have missed something vital in their conversation. Was he actually going to allow Ogiers – his brother's spy – to winter within the walls of Marsay? What had come over him? And was this connected to what she'd heard earlier? Why even—

By the gods!

Selar was actually going to do it. After thirteen years, he was finally planning to go through with it. He must be mad!

He must be stopped.

Calmly now, Rosalind turned an attentive face towards the lords and listened carefully. She would find someone to tell, someone who could do something.

With treason in her heart, she could only hope her courage ran as deep as her horror.

*

The Guilde chapel fell almost silent as the last of the initiates filed out. In their absence, Osbert couldn't help glancing up again at the south transept window, which glowed with the first sunlight they'd had for a week. The stained glass told the story of Saint Bartholomew and his work with the poor and sick. The saint himself had never interested Osbert, but the window, now over a century old, was made of some of the finest glass he'd ever seen, a tribute to the Guildesmen who had crafted it. With a smile, he turned back to the priest who remained behind the altar, putting the last of the ceremonial plate away.

Deacon Godfrey was one of the few priests Osbert respected. By the age of thirty, Godfrey had worked his way to an enviable position within the Church, through hard work and not a little brilliance. His sharp dry wit was well known, as was his keen perception. He served the Church with a devotion not often found in these times; his tall, rangy figure was often to be seen at the side of the ancient Bishop Domnhall. But, much as he admired Godfrey, Osbert found it difficult to get to know him. Like most of the Church these days, Godfrey kept his distance from the Guilde.

With a brief sigh, Osbert glanced once more up at the window of Saint Bartholomew then turned towards the altar. 'I always forget how lovely they look until the sun comes out. A pity there's no way we can make the sun shine all the time.'

Godfrey shot a quick look at the window, then at Osbert. 'If you could, Governor, I fear you would soon grow accustomed to the beauty and then nothing would be left to draw your attention to it.'

Osbert chuckled companionably, drawing his yellow robes about him. 'You're right, of course. Still, it would be nice – if only for a while.'

'We do already have that while.' Godfrey gathered his things together and made to leave. 'It's called summer.'

Osbert nodded with a smile then raised a hand, 'I believe

Bishop Domnhall is unwell. Please pass on my wishes for his speedy recovery.'

Godfrey raised both eyebrows above his dark eyes. Obvious disbelief wafted across his long, grim face. His reply however, was polite, 'Of course, Governor. If you will excuse me.'

Osbert watched him leave and as the door closed behind the priest, he turned to his left. 'So, Gellatly, what have you got for me?'

Two men appeared out of the shadows, both dressed in the grey day robes of the Guilde. The first, a man whose build could have him confused with a blacksmith, bowed as he approached Osbert. The second man was taller and younger, with a head of shiny black hair. He remained in the background, folding his hands together in a patient gesture as he waited for Gellatly to speak.

'Unfortunately, my lord, we have very little. If there is anything going on, it's being done under the greatest of cover.' Gellatly shrugged his massive shoulders. 'Nash here disagrees but I doubt it will be possible to gain anything definite until the spring.'

'The spring!' Osbert exclaimed with a deep frown. Waving his hand for the men to follow him, he strode down the length of the chapel until they reached the door at the end. 'Have you any idea what the Proctor would say if I told him that? By the gods, Gellatly, Vaughn will have you flayed alive if he finds you at fault in this matter. I will accept no excuses, do you hear?'

'Yes, my lord.' Gellatly's response was little more than a growl and Osbert turned to face him.

'And I want to hear no more of your dissension over the King. I don't care if you do hate him, Gellatly. We still serve Selar, regardless.'

Gellatly stuck out his jaw. 'I was taught the Guilde's sacred duty was to serve the gods.'

'Don't start arguing semantics with me, man or I'll flay you myself!' Osbert snapped, his previous good humour gone. 'You're no good to me if you can't follow my orders.

Whether you hate the King or not, this matter affects the future of Lusara and it would do you good to remember that.'

Nash placed a hand on Gellatly's shoulder to forestall any further comment. He bowed his head with noble dignity and murmured, 'We do remember, my lord Governor. It is merely out of concern for Lusara's security that my friend speaks in this manner. He means no disrespect.'

Osbert's gaze narrowed as he looked from one man to the other. He knew he could trust Nash, but Gellatly was becoming a problem. Perhaps it was time to replace him. He nodded abruptly. 'See to it that it stays that way. There is something else I need you to do. Ogiers of Mayenne. He's to stay at court for the winter. For form's sake, the King has allowed it. But you must know he would rather Ogiers were anywhere else – and by his own choice. The King cannot send him away.'

Gellatly nodded. 'What would you have us do?'

'Use your imagination, if you have one!' Osbert snapped. 'Watch him, find out all you can of his real intentions. Report to me in two days. By then I may have worked out how to get rid of him. But use discretion, I warn you. I know Ogiers of old and he's no fool. If he finds you're watching him he's sure to make use of it.'

The two men bowed obedience and Osbert turned for the door. He had an appointment with Vaughn and he didn't want to be late.

Godfrey returned to the Basilica and spent a few minutes putting away the things from the Guilde chapel. He didn't hurry, there was still some time before the others would arrive and Father John would surely have the dining table set in Hilderic's study. He could change out of his vestments and be with Hilderic before the first guest.

He placed the plate and chalice inside the sacristy cupboard and locked it with the key hanging from his belt. Taking a taper, he lit two candles against the encroaching dusk and placed them on the robing table. He was about to remove the embroidered stole from around his neck when there was a brief knock on the door.

'Come.' Godfrey turned and waited, but nothing happened. 'Who's there?' he demanded.

Now the door opened and a woman entered, dark cloak drawn dramatically around her face. She came forward only far enough to close the door behind her then stood silent, her hands beneath the folds of her cloak.

His patience wearing thin, Godfrey took a deep breath, 'How may I help you, daughter?'

The voice beneath the hood was muffled. 'I am in need of confession, Father.' The hands reappeared and drew the hood back from her face. As she looked up at him, Godfrey sank to his knees.

'Your Grace! I had no idea! But why are you . . .'

'Forgive me, Father,' Rosalind whispered, taking an indecisive step towards him. 'I have very little time before I am missed. You are the only one I can trust.'

'But surely your Confessor is qualified to help you?'

Rosalind stopped him with a sharp shake of her head. Her eyes went back to the door and in response, Godfrey rose to his feet, moved around her and locked it. Her eyes smiled gratitude but her hands twisted together in agitation. She paced up and down a little then stopped and faced him again. Godfrey didn't need to be a priest to see she was deeply troubled.

'I see you wear the stole, Father,' Rosalind began, her voice hesitant. 'May I ask . . . can you hear my confession without it on?'

'Of course. It merely symbolizes the seal placed on your confession.'

'And if I do not wish my confession to be sealed?'

Her eyes searched his. What was she asking? Was this some kind of trap set by the King? No, Rosalind was Selar's prisoner – not his pawn.

Godfrey nodded slowly and crossed the room. He stood before her, his impatience gone. 'Your confession is as sealed as you wish it to be. If there is something you wish me to discuss with my brothers then you have only to say so.'

'Then I do say so, Father,' Rosalind replied emphatically. 'I am afraid that . . .'

She paused and Godfrey took her hands in his, willing her calm. 'Tell me, daughter. What troubles you?'

'I . . . I'm sorry, father, but this is difficult. I do not know if I am doing right coming to you like this. If the King should find out . . .' she paused again and took a deep breath. When she spoke this time, her voice was firmer, as though she'd finally made her decision.

'I have discovered something you must know, Father, but the conclusions I have drawn fill me with fear. I hope I am mistaken. Yesterday I overheard a conversation which directly concerns the Church.'

'Who was speaking?'

'Vaughn and . . . the King.'

Godfrey felt the breath sucked out of him. It was treason for her to be telling him – and treason for him to listen. But he didn't stop her. It had cost her a lot to come here. 'And what did you hear?'

'In return for some favour, the King has agreed to support Vaughn in a new enterprise. He . . . intends to take hospice work away from the Church. He says that such science belongs to the Guilde and has no place among the holy. Vaughn is quite determined, Father and it scares me. If they . . .'

'If the Guilde takes on this work, they will deny it to the poor for they would be unable to pay, yes, I know. They would also take away great amounts of Church land in the process.' Godfrey turned away, his mind reeling. Where had the traditional brotherhood gone between Church and Guilde? For a thousand years, the two had worked together, side by side for the common good. Now it seemed Vaughn was willing to sacrifice that ancient bond for his own ends. This was terrible!

'Do you know what the favour is? What did the King want in return for this support?'

27

'I was unable to hear clearly, but I fear it has something to do with the embassy from Mayenne. You know the Duke is to stay the winter in Marsay? I am unable to believe this is innocent, Father. It is not widely known but the King has always secretly desired to take back the throne he was cheated out of – that of Mayenne. I ... believe his decision to embrace Ogiers is purely to put Tirone at ease over their relationship in order that he might better prepare himself for war.'

Godfrey met her gaze. She was serious. She believed it with all her heart. The worst part was, it made sense – too much sense. If Selar intended war against Mayenne then taking Ogiers in and treating him with all honour would be a natural first step. Lull Tirone into a deeply false sense of security. Then, when the moment came, Selar could strike . . .

'But the King must know that the people of Lusara would never go to war for him,' Godfrey objected, clinging on to the first thread of logic that came to him. 'And certainly not to invade Mayenne.'

Slowly, Rosalind nodded, 'Yes, you must be right. I have misunderstood. He would not make so grave an error as that when there is so much at stake. But still, Vaughn is determined to succeed with the healing work. I beg you to tell Bishop Domnhall. He is the only one who can stop it.'

'And I will keep your name out of it, Your Grace. You have already risked much to tell me this. Now you must go, before you are missed.'

Rosalind actually smiled and for a moment, she was a young girl once again, untroubled by her fate and her future. Then it was gone, the hood replaced about her face. Godfrey opened the door for her and checked that the corridor was empty. In a second she was gone, leaving nothing but her scent.

Minutes later Godfrey was on his way to Hilderic's study.

He was late and the old man favoured him with a frown as he slipped into the room. The others were already present: McGlashen, Payne and the stalwart abbess of Saint Hilary's,

Eluned. Mumbling apologies, Godfrey drew the archdeacon into a corner and, in a few moments, apprised him of what Rosalind had said.

Hilderic's eyebrows shot up. 'You can't be serious! Dammit, Godfrey, if this is one of your jokes . . .'

'It is no joke, Brother,' Godfrey whispered, his eyes darting back to the others. Eluned could be trusted – but the lords? Did they already know? Would they help? 'At least my friend's conclusion about war is misplaced. We are to be spared that.'

'Really?' Hilderic murmured, attaching his formidable mind to the problem. 'McGlashen was just telling me about the problem with these nomadic raiders stirring up trouble in the west. They're moving east and no one knows anything about them. It is said they come from Mayenne but there's no proof. If Selar wanted a war with his brother then this would be a useful way to gather support from the people.'

Godfrey considered that for a moment then shook his head. 'This is nothing more than speculation, Brother. We could be completely wrong. We've no evidence at all . . .'

'No? Think about it, Godfrey. There was only ever one man who was a good influence on Selar, but he's gone now and never likely to come back. If Selar wanted war, who better to help him than Vaughn? He's ambitious, greedy and entirely self-serving. He's completely capable of arranging these raids as a deliberate reminder of those during the Troubles. From what McGlashen says, these raids are very similar to those fifteen years ago. Back then there was barely a House in Lusara which didn't suffer as a consequence. Raids and those evil abductions. Children of the great Houses taken and never seen again. McGlashen's cousin Peter was one such – taken when he was only four years old. The child's father died in the battle of Nanmoor fighting Selar, and his mother in childbirth only months later. Don't tell me Selar can't be behind this.'

'Then what do we do?'

'For the moment, nothing – and not a word to these others here. We don't dare compromise McGlashen and

Payne. Their presence on the council is too important. The people have already lost their most beloved champion, we cannot afford to lose more. After we've finished here, I'll go and see Domnhall. After that...' With a shrug, Hilderic turned back to his supper guests and ushered them to their seats around the table.

Godfrey moved to the sideboard and poured himself some wine. As he brought it to his lips, there was an urgent knock on the door. Hilderic's secretary, Father John, entered breathless, his eyes casting about the room.

'Archdeacon,' he gasped, bowing quickly to the others. 'The doctor asked me to send for you. Bishop Domnhall has collapsed.'

Nash waited across the courtyard, wrapped in a old wool cloak. In the darkness he knew he was almost invisible unless someone looked directly at him. Not that anyone was about. It was a cold night and for the last hour light drifts of slushy snow had fallen from the sky, making the night altogether too miserable to contemplate. This was the first snow Marsay had had this autumn and it boded ill for the coming winter. With his eyes on the small ornate door opposite his sheltered corner, Nash let his mind wander for a moment. Inevitably, his thoughts returned to Gellatly – and Osbert.

He had a problem. It was not insurmountable – but it was a problem, nonetheless, one which required delicate handling and very careful timing. Gellatly had that afternoon once again drawn Osbert's wrath on the subject of the King. The governor's attitude had been stern but even so, was more generous than the official Guilde position. However, Gellatly had obstinately stuck to his strict moral code, endangering his position with Osbert – and handing Nash a singular opportunity.

To further his ambitions, Nash needed to rise. Not quickly – at least, not too quickly. In order to get close to Osbert, and therefore Vaughn, he had to remove Gellatly. A small step in his schemes, perhaps – but a necessary one. But there were difficulties. For one, Nash could not afford to involve himself in the eyes of the Guilde, and so his actions needed to be subtle. Then, of course, he had to ensure there was no real danger to the King. It would not do after all these years of work for Nash to remove the one person he needed most – especially by accident. Especially if . . .

Nash paused – then a slow smile spread across his face. There was a chance here for him to take more than a single step forward. In all his plans he had avoided the temptation to jump too far ahead of himself. He'd made that mistake before and suffered for it. He'd lost too many years by acting precipitously. But this time, there was the distinct possibility that he could do so without genuine risk. As long as his methods remained subtle, there was every chance he would succeed. Of course, it all depended on Gellatly. It all depended on how much he really hated Selar – and on how much he trusted Nash. And in the process, he could give Osbert and Selar exactly what they wanted. Yes!

As though on cue, the big man chose that moment to slip through the ornate door opposite. He paused long enough to pull his hood up against the snow, then made his way across to Nash.

'Well?' Nash enquired quietly.

'Hah!' Gellatly frowned and glanced around at the empty courtyard. 'The monsters would annihilate us all if we gave them the chance.'

'Ogiers?'

'Not just him or his puffed-up advisors,' Gellatly growled, 'but all of those heathens from Mayenne. You can't get away from them. They've worked their way not only into the court, but the Church and even our beloved Guilde. Pretty soon, we'll have nothing left. All the things that made our country great are now riddled with them, like maggots on a dead dog. And the carrion of Sadlan and Tusina hover over our borders waiting to pick over the corpse!'

Nash kept his voice soothing. 'That's dangerous talk, my friend. But come, let me buy you an ale before you get yourself all agitated. There's a new tavern opened up down in the town. I hear their ale is the best in Marsay.'

31

He put an arm around Gellatly's shoulder and drew him away. 'Come. You can tell me all about it.'

The great hall was packed with courtiers, merchants, clergy and Guildesmen for the first official presentation of the envoy from Mayenne. He had gifts to give, good wishes to impart and there was hardly a soul at court who did not desire to be present for this historic occasion.

Godfrey made his way through the press of people with polite but firm resolve, moving to the right side of the platform where Hilderic stood. As he gained the Archdeacon's side, Hilderic glanced dryly at him.

'You took your time. I thought you'd be too late.'

Godfrey shrugged, 'He had a lot of questions. What was I to say? Sorry, Bishop – I have a banquet to attend?' He took his gaze from the bustling throng waiting below and turned it on the old man beside him. Hilderic was shorter than Godfrey, with a square stocky face which matched his build. The tonsure he'd once worn as a monk had now disappeared, along with most of his hair. All that was left was a narrow band of grey steel which matched his eyes. Hilderic was old, but by no means frail. Despite the differences in their ages, the two men had become close friends over the years, although few would guess at it to hear them talk.

Formidable in his knowledge of Church law and custom, Hilderic had been instrumental in keeping the Church together as Domnhall's ill health suspended much of his work. With the traditional alliance between Church and Guilde in tatters around their feet, that work was growing more difficult by the day. Godfrey had worked alongside Hilderic, taking as much of the administrative burden from his friend's shoulders as he could. Still, it often didn't make any impression on Hilderic's mood.

With a grim frown, Hilderic murmured, 'And how is he?'

'Still lucid, although his attention drifts from time to time. I told him you'd visit this evening, after these ... festivities. He still knows nothing of the matter we discussed. I don't know when he'll be well enough.'

'Then pray, brother. Not only for his sake, but for ours. We need him more now than at any other time.'

Godfrey nodded but was prevented from saying anything else by the appearance of Selar at the huge double doors at the end of the hall. Along with the rest of the court, Godfrey bowed deeply as Selar progressed towards the throne. Beside him was his gentle Queen, Rosalind. She wore a gown of sea green laced with gold thread. As he straightened up, Godfrey's heart went out to her. She was too young to be so ill-used. Rosalind held her head high and, as always, moved at Selar's side with grace and dignity.

The man beside her walked with a different kind of dignity – one born of power. The King had chosen his clothes carefully: a sky-blue cape lined with white fur over a long tunic of crimson and gold tied in with a low belt of jewelled blue kidskin. He wore a sumptuous gold circlet on his fair head, decorated by small rubies. A heavy brow shadowed his bearded face but the eyes deep in their sockets had not softened over the years. At forty-two, Selar's tall, solid figure towered over his Queen and was still powerful enough to command respect where none knew of his reputation for ruthlessness.

Godfrey kept his eyes dutifully on the King as he took his throne, then glanced around the hall once more. There was a full Guilde presence in the traditional place by Selar's right hand. Vaughn looked like he would rather be somewhere else, continually brushing a strand of thinning grey hair back from his eyes. Eachern, Kandar and other councillors flanked the throne. As one they turned to face the door where Ogiers of Quels was making his entrance.

Was it possible that it was Tirone and not Selar who was responsible for those raids? If Tirone meant Lusara ill then surely the best way to disengage suspicion would be to send one of his most trusted and respected advisors. That man would also be able to report back to Tirone on the strengths and weaknesses of Lusara, of Selar. This envoy could be the bringer of war on both sides of the border.

If so, it was unlikely Ogiers knew anything about it. His

reputation spoke only of his honour, his courage and his skills at peacemaking. He had been solely responsible for re-opening the northern trade routes between Mayenne and the war-loving nation of Sadlan. The effort had taken him five years – and none too few grey hairs.

Ogiers had brought his gifts and now had them laid out before the dais. He stood to one side as a chest of rare Alusian crystals was displayed. In response, Selar had risen from his throne and was even now reaching down to touch them.

Suddenly there was a flash of movement from the other side of the hall and a roar of rage. Godfrey turned in time to see a yellow-clad figure lunge towards Selar, the glint of steel in his hand. There were cries of horror as people backed away, but Godfrey found his feet taking him forward. The man raised his hand to strike at the King, who, shocked at this outburst, had no time to move. Abruptly another man lunged forward, placing himself between the King and the knife. There was a scream of pain and the attacker fell slowly to the floor.

For a second nobody moved. Then Godfrey fell to his knees beside the fallen man. Blood oozed out of a gaping wound in his chest but his eyes were full of nothing but sorrow. With his last gasping breath, the attacker grabbed hold of the trium which hung on a chain around Godfrey's neck. Then he fell back, dead.

'Who the devil is he?' Selar was demanding. 'Vaughn? He's wearing Guilde colours! What's the meaning of this?'

The Proctor pushed his way through the crowd and stared distastefully at the bloodied corpse. 'His name is Gellatly, Sire, and I have no idea what he intended.'

'Well, it's damned obvious what he intended,' Eachern snapped, bending down to take the knife from the dead man's hand. 'He intended to assassinate his King! Are you going to tell us you knew nothing about this?'

Vaughn opened his mouth but no words came out. He shut it again, took a deep breath then said, 'I do not like your tone, my lord. Are you accusing me of treason? If so, may I remind you that it was also one of my own men who saved His Majesty's life – while you stood idle. Perhaps this is some scheme of yours.'

'Enough!' Selar blasted at them both. With a thunderous frown, he glared at the faces of those gathered around, finally landing on a man who stood silently beside Governor Osbert – the man who had saved his life. 'You. What's your name?'

The man bowed deeply, 'Nash, Sire. Samdon Nash.'

Selar's gaze narrowed, 'Well, Samdon Nash, it seems I owe you my life.'

'No, Sire. I did nothing more than my duty.' Nash was the picture of calm, his eyes downcast before his sovereign.

'More than these other incompetents,' Selar jerked his head. 'Do you know this man?'

'Yes, Sire.'

'You do?' Selar took a step forward, his eyes level with Nash. 'Then you knew he was going to do this? Come, speak up, man.'

Nash raised his eyes and held Selar's gaze. 'No, Sire, I did not know what Gellatly intended. However, I cannot say I was surprised when I saw him move. I suppose that's why I was able to react so quickly.'

'And why were you not surprised?'

At this, Nash glanced first at Vaughn and then at Osbert. When Osbert nodded, he replied, 'It was no secret that Gellatly did not hold the greatest love for you, Sire. Only a few days ago, when he was speaking to His Grace the Duke of Quels, Gellatly repeated that he would love to see you lose your throne. I'm sorry, Sire, but I had no idea he was that serious. I would have said something otherwise.'

'Yes, I'm sure you would,' Selar hissed. He turned very slowly until his eyes landed on his brother's envoy. Ogiers' smooth composure was noticeably shaken and his eyes widened as they read the unspoken question in Selar's eyes.

With great dignity, Ogiers drew himself up, 'If you wish to involve me in your domestic squabbles, Your Majesty, then I suggest you say so openly. Otherwise, with your leave, I shall withdraw.'

'Oh, believe me,' Selar intoned menacingly, his eyes glinting in the candlelight, 'you have our leave. And you can tell my brother that he will have to try much harder next time.'

Ogiers stiffened, his jaw jutting out in defiance. Without a word, he turned and stalked out of the hall, his retinue trailing behind.

Forgotten in the argument, Godfrey now rose to his feet. Selar glanced at him then jerked his hand towards the body. 'Get that thing out of here – and clear this room!'

With a final bellow to Vaughn and his council, Selar strode away. The crowd around the body began to break up and soon Godfrey was one of the last remaining. Hilderic joined him, his face pale and ashen, but it was the Queen who drew Godfrey's attention. Cursing himself, he moved quickly to her side.

'Your Grace, please allow your ladies to take you away. You should not have seen this.'

The Queen tore her gaze away from the body. She looked shocked but her voice was steady as she said in a whisper, 'Father ... I can't help it. Why did he do it? What would make him ... he must have known he would be stopped.'

Godfrey took her hands in his, dropping his voice until it was audible only to her. 'Who knows what makes a crazy man act? But you, daughter,' he added pointedly, 'must not be sorry he failed.'

She met his gaze for a moment then nodded slowly, the briefest hint of a smile gracing her sweet face. 'Oh, Father, I would that you were my Confessor. You chide so gently.'

'I do so for love and care of your immortal soul, daughter. The gods bless you where you least expect it. But please, leave now.'

She nodded and turned away. Gathering her ladies together, she left.

Godfrey turned back to Hilderic as three soldiers lifted and carried Gellatly's body out of the hall. The two priests stood alone as a great silence descended like a shroud. In his mind, Godfrey saw again that moment when Gellatly had lunged forward. Now he could remember the look on the man's face – a look of pure hatred. Nash had been diplomatic to say the least – a rare talent these days.

With a sigh, Godfrey looked to his friend, 'I must say, I'm glad the Bishop didn't keep me any longer than he did. I would have hated to have missed all this fun.'

Hilderic's eyes rose heavenward. 'Oh, stop it, Godfrey! I've never been able to understand your twisted humour.'

'Perhaps not, Brother,' Godfrey replied amiably, 'but sometimes, I fear the joke is on me.' Taking the Archdeacon's arm, he walked across the open space towards the door. 'This will be the first time in my life that I will do penance for sharing the wishes of a Queen.'

# 2

There was no doubt about it – he was stuck.

The tree was sturdy but Micah had now climbed so high that its branches were lighter and their strength questionable. Pine needles rustled under the strain of his weight while the bough beneath his feet groaned in protest. With growing alarm, he cast about for a surer hold, careful not to crush the eggs nestled under his padded tunic.

He grabbed a handy stump which jutted out from the trunk then shifted his feet in order to gauge the next step down. But it was no use. The only way he could reach the lower branch was to slide down with his stomach against the trunk – and thereby crush the eggs he'd climbed to collect.

Micah glanced down. His master stood beneath him, adjusting the load on the pack horse. With a sigh, Micah attempted to address the question that had been tossed up to him with such ease. 'To be honest, my lord, I really don't know.'

Dunlorn glanced up with raised eyebrows. 'You don't know? You've had three years to think about it, Micah – surely you must have some idea how your family is going to react to your sudden return. They will have missed you – especially your mother.'

'Aye,' Micah nodded without enthusiasm. 'My mother will also have been busy, I'm sure, making sure my sisters are properly married and keeping an eye on my brothers. She was never able to quite get the idea that they were grown up and could look after themselves. Apart from anything else, I'm sure I must have an army of nieces and nephews who know nothing of my existence.'

'One of the trials of being the youngest child?'

'With five brothers and two sisters at home I seriously wonder if they've even noticed I've gone!'

Dunlorn turned back to the horse with a chuckle. 'Oh, I think they'll have noticed. And your father?'

Micah turned his gaze to the tree-top above him, ignoring for a moment his uncomfortable predicament. It was all very good wondering how the rest of his family would take his return – but Micah already knew with heartfelt certainty how his father would react. By now it was entirely possible that his father had formally disowned him. His stomach sank at the thought. If it wasn't for that, he could immerse himself utterly in the joy of returning home.

Dunlorn interrupted his reverie, 'I'm sorry, Micah, but just what are you doing up there?'

'Getting supper, my lord.'

'Supper? But it's still morning.'

Micah took hold of the trunk once more and turned outwards. Shuffling his feet along the branch a little, he strained his neck trying to see the other side of the tree. 'Eggs,' he said.

'At this time of year?'

'Aye. The grey-eyed flosson lays its eggs in early autumn.' Micah's words were punctuated with gasps and grunts as he lowered himself to a sitting position. From there he tried to reach the nearest branch, which was tantalizingly close. 'Actually, I was lucky to find them. They don't normally nest this far south.'

'Oh. So why are you still playing around up there?'

At this, Micah paused in his struggles and looked down at his master. 'Your assistance would be better served by securing me a way down rather than spending time—'

'Asking stupid questions?' Dunlorn laughed. Placing his hands on his hips, he added, 'I would like to help you, Micah, but as you can see, I don't seem to have a ladder about me and we're leagues from the nearest village. Can't you just come down the way you went up?'

Micah gritted his teeth, but his patience was wearing as

thin as the branch he sat upon. 'If I could do that I wouldn't be stuck.'

'No, I suppose not.' Dunlorn's smile faded as he glanced around the forest floor for inspiration.

Watching this futile gesture, Micah reached a hand into his tunic to check the eggs. 'Well, can't you do something, my lord?'

'What do you suggest?' Dunlorn looked up again, spreading his arms wide in helplessness, but unable to suppress a chuckle.

Micah sighed and leaned his head back against the tree trunk. At this rate, he'd be spending the entire day up this tree. 'I'm wounded you find so much merriment at my expense, my lord,' he said with as much dignity as he could muster.

'Look,' Dunlorn began, his tone practical, 'there's a branch there, just behind the trunk. You can't see it but if you put your foot to the left ... no, the other foot ... yes, that's it. Now let go your hands.'

Micah did as he was told, his foot searching out the supporting limb – and felt nothing. In a panic he tried to regain his hold on the branch above but missed. With a sickening lurch, he fell like a stone, landing flat on his stomach, pine needles pricking his face. He lay there for a moment, forcing air back into his lungs. As his head cleared he felt a cold, cloying wetness spread through his shirt and across his skin.

'Are you hurt?' Dunlorn knelt beside him, all humour gone.

'No.' Opening his eyes, Micah pushed himself up, taking the hand Dunlorn held out to help him to his feet. Gingerly, he reached inside his tunic and brought out a piece of sticky egg-shell. 'I'm afraid, however, that supper will have to take some other form.'

'I didn't know you knew so much about birds.'

'Neither did I,' Micah replied, fishing the remains of the eggs out of his tunic. 'Not until I'd had salted beef for the

40

sixth day in a row. It's amazing the things you remember when you have to.'

With a raised eyebrow, Dunlorn replied, 'And the things you forget. Come on. Let's take a proper look at this forlorn little country of ours.'

Leaving the horses in the copse, Micah followed his master through the trees to the base of a nearby hill. A fragile breeze drifted through the tree-tops behind him but despite the chill, it felt more like spring than autumn. The slope above them rose steeply to a clear blue sky and Micah grinned as he began climbing the hill. Rocks and pebbles skittered down under his feet but he grabbed tufts of wet grass and made steady progress until, with a last lunge, he gained the top.

The view was breathtaking. Ancient hills topped with scrawny trees crowned the wide valleys, populated with clusters of farms and villages. It mattered not that the country was gripped by the onset of winter, rather, it gave the land a crisp beauty. From the windswept downs in the west to the smoky shadowed mountains in the east, the country was bathed in a blanket of golden sunshine.

As the breeze tossed the cloak about his legs, Micah turned to take in the rest of the magnificent view. Facing north, the mountains seemed closer as the range curved west. It would take them two more days to reach the foothills. And before the mountains, beyond the copse below them, was the forest.

His gaze dropped to the dark living mass of Shan Moss spread out before him. It was the largest and, to his mind, most beautiful forest in the country. Now, in the middle of autumn, Shan Moss was bathed in a furnace of colour and stretched from his far left, across the downs and right up to the foothills of the mountains themselves.

It didn't seem like three years. Not now.

Micah turned to his master. Dunlorn stood beside him, gazing at the view, his expression – as always – entirely unreadable. What thoughts were hiding behind that mask? What questions was he asking himself that he would never voice aloud?

Was Dunlorn perhaps wondering whether they would leave him alone after all?

Micah had known this man almost all his life, had served him, worked and fought alongside him and followed him on his self-imposed exile. But even after all this time, Micah could not honestly say that he understood the man, that he really knew what drove him, why he had taken a seat on Selar's council in the first place – and most especially, why Dunlorn had dropped everything and, in the middle of the night, taken his leave of Marsay, Selar and Lusara.

Oh, Micah had his theories. Robert was a man of immense intelligence and was a natural – if reluctant – leader. To many, his outward calm, his confidence and charm bespoke a greater inner peace, but Micah knew better. Whatever belief Robert had held in his own abilities had slowly crumbled as he saw himself fail again and again to contain the excesses of the King, to restrain Vaughn and the Guilde. And failure – his own failure – was the one thing Robert could not forgive. Honour and truth were not merely words to him. They were alive, in his very blood. Admitting that failure and accepting the consequences was something that had changed him deeply. His honour alone would demand he remove himself from the field of battle.

That, at any rate, was what Micah believed. He was fairly certain that if he ever asked the question outright, he would get a straight answer. But Dunlorn had never volunteered the information and Micah believed there was a good reason behind that. Reasons that ran deeper and drew more blood with each telling. Micah knew the facts: the argument with the King, the battle with Vaughn. In fact, Micah probably knew more than anyone else. But the one thing he had never done – and would never do – was to ask why.

It did nothing to relieve his curiosity – a trait his master often made light-hearted fun of. But Micah didn't mind – and after all, his curiosity had saved their lives on a couple of occasions.

'Well, what do you think of it?' Dunlorn asked quietly, turning a gentle smile on him.

42

Micah grinned. 'It feels good to be back.'

'You've missed it so much?'

'Yes and no,' Micah shrugged. 'I'll confess there were moments over the last three years when I wished I'd never asked to go with you.'

'Like that night in Cartha,' Dunlorn added evenly, 'when you overturned a cartload of the Emir's favourite wine and were chased out of town by a brigade of his finest?'

Micah felt his face colour and he looked away. 'As I said – there were moments. But for the most part, no, I'm glad I went along. Missing home was never so bad that I was sorry I left.'

'And your father?' Dunlorn queried softly, turning back to the forest. 'You know, Micah, you haven't mentioned him once in three years. You've talked about everyone else at great length – but not him. I'm sorry to be the cause of that.'

'No, my lord!' Micah shook his head vigorously. 'It's not your fault my father will not forgive me. My decision to serve you was mine alone – as was the decision to leave with you. My father chose to forbid it. It was not your doing.'

'No?' Dunlorn glanced sideways at him, an eyebrow raised in irony. 'Even though he believes that I am a traitor? That the moment I befriended Selar, took a seat on his council, your father, along with many others, believed I had betrayed my country? No, Micah, I fear I am very much to blame. In his eyes, my treachery has tainted you. I only hope that with your safe return he will be able to find it in his heart to forgive me and welcome you.'

Micah frowned. Could that possibly be the reason why Robert had decided to return to Lusara? Because of that? It was inconceivable!

Taking a deep breath, Micah began to ask – but before he could, Dunlorn smiled. 'There are a number of reasons why I decided to come back, Micah.'

'I wish you wouldn't do that,' Micah shook his head.

'Do what?'

'Don't change the subject, my lord. You know what I'm talking about.'

Dunlorn shrugged. 'Would it be so bad if your father was the reason why we returned? Am I not allowed to give you anything in return for your loyalty? You undervalue yourself, my friend. Oh, I admit there are indeed many reasons why I decided to come back. Of course, things have changed and I might end up regretting the decision completely. Who knows?'

Micah nodded and took a deep breath. 'And do you think, my lord, that perhaps Dalzie Kerr might not be right? He said things had changed for the worse. Perhaps the King will not be willing to leave you in peace.'

'I think,' he said eventually, 'that Dalzie and the rest seriously overestimate my importance to Selar.'

'But you were once the closest of friends.'

'Yes, but that was a long time ago. And besides, I've been away, completely out of their sight for more than three years. My deeds, my purpose and influence will have long been forgotten. The King, the Guilde and all the others will have more things to occupy them than worrying about me.'

Micah glanced sideways at him. 'And just to make sure, you arrive on the very threshold of winter so they have a good four months of bad roads and terrible weather before they can even approach you at Dunlorn.'

'Exactly.' Robert nodded and flashed him a smile.

'And what about the rest?' Micah asked before he could stop himself.

'The Enclave?' Dunlorn shrugged lightly. 'I think they'll consider themselves well rid of me. That, at any rate, is what I hope.'

He took one last look at the view, then said, 'Let's move on. We'll go into the forest from here. If I remember correctly, there's an old ruin to the north we could shelter in tonight. If the gods are with us, I may even be able to find it.'

Finnlay was definitely not having a good day. In fact, if he stopped to examine the last week, there would doubtless be some kind of pattern forming. Not that he had time really to stop at all – darkness was little more than an hour away and after travelling for the better part of two days, he now accepted the unpleasant fact that he was quite hopelessly lost.

The forest around him squeaked and twittered in autumn harmony – and gave absolutely no indication of which way he should turn next. To Finnlay's tired and frustrated eyes, every tree, every copse, every valley of this damned demesne looked exactly the same – and had done for the last forty-eight hours. He guessed he was heading south – roughly, but even with the autumn fall of leaves, it was difficult to see the sun through the forest canopy, and even harder to guarantee that his course remained southerly. For all he knew, he'd been going around in circles.

He came to the edge of a gentle drop in the forest floor. Below him was a natural clearing with a narrow stream flowing through the middle. It looked as good a place as any. Turning his horse down the slope, however, it stumbled and, regaining its balance, came up lame.

'Well, that's just perfect!' Finnlay snapped, jumping down from the horse. He led it carefully down to the clearing then bent to examine the leg. The grey gelding's near front hoof was tender to the touch but not badly injured. Finnlay straightened up and looked the horse straight in the eye. 'If I didn't know better, I'd say you did that deliberately.'

He turned to the stream and dug around a bit to find some clay mud and moss. Packing it into his palms, he smeared it over the horse's hoof and up towards the knee. The compress would reduce the swelling and with any luck, by morning Finnlay could be on his way again. But . . . on his way where?

He looked around the clearing then back up the way he had come. Even from here, he could only just pinpoint where the sun was and soon it would disappear behind the rise and an evening chill would descend. He should have begun building a fire – but he didn't. Instead, he found the nearest log and sat down to think.

When he'd left Arlie and Martha yesterday morning,

they'd been travelling almost due east towards Solmoss. Now, if Finnlay had turned south at that point and kept in a near straight line, then surely by now he would be close to the southern border of Shan Moss. Of course, if he'd not gone in a straight line he could be just about anywhere! And it was entirely his own fault. Arlie had warned him about the forest but Finnlay had been so sure about that touch – so certain . . . of course, he had mentioned nothing to Arlie and Martha about it. It would not do to get them all excited over what could turn out to be nothing. When he'd left them to travel to the Gathering on their own, Finnlay had merely told them he had something he needed to take care of and that he would rejoin them later. In his haste, he had hardly noticed where he was entering the forest, nor which direction the maze of hills and valleys would take him.

Then the touch had gone – and no matter how hard he'd tried, he'd not been able to resurrect it. So now the question was, had he imagined it? Or, despite all logic and sense, had his brother really come back? Was he somewhere in this damded forest, on his way home? Or was he still wandering the lands of the southern continent, determined never to return to Lusara?

Finnlay glanced up at his horse as it stood silently by the stream edge. 'Why don't you Seek him out, eh? If I told you what he looked like, could you find him?'

It was, of course, pointless talking to the horse but – suppose he'd been right. Suppose, for one moment, Robert was somewhere in Shan Moss, that he'd come back and was even now, close enough for Finnlay to find him. Would that make it any easier for Finnlay to convince him? There was no certainty at all that Robert would even speak to him.

With a sigh, Finnlay played idly with the twigs in his hands. Marcus was dead. There was no getting around that. Marcus was dead and the Enclave needed a new leader. Even now they were all gathering together in preparation for Standing the Circle. Arlie and Martha were getting closer by the day – and that was exactly what Finnlay should be doing right now instead of chasing his tail in a cold and friendless forest, looking for a brother who was probably not even there.

But he'd had to try. With Marcus gone, Finnlay knew the Enclave was in deep trouble. Now more than ever they needed a strong leader – and when he'd felt that touch, the touch of his brother's presence two nights ago, he'd had no choice but to follow it. If he could just find Robert and convince him to Stand the Circle then perhaps, after all this time, the Enclave would finally be able to fulfil its destiny. It was too much of a coincidence: Marcus dying ten days ago – then Finnlay finding Robert (it seemed) back in Lusara. Surely the gods had intended it – surely it was time for Robert to put aside his objections to the Enclave and join them fully. Surely . . .

Surely the last person Robert would ever listen to was his younger brother. No, Finnlay sighed again, and came to his feet. This was a hopeless quest. In the morning, when his horse was better, he would climb the nearest rise, get a good bearing on the sun and head north again. Even if Robert was back, Finnlay would never find him in this maze of a forest – and should he do so, Finnlay no longer had the words to convince him of anything, let alone the Enclave. Bitter disappointment welled up inside him and he kicked out at the log, sending clumps of moss flying. If only there wasn't so much depending on someone like his brother taking the leadership, so much at stake. The Key – the Calyx – all of it.

No. He would have to find some other way—

A noise behind made him stop in his tracks. He whirled around and tried to peer through the trees. At first he could see nothing, then his ears caught the sound of a horse – no, three horses coming towards him. He froze and waited – then blinked in surprise. There, getting closer with every step, was Robert!

For a moment, Finnlay couldn't believe his luck and almost laughed. After all that time and effort, his brother comes across him by accident! Perhaps he'd been right after all – perhaps the gods did mean his plan to work. With his heart filled with renewed confidence, Finnlay strode forward as Robert's horse broached the clearing. 'Serin's blood, Robert, but you're a hard man to find!'

His brother was frowning at him in obvious surprise. 'Finnlay! What are you doing here?'

Finnlay grinned. 'Looking for you.' He glanced behind his brother and caught sight of a man his own age riding the second horse – a man with glowing red hair and sun-drenched freckles. 'Micah? Is that you?'

'Aye, my lord. It's good to see you again,' Micah replied with a smile.

Taking Robert's bridle, Finnlay held the horse as he dismounted. 'And it's damned good to see you, too. How's life treating you?'

'Very well, my lord.'

'And my brother?'

Robert took the bridle from Finnlay's hands and led the horse to the stream. 'How's life treating me or how am I treating Micah?'

'One follows the other, does it not?' The words were out before Finnlay could stop them.

Robert glanced at him but said nothing. Instead he turned his attention to Finnlay's horse. He bent down to examine the injured hoof, running a sure hand up the leg and chest of the animal to give it a companionable slap on the neck. He then turned back to Finnlay, his expression a little gentler, but not yet compromising. 'You look well, brother. How has life been treating you?'

There was no suggestion of mockery in Robert's tone but there was something in his eyes. Finnlay answered anyway. 'Fine. Everything is fine, really.'

'And mother? How is she?'

'I saw her at Saint Hilary's a month ago and she was in perfect health.'

That elicited a small smile from Robert. He nodded. 'And what about the rest of the family? Uncle Oliver? Have you seen him?'

'Not recently. Everyone is fine, like I said. Except...' Finnlay paused and studied Robert for a moment. He'd changed little over the last three years. His hair was longer, certainly; he was more tanned and perhaps a little leaner – but it was the gaze buried within those sea-green eyes which made Finnlay pause. There was something ... wrong here but he couldn't put his finger on it.

'Except?' Robert prompted.

Now that it came to it, what exactly was Finnlay to say? It seemed they could talk – which was a start – but talking to Robert about anything important had always been difficult. For one thing, Robert never seemed to take anything seriously – and on the odd occasions when he did, it was impossible to predict how he would react.

Taking a deep breath, Finnlay moved closer and said, 'Robert, we need to talk.'

'About what?' Robert had turned to the packhorse and pulled a flask from one of the bags. 'How did you know I was back?'

Finnlay watched him warily. 'How do you think?'

A smile played about his brother's face for a moment. 'Don't tell me you've been practising. Oh, Finn, if only I'd known.'

'But you did know. You started shielding almost the moment you arrived.'

'Did I?' Robert pulled the stopper out of the flask and held it out to him. 'The last of the Rennish ale. Would you like some?'

Finnlay stared at the flask. Yes, something wasn't right here. Robert was behaving as though he'd never been away – as though he'd seen Finnlay only last week. He was acting as if he'd never promised never to return to Lusara.

Taking the flask, Finnlay swallowed the bitter liquid, using the time to get his thoughts back in order. Regardless of what his brother was thinking, there were still important matters to discuss. There would be time to work out what was wrong later.

Finnlay handed the flask back and tried again. 'Robert, I have to tell you something.'

'Oh?'

49

'It's about Marcus, Robert. I'm sorry, but he's dead.'

Robert froze in the act of taking a drink from the flask. Slowly he lowered it from his mouth and closed his eyes.

Micah came around the horses and stood between them. 'When? How?'

'Almost two weeks ago, from a fever. He fell ill then three days later he was gone.'

'Mineah grant him peace,' Micah whispered.

'Aye,' Robert looked back at Finnlay. 'And Ayn? Have you seen her? How is she?'

'I don't really know. She sent me a message. She seemed to be taking it well.'

'Aye, she would.' Robert turned away, his head lowered.

Finnlay glanced at Micah then, unable to help himself, blurted, 'Robert, there's to be a Gathering, to choose a successor to Marcus. You must come.'

Robert kept walking until he reached the fallen log. There he sat, resting his elbows on his knees. 'I know what you're about to say, Finn. I don't want to discuss it again.'

'But you know what will happen if you don't . . .'

'I said I don't want to discuss it,' Robert interrupted wearily. 'If you've exerted yourself to find me only to have an argument, then I'm afraid you'll be disappointed.'

Finnlay stared at him. Suddenly, all his calm, all his good intentions – all the peace of the last three years drained away – and was instantly replaced by the same blinding anger which had always dominated their relationship. Anger from Finnlay and a flat calm from Robert.

He strode forward, his heart racing. 'I don't believe it! After three years you still care so little?' He spat the words out, daring his brother to respond.

And Robert did. He glanced up from his seat and pinned his younger brother with a gaze of steel. 'Then you haven't changed, have you? For a moment there, I allowed myself to believe the impossible. Still, you have your heart fixed on an argument, brother. By all means, don't let me stop you.'

Finnlay couldn't hold the gaze and looked away. He saw Micah take up the horses' leads and move them away from the stream. As always, Micah was either unconcerned or unaffected by the obvious rift between the brothers. For some reason, Finnlay found that comforting – just enough for him to get a hold on his fury. When he finally turned back to Robert, his anger was under control – mostly.

'You know the Enclave needs you, Robert,' Finnlay began, still determined to have his say. 'And with Marcus gone, they need direction – your direction. You must Stand the Circle and take his place.'

'I must?' Robert whispered.

'By the gods, yes! How long is this to go on?' Finnlay shook his head, totally bewildered. There was no fight in Robert at all! With growing fear, he continued insistently, urgently, 'While you still had a seat on the Council we could understand the good you could do – if not the means by which you chose to do it. And when Berenice died it was understandable. But it's been three years, Robert. How long will you keep up this . . .' Finnlay's voice trailed off, words failing him at the last.

'What?' Robert queried softly, 'This charade?'

Finnlay couldn't speak. This was too close to the truth and despite his best resolutions, he found he couldn't actually come out with the words.

Robert shook his head sadly, taking the silence for an answer. Finnlay inwardly kicked himself for his stupidity.

'The Enclave will survive without me,' Robert added, not looking at his brother. 'It has before and it will again. It doesn't need me, nor the trouble I would bring it.'

'I'm not the only one who wants you there. Ayn said that Marcus's last words were of you. He wanted you to take his place.'

Robert raised his eyebrows in self-mockery. 'It must have been the fever.'

'Damn it, Robert, how can you joke about it? Those people need you. You're the most powerful of us all but all you can do is sit there making jokes and somehow remain untouched by it all. You know, if you weren't my brother . . .'

51

'Yes?' Robert stood and carefully replaced the stopper in the flask.

'If you weren't my brother I would say you had ceased to care at all!'

Robert took a long time to reply. He shook his head and a small smile softened his face. He came closer and placed a hand on Finnlay's shoulder. 'What purpose is there in caring about things I cannot change? We're travelling a little further before we stop for the night. If you like, you can take the pack horse and come with us. It won't take a moment to change the saddle over. If not?' He shrugged and dropped his hand, 'then I suppose I will see you at Dunlorn for the winter. I hope that's . . .'

Robert's voice trailed off and Finnlay frowned. 'What is it?' Danger?

The answer was immediate. The forest around them began to rustle and seconds later they were surrounded by a squad of mounted soldiers. They wore no identifiable blaze but the drawn swords and the speed of the ambush meant only one thing. Trouble.

Instinctively, Finnlay watched Robert out of the corner of his eye. His brother appeared relaxed and unruffled, his hands held loosely at his sides. He made no move towards his sword but that meant nothing. Robert could move very fast when he needed to.

One soldier detached himself from the group and rode forward. 'Who are you? What are you doing here?'

Robert shrugged, 'Just travellers, sergeant. Nothing more.'

'Travellers, eh? From where? What's your name?'

'Does it matter who we are?'

The sergeant obviously didn't like that at all. He tugged his reins and with a nod to his men, grunted, 'Bring them.'

Disarmed and bound, they were led on foot through the forest and down a steep track until they reached a valley. In the centre was the ruin of a stone building surrounded by tents, fires and at least five dozen more soldiers. Finnlay watched Robert, waiting for some sign that he was about to move. But there was no opportunity, no opening, and even Micah looked worried.

As they approached the tents, another more senior soldier strode up to them. The sergeant gave his report to the captain, who looked the captives up and down.

'Where did you find them?'

'Over the ridge, sir. They claim they are just travellers.'

'I see.' The captain nodded then turned to Robert. 'Who are you?'

Finnlay clenched his fists, hoping to warn Robert against giving his name. There was no way to guess what would happen if these men found out his brother's identity. There were too many variables. Robert had been gone so long he would have no idea whether these men were friends or foe. And if they were foe?

Robert took in the makeshift camp then turned back to the captain. 'My name is Douglas. Robert Douglas.'

A tiny frown creased the young captain's brow. 'Douglas?' For a moment he appeared to struggle with his memory – then abruptly his eyes widened. 'My lord! I apologize if my men mistreated you. Sergeant, get rid of those bonds. If you will come with me, my lord? His lordship will be happy to see you.'

'Oh?' Robert shot a perplexed look at Finnlay before adding, 'And who is your master?'

The captain smiled and drew them across the compound, 'Why Baron Blair, of course!'

Blair met them outside his tent and instantly clapped his hands on Robert's shoulders. With a bellow of laughter he demanded, 'By the gods, Robert, what are you doing back? When did you arrive? And Finnlay? I haven't seen you for months! But how . . .'

He paused with a glance at the captain who waited behind them. The man quickly explained and Blair gave a small cough and tugged at his shaggy beard. 'Sorry about that, Robert. We've . . . er, had a bit of trouble with a band of raiders. My men have orders to bring in anyone looking suspicious. Come inside, close by the fire. You must be frozen!'

Inside the tent was a huge brazier glowing with welcome warmth, a long table, a rug on the floor and a scattering of chairs. Blair poured them all wine, but kept throwing puzzled glances in Robert's direction. Finnlay drew Micah close to the fire but Robert stayed by the table, his eyes on Blair.

'I tell you, Robert, it will take me days to get over the shock of seeing you again. That's not to say I'm not glad to see you – but where have you been the last three years?'

'Here and there,' Robert replied with a shrug, then smiled to soften the evasion.

'To be honest, I never thought I'd see you back here. Not after . . .'

'No,' Robert replied, cutting Blair off. 'Nor did I.'

At that moment, Finnlay's attention was caught by a new arrival. Flowing white hair, broad muscled shoulders and a gaze that could split oak.

'Uncle Oliver!' Finnlay blurted, at once delighted and bewildered.

In response, Robert turned around to be caught up in a rough bearhug. 'Robert! It's so good to see you! We just heard you were here. But I don't understand. I thought you'd quit Lusara for good.'

Despite his obvious shock, Robert managed a smile, 'I can't say I expected to see you here either.'

Finnlay greeted his uncle, unable to disagree with his brother. That Blair should be here with his men looking for raiders was no real surprise – that Oliver Sinclair was with him, was. Finnlay stepped back to the fire and watched the man who had, over the years, become almost a second father to him and Robert. Oliver Sinclair had been many things in his long life – a soldier, King's councillor, battle hero – not to mention Duke of Haddon and the older brother of Finnlay's mother. Finnlay's earliest memories held images of this quiet, wise old man, whose hair seemed always to have been the purest white. Over the years he had done much to fill the place of their lost father and in some respects, they had filled the place of the children Oliver had never had.

'A touching reunion,' came a dry comment from the door. Finnlay glanced up and recognized the pinched, sallow face and narrow grey gaze of Roy Seaton. Great, this was just what they needed.

But Robert was talking to Oliver and only glanced a greeting in Seaton's direction. 'You're a long way from home, Uncle. My mother is well, I hope?'

Oliver nodded with enthusiasm. 'She is indeed – though I haven't seen her myself since the spring. You know how hard it is to get to that damned abbey, Robert. She'll be delighted to see you back, safe and sound, my boy. I'm surprised she didn't write and tell me you were on your way.'

'That would have been difficult – since she didn't know.' Robert paused, glancing at Blair but avoiding Finnlay's eyes. 'In fact, nobody knows.'

An awkward silence descended on the room. Finnlay was tempted to fill it with some casual comment but there was an undercurrent to the silence he found fascinating. Something in the way Blair glanced at Seaton – and Oliver avoided them both. Finnlay looked to see if Robert had noticed, but his brother's face was typically shuttered. After a moment, Blair picked up the wine jug and began refilling their cups. As he did so, Oliver sank into a chair close to the fire, his eyes on his eldest nephew.

'Are you saying you've come back in secret?'

Robert shook his head. 'No, not at all. I see no point in secrecy. I'm not wanted for any crimes. There's no warrant out for me – unless something has transpired in my absence?' He cast a questioning look at Blair, who shook his head.

Seaton strode across the room and helped himself to some wine. He grunted, 'I'll dare say there are a few who will not be as welcoming of your return, Dunlorn. Not that I would take any notice of that. These days the usurper's council is made up of either traitors or slavering cronies. I wouldn't give tuppence for the lot of them!'

'Hold your tongue, Seaton,' Oliver chided gently. 'My nephew has been away a long time. I'm sure he has other things on his mind than your fine opinions.'

'My apologies, Your Grace, I meant no insult,' Seaton bowed stiffly but his face betrayed his real thoughts.

'No insult was taken,' Robert replied with a quick glance at his uncle. 'But I'm curious – your calling the King a usurper?'

Seaton raised his eyebrows defensively. 'Well, he is – it's a fact we all acknowledge – even Selar himself. What of it?'

'Well, nothing really,' Robert's tone was casual. 'It's just that you never used to call him that. I can't help wondering what has changed.'

'Oh, please, Robert,' Blair raised his hands in appeal, 'don't let him get started.'

'Forgive me,' Robert smiled, 'but I have a lot of catching up to do.'

Seaton snorted in derision. 'That's what you get for turning your back on your country and your people when they most need you. I'm surprised you're even asking the question – or that you bothered to return at all!'

'Seaton!' Finnlay took a step across the room, 'there is no need for—'

'What?' Seaton snapped, 'Disrespect? Well, tell me, Finnlay, how am I supposed to respect a man like your noble brother, here? He was once our sole voice to the King – our single representative on the council and the one man who was capable of standing up to that fool of a Guilde Proctor. A battle hero, even, and the beloved champion of the people. Where should respect lie when that same man then just walks away? A man who, the moment when things begin to get really difficult, just runs in the opposite direction? By Mineah's teeth, he didn't even tell us why he went!'

Finnlay opened his mouth, trying desperately to control his fury. But his brother took a deep breath and murmured, 'Leave it, Finn.'

Robert then turned a steady gaze on Seaton, who was frozen under that intense scrutiny. Finnlay almost felt sorry

56

for the poor fool. Many men before him had been rooted to the spot by that same gaze and more than a few of them had felt just as intimidated as Seaton obviously did now. It was a strange talent Robert had, and one he used unconsciously. It made men both admire and fear him.

Robert paused as though choosing his words with care. When he spoke it was with his usual even tone, untainted by anger at Seaton's attitude. But then again, Robert never did get angry at anything. 'Do you think my staying in Lusara would have helped? Do you really think that if I'd stayed you would not have lost those lands outside Emaine?' He skilfully ignored the sharp look he got from his uncle and continued, 'I doubt I would have had any effect on that dispute.'

'And what do you know about it?' Seaton blustered. 'You've been away for three years!'

Robert shrugged. 'I still heard things. As for the rest, my reasons for leaving were between the King and myself and not the business of anyone else. You're entirely within your rights to be angry at what happened to your lands but please – don't lay the blame at my feet.'

'So,' Seaton drew the word out, 'you won't stand against him. I might have known you'd turn your back on us again.'

'As you have so rightly pointed out, I have been away. If you wish to blame me for what happened, then by all means go ahead, if it makes you feel better. I've been held to account for many worse things in my time. But understand this: I am not a part of your argument and never will be. But even if I was, I swore an oath of allegiance to Selar when I joined his council and nothing – neither your anger nor your contempt – will ever convince me to break that oath.'

Seaton glared at him for a moment then without another word turned and stalked out of the tent.

Blair sighed into the silence and glanced at Robert. 'I'm sorry about that. Those lands had been in his family four generations. There's been quite a lot of that sort of thing happening lately. Seaton's still bitter about it.'

Robert remained where he stood, his eyes still on the door where Seaton had gone. 'Yes, I'm sure.'

Blair came across the room and slapped a hand on his shoulder. 'Will you spend the night with us here? It's the least I can do after the trouble my men caused you.'

Robert shook his head. 'No, thank you. I want to get a little further before we make camp. We've still got a long journey ahead of us. I want to cross the mountains before the first snows.'

'Well, it's good to have you back, anyway. My men will have your horses ready.'

Oliver stood, 'I'll walk you out, Robert.'

Saying goodbye to Blair, they left the tent. Micah went off to retrieve the horses, leaving Finnlay, Robert and their uncle alone in the centre of the compound.

Robert was silent for a moment then murmured, 'Well?'

Oliver raised his eyebrows and ran a hand through his mane of hair. 'Please don't jump to conclusions, Robert. There's so much you don't know. A lot has happened while you've been away. I beg you, be patient before you act.'

'Act?' Robert arched an eyebrow. 'I have no intention of doing anything. I just want to know what's going on. Why did Seaton lose those lands? And why are you here? And the others? What's this all about? What conclusions, exactly, do you want me to avoid?'

'Look, Robert,' Oliver leaned forward, his voice dropping, 'if I were you, I would stay clear of Blair and Seaton for a while. At least until you have a better idea of how things lie.'

'Is this a warning?'

'No, nothing like that. But as for that other thing . . .'

'What other thing?'

Oliver waved his hands irritably. 'You know very well what I mean. You'd never heard about Seaton losing those lands and I doubt your brother here told you either. You picked it out of Seaton's thoughts. Don't try to deny it – I've known you too long. I don't know what things you got up to while you were away but you can't continue to do them now. Not if you intend to live long enough to get into any real trouble.'

'But I . . .'

The old man frowned. 'I know what you are, Robert – you and your brother. Fortunately, I don't think anyone else knows and for that I thank the gods alone. But whatever you do, I beg you to be careful. If not for your sake, then at least for your mother's.'

The moon was long gone behind a swathe of clouds before Finnlay heard Robert call a halt at the bottom of a narrow gully. He was glad. Tired, cold and saddle-weary, he slid down from his horse and let it drink from the shallow stream. In the darkness, he could only just make out the faces of his brother and Micah. Both looked equally tired. He would have to broach the subject of Oliver's extraordinary revelation in the morning.

On the other hand . . . 'I suppose,' Finnlay murmured, 'the good side was that you at least found those ruins.'

Micah managed a weary chuckle but Robert turned swiftly and pointed a finger directly at Finnlay's chest. 'Not one word, brother. Take this as clear warning – not one, single, solitary word. For once in your life, have the sense to know when to leave something well alone.'

Taken aback, Finnlay spread his arms, the image of innocence. 'I wasn't going to say anything, Robert, honest.'

'I'm going to say this just once, brother, so listen very carefully. I have not come back to Lusara to return to court – or to join the Enclave. I don't know what Seaton and Blair are up to and I don't want to know. If you wish to get involved, then that's your problem. But I will not now, nor ever, become involved in it all again. I'm going home and I intend to stay there. If you can't live with that, then I suggest you think about taking up permanent residence at the Enclave – or learn to keep your mouth shut. I suspect the former is more likely than the latter. Any questions?'

Finnlay let out the breath he'd been holding and did his best to meet Robert's gaze. 'Just one. Why?'

For a second, he actually thought Robert might answer but instead, his brother burst out laughing. 'Why? Is that all? Is that the best you can do? Oh, Finnlay, really.'

As Robert turned away, Finnlay pursued him. 'It may be a lame question but I still want an answer. Why? Why did you go? Why come back and why are you determined to turn your back on everything you care about?'

'But you said I cared about nothing,' Robert replied offhandedly, reaching up to unsaddle his horse.

'By the gods, Robert – just answer the damn question! Why?'

'You don't really want to know. You're just hoping that in my reasons you'll find something you can use to change my mind about the Enclave.' He paused and turned around to face Finnlay properly. There should have been disdain in his eyes but there was nothing – not even patience. Just a dead, flat and unbroken façade. When he spoke again it was into a cold silence.

'Trust me, Finn, it doesn't matter. Not only do I not want to Stand the Circle – but I cannot. I had hoped you'd understand that by now. You, the Enclave and indeed the whole country will have to learn to get along without me. Believe me, it's better this way. And it's better too, that you even forget that I am a sorcerer.'

So there it was. The declaration. Even as the words were spoken, Finnlay felt the finality behind them, like a wall of stone for ever separating them. There was a bitter taste in his mouth, of disappointment and futility. All the hopes he'd held for the past few days drained away from him and he felt empty and cold. Robert may have returned to Lusara, but this return was a greater rejection than his exile had ever been.

Finnlay couldn't look at him any more. He was afraid to. Instead, he turned back to his horse, words of acceptance on his lips. But he never got to say them. At that moment Micah moved, his voice hushed.

'My lord?'

As Finnlay looked up, Micah pointed towards the forest, his face stern with warning. 'Someone's coming.'

# 3

Micah heard the horse coming towards them at a stumbling gallop, but he couldn't see anything through the pitch black forest. And there was another sound too, one further behind—

'A chase,' he murmured. 'Your uncle?'

Robert turned swiftly. 'No. Something else. Get the horses back from the water.'

Seconds later a horse crashed through the undergrowth and pounded across the stream, sending sheets of water into the air. On seeing them the animal reared, but its rider fought and won control. Without hesitating, Micah stepped forward and grabbed hold of the bridle while a voice above him gasped out, 'Please help me! Robbers ... chasing me. Please ... need to hide.'

Instantly, Robert moved. 'Come down off there. Micah, help her up that tree. Quickly!'

The girl jumped down. Micah lifted her on to the lower branch and stepped back. She was invisible in the darkness. He turned around to find his master had already sent the horse on its way. Finnlay had tied their own horses up and was sitting casually with his back to a tree stump. With a nod, Micah grabbed an armful of firewood from the forest floor and squatted down to prepare a fire – as though he'd been there all along.

He was just in time, too. The forest opposite them parted again and three horses sped across the stream, coming to a stumbling halt in front of his master. But these men were not robbers. All three riders wore the unmistakable yellow blaze of the Guilde.

'Did you see a rider come through here?' their leader

demanded, gruff and out of breath. 'Moments before us? A criminal and horse thief?'

Robert placed his hands on his hips and nodded slowly. 'Certainly did. Rode right past us, headed that way. He nearly knocked us down.'

'That way?' the man pointed in the direction Dunlorn had sent the horse.

'Yes. I hope you can follow its tracks. People like that should be stopped.'

'Right, come on!' As one, the soldiers turned and took up their pursuit, but Robert stayed where he was until the sound of the horses disappeared into the night. Then, with a warning glance at Micah, he called up to the girl, 'Come down. Quickly. Finn, get that saddle back on my horse. They could return any minute.'

Micah wasted no time and rounded up their horses, coming back to his master. 'What next? These poor animals are too tired for flight.'

'I know. Take them and the girl further up this gully. There's bound to be a cave or something you can shelter in. Finnlay, go with them. Try to keep the horses quiet and no talking until I return.'

'And if they come back, my lord?'

Robert gave him a lopsided smile. 'Just go, Micah. Now.'

Micah nodded and led the others along the stream. Limestone walls rose on either side of them, covered in clumps of determined bushes. The night was so dark, Micah had a lot of trouble keeping to their path, finding eventually that it was easier to walk along the stream bed instead. He scanned both sides of the rising cliffs but could see nothing of any use. Then Finnlay tapped his shoulder.

'There, behind those bushes. A cave.'

With a breath of relief, Micah gained the bushes and led the horses into the cave. It turned out to be big enough to hide them all. The girl stood beside Finnlay, her eyes fixed on the cave mouth. In silence they waited, listening to the night. With a bit of luck, those soldiers might not even return.

62

After ten minutes however, Micah began to worry and curse himself for not staying with his master. Sure, Dunlorn was a mighty swordsman, but it was dark and he was tired. Alone, he might not be able to overcome those men if the slightest thing went wrong. Micah shot a glance across the cave to where Finnlay stood. He would know. If anything happened to his brother, Finnlay would know. At least, that's what Micah hoped. So far, he appeared unconcerned – not that Micah could really see his face, but Finnlay hadn't moved and that was sign enough.

The minutes dragged by until Micah was about ready to leave the cave, when he heard a splash in the water outside. He froze. His hand instantly went to his sword but Finnlay caught his eye, shook his head and visibly relaxed. Moments later, Robert stood in the cave mouth, gazing inwards.

'Well,' Finnlay murmured, 'you two certainly live interesting lives.'

Micah couldn't help laughing with relief. 'It's getting to be quite a habit.'

Dunlorn came into the cave and glanced about him. 'Well, it could be worse.'

'Considering the fact that those were Guildesmen you just lied to, brother, I don't really see how.'

Spreading his arms expansively, Robert replied, 'It could be snowing.' With a grin he turned to Micah. 'Those men won't come back. Let's get a fire started. I'm cold!'

With a blaze going in the middle of the cave, the horses unsaddled and stalled at the far end, Micah pulled one of the bags across to the fire and began to prepare some food. Robert sat down on the other side of the fire and reached out his hands towards the flames. With a glance in Micah's direction, he waved the girl forward from where she stood by the cave mouth.

'All right, child,' Dunlorn began quietly. 'Do you want to tell us your name?'

The girl moved forward hesitantly, glancing at each of them before taking a seat by the fire.

'I'm more curious to know why she lied to us,' Finnlay

grunted, taking the piece of bread Micah handed him. 'Unless I'm mistaken, robbers don't go around dressed in Guilde robes – although few people would be able to tell the difference.'

Robert hid a smile and turned back to the girl. 'Well?'

She gazed at him for a moment, not speaking. Now that Micah could see her properly, he realized she was not as young as he'd first thought. Perhaps sixteen or seventeen. Nor was she dressed so poorly. Although her cloak was worn and frayed, the green dress underneath showed little signs of age, even if it was streaked with dust and mud. Her thin, oval face was tanned and made her deep blue eyes almost glow in contrast. A ragged braid of thick black hair tumbled down her back. Although she was obviously wary, the girl appeared strangely unafraid and moved with a confidence beyond her years.

'You can speak, can't you?' Finnlay prompted, his patience wearing thin.

'Yes,' she murmured with a little laugh. 'Of course I can – and I'm sorry I lied to you back there. My name is Jenn and I thank you for your help. I don't think that poor horse would have taken me much further. He was already winded and stumbling when I came upon you.'

'And why were they chasing you?' Finnlay asked flatly.

She dropped her gaze for a moment. 'I guess I insulted them. I'm no horse thief, I promise you.'

'Are we supposed to believe that?'

'Finnlay, please,' Robert chided. Micah handed out cups of ale, then settled down with his back to the wall of the cave, his feet toasting nicely before the fire.

Finnlay took a swallow, then wiped his hand across his mouth. 'Then that horse was yours?'

'Not exactly. I . . . borrowed it.'

'Borrowed it? From whom?'

At this, she smiled a little. 'I don't know. I didn't have time to ask. When those men came at me I just leaped on the first one to hand. By then it was too late.' The smile vanished, replaced by a frown. 'Do you think they will have found it by now? Do you think those soldiers will return it to its owner?'

Finnlay blinked at her unveiled anxiety. If she was trying to fool them, she was doing a very good job. However, Micah didn't think she was. There was, after all, no reason for her to lie now – after they had helped her.

'I don't know,' Dunlorn answered lightly. 'Perhaps next time you'll learn not to insult the Guilde. It can be dangerous. Men have been killed for less. But I'm curious. What exactly did you say to them?'

'Well, er . . . have you heard the story about the hermit of Saint Cuthbert's?'

'By the gods,' Finnlay rolled his eyes and leaned back on his elbows.

'Ignore my brother,' Dunlorn smiled companionably. 'What hermit?'

'I don't know him personally, of course, but this hermit was once a Brother at Saint Cuthbert's and has spent the last twenty years living deep in this forest. A few weeks ago he suddenly returned to the abbey and told the Abbot that he'd had a vision of Mineah – and of a dark angel who has come to the land to tear the Church in two. Having made this dire pronouncement, the hermit then left and disappeared again. As you can imagine, this story went around like wildfire. I mean, it's been decades since anyone had a proper vision of Mineah. I even heard someone say that it means she's about to take on human form again – just like she did five hundred years ago when the crumbling empire destroyed the last of the sorcerers. Back then, when the goddess helped the empire, they built a shrine to her in Alusia – so you can imagine how much people hope she is coming back now.'

'I'm sorry,' Finnlay interrupted, 'but do we come to the Guilde somewhere in here – or is this just a history lesson?'

Jenn turned her head until she faced him squarely. 'A pity it's not a lesson in good manners.'

Robert burst out laughing. And while Micah chuckled, Finnlay just looked sour.

'Never interrupt a storyteller, brother! Please, Jenn, go on.'

'Well,' she began again, 'I was working at the tavern in Westmay, near the monastery. Those Guildesmen came in and started giving the innkeeper a lot of trouble. He's a friend of mine, you see, but he couldn't do anything to stop them. So I just told them that perhaps this dark angel in the hermit's vision was not an angel at all, but the Guilde itself!'

Micah's eyes widened and even Finnlay choked.

Robert shook his head in wonder. 'By the gods my girl, but you do live dangerously!'

Jenn shrugged. 'They're so sour these days. I just got annoyed. I couldn't help it.'

'Obviously not! Were they stationed in your village? Will they be waiting for you when you go home?'

'Oh, it's not my home. I was just staying there for a while before I moved on. I don't really have a home.'

Micah looked up at this. 'No home? What about your family?'

In answer, she just raised her shoulders.

Robert frowned slightly then shot Micah a warning glance. 'I think it's time we all got some sleep. It's late and I want to get moving by dawn.'

Bushes rustled against the cave mouth as a brisk wind whistled down the gully. It had started as a light breeze two hours before dawn but now, as the first glow touched the heavens, it warned of darker weather to come. From where he lay, he could see only a thin strip of sky still bleak with night, but on the western face of the gully opposite, he started to make out details by the light of the coming dawn. Thin, stringy plants clung tenaciously to the cliff face and draped their long roots towards the water far below as though desperate to drink.

Slow and silent, Robert pulled his blankets back and rose from his bed. Behind him, the others slept on undisturbed. He moved carefully forward to the cave opening and looked up. It was still blissfully dark but there was just enough glow in the east to make out the shifting clouds tumbling across the sky. There would be rain later – a lot of rain.

He glanced back inside the cave. The fire was little more than a glow, banked against the morning. Around it were three bundles of black, his sleeping companions. Beyond them, standing silently in ignorant peace, were the horses.

*Thus he returned in stealthy sorrow, quiet and black with the night. Unfinished and unending . . .*

The quote was ancient, from *The Chronicle of Banderic*. Six hundred and twenty-three years old. Amazing.

Not so amazing, really. He must have read that book a dozen times by the age of fifteen. A sweeping tale of adventure and bravery, of exploration and discovery. Even now, some of those place names could conjure up a feather-touch of excitement, remind him of the boy he'd once been. What was the rest of the quote?

*Imperfect and eternal, the rage unquelled in his breast, there to die a forgotten peace. Untempered flame of unholy passion will guide his path though wisdom itself will fail him at the last . . .*

Was it really so long ago since that awful day when he'd stood before the Key, an innocent child of nine? Had the years passed so quickly that he'd not noticed? Within the age of the Enclave, it was a grain of time but to Robert, everything came down to that one moment. Those few seconds suspended at the edge of his childhood had changed his life and had brought him to where he was today, standing in a cave somewhere in Shan Moss. How could one single moment determine the course of an entire life? How had he allowed it to?

He walked forward out of the shelter. He felt the wind immediately and turned his face into it, revelling in the fresh cold touch. It had been so long since his flesh had caught a wind like that. And the smells – so familiar and yet so different. Invisible reminders pricked at his memory, touching things here and there. So much he'd forgotten. So very much.

But it hadn't just been that one moment, had it? In all, his life had been a series of moments, all equally to blame, all equally leading him to damnation.

No, they would leave him alone. He would make sure of it. This was one thing he would not fail at. There was nothing – absolutely nothing – they could say or do that would change his mind.

He bent down and trailed his fingers in the water, feeling them tingle and go numb. He wanted to reach out to the numbness, make it course through his veins and into his very heart. He wanted to wrap it around his soul, to drown in it. Anything that would finally grant him some peace.

But peace was not so easily gained. Three years wandering the southern lands had taught him that. There was no peace. He would just have to go on feeling, regardless of his will. He could no more stop it than tell the wind to stop blowing. It was inevitable, that failure. Just as inevitable as this return to Lusara.

Why hadn't he seen that before? But three years ago, in the black pits of his frustration and despair – when rage had threatened to overwhelm him – thoughts of any return had been beyond him. And now looking back on it ... on Berenice ...

No! Not that. He would not – could not – afford to think about her.

Then what about Marcus? Faithful, exuberant, wise. Gone now. Gone before Robert had even seen him again. Gone for ever. Another friend lost, another voice silenced. A sombre welcome back to Lusara.

So – what was he to do about Finnlay? Send him on his way? Do as he asked and go to the Gathering? Or continue as he had always done and keep trying to make his brother understand. But was there anything left – any words remaining to convince his brother and all those like him that Robert was not the man they thought he was? That to put their faith in him was to guarantee failure – and worse?

But he already knew the answer. Finnlay was his brother and for all his faults, Robert loved him. As long as Robert had breath to command, he would continue trying to teach his passionate, fiery sibling all he could. And perhaps, somewhere in there, at some point in time, Finnlay might just be able to forgive him his great crime.

Yes, forward. He must continue forward. The past was gone. The future would not be so bad that he couldn't bear it. It only required a modicum of strength – and a cartload of determination. It could indeed be much worse.

He straightened up and turned his eyes towards the sky once more. It was almost dawn now, with that crisp grey half-light which characterized the moments just before the sun rose. That delicious moment of renewal, when the earth refreshed itself before diving into the coming day. Yes, it was time to move. He took a step back from the water – and stopped. A sound from the cave, movement and a light whispered voice.

Robert smiled. 'I wouldn't bother taking that horse. It's lame.'

The girl's face snapped around towards him in surprise. She remained frozen in the cave mouth, her hand on the horse's bridle, then, giving in easily, she shrugged. 'I didn't think you would miss it.'

'I sincerely hope you don't make a habit of borrowing horses. Next time there may not be anyone around to rescue you. Do you?'

'What?'

'Make a habit of it?'

She raised her eyebrows and for a brief second, Robert had the strangest feeling that she looked familiar. The moment was fleeting however, and didn't last long enough for him to pinpoint why.

'You don't look very surprised,' she replied evenly. 'Were you waiting for me?'

'No, I was watching the sunrise – and you didn't answer my question.'

'No, I don't make a habit of it. Despite what that Guildesman said, I'm not a thief. Look, put yourself in my place. I don't know who you are – or why you helped me.

69

It's a matter of survival, after all. For all I know, you could be murderers.'

Robert nodded deliberately. 'Aye, we could indeed. What do you want? Back to your village?'

'Would you take me if I asked?'

'That would depend on how much I trusted you.'

'Or on how much I trusted you.'

Despite his best intentions, Robert had to laugh. Jenn said nothing, merely watched him. She was no innocent, this one. Instead, she seemed to face life with a shameless bravado. 'Where, then?' he said.

'Well, if you gave me the horse then I wouldn't be stealing it, would I?'

'But it's not my horse. It belongs to Finnlay, so you'd have to ask him. Any other suggestions?'

She gave him a measured look then glanced away. 'Are you heading across the mountains?'

'Yes.'

'Would you take me to the other side?'

'Who are you running from – apart from the Guilde?'

'No one.' She frowned up at him. 'Why should I be running? I've just always wanted to see the other side of the country. I know I've probably annoyed your brother, but really, I could be useful. I can cook better than your sunny-faced friend in there.'

Robert had to concede there was some virtue in her travelling with them. While this stranger was around, Finnlay would have no choice but to keep quiet. There was no way Finnlay would endanger the five-hundred-year-old secret of the Enclave by speaking about it in front of the girl. Indeed, she could be more useful than she thought.

'Well, don't expect him to be happy about it,' he smiled. 'Finnlay has a bad habit of letting things smoulder away. Don't be surprised if he hardly says a pleasant word to you.'

She waved a hand in the air. 'Don't worry. I'll win him around.'

Robert reached up and took the horse's bridle from her. 'You can ride this horse if you like.'

'But you said it was lame!'

He tossed her an apologetic smile. 'Well, it was – yesterday. Come on, let's wake the boys up.'

But Finnlay was already awake and immediately herded Robert to the back of the cave, out of earshot. In a hushed voice he hissed, 'You can't be serious! We don't know who she is. Last night the Guilde were chasing her. Do you want to bring them down on you so soon after your return? And to take her across the Goleth? Right past . . .'

Robert lifted his saddle on to his horse and spared Finnlay only the briefest glance. 'What do you expect me to do? Just leave her here? Send her back into the waiting arms of the Guilde? Abandon her at the first village we come across? You've sworn the knight's oath, brother. She's helpless and alone in the world. It's our duty to protect her.' He finished with a smile hoping to break Finnlay's mood but it didn't make any difference.

With a scowl Finnlay straightened up. 'I see. Well, I'm sorry, brother but it's not that simple. You won't get rid of me that easily.' Without another word, he turned and made for his saddle.

Robert shook his head. Where did Finnlay get these strange ideas?

The day wore on, cool and dark as the persistent clouds that hung ominously above. More than once, Micah peered through the golden canopy of forest hoping for some break in the grey sky. And now, with midday just past, the wind had freshened, threatening a storm.

He rode behind Robert and Finnlay, keeping Jenn company – or rather, she kept him company, for she was an interesting, intriguing companion. She had a quick mind and, it seemed, a fearless tenacity. Nevertheless, Micah felt it his duty to find out as much about her as possible. Besides, she made him laugh.

'You look so grim, Micah,' Jenn murmured gravely, her azure eyes fixed upon him. 'What are you worried about now?'

'The weather, nothing new. I suppose I'd forgotten just how quickly it changes here. And it's so cold. Aren't you cold?'

'Not particularly.'

Micah shook his head and flexed his fingers a few times. 'So,' he tried again, 'if Westmay was not your home – where do you come from? Where is your family?'

Jenn laughed. 'So curious, Micah. All questions, questions.'

'Have you something to hide?'

'We all have something to hide.' With a meaningful look at the two lords ahead of them, she leaned towards Micah conspiratorially. 'I'll tell you if you tell me why those two hardly speak. Why is Finnlay so angry with his brother?'

For a moment, Micah actually thought she was serious, then he saw the way her eyes sparkled with mischief and he relaxed. 'How should I know?' he asked.

'You travel with them. They trust you. You must know. The only thing I don't understand is why Robert is not angry in return.'

'He never gets angry,' Micah shrugged.

'What, never?'

'No. He says that anger is the one emotion that makes a man ultimately vulnerable and ultimately dangerous. He says he has no desire to be either.'

'But why is Finnlay angry with him in the first place?'

Micah turned his head to look at her. Yes indeed, the same mischievous glint in her eyes. Instead of replying, however, he said, 'You're trying very hard to change the subject.'

She lifted a shoulder idly. 'Not that hard.'

'We were discussing your family.'

'Were we? I thought we were discussing your master.'

Micah grinned. 'As I said, you're changing the subject.'

'But there's no mystery there, Micah, honest. I grew up in a tavern on the other side of Shan Moss. When I was twelve, my father died and my mother went mad. They took away my brother and hanged him as a thief. As I was only a child, they took away the tavern and I was left to find my own way. Since then I've wandered the countryside, working where I can. My goal is to see the whole country before I die.'

Micah coughed. 'Is that the truth?'

'What?' she glanced at him with eyes of pure innocence. After a moment, she softened, 'Well, mostly – all right, not much, but I did grow up in a tavern with my father. When he died I was sent to his sister's farm but she had no room for me and after a few months, turned me out. I lost the inn and my father. I've been travelling ever since.'

'And your mother?'

'I never knew her. She died when I was born.'

'You are a storyteller, aren't you?' Micah laughed.

'I'm learning,' she grinned. 'That's why I travel – to collect stories. You'd be amazed at the things people tell me, the things I hear by accident.'

'Such as?'

'Well, like the hermit and his visit to Saint Cuthbert's. I'd like to hear stories you've heard on your travels. Like when you were on the southern continent. Did you see Alusia or the Palace of Bu?'

'You've heard of the Palace?' Micah demanded, shocked.

'Of course. It's said the place was built by sorcerers centuries ago – but I don't believe everything I'm told.'

'Well, it looked to me like it was built by ordinary folk.'

'Oh?' Jenn shot back, 'how could you tell?'

'I just know about these things,' Micah ventured a casual smile. 'I even met a sorcerer once.'

Jenn laughed in disbelief. 'That's what everybody says.'

'Well I did – and if there had been any wandering around the Palace of Bu, I would have known.'

Shaking her head, Jenn turned her gaze to their path and fell silent a moment. Then, with her hands folded together on the pommel of her saddle, she said, 'I heard another story once, about a legend.'

Something about her composed manner and the subtle change of subject drew his attention. 'What legend?'

73

'It's an old story though I've heard it many times from many different people. Of course, the details vary depending on who was talking – and why. It has to do with an evil King and a young lord who befriended him. The young lord worked hard, turning the King's hand away from destroying the people. In return for helping to bring peace to his country, the king bestowed many honours on the young lord and held him high above all others. From these new heights the lord took the armies of the King and fought many battles along the northern border of the country, quelling invading armies and bringing security to those who lived there. The King, full of gratitude, granted the lord many requests to help the people and in return they loved the young lord and took him into their hearts. But jealousy and intrigue ate away at the souls of those around them and one day, the young lord turned his back on the King and left his people alone. Some say he was driven away – some say he left in fear. Others believed that one day he would return with a conquering army, destroy his old friend and take the throne himself.'

Micah kept his silence and waited for her to finish. There was nothing, after all, that he could say.

'As it turns out,' Jenn continued with a glance in his direction, 'they were all wrong, weren't they, Micah?'

He couldn't meet her gaze. 'Why ask me? It's your story.'

'Because that young lord is your master – Robert Douglas, Earl of Dunlorn.'

Micah let out a pent-up breath and turned to study her for a moment. The inevitable question came out: 'How did you know?'

'Two brothers, five or six years apart? One called Robert, the other Finnlay? The way your master took command the moment I begged for help and the fact that Finnlay was so annoyed that it was the Guilde chasing me. Robert's been away for a long time, on the southern continent.' She paused with a shrug. 'It wasn't that hard. His return is not supposed to be a secret, is it?'

'No, not exactly. However, my master would like to get

back to Dunlorn before it becomes common knowledge.' He watched her. Was she trustworthy? She returned his gaze without artifice, no glint in her eye, no suggestion of mischief. This was her true face, her honest face – and he believed her. He stored the memory away for future reference. There was really no telling otherwise when she was . . . enlarging on the truth.

Reading his unspoken question, she murmured, 'I'm no danger to your master, Micah. As a storyteller, I'm more interested in how the legend came to be, rather than the destruction of it. Your master is very important to the people. Even today. I hope he understands that.'

Micah nodded absently. It was all very well and good her saying that – but she only knew the story and not the truth. What would she say about the legend if she knew that at its heart was the secret of forbidden sorcery and a whole world beyond her vivid imagination?

His gaze returned to the two men who rode in front, in silence. Jenn had seen Finnlay's anger but his vow to the Enclave and his Sealing would prevent him from saying anything about why.

The tales of sorcery had died out along with the last of the old order and now were little more than stories with which to frighten children. No one remembered any more just what sorcerers had done. All they knew was that once sorcerers had flourished and worked alongside the old empire until one day they had turned against it. The facts, along with most of the details, had faded with time, but it was a matter of great pride to most people that the sorcerers had been defeated in the end. They'd been hounded, caught and tortured throughout the world until the last had given up his life.

All that had happened over five hundred years ago. Sorcery had died out along with the last remnants of the empire. Everybody knew it, everybody believed it. It was a fine story – a great and triumphant history – but Micah knew it was also a lie.

Not all the sorcerers had taken part in that last battle. In fact, not all of them had taken part in the rebellion against the empire. A small few had refused to be a part of the conflict and rather than help or hinder, had simply left. When the final battle against the empire was lost, some of the survivors joined them. Together, hidden by their awesome powers, they had come to Lusara and founded the Enclave. Five centuries later their secret was still intact, their powers unseen.

And this girl wanted to know why Finnlay was angry! What would she say if he could tell her that Finnlay raged because Robert had turned down a greater power than any of them could possibly imagine?

As they emerged from the forest, Robert called a halt and took his first unhindered look at the Goleth mountains spread out before him. From this point they ran a further eighty leagues to the north and almost a hundred leagues south to the coast. It would take them five days to cross the range if all went well, but first they needed some supplies. And there, perched on the side of a crumbling foothill, stood the village of Solmoss. Buildings were cramped together in a scar of brown against the grey stone, dwarfed by the expanse of Shan Moss below, the peaks beyond. These people were poor, scratching a living from the wild goats that lived in the mountains and what game they could find in the outer reaches of the forest. Few people ventured further in or high into the mountains. Superstition kept them out of the forest – and something else entirely kept them out of the Goleth.

'Do we stop for the night or go on?' Finnlay asked without preamble. 'I don't like the look of this weather.'

Robert nodded, 'It's too early to be stopping but I agree, it looks like it's going to turn very sour. We'll stay the night and give the horses some rest before they tackle the mountains. We can get a good start in the morning.'

His expectations were shared by the villagers. Down every narrow street, people were closing shutters, taking belongings inside. They knew the mountain weather well and their preparations made Robert more than a little uncomfortable.

He couldn't afford a long delay. If it should snow it would be impossible to cross the mountains before spring. As they dismounted before an inn, Robert prayed silently this storm would last only the night.

'Micah, you take care of the supplies. Get enough to last us a week. We'll be across the Goleth by then and I don't want to weigh the animals down too much.' He paused, noticing Finnlay's eyes on him. He wanted to talk. Not only about the Enclave – but about Oliver too. Well, Robert wanted to talk as well, but not now. Now there were more practical things to worry about. 'And we need to find Jenn something warmer to wear.'

Jenn glanced at him, startled, but said nothing. As Micah went off about his chores, Robert headed up the busy street, Finnlay and Jenn following behind.

Solmoss had grown little since Robert had last been here. There were a few more houses further up the hill but the local shrine still stood alone. Beyond and hidden by the scrubby wood was a deep ravine and the only pass through the range. A few market stalls squatted on the edge of the village, as if shrinking back from the shrine built to protect them. It was here that Robert stopped to find a new cloak for Jenn. Most of the stalls were now closing in preparation for the coming storm, but Robert displayed a few coins for encouragement and soon he found something useful.

'This one will do,' he murmured, reaching for a thick brown garment of rough-spun wool. He turned to show it to her, but she wasn't paying attention. 'Jenn?'

At the sound of her name, she stepped back, bumping into him. 'Look – the shrine. The Guilde!'

Robert turned. A little further up the hill, perched on a single rock outcrop, stood the wooden trium, the same as in any village in Lusara – but this one was surrounded by at least a dozen Guildesmen and their attention was focused on one thing.

'By the gods!' Finnlay breathed. 'They've got Arlie Baldwyn!'

There were a few people standing around, watching as the

Guilde dragged the man to the trium and tied his hands to the triangular arms, bound his feet at the base. The fair head was raised and fixed defiantly on the nearest Guilde guard. His wife Martha was nowhere to be seen.

Robert started forward but events moved too quickly. Arlie's head was pulled back, his face a grimace. There was a flash of steel and Arlie screamed as his left hand was severed at the wrist. Robert grabbed Finnlay's arm. 'Find Micah! Get the horses and bring them around the village to the wood, there. Do you see it?'

'But . . .'

Without pausing, Robert gripped his shoulders hard. 'If we don't get Arlie down they'll leave him there to bleed to death! Move. I'll find Martha.'

Without another word, Finnlay turned and headed back down the hill.

When Robert looked back the small crowd was dispersing from around the trium and the Guildesmen were returning to the village. Four were left on guard.

There was only one way they could do this – but first, he had to find Martha. Quickly. He took in a deep breath and marshalled his concentration. Reaching deep inside, he awoke his Senses, sent them out into the village. He focused on one single thing, one aura – and there! Martha, hiding behind the building just opposite. Finnlay would come across her as he returned. Good. That made things so much easier. Now to get Arlie out.

Robert glanced back at Arlie, silently willing his friend to hold on. Then he turned to Jenn. 'I need your help.'

She didn't answer. Her eyes were fixed on the shrine and the blood falling down Arlie's bound arm.

'Jenn?' Robert reached out and touched her shoulder. She jumped and turned a look of sheer panic on him. He kept his voice calm but couldn't extinguish the urgency. 'I need your help. They're leaving him there to die, Jenn. He's my friend. I have to help him.'

There was no apparent reason for it, but the panic died

from her eyes. She took a deep breath. 'What do you want me to do?'

He gave her a quick smile of encouragement then led her across the street and into the wood. They waited in the shelter of a scrawny tree as the first drops of rain began to fall. The last of the market stalls closed up as everybody headed indoors. 'I need you to create a diversion. Those guards there, go up to them, talk to them – whatever. But draw them away from Arlie.'

'Now?' she murmured, her eyes still on the yellow uniforms.

'Not yet. When Finn gets back with the horses. We can't get far without them. We've got a few minutes.'

Jenn nodded calmly, but her hands were shaking. Robert reached out and took them. Her fingers were cold – he never did get that cloak. 'Are you all right?'

'Why?' she murmured, rigid with fear – or was it anger? 'Why did they do that to him?'

'I don't know,' Robert frowned. Familiar seeds of frustration and helplessness gnawed at him as though the last three years had never passed. 'He must have broken some Guilde Law.'

'But cutting off his hand? What book of law does that come from?'

What indeed? And why the left hand? What had Arlie done?

But Jenn wanted an answer. There would be time to deal with other reasons later. 'The punishment I've heard of goes back to the days when sorcerers still walked the land and were feared and hated. It was said that cutting off the left hand would stop their powers – something about a talisman they used. It was then supposed to be easier to kill them. But I don't know why the Guilde have suddenly started using such a thing after all this time. I mean, everyone knows there are no sorcerers any more. It must be some new law.'

At that, Jenn turned to face him. 'Why didn't you stop them?'

The question threw him. 'There was no time.'

'No. I don't mean today.'

No, she didn't. She meant something else entirely. 'You know who I am,' he stated flatly. 'How did you know?'

She took a step closer and her eyes searched his face. He could only guess what she was looking for. 'Why didn't you stop the Guilde?'

He met her gaze for a long moment, then looked away. A thousand answers raced through his mind – answers he could and had given out as easily as prayers at Caslemas. Quick, simple, pat answers that hinted at but never actually told the truth. For some reason though, he could utter none of them. He opened his mouth in an effort to do so, but the only thing that came out was the truth. 'Because I couldn't.'

He gave her no further opportunity to ask questions. Finnlay and Micah had found Martha and were now coming through the woods towards them. It was time to move.

'Get the guards as far to the other side of the shrine as you can manage and then be prepared to run. Don't worry, I won't leave without you.'

'But can you get him down without help?' Jenn's hands started shaking again but she was in control.

Robert smiled. 'Don't worry, I'll have help.'

As Finn arrived, Jenn headed out of the wood and into the rain. The wind whipped at her gown, caught her hair but she continued doggedly. Boldly she strode up to the nearest guard.

'What's she doing?' Finn whispered.

'I don't know. Just listen.'

From beneath the wind, he could hear Jenn. As she spoke, the other guards gathered around her, all captured by her disarming smile – and yet, even with the wind and the rain, Robert could still hear that tremor of fear or anger in her voice.

'I sincerely hope you have a very good reason to do such a thing to this criminal,' she said. 'From what I've heard, this punishment is reserved for sorcerers . . .'

'Oh hell,' Finnlay groaned in Robert's ear.

But Robert wasn't listening so much as watching what Jenn was doing. Almost with each word, her weight shifted a little and she drew the guards away from the shrine. Not far from it – but almost far enough.

'You'd better hope,' she went on, 'that he's not a sorcerer or you could be sorry.'

'He'll be sorry!' One guard laughed and his mates joined in.

'Because I've heard stories about things like this,' Jenn continued, unperturbed. 'About ghosts that have risen from the trium and haunted their murderers for years afterwards. For some reason, cutting off the hand like that ensures a man will become a ghost when he dies. I even heard one story about a Guildesman who threw himself from a cliff because a ghost had haunted him every night for ten years. If that's what a normal man would do, just imagine what will happen to you if this man is a sorcerer.'

Robert tensed as each of the guards turned to glance at Arlie. Then they looked back at Jenn as she regaled them with more tales. Now was the time to move.

He strode out of the woods into a deserted space, slashed by wind and rain. The guards seemed oblivious to it – and Robert reached out to help them a little. With the smallest brush, he pushed their attention away from Arlie.

He gained the shrine in seconds. Thunder rolled above him as his knife came out and cut the bonds holding Arlie. He left the rope around the man's left wrist to stem the flowing blood. As the last thread was cut, Arlie fell forward and Robert caught him. With a silent grunt he hefted Arlie on to his shoulder and turned back for the woods where Finn was waiting. Together they got him on to a horse with Martha mounted up behind to hold him steady.

'You get moving. We've got seconds, no more. Head up the track to the river. If we can get over the bridge before they reach us we'll be safe.' Robert sent them on their way then turned back to see where Jenn was.

At that second, lightning flashed across the sky – and Jenn raised her hands as if to put a curse on the men before her. Then with a kind of manic laugh she turned and ran further up the hill – away from Robert. Two of the guards moved to follow her but the others glanced back to find their prisoner was missing. Instantly the alarm was called and Robert took off.

He ran through the woods, higher up the hill, until he found Jenn, panting for breath. He grabbed her hand and together they raced on until they reached Finn and the others. Through the storm they could hear the sounds of pursuit. They had to get to that bridge.

They trotted the horses along the track but as quickly as they moved they were still too slow. The guards would be on them in minutes – with the rest of their number. This was not going well.

'There!' Micah shouted suddenly, 'the bridge!'

The wood ended abruptly with a wide canyon carved through the rock. A raging river tore through its heart, spanned by a frail bridge too narrow for more than one horse at a time. Trestle legs supported the bridge but it was the rope railings that held it high above the water. On the other side was the path into the mountains and safety.

'Take Arlie and Martha across, Finn. Go with them, Jenn. Take the horses.' Robert had to shout over the storm. The bridge creaked under the weight, but one by one they crossed safely. 'Your turn, Micah!'

But no sooner had he stepped on to the first slat than the guards finally came upon them. Robert whipped out his sword and blocked the entrance to the bridge. Micah was ready to turn back to help him, but Robert shouted for him to go. As Micah stumbled across, Robert swung his sword, desperate to keep the guards from the bridge, but there were too many of them. He killed the first but his place was instantly taken by another. Robert swung again but as the man fell, another rushed past and began hacking at the bridge rope. Micah was still out there and the violence of the blow made him slip. Robert rushed to stop the attack but he was too late. The first rope snapped and the bridge tilted. The wooden supports strained against the water's current and, desperately, Micah scrambled to hold on.

Robert turned back to the bridge but the guards were on him, crowding him, determined. He inflicted damage but he was outnumbered. Another gained the bridge and began hacking at the remaining rope. Robert tried to fight his way through but couldn't get near. He shouted a warning but even his own ears heard nothing over the storm. Suddenly the last rope snapped and the bridge was left to stand alone.

It wasn't made for this kind of misuse. Slowly it began to tilt further, then, with a jerk, fell sideways. With a yell, Micah slipped completely and fell, knocking his head. Through the rain, Robert could see the smear of red blood across Micah's face, saw him slide over the edge of the bridge, unconscious, his left arm hanging useless at his side. The bridge tilted again and the river tugged at Micah's feet. Robert strained to get to him, but he was cornered, fighting for his life. In agony, he watched Micah slide closer to death, when suddenly he stopped falling. A hand grabbed his clothing, two hands, desperately. Jenn!

Flat on her stomach, she held on to Micah against the river. But she wasn't strong enough to pull him back up. She needed help – but if Finn went out there, the bridge would surely fall.

Robert ducked a blade aimed at his head and slipped on the muddy precipice. He tumbled down to a rock ledge and had a moment's respite as the guard scrambled to follow him. In that second, Robert turned, haphazardly gathering his powers to hold the bridge but—

The bridge moved again. With Micah dangling over the side, Jenn holding on to him, the bridge shifted, shuddered and moved – *against* the current. Slowly it rose until it was almost level. Jenn hauled Micah alongside her, her face screwed up with the effort. Instantly Finnlay dashed out to her. Together they dragged Micah's body to safety. The moment they hit the mud, the bridge groaned again and collapsed completely.

As the last splinters of wood floated down into the canyon, Robert glanced back at the guard. They were upon him now, the first blade swung in his direction. He parried it, pushed the man back – then turned towards the river . . .

And jumped.

# 4

Pain.

Over and over he tumbled. Breathe ... water ... cold! Hold on, Robert. Concentrate. Find the other side. Move. Ignore the pain. Concentrate. Focus. Reach out. Reach out.

Pain.

Focus, damn you! Focus. Find the other side! Do it! Forget the bridge, forget the Guilde. Find the other side. Concentrate. Reach out, gather your damned powers you idiot! What good are they if you can't find the other side of the canyon!

So this was how Selar had felt ...

Focus! You'll drown if you don't focus!

*Robert, honest, I didn't touch the bridge ...*

That's it, push the pain down. Focus, concentrate. Reach out and there – there's the rock. Kick. Ignore the cold. You're getting closer. Touch the rock. That's it ...

Robert's head came above the water and icy air ripped into his lungs. Inch by inch he pushed himself up on to the rock and out of the torrent. For a minute he lay there, unmoving, until the pain resurfaced, the cold. He turned and looked back up the canyon. The bridge, the wood, the Guildesmen were nowhere to be seen. He must have been washed some way downriver.

With a groan, he climbed to his feet. No broken bones, nothing but a few bruises – and the hideous cold. He had to get moving before the cold could kill him. Before him rose the canyon wall, grey, wet with rain and beaten by the wind. But there was a path. All he needed to do was get to the top. Finnlay would find him. Finnlay was a Seeker. He would come and find him.

The rockface cut into his hands but they didn't even

84

bleed. At least the cold dulled the pain. His sodden cloak dragged him back, shuffled around by the wind like a mighty millstone. He wanted to tear it off and let it fall to the river and be swept away but he couldn't stop long enough. He had to keep moving, had to keep some warmth in his body.

*Why didn't you stop them ...*

*I know what you are, Robert ...*

Oliver! How had he known? Not just about him, but Finn as well. How? They'd never given anything away, never shown him, never told him. How had he known?

What was he doing with Blair and Seaton? Plotting treason?

Robert kept climbing. If only his thoughts could be as dulled as the pain in his hands. Further and further he climbed, but still the words tumbled in his mind.

The bridge.

He hadn't touched it. Hadn't even been able to marshal his powers to reach out and hold it. But it had moved! By itself?

Impossible. Then how? Only one way – and only one person. Finn would never be strong enough to do something like that. Arlie? Martha? No. And not Micah.

With a final scramble he gained the top of the cliff and landed on his face. He rolled over away from the edge and paused to catch his breath. Now he just had to stay awake. Finnlay would never find him if he slipped into unconsciousness. Stay awake and think about – what?

The Guilde. Oh, yes, things had changed in his absence. Somehow the Guilde had resurrected ancient laws and started applying them to normal people. Of course they'd not known Arlie was a sorcerer – they would have burned him at the stake if they had. No, Arlie had committed some small crime and they had cut off his hand in punishment. By the gods, Selar, what are you doing?

'There he is! Quickly now!'

Finn's voice, coming from where?

Robert tried to get up, but the cold had drained the last

of his strength. He was beyond shivering, beyond feeling. Blessed peace at last.

'Come on, Jenn,' Finnlay's hands were on him. 'Hold his shoulders while I lift him on to the horse. That's it. Now let's get him back to the fire.'

In a haze of grey, Robert peered through the rain at Finnlay's familiar face. In a croak, he murmured, 'It was Jenn, Finn.'

Finnlay laughed harshly. 'They're all right, Robert. We found a deserted shack. Martha's looking after them. We'll have you there soon. Just hold on.'

Robert just nodded. Finnlay hadn't understood – but it didn't matter. He soon would. They all would.

It was the pain that sent him to sleep – and the pain that woke him. Aching, blinding pain in every fibre of his body. At least he was still alive.

'Come, Robert, sit up and drink this,' Martha's lovely face beamed at him, her hand lifted his head. 'It will warm you, wake you up properly.'

Liquid poured down his throat and he swallowed greedily. It tasted good. 'What is it?'

'Never mind that.' Finnlay appeared behind Martha and Robert pushed himself up. He was lying on the floor of a shack, warmed by a crumbling fire. By the other wall lay Arlie and Micah, tended by Jenn.

'Arlie will be fine, Robert,' Martha smiled, bringing the cup to his lips again. 'And Micah will be up and about by morning. He's got a nasty gash on his head but it will heal. The important thing is that Arlie will live, thanks to you.'

'But we've got a problem, Robert,' Finnlay added, dropping his voice. 'The storm will die out before morning. We can't move Arlie that soon and if we stay here, those Guildesmen might find a way to get up this ridge.'

Robert took the cup from Martha and warmed his hands on the smooth pewter. Now it all made sense. 'I'm sorry, brother, but even if I were completely fit, I couldn't hold a mask for a whole day. Nobody could.'

'You're still not thinking clearly. You don't need to hold it for a whole day. Just when I sense them coming up the ridge. The point is, they could come at any time. You need to be up and ready if they do.'

Draining his cup, Robert nodded and handed it back to Martha for a refill. 'How much time have we got?'

'A couple of hours, perhaps more. I don't know. The wind has dropped and the rain alone won't stop them. I've scouted the track up the ridge. If we can make it to the first pass before they find us, we'll be able to hide on the plateau. After that, they won't want to follow us any more.'

'No.' Robert's eyes returned to the other side of the shack. Arlie lay propped up against the wall, his severed wrist bound against his chest. His face was pale and although his eyes were a little glazed, he watched Robert with something that resembled expectation.

Even after three years away it didn't stop.

'Where are the horses?' Robert turned back to Finnlay and finished off his brew.

'There's a lean-to just outside the door. I've dried them off and fed them but I haven't had time to rub them down properly.'

'Well,' Robert sighed, 'help your poor old brother to his feet, Finn. The exercise will warm me up.'

It was warmer in the lean-to than the shack – but six horses will do that, even in a storm. Robert tended to the nearest animal while Finnlay took the last. With every stroke of the brush, Robert's muscles ached, but as he worked, the pain subsided and eventually disappeared. He was on the third animal before Finnlay spoke.

'That was some effort – what you did with the bridge. I mean, I know you're the most powerful of us but I've never seen you do something that big before. I thought Micah was dead.'

'So did I,' Robert didn't pause, 'and I'd like to take credit for it but it wasn't me.'

'But—' Finnlay straightened up, utterly confused.

Robert couldn't help it. 'You mean it wasn't you?'

'Robert, honest, I didn't touch the bridge ... What are you saying?'

Ducking under the horse's head, Robert began brushing the other flank. Long even strokes helped organize his thoughts – even though those thoughts dismayed him. 'I'm saying that Jenn did it. She has powers – and before you start arguing, think about it. Neither you nor Martha are strong enough for something like that and even if Arlie had been conscious, it would have been beyond him also. We know Micah has no talents – so it has to be Jenn.'

Finnlay's face drained of colour as the idea sank in. 'And I'll bet she has no idea of what she's done, either.'

'No.'

There was a brief pause – then a complete change. 'She'll have to be Sealed, Robert. You know what this could mean?' Finnlay was all for going straight back to the shack, but Robert stopped him.

'No.'

'Damn it, Robert!' Finnlay slammed his hand against the frail wooden wall, making the horses jump. 'She'll have to be Sealed – there's nothing else for it. Don't pretend you think we can ignore this. She's strong – very strong. Strong enough to move a bridge that size. Could you have done it?'

'I don't know. Perhaps. The point is, I didn't.'

'Either way, I'll have to Seal her.'

'No.'

Finnlay came to a complete halt and stared at Robert. 'Are you serious? You really want her to go on unsealed and unprotected? What if she meets Malachi? Without a Seal she'll have nothing but raw shielding. I don't care how strong she is, untrained, she'd never avoid detection by the weakest Malachi. Mineah's breath, Robert, the Enclave itself is a day's journey from here. The danger ...'

'For pity's sake, brother, will you please calm down.' Robert sighed. 'Sometimes I wonder how you ever made it to Adept status. You have enough trouble controlling your temper, let alone your powers. I didn't say she wouldn't be Sealed – but you will not do it, I will. I sincerely doubt there are any Malachi around here. They, more than anyone else, believe the tales of monsters and such which have always been associated with the Goleth, so you can calm down. Of course I have no intention of letting her loose on the countryside without any protection. She, like all of us, needs a Seal to warn her if Malachi approach her.'

'And if you Seal her,' Finnlay added, 'she'll be your candidate and since you're not a sworn member of the Enclave you're under no obligation to take her there. She'll be under your protection alone. She won't meet others of her kind and won't join us. Despite the fact that Micah needs medical attention – which he could easily get at the Enclave – you're still determined not to attend the Gathering, regardless of the circumstances. Is that it?'

'If you like,' Robert nodded wearily. 'On the other hand, I could point out that she doesn't like you very much – a fact for which you only have yourself to blame. And if she doesn't like you, she's hardly going to trust you, is she?'

Finnlay's jaw jutted out in defiance but he didn't pursue the point. 'When will you do it?'

Robert shrugged, 'Have you tried Seeking out those Guildesmen yet? Are they on their way up?'

'Last time I tried was just before you woke up. There was no sign of them.'

'Well,' Robert ducked his head out of the lean-to and glanced up at the dark sky, 'the rain has stopped. We've about an hour before sunrise. I'll do it now.'

Martha looked up when they got back into the shack. She glanced at Arlie then rose to speak to Robert. 'I have to thank you, Robert. If you hadn't helped us, Arlie would be dead.'

'What happened?' Robert drew her close to the fire and put another damp log on to the flames. 'How did they pick you up in the first place?'

'We were waiting for Finnlay. He'd said he might catch up with us in Solmoss. I didn't realize he'd gone to look for you. There'd been a fever in the village. It had already killed one child and three more were sick. You know what Arlie's like, he can't stop himself helping people if he can. So he made up a tonic – nothing more. He gave it to the children and they got a little better. Then those Guildesmen came into the village and started asking questions. They said it was against the law for anyone outside the Guilde to practise healing.'

'What? When did this happen?'

Martha replied. 'I don't know but they were very serious about it. The children were getting better but Arlie refused to leave them. So they arrested him. They didn't even wait for a judge – they just tied him to the trium and . . .' her voice trailed off.

Robert nodded. So the Guilde had finally made a move against the Church. They wanted the hospice work out from under Church care. And why? Because any service offered by the Guilde had to be paid for – and they would have no rivals. At least, not under Vaughn. And Domnhall had been unable to stop them.

What had he come back to?

'Anyway, Robert, I just want to say I'm glad you're back in Lusara. We were afraid you would never return. As it is, you chose a good moment.'

'Did I?' Robert couldn't look at her, couldn't address the unspoken questions in her eyes. Instead he turned his attention back to the most pressing problem. This would have to be handled very delicately.

Jenn was seated beside Micah, spooning broth into his bruised mouth. Robert couldn't help noticing how small and young she looked – even if she was a little old to be developing her talents for the first time. Usually this sort of thing happened at around ten or twelve or even younger. Jenn would have to be at least sixteen, if not older.

'Well, Micah, you look a little better. How do you feel?'

Micah glanced up, then winced. 'Not so bad considering I'm still alive, my lord.'

'You should keep still,' Jenn chided him, bringing another spoon of soup to his mouth. 'Eat, you need your strength.'

'Listen to her, Micah,' Finnlay added pointedly, 'she knows what she's talking about.'

Jenn glanced at him quizzically, but it was Micah who asked what he'd meant.

'I can't really tell you, Micah,' Finnlay shrugged. 'I'm not the one who can move bridges.'

'Finnlay,' Robert said wearily.

'My lord?' Micah frowned.

Robert settled on the floor by the fire and sent a warning glance to both Arlie and Martha. She sat beside her husband, taking his good hand in hers. Unlike Finnlay, she seemed to sense the need for quiet.

But Finnlay couldn't keep silent. 'Jenn saved your life, Micah. She pulled that bridge back together long enough to get you to safety – using sorcery!'

'That's enough, Finn!' Robert snapped, but the damage was done. Over the space of a few seconds, Jenn turned pale and her eyes widened. His brother was ham-fisted and belligerent – and had absolutely no sense of timing. If they weren't careful, they would scare the poor girl half to death. When would Finn learn that his way was not the only way to do something?

'Me?' Jenn murmured vacantly. 'What do you mean – sorcery? I don't understand . . .'

Robert shook his head slowly, throwing a searing glance in Finnlay's direction. 'No, I don't think you do.'

Her hands trembling now, Jenn laid the bowl down on the ground. 'You're accusing me of sorcery? But everybody knows there's no such thing any more. All the sorcerers were killed off centuries ago. It's been more than a hundred years since anyone even saw one. How could I . . .' her voice trailed off as she glanced away. When she turned back, there was a mixture of anger and defiance in her eyes. 'You would turn me over to the Guilde after all?'

'By the gods, no!' Robert held up his hands. 'I, of all people would never do that.'

'Then what are you talking about?'

Micah eased himself up to half-sit against the wall. 'I'd

like some more of that broth if you don't mind.' As Jenn tore her gaze away from Robert, Micah added, 'My lord, are you sure about this?'

Robert nodded, emptying his bowl. 'I'm afraid so. Jenn, do you know what happened at the bridge?'

She glanced at him, still suspicious. 'It was falling. That's all.'

'What about the moment it moved level again. Do you remember that?'

'I . . . remember wishing it would – that's all, I swear. I just wanted to get Micah to safety. What's the harm in wishing for something?'

'Aye, what indeed?' Robert almost smiled at the innocent question – but stopped himself in time. Instead, he reached into his bag and brought out a flask of wine. 'So you don't remember doing anything . . . more? Anything unusual?'

'Like what?'

'So you just wished the bridge would hold?'

'Yes. Didn't you?'

Robert glanced at Finnlay who raised his eyebrows and asked, 'That's it? No preparation? No *ayarn*?'

Robert held up a hand to quieten him. 'It seems so. I don't suppose you've ever done anything like that before?'

'All I did was wish the bridge would hold. If that's a crime then, no. I'll never do it again.'

This time, Robert did smile. 'Oh, I think you will. But have no fear, we won't be handing you to the Guilde. You see, what you did tonight is, well – here, let me show you.'

Not taking his eyes from her face, he flicked his left wrist in a movement so familiar now he could do it in his sleep. He held up his hand for her to see. 'Do you know what this is?'

'It looks like a stone from a river. A white stone,' she replied, edging closer despite her obvious wariness.

'That's exactly what it is – or rather, what it was. Now, with some help, it has become an *ayarn*.' He paused. This was the point of no return. Taking a deep breath, he continued, 'It is a tool sorcerers use to focus and direct their powers. It can also act as a shield to hide discovery by another sorcerer. It's nothing special in itself, nothing more than a common stone – but no sorcerer is ever without one.'

Her mouth opened – then snapped shut as the meaning of his words sank in. Abruptly she said, 'I don't believe you. Sorcery doesn't exist any more. If it did people would know about it – and they don't. This is just some stupid game.'

Robert shook his head slowly. 'Just watch.' He took another deep breath and focused his eyes on the stone. With comfortable familiarity, he reached down deep inside himself to the place where his power dwelt. Raw and formidable, its strength was controlled only by the *ayarn* – and years of practice. Even now, after all this time, Robert was still awed by the potency of its force, the ease with which he wielded the power. It provided him with his sharpened Senses, the strength to perform the impossible – and more problems than he cared to admit. Nevertheless, he would never choose to be without it. It was too much a part of him, of his soul.

Feeling Jenn's eyes upon him, Robert pushed the power into action, sent it through the *ayarn*. As the seconds passed, the firelight died away.

Then – slowly – a tiny blue light appeared in the centre of the stone. At first it grew only gradually, then quicker, until it became a narrow rod rising from his hand. It rose higher and higher until it almost reached the roof and then it suddenly burst, plunging them all into darkness again. There was a breath of wind and the fire sprang to life once more.

Robert looked up from the *ayarn* and found Jenn staring at him, her eyes open in wonder. 'That . . . that was sorcery? That's why you think I moved the bridge? Because you're a . . .'

'Exactly.'

She put the pieces together. 'That's how you knew about Arlie's punishment – because it's not just a story to you – and that's why you helped me even when you knew it was the Guilde who were chasing me? Because it was the Guilde who killed the last of the sorcerers.'

She stopped for a second, glancing away. Then her eyes darted back to him. 'Is that what happened before you left Lusara? Did the Guilde find out what you are?'

'What?' Robert scrambled to keep up with her but she'd already moved on.

'And you think I am a sorcerer?' She laughed ironically. 'I'm sorry, but I don't see how you think I did something to that bridge. Why could it not have been you? Or your brother?'

'Because once you know you have powers, you know when you're using them. Often the first time comes as a surprise. It did with me – of course, what I did was nowhere as spectacular as what you did today.'

'And you're sure it was me?'

'Positive.'

She shook her head again and slumped back against the wall. Beside her, Micah companionably reached over and patted her hand. 'Don't worry, you'll get used to the idea.'

She turned on him, suddenly suspicious. 'Not you, too?'

He shook his head, 'Alas, no. Sometimes I feel quite left out.'

Jenn stared at him for a moment then began laughing again.

'I don't see what's so amusing,' Finnlay grunted.

Jenn ignored him. 'So I pulled the bridge back long enough to get Micah across?'

'Yes,' Robert replied. 'You did it using the same kind of power that my brother and I have. There are not many of us around any more and we like to keep our existence secret – for obvious reasons.'

She thought about that for a moment then, frowning slightly, she moved forward. 'And what was that thing you had, that stone? Can I see it?'

Feeling Finnlay's eyes on him, Robert held it out for her to take a closer look. With any luck, this wouldn't be too difficult.

Her hand reached out but she paused. 'May I touch it?'

'Of course,' he said casually, 'it's just a stone.'

Moving a little closer she said softly, 'But how did you make that light? How . . .'

Her fingers hovered above the *ayarn* and Robert felt a strange tingle in his hand. He frowned, not recognizing the sensation. The tingling intensified as her hand came closer and he was about to say something when she touched it – and a flash of light shot out of his palm throwing him back hard against the wall. For a second he lay there dazed, then everything went black.


'Robert! Robert, can you hear me?'

Grey fog clouded his eyes, a morass of wallowing shadows. He struggled against them, trying to clear his vision. As they gradually subsided he became aware of a searing pain running up his left arm, pounding in his head.

'Robert!'

'Yes . . . I hear you . . . Finn,' he croaked. Turning his eyes towards the voice, Robert could see the concerned face of his brother and above him the thatched roof of the shack. He pushed himself up and groaned as the throbbing in his head intensified.

'Don't move.' Finnlay reached over for a water bottle and held it to Robert's mouth.

The cool liquid was like a balm on his burning throat and he drank greedily. As he handed the bottle back to Finnlay, he turned to the other side of the room. 'Jenn,' he said suddenly, moving to get up. 'Is she . . .'

Martha crouched over the girl. 'She's alive. Unconscious, but alive.'

'It didn't touch you?'

'No. Just you and Jenn. I've never seen that happen before. What was it?'

'I don't know.' The pounding in his head subsided to a dull throb and with Finnlay's help, Robert stood. His left arm still burned but he had to see Jenn, had to know she was all right.

As he knelt down beside her, Micah glanced at him with

a look which, despite his shock, bordered on wry humour. 'I thought you knew what you were doing.'

'Aye, so did I.' Turning to Jenn, Robert tried to find any sign of life in her face. Eyes closed and with a face as white as snow, Jenn barely breathed. Not daring to touch her, he leaned forward and called her name.

Slowly, her eyes opened and locked on his. They focused and she gave him a weak smile. 'Yes?'

'How do you feel?'

'I feel fine,' she whispered. 'But you . . .'

'Don't worry about me,' he shook his head. Strictly speaking, she should be dead – a flash like that would be enough to kill. Not that it had ever happened before – at least, not to him. And why should it happen now? There was no reason at all. He reached out to help her sit up but the moment he moved his left hand pain flashed through him like lightning. He gasped, suddenly dizzy, and Finnlay scrambled to his side.

'By the Gods, Robert, look at your hand!'

Robert lifted his arm to the light. His hand was red and burned, his fingers clenched in a tight fist. Steeling himself against the pain he slowly released the fist, opening one finger after another until his palm and the stone that laid there were revealed.

'Serin's blood!' Finnlay swore, and with good reason, for the smooth river stone which had once been alight with fire now lay broken in two, split through the centre.

Robert stared at it for a long time. That small familiar shape was now gone and replaced with something entirely different. He could hardly recognize it, and yet he knew it was his own *ayarn*. The pain in his head subsided and was replaced with a sensation less familiar but no more welcome. But fear was a healthy thing and he took a deep breath before turning his gaze back to Jenn.

'How did she do that?' Finnlay murmured breathlessly. 'No one can split an *ayarn*. It's impossible!'

'Obviously not.' Robert sat back and, with his right hand, carefully picked up the pieces of the stone. He slipped them into a fold of his shirt and got to his feet. 'It seems we'll be going to that Gathering after all.'

Finnlay kept watch all through the day, mostly in the shelter of the lean-to, where it was warm. He kept his *ayarn* out, not daring to let an hour go by without scanning for that guard. But still they did not come. The weather had cleared to a fine drizzle, so he was happy they were not actually travelling.

As the light began to fade, Robert came out to him with a mug of warmed wine.

'Still no sign?' he said, turning his gaze to the ridge.

'Nothing. I don't understand it.'

'Perhaps they thought we'd be too far ahead to catch by now. On the other hand, they may have come to the same conclusion about the bridge as we did.'

'By the gods, I hope not!' Finnlay sighed. 'The last thing we need right now is a confirmed sighting of sorcery. I just hope they didn't recognize you.'

Robert shrugged and leaned back against the wall. His face, as usual, was impassive, his tone casual. He gave no outward sign that he was concerned about anything. How did he do that? How could he just ignore the situation? After all, it was a good thing that guard wasn't coming up the ridge because without his *ayarn*, it would almost kill Robert to provide a mask big enough to hide them. But did he say anything? Do anything? No. He just stood there as though he didn't have a care in the world.

Irritation grated at Finnlay. He wanted to shake Robert's almighty calm, wake him up to the reality of life – Lusara, the Enclave, the bloody Guilde. He took in a swift breath. 'What do you think Oliver is up to?'

There was almost no reaction. Merely the shift of Robert's gaze from the mountains. 'I don't know. He's a grown man, Finn. I have no say in his decisions.'

'Then you think he's plotting something with Blair? They're a powerful combination, you know, but not remotely strong enough to overthrow Selar. They wouldn't

97

be able to get the support they needed – but if you joined them . . .'

Robert turned and began walking away, down the ridge. Finnlay dropped his cup and hastened after him. 'If Oliver is mixed up in treason it's because you refuse to do anything about Selar. He's only involved now because of you. And don't forget, he knows about us – don't ask me how, but he does. That makes it even more dangerous to leave him alone. He should be Sealed, too. We should have stayed and done it, then, if he's ever captured he can't tell anyone what he knows.'

Robert came to a halt on the edge of a sharp drop and gazed down along the ridge. His hair was black with the rain and sticking to his face but he seemed oblivious to it – along with everything Finnlay had said.

'I wish you'd make up your mind, Finn. If we'd stayed, Arlie would be dead now. If I go and join Oliver then I could never Stand the Circle and lead the Enclave. As it is, I've said I'll go to the Gathering.'

'But you won't Stand, will you?'

'No.' Robert turned to look at him, his green eyes dark and full of something Finnlay could not understand. 'You don't *know* Oliver is involved in treason, but even if he is, I can't do anything to stop him and you know I won't join him. When will you learn, Finn, this is a battle you will never win?'

With that, Robert turned and headed back towards the shack. But Finnlay couldn't leave it there. 'And what about Jenn? Your *ayarn*?'

Robert stopped and faced him again. 'What about her?'

'We're about to take her to the Enclave – through the gate. After what happened with your *ayarn*, we have no idea how she'll react to the screens.'

'I suppose it would be rather disconcerting if she managed to blow the top off the mountain.'

Finnlay stiffened. 'That's not funny. Sealing is supposed to keep the secret of the Enclave so that it's impossible for someone to talk about it with anyone who's not also Sealed. But how do we know it worked with Jenn?'

'We could test her.'

'You Sealed her, Robert, and therefore only you can test it. Without your *ayarn* you can't even do that much. Think about it. We're about to reveal a secret that's been kept safe for centuries. For all we know she could walk out and tell the first person she meets. And that, as I'm sure you know, would mean the end of us all.'

Morning came, and with it, a low cloud of fog which hung about the mountains like a funeral cowl. Soft and eerie, it damped every sound so that even the movement of the horses along the rocky path was deadened. Tall granite towers lined their passage through the mountains, appearing like ghosts through the mists. Going right through her thick woollen cloak and heavy dress, that same fog seeped into her bones – and into her soul.

Sorcery!

Was it possible? Was the legendary Earl of Dunlorn really a sorcerer? It was inconceivable! And why had she never heard about it before? He must have some trick to hide it. They all must . . .

And she was now one of them.

All night she'd lain awake going over what had happened at the bridge. Over and over until she finally found the moment. That's all it had been, too – a single moment. With Micah hanging over the side, she'd cried out to the gods to make the bridge hold fast so they could get Micah to safety. Just that – a tiny, single second in time. That's all it had taken. And that was sorcery?

But there was no such thing any more. It was history – fact! How could it be a lie – for five hundred years? Oh, Robert had been so perfectly calm telling her – bringing out his stupid *ayarn*, and for what? So he could almost kill them both?

And now she was travelling with them, the Guilde searching for them. The Guilde . . . those monsters . . . And where was Robert taking her? To meet more sorcerers? Would they let her go afterwards?

No. They wouldn't. If there were so few of them around they'd want to keep every one they found. She would be a prisoner – their prisoner. A prisoner of sorcerers. A prisoner of evil for ever hunted by the Guilde.

But it was not too late. If she found the right moment, she could slip away. If she could find her way back down through the mountains she would be free of them. But she had to do it now, before they went too far.

She looked around. They were travelling along a narrow track which wound along the mountainside. Micah had ridden beside her all morning. It was impossible not to like him. His sunny face and guileless blue eyes held nothing but warmth and concern for her welfare. As though sensing her disquiet, he'd stayed by her side, almost willing her to be comforted. But he was nursing his wounds and although he made light of them, she knew he must be in pain. On the other hand – that could be useful. Micah would be less likely to notice her absence if she just slipped away. The others rode in front, Martha supporting Arlie and Robert leading the trail.

Hardly daring to hope, Jenn let her horse slow down little by little until the others disappeared around a corner of the track. She came to a stop and waited. With a little smile she turned her horse and headed downhill. She had to move slowly and quietly. Just a little further, past this granite tower . . .

The bridge.

There was no other way down without crossing that canyon – or was there? She stopped again and quickly ran over in her mind every turn they'd taken since leaving the ridge. Yes, there was a way. A path that would lead down into the valley.

When she found it she almost laughed. It was steep, across the slope of a ridge, but they would never catch her – especially if she wasn't on the same trail as them. The fog swirled around her, but now it had become her friend, hiding her more and more as she travelled further away from them. She couldn't see very far ahead, the mists were too thick but here and there, great boulders appeared out of the gloom like sentinels guarding her path.

Then abruptly the trail died out – but it continued a little further up. Turning her horse towards it, she saw the old path had ended in a cliff dropping away so far she couldn't see the bottom. It was lucky she'd been paying attention. She continued on the new path for a while when suddenly the horse lurched on the shifting rocks. She gasped, grabbing a tight hold. The horse stumbled again, unable to find a solid footing. Stones tumbled down the slope beneath her as the horse began to panic. With a scream, it reared and she fell to the ground.

The horse reared again and she scrambled to catch the dangling reins, but the rocks worked against her. Falling now in a sliding sheet, the rocks beneath the horse rumbled downwards, taking the poor animal with them. With a final scream, the horse went over the drop and disappeared.

Jenn closed her eyes and tried not to listen to it land. A dull thud came seconds later, going right through her heart. How could she have been so stupid? So careless? So full of herself, she'd managed in less than half an hour to kill that pitiful horse – and in such a terrifying manner. And where had her so-called sorcerer's powers been? Had she managed to save the horse? No!

She lay there for a moment, not even bothering to hate herself. Then with a sigh, she moved. There was nothing for it now but to continue on foot. She got to her feet, steadying herself with her hands. She took one step forward but the rocks slid again. With a groan they shifted and she stumbled, landing on her knees. She would have to turn back before this whole mountainside collapsed beneath her.

Terror gripped her. Heart pounding in her ears, she came to her feet once again. She turned slowly but the moment her foot came down she lost her balance and fell flat on her face. She scrambled for some purchase but the entire slope was moving, dragging her down. With the drop only feet below her, she screamed—

And something grabbed her arm. She stopped sliding, gasping for breath as the rocks beneath her continued their journey over the cliff.

'Keep still!'

It was Finnlay. He had hold of her. She tried to look up. She caught a glimpse of him stretched out on his stomach, his strong hand gripping hers – the other hand holding his *ayarn*. Behind him, on the solid path was a shadow – horses, people . . .

'I said keep still – this isn't easy, you know!'

Slowly the rocks around her stopped moving, but he didn't let go.

'Now, put your feet down – there, where it's solid. Be quick, I can't hold it for long.'

She dug her toes into the rocks again, but this time they stayed firm. Grabbing the nearest handhold, she dragged herself upwards, feeling Finnlay pull on her arm at the same time. Her knees and legs scraped against the sharp rocks but she hardly noticed. Inch by inch she moved upwards, not daring to look.

'Keep coming. Just a little further.'

Finally, she managed to get on to her hands and knees and clambered back to the original trail. Finnlay sat beside her, getting his breath back. She dropped her head, gulping in air and fighting back tears. Her hands were shaking, but suddenly there was an arm around her shoulders and Micah's murmured words of comfort. She turned and buried her head in his chest. Freedom or death. It seemed she had no choice at all now.


'You have to admit, it was a pretty stupid thing to do.'

Jenn turned in the saddle and tried to see the expression on Micah's face. He wasn't angry – merely pointed. For hours they'd shared the horse and in all that time he hadn't spoken, but then, neither had she.

'You could have got yourself killed along with your horse,'

Micah continued. 'It also wasn't very nice of you to get me into trouble like that. I was supposed to be looking after you. I'm sorry I didn't do a better job.'

'But it wasn't your fault!' Jenn replied before she could stop herself. 'I didn't mean . . .'

Micah reached forward and patted her arm. 'I know, Jenn, but you should know, these are good people. You have nothing to fear. They will never harm you.'

'I wasn't afraid.'

Micah didn't reply and they sank into silence for a while. But Jenn didn't want the silence. She wanted to know . . . so much. 'How did you find me?'

'Finnlay found you. He's a Seeker.'

'What's that?'

'I could tell you, but the question is, should I? Do you really want to know or are you just making conversation?'

'She really wants to know, Micah,' Robert murmured behind them.

Jenn glanced over her shoulder at him. He was gazing unconcernedly up at the grey sky, watching the fog slowly clearing.

'A Seeker,' Robert continued, 'has the ability to search for a person he or she knows. It is a rare but very useful talent and one which takes years to perfect. A truly powerful Seeker can even detect the aura of a sorcerer he's never encountered before – but the conditions have to be right.'

'What is an aura?'

'A kind of signature, if you like, part of our powers. Every one of us is different.'

'So I couldn't have got away anyway?'

'No.' He turned his gaze on her. 'What I need to know, however, is why you would want to? Are we such terrible company? Or do you still not believe in sorcery?'

Believe? What kind of question was that? How was she supposed to respond? 'Oh, I believe. I just don't understand. How can I? What have you told me? Nothing. You didn't even ask if I wanted to know.'

Robert brought his horse alongside but kept his gaze on

the others ahead. He smiled. 'An interesting concept – asking you if you want to know something without telling you what it was. I assume, though, what you really want to know about is sorcery.'

'Wouldn't you?' Jenn demanded, annoyed by his tone.

'No question – I did when I was in your position. But I do apologize, I really should have told you more yesterday.'

'Then tell me now!' If Jenn had been standing she would have stamped her foot, but she contented herself with a simple glare. 'Where are we going? Why me? Why doesn't anybody know about sorcerers?'

'About us, you mean?' Robert smiled again. 'That's deliberate. We keep our powers secret because we'd be destroyed otherwise – just as the history books say. And yes, before you ask, we can be destroyed. We nearly were once. A few survived and came here to Lusara to found the Enclave. With the help of an object called the Key, the Enclave has remained a secret and its defences still stand today, five hundred years later. The Enclave is a community of sorcerers. They survived the early years but not without loss. Within a year of its founding, the Enclave suffered a great tragedy, a fire, which almost destroyed the library they'd brought with them. As a result, much of what we once were has been lost. One of the Enclave's great tasks has been to regain what was lost.'

'And all the sorcerers joined this Enclave?'

'Not exactly. Some were killed, others left and drifted into obscurity.'

'And some,' Micah added, 'became Malachi.'

'Indeed,' Robert nodded, 'but I'll go into that another day. As to why you are a sorcerer? Again, I don't know. As far as we know, talent is not passed from parent to child. My brother and I have powers, but neither of our parents did – in fact, nothing in my family history even hints at it. That's why we have Seekers. It seems that sorcerers develop their talents as they come into adulthood. As I said, often the first experience is a shock. Seekers go out into the country looking for these people and hopefully bring them

104

back into the fold. Only about half of our sorcerers have children with talents.'

'And we're going to the Enclave?' Jenn asked quietly.

'Yes.'

'And will I be allowed to leave?'

'Of course! It's not a prison. You're just as free today as you were yesterday.'

'Then why are we going? Because I broke your stone?'

'You've made Finnlay quite happy. He despaired of ever getting me to this Gathering. But I suppose it could be worse. It could be snowing!' He laughed and shook his head. 'It's funny how things work out. I help you out of a spot of trouble with the Guilde and in return – you give my brother something he's wanted all his life. Still, I'd better go and slow him down, otherwise we'll lose him in the fog. As things are, I would not be as efficient as he at finding him on this mountain.' With that, he kicked his horse and cantered along the track.

Jenn frowned. 'Is he always like that?'

'Yes,' Micah nodded. 'As long as I've known him. He seems to have the most extraordinary inability to take himself seriously. Sometimes I almost despair.'

Despite herself, she smiled. 'And what did he mean about things being as they are? Is he not a Seeker?'

'Most certainly. My master is the most powerful sorcerer within the Enclave, stronger than any in its past. Finnlay, however, is a more powerful Seeker. It's the only thing at which he excels, since Finnlay is relatively weak in his other powers. Aside from that, my master has lost the use of his *ayarn* and therefore cannot use his powers.'

'Why not?'

'The *ayarn* is a tool for focusing power, as he told you. But it also shields the user from over-exertion. To use your power without one could kill you. However, you moved the bridge without one and suffered no ill effects. I believe that's why he wants you to go to the Enclave.'

'But I . . .' Jenn shook her head. She was used to surviving difficult situations, but this was all too much. 'Oh, I give up!'

Micah chuckled but Jenn couldn't take offence. 'All right, tell me. Where is this Enclave?'

He reached forward and pointed out across the deep valley they were approaching. 'See that peak yonder? The sharp jagged one? That's the Goleth itself – and that's where we're going.'

The valley rose almost vertically on either side, topped by seemingly impassible needle ridges. Between them, dusted with a fine layer of cloud, was a single peak, grey and forbidding. No plant lived there, no trees or animals. A bleak grey rock, towering above its neighbours. The Goleth.

The Enclave.

# 5

Ayn returned to her seat at the end of the council chamber and faced the children. They sat on both sides of the long table, wide-eyed, curious and not a little in awe of this room where their history was painted on the stone walls surrounding them. Some of the most famous Enclave debates had seared the air of this room – not to mention some of its most infamous decisions. This was the heart of the Enclave Council of Elders, and Ayn had brought them here to explain some very particular lessons.

She folded her hands together and looked at each of the children in turn. Their waiting faces were illuminated by candlelight shining from the tall stands in each corner of the room and the silver star-shaped holder lying in the centre of the table. Ayn let her eyes drop to the star and the eleven lit candles standing on its points. There was one more candle, but it was unlit and would remain so until another elder had been chosen to take Marcus's place.

Ayn drew in a breath and began speaking. 'Upon these walls you see our history; these are the years after our people came to this mountain. The story you are now beginning to learn. Before that lies a greater history, that of the centuries before we came to this place, of the time before we had to hide our talents for fear of death. Despite our best efforts, to this day sorcery is still believed to be the greatest power of evil by those outside these walls. You, children, are the new generation. By the next moon, you will all move up into your next class and begin the training which will define your adult lives, but before you do, it is my duty as an elder to make you aware of some of the most important aspects of your life here.

'We live on the precipice of mortal danger. This Enclave

– these caves we live in – was created out of bare rock to house and protect us. It does so with the aid of the skilled members who live here – but that does not mean it will always remain so. It would take so little for our home to be discovered and once done, we would be destroyed. Yes . . .' She paused, taking in the doubtful glances of the children. None of them were much above twelve years of age, still fresh in their enthusiasm and new to their powers. For such as these, dire warnings held little weight. 'There are still those within the world who desire nothing but our blood. And then there are the Malachi.'

Ayn paused and leaned into the back of her chair. This was such an unpleasant task, but it was about the only one she felt capable of attending to. This was a grim speech – she was in a grim mood.

'Soon after our forefathers came to this continent, there was a tussle for power between those remaining who had together created the Key. Two groups emerged, one led by a man called Edassa, whose father was reputed to have created the Word of Destruction. Edassa, embittered by guilt for abandoning our ancestors to fight the empire alone at Alusia, wanted to take the Key and make the empire pay for having turned on them. The Key, however, chose another path. It struck down Edassa, paralysed him until he was barely able to speak. Then our forefathers left Edassa and his followers and came here to found the Enclave. Edassa and his people travelled elsewhere. Over the last five hundred years, we have come to know them as the Malachi – and that their sole intention is to eliminate us all and regain the Key. They called us the *Salti Pazar*, in our ancient language, the Treacherous Ones. Out in the land, a Sealed sorcerer cannot be sensed by a Malachi, though lessons you will learn here will help you to sense them. Never forget, however, that the Malachi have sworn to destroy us. And why?'

She looked at each of them in turn but didn't receive an answer. Good: they were listening.

'Because they want the Key and its power. They would use it to find the lost Calyx and unleash a terrible power upon the land. They would discover the Word of Destruction and then there would be no power on earth that could halt their domination. Even as we rely on the Key for our safety, we are also entrusted with its safekeeping. Although we do not possess a sorcerer powerful enough to wield the Key to its full potential, we live in the knowledge that one day there will be among us one who will rise and speak to the Key. Legend tells us that on that day, we will find where the Calyx is hidden. From that day we will have the power to emancipate ourselves from this prison and be free once again to walk the land as sorcerers.'

Ayn rose to her feet. The children came to theirs also. Not a single one shifted or fidgeted or murmured. 'Until that day, you must all learn, study, practise – and most importantly, obey the laws governing us all. To that end,' she paused and looked directly at the fair-headed boy on her left, 'I must warn you: under no circumstances are any of you to attempt the kind of dimensional shift you tried this morning. It is dangerous – to you and anyone close by. But whether it's dangerous or not is irrelevant. The point is: it is forbidden.'

The boy lifted his chin defiantly but said nothing. She would have to keep an eye on him. She was about to continue when there was a knock at the door. She turned to find her friend and fellow councillor, Henry, sticking his head into the room. His bushy eyebrows framed his face like a ledge on a cliff, but his face wore a grin.

'I'm sorry to disturb you, Mistress Ayn, but somebody has come through the gate.'

Ayn frowned. 'Of course they have. People are arriving all the time. Or have you already forgotten about the Gathering, Master Henry?'

'I think you'll want to see this for yourself.'

Ayn studied him for a moment. Whatever it was, it was obviously nothing bad. Well, she was about finished anyway. She dismissed the children and followed Henry out into the main cavern. As they took the corridor to the surface she couldn't help glancing sideways at him, but his face was merely smug. Ayn was not amused, but she refused to ask. Instead she said, 'How many candidates have we ready to Stand the Circle so far?'

'Six – the same as this morning. What are you hoping for – a miracle?' There was a twinkle in his eye but Ayn ignored it.

'I always hope for miracles, Henry, otherwise I wouldn't keep talking to you.'

His laughter echoed along the stone walls and vanished into the sunshine beyond. Ayn limped up the incline, cursing the pain in her hip. It always got worse as winter approached. Normally Marcus would be able to ease the pain a little. But now Marcus was gone and this winter she would have to cope without him. She would have to cope without him for the rest of her life. They'd been together so long that it was still difficult to believe he was no longer around. Their daughter Fiona had been a great comfort over the last few weeks, but even so, Ayn still found it difficult to talk openly about her loss. There remained something very private about the whole thing.

But it was early yet. Time would dull the pain, if not remove it. The real problem was surviving until then.

'There,' Henry said as they came out into the sunshine. He pointed across the wide green bowl which sat atop the mountain like a crown. With the jagged edge of the peak lining the outer rim and reaching to the sky, it was sometimes difficult to remember that there was a world outside to worry about.

Ayn squinted in the dwindling light, but all she could see was a knot of people gathered around the entrance to the gate. 'Who is it? Damn this secrecy, Henry, and tell me!'

He didn't, though. He just took her arm as if she was an invalid and walked her across the grass, stopping only when they reached the knot of people. His behaviour irritated her, which is why she didn't really grasp what she was seeing. At least, not at first. Then—

'Robert!'

The crowd parted and made way for her as he turned

with a smile on his face. He strode towards her and swept her up in a hug which threatened to crush her frail old bones. 'Oh, Robert, I don't believe you've really come home to us! Finnlay always said one day he'd change your mind but I was so sure you wouldn't.'

'Actually, I haven't, but we'll get to that later.'

She stood back a little and looked up at him. She'd forgotten he was so tall. With his broad shoulders draped in an old black cloak and his wavy hair tousled from the wind, he was a commanding presence. And the rest? The warm smile, the confident bearing and the laughter in his voice did nothing to hide the shadow around his sea-green eyes. She was burning to ask him why he'd returned, but for now it was enough to know that he had.

She turned her gaze to the others with him. 'Micah! How you've grown. Martha, Arlie? What happened?'

The joy of Robert's return paled as he told her. She quickly gave orders for Arlie to be taken to the healers and soon they were left alone. With a grim face, Ayn turned back to Robert, then paused as she noticed the girl standing behind Micah.

'Who's this?'

Robert shrugged. 'This is a problem.'

'That's no kind of introduction, Robert! But come, my bones are too old to stand outside like this. Let's go in.'

Half an hour later, with the others shooed off to find food and drink, Ayn heard the rest of the story in her apartment. Robert sat on the edge of his seat with an absorbing stillness, full of concealed power and raw energy – and yet totally relaxed. As always, she was mesmerised just listening to him. Three years had changed nothing.

'That's really all I can tell you,' Robert finished, leaning back in his chair. 'And Micah's wounds are nothing compared to the bruise to his dignity. Still, it could have been so much worse.'

'What about your burns?'

'It's nothing. They heal well enough. It just means I'll have to wait a little before I make another *ayarn*. It doesn't matter – after all, I doubt I'll see much more trouble between here and Dunlorn. What does concern me, however, is the girl.'

'You were right to bring her here. You didn't . . . help her in any way?'

'How could I? I couldn't even marshal my own powers to save Micah. You know what it's like, how much concentration it takes to do something that big.'

Ayn smiled. 'Actually, I don't, since you're the only person I know who could have done it, but I'll take your word for it.'

'And another thing – why didn't we pick up on her before now? You've often Sealed candidates long before any physical sign of their powers has manifested.'

'Our scans are not infallible, Robert. We would never have found you at all if it hadn't been for that little accident you had all those years ago.' Ayn smiled. 'I'll call a meeting of the Elders. I'm sure they'd like to hear your story firsthand – and meet our newest candidate in person. I assume that's the reason you came to the Enclave?'

Robert raised his eyebrows as though the truth was something he should apologize for. But Ayn knew him too well, and despite her disappointment she managed a smile. 'And what have you done to annoy Finnlay so much, eh?'

Robert glanced sideways at her. 'I'll give you one guess.'

'He wants you to Stand the Circle? It's only natural. You shouldn't hold it against him.'

'But you saw those people just now. Greeting me and celebrating my return like I was some kind of conquering hero, when we both know I'm nothing of the kind. I know what they expect from me, but I just can't give it to them.'

Ayn was silent for a while. It amazed her that after so many years, this extraordinary man was still incapable of seeing the obvious. They loved him because of who he was – not for what he could do for them.

'Finnlay and the others want you to Stand and let the Key choose you. Find the Calyx, give us our freedom. Until you do, I fear your brother will never give you peace. He believes

112

you're the one to wield the Key. So far it has given us little of what we need, and yet we know it holds so much more. But none of us here has the ability to control it well enough to find those answers. Marcus nearly killed himself trying, and he was strong. We know so little: the Key holds our answers.'

'So you agree with Finn?'

'Robert.' Ayn paused, framing her words from shreds of instinct. 'You've become a man without a path in life. You have no goals, nothing to work for. You're like a lost child wandering a dangerous forest. Your enormous talents are wasted, yet all around you, people cry out for your help.'

She stopped as he turned to look at her. His green eyes held a fathomless light that she could neither touch nor understand. 'Why can't you feel anything any more?'

Robert held her gaze, unyielding. Even his breathing stopped and for a moment, Ayn was powerless to move a muscle. Then abruptly Robert smiled, breaking the moment. He stood and bent down to kiss her forehead. 'Go call your meeting, old woman. I'll be with Patric if you need me.'

'And you really saw the Palace of Bu? In the flesh, as it were?'

Robert gazed across the cluttered room at his friend. Patric Ferguson was his own age, and quite a powerful sorcerer. But there the similarity ended. With the exception of their shared love of books, Patric was almost his total opposite. He had an incisive mind possessed of an extraordinary ability to take huge leaps of logic – and generally end up with the right answer – usually quite some time before Robert. But where Robert was tall, Patric was a little less than average height, slightly built and with the translucent white skin of a man who sees little sunlight. Patric didn't like going outside – he never had. He'd been born in the Enclave and would die there, without ever having had any real desire to go anywhere else.

Right now though, his keen dark eyes were alight with excitement and he kept running his hands through his messy

113

blond hair. 'Was the Palace as you expected it to be? I mean, I'd have thought that after five hundred years of neglect it would be little more than a ruin.'

'Certainly not!' Robert laughed, lifting a pile of manuscripts from a chair to make room to sit. 'It's virtually untouched. I guess the stories of sorcery are so established now that people avoid it at all costs. It's eerie though, walking through rooms which are almost as they were left, days before the last battle. Really, Patric, you should go and see it for yourself. You know far more about it than me. I'm sure you'd be able to make sense of it.'

Patric leaped from his chair and grabbed a bottle of something, then paused in the middle of the room, absently looking around for cups. 'I thought we had a deal, Robert. I never hound you about Standing the Circle and you stop telling me to go out into the big wide world.'

Robert found a pair of empty cups by his elbow and held them up. 'Did we have a deal? I don't remember anything of the kind. On the other hand, I do remember you promising that one day you'll come and visit me at Dunlorn – or are you now going back on that?'

Splashing wine into the cups, Patric shook his head vigorously. 'Not at all – I just never said when. Of course, I would've gone last Caslemas – but you weren't there, so what can I say?'

'You're lying through your teeth, Pat, but I forgive you.'

Handing Robert a cup, Patric watched him through a fringe of hair, quiet for a moment. Then, without any preamble, he murmured, 'Why did you come back to Lusara?'

Robert found his gaze drawn to the depths of his wine. He felt no desire to form any kind of reply and yet he'd known this question would come – particularly from Patric.

'Oh come, Robert, or I'll start saying you got tired of running away!' Patric shook his head but persisted, 'I don't think you could stand it any more, could you? Not knowing what was going on? Not being here to see it for yourself? Not being able to do anything?'

Robert consoled himself with a noisy swallow of wine. 'If you know so much, why ask me?'

'Because you never let anyone inside your head, do you, you old fool.' With a chuckle, Patric plumped back into his chair. 'Actually, to be honest, I'm not that surprised to see you. I always knew you'd come back.'

'Conveniently wise after the fact?'

'Not at all.' Patric shook his head again – then had to brush away the hair that landed in his eyes. 'You see, about six weeks ago I was studying this old book on Bonding. You know the one, green binding, from Hastmere? Anyway, I found this interesting dialogue on the patterns of Bonding between families of the upper hierarchy in the last century of the empire and it was really engrossing. Next thing I knew, I'd fallen asleep with my head on the book . . .'

'Which you do every second night . . .'

'Which I do every second night,' Patric continued without missing a beat, 'but this night, I had a bizarre dream. I saw you standing on a rock overlooking a golden desert. In front of you was a horde of the ungodlies, armed to the teeth. But they weren't attacking or anything – they were just standing there, looking up at you. You stood there with your hands on your hips, shaking your head. Then you said, "Well, if you're going to be like that, I may as well go home."'

Robert burst out laughing. 'Where on earth did that come from? And you believed it? You saw it as a sign that I was coming home? By the gods, six weeks ago I hadn't even thought about coming back.'

'Oh really?' Patric eyed him without humour. 'Then I suppose it was just a coincidence.'

Robert held up his hands in appeal. 'Oh, please, don't start that again.'

'And I suppose it was just a coincidence you happened to be in the right place at the right time to help this strange girl get away from the Guilde? And yet another coincidence that she happens to develop powers the moment someone is in danger? And an even bigger coincidence that she split your *ayarn* when you were only hours from the Enclave?'

'What do you know of it?'

Patric shrugged and folded his arms. 'I went and had a chat with Micah at the healer's while you were closeted with Ayn. I thought I'd save you the trouble of telling the story a second time. The girl was with him. She didn't have much to say for herself but that's not surprising, really. I should point out, Robert, that your arrival with her in tow has caused quite an uproar around here. My advice is to stick around until spring while they sort her out. Besides, you and I have some work to catch up on. I've discovered some interesting literature on the legend of the Word of Destruction written by Amar Thraxis. You have no idea how many books remain from the devastated library, and hardly anyone ever looks at them any more. Mainly because they don't give up instant answers to immediate problems. They're all hooked on trusting the Key. It's such a waste. I could show you now if you like. It's quite amazing . . .'

'Slow down, Pat,' Robert placed his cup on the floor. 'I can't afford to stay any more than a couple of days. Long enough for the Council to have a good think about Jenn. Whether she decides to stay here is her choice but I have to go home. I'll attend the Gathering only because I'm here anyway, but don't start getting ideas. If you want to catch up on work, my friend, then I suggest you try fulfilling your promise and come with me to Dunlorn.'

Patric was silent for a while, his eyes fixed on the cup in his hands. Then he said quietly, 'They won't leave you alone, you know. Selar, Vaughn or the Enclave. They'll never give up until they've squeezed the last drop of blood out of you. The Enclave has never forgotten the first day you came here and they're determined one day to get to the truth. If you really want to avoid that kind of involvement then I suggest you go now, while you still can. Go and leave Lusara for ever because, my friend, the time will come when you no longer have a choice.'

Jenn sat in a quiet corner, content to watch the casual comings and goings of people through the great cavern.

116

Beside her, Micah leaned back against the limestone wall, slowly making his way to the bottom of a mug of nutty brown ale.

She took in a tired breath and murmured, 'So if all these people are sorcerers – or most of them – what do they do here? Sorcery?'

'Many things. There are those who work to keep the community going and there are others who are engaged in studies about sorcery and its history. For all that sorcery is feared and considered heresy by outsiders, sorcerers themselves are limited in what they can do. Most of them here believe they are capable of much more. Their studies are aimed at learning about their powers. They also strive to find the fabled Calyx, which is said to hold all the answers.'

'What's a Calyx?'

'I'm told it dates back to the Dawn of Ages, when the first sorcerers walked the land. There are two books which mention its existence and what it can do, but no one here has ever seen it, nor even knows what it looks like. It is said it was lost before the battle with the empire, but Master Patric isn't convinced. A lot of his work is involved in finding the Calyx.'

'And Finnlay?'

'He's been obsessed with finding it from the moment he joined the Enclave. A lot of his journeys away from Dunlorn have been to search for other books, references, following any little trace he finds. It's never far from his thoughts.'

'And that's why he wants Robert to Stand the Circle? So he can help?'

Micah nodded. 'There's a whole wealth of lore belonging to these people, but a lot of it was lost in the fire. What they have now has been pieced together over five centuries. Really you would be far better off asking my master these questions. He knows all about it. He's been studying it for years, along with Master Patric. Between them I think they probably know more about the history of sorcerers than anyone else here.'

Jenn nodded and glanced again at the door opposite. The

cave ceiling came down in a rough curve and was met by a line of oak panelling going the length of the cavern. It was unusual in that it was the only room she had seen so far which had something so decorative. The door stood in the middle of the panelling, richly carved with images she could barely see in the candlelight. On the other side of that door, Robert and the Enclave council were talking about her – and had been for over an hour.

She sighed. It was pointless wondering about what would happen next, but that didn't stop her chewing it over like a piece of tough beef. She couldn't help it. The last few days had long surpassed her wildest nightmares. Glancing up at the man beside her, she said, 'Micah, is it just me, or does this whole situation look unusually peculiar to you?'

Micah let his back slide down the wall until he was sitting on the bench seat beside her. 'No, it's not just you. It is unusually peculiar.'

Jenn laughed. 'Oh, good. I feel much better now. Now I know I'm not really crazy, but in a lot of trouble instead.'

'Well, in the immortal words of my master, things could be worse.'

She looked sideways at him for further clarification.

'It could be snowing,' he finished, deadpan.

'And that makes a big difference?'

'Certainly does. Can you imagine the mess it would make in here?' He shook his head as she laughed. 'Besides, you're not in trouble. They just don't quite know what to make of you.'

'Really?'

'Yes. It happens from time to time. I believe they had a similar problem with my master. Of course, I wasn't around at the time but apparently there was some considerable consternation over how much more powerful he was compared to everyone else. For a while there, they thought things had taken a leap forward.'

'But?'

'Well,' Micah replied seriously, 'in some ways he works with these people, but the truth is he's not really a member

118

of the Enclave. He's never fully committed himself, never sworn the oath – that's part of why Finnlay argues with him so much.'

Jenn sighed. 'I don't know. This is all so confusing. I'll never understand it all.'

'It doesn't matter,' Micah said, and drained his mug. 'You have plenty of time to get used to your powers – if you choose to use them again. And then you can decide whether to stay and work here or continue on to wherever you want to go.'

'But if I . . .' but she never got to finish the sentence. At that moment, the door opposite opened and Robert waved them inside.

His gesture was simple, but for some reason the movement sent an uncomfortable tingle up her back. With Micah a step behind, she walked to the door. Inside the room was a long table around which were seated a dozen faces she'd not seen before and three she had, Finnlay, Robert's friend Patric and Ayn. All of them were turned to watch her arrival. Behind them, the walls were covered with paintings, richly coloured and undimmed with time. She wanted to pause and examine them, trace the detail with her hands, but the faces around the table were too compelling.

Robert closed the door behind Micah and moved to the head of the table.

'This is Jenn,' he said by way of introduction.

Jenn tried to study each of these people as they turned to study her, but the tingling in her back was worse now that she'd moved. It nagged at her attention, demanding she stretch to be rid of it.

'We've been told of your extraordinary effort at the bridge,' an old man to her left began. 'It was a most courageous act.'

Feeling the intense scrutiny of those around the table, Jenn shifted from one foot to the other, hardly able to frame a thought, let alone a response.

'Can you tell us how you did it – or what made you think of it in the first place?'

119

'I . . .' Jenn began, trying to shake off the distraction which was now working its way up her neck, 'I didn't really think about it at all. I only thought about Micah.'

A murmur arose as glances between the strangers were exchanged.

'But did you feel the power as you pushed the bridge back?' A man on the opposite side of the table asked.

Like a finger touching the crown of her head, pain erupted in her skull. She reached for the empty seat in front of her and sank into it. 'I felt . . . nothing . . . except—' she gasped and closed her eyes.

'Enough!' Robert moved quickly to her side, placing a hand on the back of her chair. 'I warned you this wouldn't work – now stop it!'

The pain gradually subsided to a dull throb, although her back still tingled. Slowly she breathed deeply, eventually opening her eyes.

'I said he would interfere, Ayn, but you assured me otherwise,' the man to Jenn's left grumbled.

'Oh, be quiet, Wilf. Can't you see the child's in pain?' Ayn rose from her seat. 'Robert's right. We can't force anything from her.'

A cup of wine was placed in Jenn's hands and she looked up to find Robert's apologetic face gazing down at her. She swallowed a mouthful and tried not to look at the others. What had they been doing to her? Why didn't they say . . .

'This is ridiculous,' Wilf slapped his hand on the table. 'How can we find out anything about her potential with this . . . renegade standing watch over her?'

Robert straightened up and favoured the old man with a smile. 'Well, I can always leave – but I'm afraid I'd have to take Jenn with me. She is, as my brother has so rightly pointed out, my responsibility.'

'Oh, really!' Wilf sat back.

'I told you to be quiet, Wilf, and I meant it. Robert is here at our invitation. If you think he won't carry out his promise then I must assume you've forgotten that he never makes empty threats.' Ayn reached Robert's side and, with a calm smile in his direction, she continued, 'We're faced with something we don't understand – and a child who is probably terrified by these bullying tactics – not to mention a situation she knows nothing about. May I suggest we try talking to her?'

There were a few quietly smug faces around the table at that. Then another man leaned forward and said, 'What about your *ayarn*, Robert? You said it split when she touched it.'

'Can you please,' Jenn said suddenly, wondering where the words were coming from, 'stop talking about me as though I was not here.' The pounding in her head still threatened to overwhelm her and it was only a determined effort that kept her from crying out. The insistence of these people was so irritating! But there was the comfort of Micah standing behind her – and Robert's imposing presence. Yes, she would happily answer all of their questions, but please, just let the pain stop.

There was a rustle of cloth and the scraping of a chair on the stone floor as the man rose to his feet. 'I apologize, Jenn. I did not intend to be rude.'

Beside her, Jenn could sense rather than hear Robert's soft laughter. Starting afresh, he answered the original question. 'Aye, Henry, the stone was split clean in two.'

'May we see it?'

As Robert reached inside his shirt for the stone, Jenn went to take another mouthful of wine but stopped with the cup halfway to her mouth as a strange ringing seemed to fill the room. She glanced furtively at the others but they were either accustomed to it – or hadn't heard it. Her eyes stopped on Robert, or rather, on the stone in his hand. As it came free of the cloth, the ringing grew louder and louder until the crash and tumble of a thousand church bells filled her mind. She couldn't drag her eyes away from the stone. She could hear voices, but they were far away and she couldn't really understand the words. All she knew was the stone and the bells, the tingling in her back and the pain in her head.

On and on it went as the stone was held up for the others to see, then placed on the table before her. Still she couldn't take her eyes from it. It drew her gaze like a beacon in the night, narrowing down until her entire world was encompassed by that single river stone, smooth, washed and split in two. Then a hand – her own hand – reached out and grasped hold of the two pieces, her fingers tightening around the stone as though they had a will of their own.

Suddenly she felt trapped, like a caged animal, the touch of cold steel and brooding stone against her cheek. The pounding suddenly clarified and became the sound of a galloping horse while around her was the scent of damp moss and rotting leaves, then—

Silence. The ringing bells had gone, the pressure, the pain all vanished. Suspended in time, she breathed cool fresh air. She let it fill her lungs with new vitality, stretching to every fibre of her body. Her head was clear, crisp and sharp.

She opened her eyes.

Robert was kneeling beside her, his eyes fixed on her face. She met his gaze and for a moment – just a split second – she felt she could almost read his thoughts, almost see deep into those dark green eyes. Then she looked down at her hand and mumbled, 'I'm sorry. I know I shouldn't have touched it but . . .'

She opened her palm and held up the *ayarn*, solid and whole once more.

The room exploded in uproar. Councillors stood and rushed forward, but Robert held up his hand, silencing them all. Then, very carefully, he reached out for the stone, but as his fingers came close to it, the stone gave out a tiny, almost invisible flash of light which died as quickly as it had lived.

The stone dropped into his hand and as she let go of it, Jenn felt incredibly tired. She tried to stand but her legs had lost their will. Dizzy and sick, she stumbled and would have fallen, but Micah caught her. He lifted her in his arms and then her eyes closed and she lost herself to oblivion.

*

122

Robert stood in the doorway of Ayn's bedroom while Finnlay hovered behind. Patric and Micah waited in the next room. Ayn, leaning on her walking stick, settled the covers around Jenn's neck. Then, with a gentle hand on the girl's forehead, she turned and shepherded them out, closing the door behind her.

'She's almost asleep.'

'Are you sure that's all it is?' Robert asked, afraid to trust to so simple an explanation.

'Robert,' Ayn said wearily, 'I'm a Healer, trust me – Jenn is fine.'

He waited for her to sink into the comfort of a padded chair, then said, 'I'm sorry.'

'What for? For bringing her here? Those old fools haven't had so much fun since the day I brought you into the hall and the Key spoke to you in front of them all! Things do get a little dull around here sometimes, you know.'

Robert perched on a stool and clasped his hands together. 'Yes, I suppose you're right – and things could be worse.'

'Please,' Micah raised both hands in appeal, 'don't say that again.'

Laughing softly, Robert nodded submission.

Finnlay had hardly moved from the bedroom door, but now he took a few steps forward to a seat opposite Robert. 'So what did she do? How did she put your *ayarn* back together?'

'I don't know. I mean, how did she split it in the first place? If we knew that, we'd be halfway to understanding.'

Patric leaned back against the wall and folded his arms. 'Well, since she obviously doesn't need an *ayarn* as we do, then perhaps she has some kind of antipathy towards it. Then again, that doesn't explain her putting it back together again. Robert, have you tested it? Does it still work the way it used to?'

Robert briefly closed his eyes and sent his senses out through the door and into the tunnels of the Enclave. Here and there he caught familiar auras. After a few seconds he returned, and opening his eyes again, said, 'Yes, perfectly.'

Ayn was staring at him with a frozen expression, but it was Patric who spoke. 'You can do that? Without even taking your *ayarn* out?'

'Come on, Patric, don't digress,' Robert shook his head. 'We were talking about Jenn. Whatever she did to my *ayarn* seems to have had no effect on it.'

With a huge sigh, Patric shook his head, 'Then we're back where we started.'

'I just want to know one thing,' Finnlay held up his hands and sat forward, his gaze intent on Robert. 'What are you going to do now?'

'Do?' Robert passed a weary hand over his forehead. He could be wrong, but he had a sneaking suspicion another argument was brewing. But this time he was not in the mood.

'About Jenn.'

'I'm sorry, Finn, but I don't understand the question. Are you under the impression that there is something I should do?'

'Oh, for Mineah's sake, Robert! I'm asking if you still intend to take her to some town in the middle of nowhere.'

Robert looked up at Finnlay. For some reason, he suddenly felt very cold. Not his flesh – his body – but inside. Deep inside. 'Yes, if that's what she wants.'

'But you can't! Think of what she could mean to us here? You've already said you know nothing about her abilities. What better place to study them than here, in the Enclave, with so many skilled people around?'

Robert turned away, unwilling to respond. Finnlay, on his feet now, carried on regardless, his ambition now raw and unfettered. 'Jenn could live here, so much better off than working as a serving girl in some tavern – and she'd be safe. You can't let her go and wander the country. Who knows what she might be able to do here? And who would know? She has no family, no friends. No one would miss her.'

The point dawned on Robert slowly. Finnlay had excitement in his eyes, the certainty of success. 'Well, that's just typical! We rescue her from a band of fanatic Guilde soldiers

– only to imprison her in a cave full of people who would use her themselves. Is that it, Finn? Who would know? Jenn would know – everyone here would know. What kind of community is it that makes decisions for its newest members without even telling them why? Is this what you're fighting for?'

Robert rose and took a step towards Finnlay, his voice no more than a husky growl. 'You want to keep Jenn here so you can study her powers, find out what use she can be. At the same time, you want me to Stand the Circle so the Key can choose me as next leader. Is that what you want, Finn?'

Still moving forward, he backed his brother to the door. He could see the edge of fear on Finnlay's face, but did nothing to ease it. This was too much – even for him.

'You want to keep us both here, knowing that the moment the Key chose me I would also be a prisoner for life, never able to leave this mountain. By Serin's blood, Finn, you wanted to know why I don't seem to care about people any more – and yet you yourself don't even give your brother or this poor girl a single thought!'

He paused, the icy hand gripping his heart. 'Get out. Get out of my sight!'

Finnlay fled the room, but Robert was blind to his leaving. It had been a mistake to come here, a mistake to think he could pass through untouched. He took a deep breath, warming the cold inside.

After several calming heartbeats, he felt a hand on his arm. 'You know, Robert,' Ayn said with a fresh smile, 'sometimes I wonder how you refrained from killing Selar all those years ago and taking the throne yourself.'

Robert turned away. 'Don't say that, even in jest.'

'Perhaps I wasn't joking.'

'Even more reason not to say it. I swore an oath to serve the King solely and above all others. To break that oath would not only dishonour myself but everything I believe in.'

Ayn edged her way forward until she stood before him, gazing up into his face. 'And is that really it, Robert? Is that why you won't join us now – because of your oath? Because you hold honour as high as that? But what price honour?'

Softening, Robert placed his hands on her shoulders. 'What would be the worth of any oath I could give the Enclave if I broke my oath to the King first? Eh? I'm sorry, Ayn, but I think you'll find that most arguments end up being circular. At least they are with me.' He glanced at the bedroom door. 'Will she be all right?'

Ayn nodded. 'Yes. You go and get some sleep. Even if you don't Stand the Circle tomorrow, your presence will still be expected.'

'And is that all that will be expected of me?' Robert asked from the door.

Ayn shrugged. 'Who can answer a question like that at this time of the night?'

The only way she knew it was morning was by the subtle increase in little noises which drifted around the caves and tunnels of the Enclave. Feet moving along sandy passages and greetings called between friends. The clink of glass and scrape of wood upon stone. Jenn had slept fitfully in the unfamiliar bed. Twice during the night she'd woken, certain she could hear the sound of horses coming towards her. But when she'd opened her eyes all she could see were the shadows cast by an oil lamp in the corner, and she knew she'd been dreaming.

Long before Ayn had come in to wake her, Jenn had lain still in bed, going over the last few days in the first peace she had had since the moment she had said those hasty words in front of the Guilde soldiers. So much had happened, and so little of it believable. Even now, in the cool fresh morning, she didn't understand what had possessed her to pick up that *ayarn* last night. At the time it seemed a reasonable thing to do – the only thing, in fact – but looking back, the most overwhelming memory aside from the pressure she had felt was the enmity of those strangers around the table. Their questions and their insistence filled her with disquiet even now and dampened her natural curiosity about the Enclave.

'I heard you talking last night,' Jenn admitted as Ayn passed her a bowl of thick meaty broth. The smell drifted to her nostrils and made her stomach yearn for nourishment. She pushed the cushions up against the bedhead and picked up a spoon. 'I couldn't help hearing, I'm sorry.'

'I'm sorry our voices kept you awake,' Ayn replied evenly. She came around the bed and sat on the side.

Jenn was silent for a while, then, realizing the old woman was noting her every move, she coloured in embarrassment.

'I wouldn't worry about it, child. There's a lot you need to learn simply in order to survive. You'll have to listen with ears more sensitive than that.'

Still only halfway through the bowl of broth, Jenn paused and rested it on her lap. She shook her head, utterly bewildered. 'You have no idea how confusing this is. Until two days ago, I'd always believed sorcerers had died out. To find now that you all live here on top of this mountain is unbelievable. But what is more incredible is that I . . . I can do these strange things. I can't help wishing that someone would just tell me what's happening!'

She couldn't continue even though she wanted to. Tears stung her eyes and her throat constricted until it hurt. She took a deep breath and wiped the back of her hand across her eyes.

'What do you want to know?' Ayn asked gently and handed her a piece of crusty bread. 'I don't know everything, but a little . . .'

Looking into her soup, Jenn suddenly found it difficult to put her questions together – which was annoying, since she'd just made such a fuss about them. Glancing up, she asked the first one which came to mind. 'Last night you said something about Robert and how he didn't kill the King – and before about how the key spoke to him. What were you talking about and what is this key and . . . what is standing the circle?'

Ayn nodded. 'The two questions are very separate. The

Key is something you'll see later this morning, when the Circle is formed. Our leader, called the Jaibir, is chosen by the Key in the ceremony. When he is chosen, his powers become permanently intertwined with the Key. The Jaibir's power keeps the Key alive. As a result, he must live for ever within the confines of the Enclave. Anyone can Stand the Circle and be chosen, but since the Key needs someone with strong powers to wield it, traditionally only the strongest of us do so.'

'Like Robert?'

'As you may have already guessed, Robert refuses to Stand. He has always remained independent of us, despite our attempts to convince him otherwise.'

'Why?'

Ayn shrugged. 'I won't pretend I understand him, child. He says he has his reasons. One way or the other, he refuses to go near the Key.'

'So, what does the Key do?'

'Many things. We use it to help decipher some of our older records, as an aid to teaching. Any important decision is usually put to the Key for approval. Its most important purpose is to keep the Enclave protected and invisible from the outside world. Without it we would have been discovered centuries ago. Our main problem is that we know it has a great many more uses, but without someone strong, we can only scratch the surface. We believe that there is a way we can live in the outside world without being destroyed, that we can be free – and that the answer is within the Calyx. But to find the Calyx, we must first wield the Key fully. Two of our major surviving records show it to be so. As it is, the Key is very helpful. It's quite a sight to behold. Grown men tremble in their shoes when the Key rises to question.'

'And is that what happened with Robert?'

Amused, Ayn nodded. 'He was nine years old at the time, but already strong in his powers. I'd found him and brought him back here – we didn't realize Finnlay had the same abilities at that point. Of course, Robert's father was still alive then. He thought his son was going to spend a month at a monastery in the hills. Robert was an odd child. Always asking questions, most of which nobody could answer – and never taking any answer he did get for granted. He had a quick temper and a ready laugh. He was open and affectionate, with an extraordinary ability to make friends with anyone. Marcus took an instant shine to him.'

Ayn paused, smiling a little, before continuing with her story. 'Anyway, I brought Robert to the hall where the Key had been set up for some work. Robert walked straight up to it. Then the strangest thing happened. We began to hear a voice speaking in a whisper. I knew it was coming from the Key because I'd heard it before. You can imagine our surprise. Nothing like that had ever happened before. The Key only ever spoke to the Jaibir – certainly never a child.'

Jenn held her breath. 'What did it say?'

'I don't know.' Ayn shrugged. 'I couldn't hear it properly – neither could anyone else. Robert knows but, true to his stubborn nature, he's always declined to illuminate us on the subject. He just says that it was personal.'

'And what did you say about the King?'

Ayn's smile faded as she drank some more. 'That's something else entirely. To be honest, I think you should ask Robert. However, be prepared for the possibility that he may not answer. He retains some loyalty to Selar and consequently cannot be drawn on the subject.'

'And now,' Jenn murmured to herself, 'he won't do anything no matter how important – because it would break his oath to the King. No wonder he's so lost.'

'Eh?' Ayn started at the comment, but as Jenn looked up with an innocent smile Ayn shook her head. 'You'd better get dressed, my girl. I've laid out a new gown for you, one my daughter has grown out of. The ceremony will start soon and you wouldn't want to miss it.'

Jenn climbed out of bed as Ayn poured hot water into an earthen bowl for her to wash. Ayn set out clean linen and soap, then disappeared for a few minutes. When she returned, Jenn was clean and dry and struggling to get into a gown of soft deep blue wool.

'Here, let me help you,' Ayn said with a motherly smile. She took the dress and dropped it over Jenn's head. It slipped down into place, then Ayn held first one, then the other sleeve for Jenn's arm. As she got to the second sleeve however, Ayn paused.

'What's that?' she whispered, her eyes widening.

Jenn glanced at the old mark on her shoulder and shrugged. 'A birthmark. Why?'

Ayn dropped her hands and stared openly at Jenn.

Feeling suddenly uncomfortable, Jenn moved to pull the sleeve up but Ayn's hand shot out to stop her.

'A birthmark? Of course it's a birthmark . . . by the gods! Don't you know what it is?'

Jenn shook her head, not understanding Ayn's reaction at all. 'No, I . . .'

'No, of course you don't. I can see it in your face. I'll have to call the Council . . .' Her voice trailed off as she moved quickly to the door of her rooms.

Jenn could hear her calling out into the cavern and as she waited, a shiver ran down her spine. She pulled the dress up around her shoulder, but the sense of foreboding which gripped her was all-consuming. She looked rapidly around the room. There must be some escape. Some way out . . . But there was no window and only the single door through which Ayn had just gone. Even now Jenn could hear feet on the steps outside and voices raised in question. Ayn was trying to explain to them.

'I tell you she has a House Mark, on her shoulder, right where it should be.'

Then Wilf's voice, 'But that's impossible! A girl with her birth can't have a House Mark. What kind of trick is Dunlorn trying to play here?'

'Calm down,' Henry said quietly. 'Do you want the girl to hear you? Ayn, are you certain about this? You know what it could mean? It's a serious matter if Robert has lied to us.'

'I can't imagine he would lie, not about a thing like this.'

'Then perhaps it's the girl,' Wilf added ominously.

Jenn listened and her stomach went cold. They were coming again, just like last night. They would push her, hurt her, trap her ... What were they talking about? It couldn't be good, not judging by their tone.

As they came closer and closer, Jenn felt more and more like a trapped animal, and the moment the faces appeared at the door, she reacted from pure instinct.

Her hands flew up in front of her and a wall of sheer white flame filled the doorway.

# 6

Ayn cried out a warning just in time, dragging Henry back from the edge of the flame. Around the doorway, the stone was already going black and the smell of burnt lime filled the little room.

'What in the name of the gods is she doing?' Henry demanded, examining his clothes. 'She can't do that in there. She'll kill herself! She'll kill us all!'

'We have to stop her.' Ayn turned quickly to Wilf. 'I'm no good at this sort of thing . . .'

Wilf shook his head and stepped as close to the flames as he dared. Raising his left hand, he brought his *ayarn* up. He stood there for a few moments, then stepped back. 'No, sorry. I don't know what she's doing exactly, but I can't break it.'

'This is my fault,' Ayn drew them back across the sitting room away from the door of flames. 'I shouldn't have reacted so badly when I saw that House Mark on her shoulder.'

'Did you catch which House?' said a voice from the door.

Ayn turned to find Finnlay moving through the gathering crowd. She shook her head. 'I don't know all the Marks, I can't tell one from another.'

'What did it look like?'

Ayn replied shortly, 'Two circles interconnecting with a diagonal bar through the lower. Look, I know you find all this very interesting, but if we don't do something soon she will incinerate not only herself but the whole Enclave. We have to get her out of there.'

Finnlay moved forward. He paused a few steps short of the fire and gingerly put out a hand to the flames. He remained there for a moment, then turned his head and said over his shoulder, 'She's not that strong. I could break this without much effort.'

'Such arrogance!' Wilf grumbled.

Henry held out a restraining hand. 'There's a chance you can, Finn, but the question is, should you?'

'Oh, don't be so lame!' Finnlay broke away from the older man's grasp and moved forward again. With a flick of his left wrist, he produced his *ayarn* and held it up to the flames. For a moment they seemed to flicker and a tiny hole appeared in the centre. Then they brightened again and the hole disappeared.

Finnlay dropped his hand and shrugged. 'Oh well, I guess she'll just have to burn.'

'Oh Finn!' Ayn spat in anger but didn't waste any more time on him. She turned to the crowd behind her. 'Get Robert in here. Now!'

Robert had heard the sound of people moving towards the upper galleries but he didn't think much of it until Micah came running to him, a look of urgency on his face. Robert knew something was wrong with Jenn; in seconds he was across the hall and taking the steps two at a time. As he neared the top, the crowd pressed back against the walls to let him pass. A narrow corridor led to the door of Ayn's sitting room and as he gained it, breathless, Micah arrived behind him.

'What is it?' Robert said, but then he saw the door to the bedroom and the wall of white flame.

'I'm sorry, Robert,' Ayn approached him, her voice frantic. 'I said something that must have scared her. Wilf and Finnlay have tried to break it, but they can't get through.'

Robert took a few steps forward and paused, concentrating on the flames and trying to see through them. He could sense a vague presence on the other side, but nothing more. 'She's all right at the moment but if she keeps it up much longer . . .' He whirled around. 'What did you say to her? Why would she do something like this?'

133

'Does she even know what she's doing?' Finnlay replied caustically.

Ayn ignored him. 'Robert, she has a House Mark on her shoulder.'

'What?' Robert froze.

'I was so shocked, I must have startled her . . .'

'Obviously! We'll discuss it later.' He turned back to the door and brought out his *ayarn*, but he didn't do anything immediately.

'I've already tried that, Robert,' Finnlay murmured. 'Not even you can break that wall.'

Robert's voice dropped to a whisper. 'Who said anything about breaking it?' Without another word he raised his hand and concentrated. Within seconds a clear bristling shield surrounded the burning doorway, strong enough to contain it. Satisfied with that, he took another two steps forward and walked right through the flames to the other side, arriving untouched as though the fire were unreal.

Jenn stood in the middle of the room, her face white and gleaming with perspiration. She watched him intently, her blue eyes glazed and bright.

Robert smiled gently, hiding his concern with a calm shrug. 'Thank you for letting me in.'

'I wasn't sure . . . But you took my side against them last night so I thought . . .' Her voice trailed off as her eyes left him for a second to glance at the door.

'Do you know what you're doing?' he asked carefully.

'No. But it's keeping them out. I don't trust them.'

This time Robert's smile was genuine. 'I don't much either. They're a strange lot, but they mean you no harm.'

'Really? What are they saying? What does it mean to have a House Mark? I just don't understand any of this. Why did you bring me here in the first place?' Jenn's voice rose in pitch.

Robert held up his hands to calm her. 'You know I had to bring you here – for your own sake, no one else's. But if you want to leave, we'll do so – right now. Just drop the flames.'

'Why?'

'Because you'll kill yourself, me and everybody within a hundred paces if you try to keep this up much longer. There's a lot you don't understand about sorcery, so you'll have to take my word.'

Her eyes were bright and burning. 'Trust you? Can I trust you? Will you tell me what a House Mark is?'

'Of course. I'll tell you anything you like. Just put the flames out first.'

'No.' She shook her head. 'Tell me first. What is a House Mark?'

'All right,' he nodded slowly. 'Actually, I'm surprised you haven't heard about them before, but I guess it's possible. You know the twenty-three major Houses in the country, those families whose ancestry goes back to the old empire and beyond? Every one has a birthmark, significant to their House. Every child born in the direct line has one, with their own individual variation, but still clearly that of their House. The House Mark is always on the left shoulder, small and there from birth. This is what I am told you have.'

'But how can I have one of those? My father was an innkeeper.'

'We'll have to investigate that later but right now . . .'

She shook her head again, 'No. I don't believe you. I have a birthmark, yes, but it's not anything like that.'

'How do you know? Look, I promise you, I'm telling you the truth. I have a House Mark myself, so does Finnlay.'

'Show me.'

Robert unlaced the collar of his white shirt and pulled the cloth back to reveal his shoulder. There beside an old battle scar was a mark, a triangle split with a double bar from top to bottom. 'That's the Mark of Dunlorn,' he said quietly, his eyes on hers. 'I am telling you the truth. Please drop the fire. I promise I'll protect you.'

She was silent a moment, then she nodded mutely. Suddenly a breath of fresh cool air wafted through the room and Robert realized the wall of flame blocking the door had gone. He turned quickly back to Jenn, half-expecting her to collapse again but she kept her steady gaze on him.

'I'm fine and – I'm sorry.'

Not taking his eyes from hers, he nodded, 'That's all right.'

Seconds later Ayn and the others rushed into the room.

Micah lifted the earthenware jug of wine and moved around the room filling the goblets with rich, spicy mead. Jenn, seated on a chair by the fire, watched him move carefully and discreetly from Ayn to Finnlay and Henry, to Wilf, Patric and Robert. She noticed the way the candlelight flickered across his freckled face, making his red hair a burnished gold. For all his sombre expression, Jenn got the impression that he was not deeply concerned over all that had happened, as though his belief ran so deep that he just knew it would all work out for the best. It was not the first time she had found his calm comforting.

Robert resumed his seat beside her and glanced at her with reassurance. He'd not left her side since she had dropped the wall of flames that morning, but she couldn't tell whether it was from concern for her welfare or for fear of her doing it again.

Right now she just didn't care. She was angry. Not just with these strangers, but also with herself. In all her life she had never felt fear strong enough to control her actions. But this morning, with those people . . . and what they had said . . . The worst part of it was, she really couldn't work out what they'd said that had frightened her so.

She never liked to admit she was scared, and had never done so aloud. She doubted she ever would – because it would be like giving up. Not just the situation, but a part of herself would be lost if she ever admitted to anybody that she was afraid. It was part of her shield, her armour against the world. Jenn is never scared, people said, and strangely enough, the less she showed fear, the less she thought about it, the less she felt it.

For a moment, Jenn closed her eyes and wished herself back home. Back in the taproom of Father's inn. The noises, the smell, the heat. So comforting, so familiar. The greatest

136

danger was a fight breaking out and tables being broken. Father had always protected her from anything truly dangerous, so fear had never been a major part of her life. Only that day when the grey-haired man had come to visit Father, only then had she been deeply afraid – but then, she'd been only seven at the time. He'd come, talked to Father, watched Jenn. He'd stayed a week and never said a word to her, though his eyes were always on her. Jenn had hidden from him in the end until he'd left, but that dark piercing gaze remained with her to this day. It reminded her so much of the way these people looked at her.

They were different, these sorcerers, different to normal people. At first she'd thought it was because they were sorcerers and she found herself understanding why people had always been afraid of them. Then she'd thought that perhaps it was because they lived way up here, away from normal society. But then she realized it *was* because they were sorcerers after all.

And now she was truly one of them.

Any last vestige of doubt she'd had disappeared as surely as if those flames had burned them away. So, they'd been right after all. She had moved that bridge and split the stone – and put it back together. It had been her. But why hadn't she known? Why had it just started? What had made it happen in the first place? She'd been in difficult situations before and nothing like that had ever happened. There had even been a couple of times when she'd wished . . .

She folded her hands on her lap and willed herself to be calm. It would not do to go losing herself again at this stage. No. Now was the time to hold on to her anger and to use it. This time she was determined to get some answers. For the moment she couldn't decide which was worse, being caught by those Guilde soldiers – or being saved by Robert Douglas, Earl of Dunlorn. Since the former would have lost her at least an arm and the latter, it seemed, her freedom, it was a difficult choice. So she kept her eyes on the comforting presence of Micah pouring wine.

'You all know what happened this morning,' Robert began.

Jenn nodded absently as Micah finished and took up a place behind Robert's chair. She turned her attention to the faces around the room. Wilf, with his creased and podgy face screwed up with what she could only assume was anger, kept his eyes firmly on the wall behind her. Henry was more subtle. His expression was one of sincerity, as though this was all just some huge misunderstanding that could be easily cleared up. Patric appeared merely interested but Ayn kept brushing her hair back from her face. Of all of them, she looked the most uncomfortable.

Finnlay sat by the opposite wall, eyes downcast and grim. Although there was a very close resemblance between the brothers, at this moment, Finnlay looked like a complete stranger. His dark hair fell across his face, obscuring his burning brown eyes. She knew they were burning – what else would they do? Without thinking, she said, 'What are you going to do now?'

Finnlay started, assuming – correctly – that the question was meant specifically for him, but before he could answer, Henry sat forward and spoke.

'Well that depends largely on you, my dear. On what you want to do.'

Jenn looked at him, appreciating his kindly face, his gentle tone. 'Me? How can I decide anything? And what difference would it make anyway? You've already decided what's to become of me. Finnlay is determined that I stay here. He thinks he can sway his brother to leave without me and it's not just him. Go on, deny it. Deny that you're all thinking how much I can do for you here.'

Out of the corner of her eye she could see Robert trying hard to conceal a smile. In that moment, she decided. She could trust him after all. If he hadn't tried to hide the smile, or if he'd said anything at all, it would have been different. But he hadn't. Instead, he seemed to hold the opinion that she had the right to determine her own future – unlike these others. Perhaps that was really why he didn't fully belong to the Enclave. Perhaps that's what he didn't agree with.

Henry slowly shook his head, 'No, I would be a liar if I said I'd not thought about how much you could help us. You must understand, child, you have a unique talent.'

'Unique? How?'

Henry raised his eyebrows, offering the question to some-one else. The others, however, remained silent. 'Well, the power you have, we all have – is inside you. You were born with it and you will die with it. We don't really know what it is exactly, or what makes one person have it and another not – but we do know that it's a raw power and one that's fuelled by your own body. If you use it too much, you'll quickly become exhausted – beyond that, it will kill you. Believe me, it has happened. That is why we use an *ayarn*. It reduces the amount of energy we use, at the same time protecting us from a backlash. The stone itself is nothing special. We choose them at random – then put them through a process which bends them to our needs.'

He paused to take a sip of wine then turned back to her. 'You need to understand all this in order to appreciate how we see your abilities. You've performed at least four workings of enormous power without the aid of an *ayarn*, or a shield of any kind. You should be dead – and after this morning, us along with you.'

There was no reproach in his voice, but Jenn held his gaze before looking away. Her eyes rested on Finnlay a moment longer, but he refused to look at her. She let him smoulder in silence. 'All right, so we're not all dead. What does that mean? Why am I so different?'

She asked the question gravely and was a little put out when Robert chuckled quietly at her side. She turned her head and said archly, 'I'm glad you find this so amusing.'

Rather than look ashamed, his smile widened. He shook his head in apology. 'I'm sorry. One day, I promise you, you will understand why I laugh. For the moment though, take no notice of me.'

There was a pause, then Henry addressed her last question. 'I don't know why you can do the things you do. Answers like that take time – and others, like why at your age you should suddenly develop powers. Normally the signs are there at a much earlier age, about five or six.'

'You're making the assumption,' Wilf grunted from his seat, 'that she is in fact a sorcerer.'

All eyes turned to him and he continued, 'After all, we know so little about what we do. Who's to say that she doesn't have some other kind of power? Something we've never seen before.'

'What other kind is there?' Jenn asked him directly.

'How should I know? I'm only saying that we know just enough to know we don't know everything.'

'I think you're trying to make this unnecessarily complicated,' Ayn murmured. 'Don't confuse her with any more possibilities, please.'

Henry held up his hand to forestall the discussion digressing. 'The point I'm trying to make is, that there is a lot we could learn about your powers if you were to stay here, with us. You would be a full member of the Enclave and receive all the training and education you need. You would have the opportunity to achieve your full potential – whatever that may be.'

Jenn couldn't miss the way Robert stiffened at this proposal. He kept his face schooled and said nothing, but his silence spoke volumes. She didn't understand his reasons, she only knew that if she asked him, he would suggest that she not stay at the Enclave. She burned to know why, but knew she would have to wait for the right moment to ask him.

She turned back to Henry. 'I understand all that. What I don't understand is why my having this House Mark should affect it all.'

Silence.

Jenn glanced at each of them, but they all found somewhere else to look. Exasperated, she turned to Robert.

He shrugged and held out his hands to the fire. 'I'm afraid I didn't fully explain the significance to you this morning. I was anxious for your safety and I didn't want to go into lengthy explanations. However, what I omitted to say was that – you have a House Mark for a reason. As I said, only those in the direct line of descent bear the Mark. I do, but my cousin does not, if you understand.'

'Yes, but . . .'

Patric suddenly lost his cool detachment and leaned forward, his eyes alight. 'For you to have a House Mark means that you must be the daughter of the head of one of those Houses.'

Jenn held her breath as his words sunk in. She hadn't really thought about it much since the morning, but now she did, of course it made sense. She glanced at Finnlay again, but his face was in profile as he stared at the stone floor. There was something going on here that she didn't know about. 'Which House?' she asked simply.

Robert took in a breath. 'From the description, I'd say an eastern one, near my own. However, considering your age and the style of the Mark, I have to say I believe you are a daughter of the House of Elita. Your father is Jacob Ross, Earl of Elita.'

Jenn's heart began to race. 'My father? But . . . how can that be? Surely . . .'

'How much do you remember of the Troubles?'

'The Troubles? What has that to do with it?'

Robert waited for her reply.

'I don't really remember much at all. The Houses were at war with each other. King Edward tried to restore order but he wasn't strong enough to do much more than watch. After three years, Selar invaded. That's all I know.' She watched him, mystified, waiting for clarification.

Robert nodded. 'Before Selar came nearly all the houses were involved in the Troubles. Feud built upon Feud. Then there is the little-known fact that raids were carried out on one House after another – raids designed not only to wreak havoc on the enemy but also to kidnap a child of each House. Preferably the heir. Those children have never been seen again.'

141

Jenn shook her head slowly. 'I've never heard that. How many were taken?'

'Seventeen confirmed kidnappings in all. The thing is, Jenn, all those taken were boys of around the age of three or four. Only one girl was ever taken. You.'

'But I remember growing up at Shan Moss. I remember my father as far back as I can. If I was taken the same as those others, why can I remember so much?'

Finnlay chose this moment to enter the discussion. 'Wait a moment, Robert. I don't remember reading anything about any girl being taken. What makes you so sure she is Jacob's daughter?'

'Apart from the Mark on her shoulder?' Robert replied quietly. 'I was at Elita the day after she disappeared.'

'What?' Finnlay sat forward as all eyes in the room now turned to Robert, but he ignored them.

'I was travelling through Elita lands and stopped to pay my respects to Jacob, who was a friend of my own father. What I found was a scene of tragedy. His youngest daughter had been playing by an old ruined mill. She'd wandered off on her own and was never found. The only thing her nurse could say for certain was that she heard a splash in the river by the mill. She and Jacob believed the child had fallen into the river and drowned, her body taken away by the swift water. After I'd heard this story I rode down by the river. I found the tracks of many horses. They went no further than the mill, then headed up into the hills. The tracks were fresh and in amongst them was a single child's footprint. I tried to tell Jacob what I'd found, but he was stricken with grief. I decided I would wait. Then Selar invaded and there didn't seem much point in telling him any more.'

Jenn shook her head, unable to understand any of this. 'So they all think I'm dead?'

'Yes,' Finnlay mimicked, 'they all think you're dead.'

Jenn's eyes snapped around to meet his. At that moment she could happily have hit him, but instead she just let him see her contempt. When he finally looked away she turned back to Robert. 'I'm sorry, but I think I'm still missing something. What has this got to do with whether I should stay at the Enclave or not?'

'Well, for a start, it means you have another option. You could return to Elita. Jacob would be shocked, but he'd be delighted to have you back.'

Jenn frowned, but couldn't completely take that in for the moment. 'Go on.'

But it was Wilf who spoke. 'What he's trying to avoid saying is that apart from himself and his surly brother here, you're the only other member of a great House who is also a sorcerer. That little fact is of great significance to us.'

'Why?'

'Well, look around you, girl. None of us can do the things you can do – and none of us, no matter how talented, is anywhere near as powerful as Robert. I would say at a guess that once you're trained, you two would be evenly matched – but that's only a guess. None of us here has really seen the true extent of Robert's powers and he keeps the facts to himself. Finnlay missed out on the greater share, so between you and Robert you could probably outdo half the Enclave put together.'

'Really?' Jenn's eyes widened. She'd not realized there was so much at stake. Now it all began to make sense. 'So coming from a major House has something to do with sorcery?'

Wilf laughed. 'By the gods, child, if we knew that we'd be halfway to finding the Calyx.'

'So, what are you going to do?' Finnlay could hold his peace no longer. 'My brother has insisted you be allowed to make the choice yourself, and no one here has the courage to gainsay him.'

Robert sighed wearily. 'Finnlay, that's enough. If you want to fight with me that's one thing, but don't take your revenge out on Jenn. I won't stand for it.'

Finnlay stood and put his hands on his hips. His glowering face was formidable, but lacked the intensity of Robert's level gaze. Though they looked alike, even Finnlay's searing fury could not match the indomitable presence of his brother.

With a sharp intake of breath, Finnlay snapped, 'I don't understand you, Robert. You refuse to be involved with anything that matters – the Enclave, your country, even the King – and yet you take the side of this girl from nowhere over an argument that's really got nothing to do with you. You're not doing a very good job at staying neutral.'

Robert climbed to his feet also. 'I've already made myself clear. I don't have to answer to you or anyone else – one of the privileges of being neutral, as you call it. If you don't understand my reasons, then I'm sorry – but that doesn't change the fact that if you want to get at Jenn you have me to deal with first.'

Jenn listened to them, hearing the anger and long held frustration in Finnlay's voice and the dark determination in his brother's. She found herself standing and moving to a position between them. 'You don't have to argue any longer. I've decided what I'm going to do.'

The air was thick with anticipation as she spoke her next words. 'I'll go back to Elita.'

'Would you help me with this?'

Robert looked up from his book to find Ayn standing in the doorway of his room, holding out a white stole in one hand and a palm full of silver studs in the other. He stared at them a moment, then pushed his chair back from the table and stood. Keeping his thoughts under tight control he murmured, 'So, you're going to Stand the Circle, too.'

She put the studs in his hand. 'Why not? I don't think the Key will choose me but I think it is up to me and others like me to give the Key some kind of choice.'

Robert took the stole and placed it around her shoulders, pinning it to her grey robe with the silver studs. 'Who do you think will be chosen?'

'I'm not the best person to ask. After all, when Marcus stood he did so for the same reasons as me – and he was chosen. I've seen five Jaibirs in my time here and I would

144

have guessed at none of them.' She paused. 'Perhaps Jenn should stand.'

Robert raised both his eyebrows as he finished attaching the last stud. 'So you broach the subject at last. You think to make me change my mind by suggesting Jenn take my place in the Circle – that if I care about her welfare I would sacrifice my own principles to save her. Interesting.'

'Oh, Robert, please . . .'

'Don't.' Robert stopped her with his hands raised. 'Sometimes you can be as bad as my brother.'

'I find myself understanding him very easily. He'll blame you for taking Jenn away, you know.'

Robert shrugged. 'He can add that to the list.'

'He will say you poisoned her against the Enclave and the place you're taking her to is far away. How will she receive any training? How will she survive as a sorcerer? Will you teach her?' She reached up and put her hands on his arms. 'Please, I beg you to reconsider. Stand the Circle and finally allow the Key to make its proper choice.'

He looked down into her familiar tawny eyes. It would be so easy to give in. So simple to do as she wanted. She asked so little – and he owed her so much. Her and Marcus. He had wanted this. In his steadfast and forthright manner, Marcus had said over and over again that Robert should take his place. But now Marcus was dead and all Robert had left of him was his widow, dear, faithful Ayn. Her eyes pleaded silently, but she used no power on him. This – this silence was the hardest to bear. To reject her now would be to tell her to her face that he did not respect the memory of her husband, that he did not love her nor care about the community she lived for.

But he did care. He cared so very much.

Even as he turned away from her, a part of him cried out to tell her the truth, explain so she could understand, so she would not hate him. Why had she of all people come to ask this of him?

'I had hoped you and I would never reach this moment.' Self-loathing made the words taste bitter in his mouth, but he continued, unable to stop now that he'd begun. 'You and Patric alone have never asked me.'

Patric had always had his own theories, his own reasons for not pushing Robert. But Ayn? Her reasons now were obvious. She wanted him to help the Enclave, to serve it as she did. To help free them from this prison. He could make her so happy – and Finnlay and all the others. All he had to do was say yes.

Robert took a deep breath, squared his shoulders and turned back to face her. Her eyes searched his for some sign, some unbending of his stubborn will. In response, he shook his head slowly, the answer coming without effort. 'I cannot Stand the Circle, Ayn. Not today, nor any other day. Please understand that I can never do as you ask.'

He saw the words hit her, like a slap. Instantly he moved forward, desperate to reassure her. 'I've been away, Ayn, but nothing has changed. I'm still bound by the same constraints I was three years ago . . .'

She twisted out of his grasp. 'Why won't you tell me the truth? Why won't you say what the Key told you? How can it possibly be personal?'

'It's got nothing to do with . . .'

'Oh really?' she snapped, 'are you sure? I am. I have to be – because otherwise, I must assume your reason is nothing more than cowardice. That you're afraid to become bonded to the Key and never able to leave this place!'

Robert dropped his hands and stepped back. So this was his choice: do as she asked or be called a coward. But it was no choice at all. The choice had been made for him twenty years before – by the Key.

Yes, it seemed she would hate him after all – both because he would not say yes – and because he could never explain why. The Key had not even allowed him that much freedom. Two things it had said to him, two disparate messages, but because it had said them, he was now forced to lose one of his closest and dearest friends.

'I am sorry, Ayn,' he replied, his voice flat and dead. 'I must be a coward.'

She waited, her mouth shut firmly as though she were afraid to speak. Then, without looking at him, she walked out.

He could hear them gathering below, in the great cavern. Hours after the scheduled time, the Enclave was preparing to wake the Key. Robert glanced down at the forgotten book on his lap and, with a sigh, snapped it shut. He placed it on his table, then rose and went out into the passageway. It led to the gallery overlooking the cavern and there he paused, his hands on the railing. He was not ready for this. His public face was not yet in place, his emotions still raw and in turmoil. At any moment he was sure he could be persuaded to change his mind. But this had to be done. He had to make his appearance so that everyone would know he had chosen not to Stand. And once it was over – he could be done with them – all of them.

It was the voice rather than his battered senses which warned him of Jenn's approach. He straightened up slightly.

'You're not going to change your mind, are you?' Jenn said quietly.

Robert shook his head, 'No. Why?'

'Well, you looked so . . .'

'What?'

'Sad.'

Robert glanced at her, wondering how much of his mood she'd seen. Her expression gave nothing away, but still he frowned, 'Do you always do that?'

'Do what?'

'Speak your mind without regard to the consequences. It's just that I've noticed it a few times – and I can guess what happened with those Guilde soldiers. I just wondered whether you'd always done it.'

Instantly her face coloured and, equally quickly, he regretted speaking. There was no need for him to be cruel to her as well. He hissed in a breath, cleared his mind completely then spread his arms wide in apology. 'I'm sorry. It's been a difficult day.'

Jenn nodded slightly, but didn't seem much comforted by his abrupt change of mood. Instead, she moved to the railing and glanced down. 'I've just been talking to Finnlay. He was trying to convince me to Stand the Circle. Me, of all people!'

Robert was jolted out of his mood by this news. 'What's he been saying now? You know I just had a similar conversation with Ayn?'

'He was very . . . how shall I put it?'

As she sorted for the right word, Robert had to smile. 'Oh, please don't be diplomatic on my behalf.'

'Determined? Will that suffice?' Jenn grinned shyly in return. 'He told me he realized that my opinion of the Enclave was largely affected by yours and that if only I was to stay here for a while, I would see how it really was.'

'Exactly.'

'He didn't seem to realize how offensive it was, suggesting I was unable to draw my own conclusions from my experiences so far.'

Robert turned to look at her with new respect. Despite the earth-shattering changes that had happened to her, she still retained an air of control, of purpose, to think for herself. An independence. Perhaps that's how she'd managed to survive her strange past – and how she managed to make so many perceptive observations.

'I have to admit your experiences so far with sorcery and the Enclave have not been . . . inviting, shall we say.'

A warm smile lit her face as she replied, 'Oh, don't be diplomatic on my behalf.'

'Oh, I don't know,' he laughed. 'Perhaps Finn's right and you should Stand the Circle. They could do with somebody with a sense of humour for a change. And I could leave knowing my brother was in good hands.'

'Why do you think I want to leave?' She paused. 'Can I ask you a question? Is it true? Am I really Jacob's daughter? Do I really come from Elita?'

Slowly he nodded. 'Yes, it's true. But come, we must go down. They're about to begin. We'll discuss your father and your home later, I promise.'

The great hall was a dome of clean white limestone, as long as a field and half as wide. People streamed in from the doors at either end. Excitement and expectation fired their hummed conversation. They knew what was at stake here.

Micah and Patric were waiting on the cavern floor. As Robert joined them the ceremony commenced with a ringing bell – the Key was waking. In the centre of the cavern stood a pyramid of oak legs covered in snake-like tentacles of intricate carving. From its apex hung the bell, both beautiful and forbidding at the same time. This was the Key, but no human hand struck the peal.

The council entered and formed a line before the Key. Together, they raised their hands high and the crowd, almost four hundred souls, were instantly silenced.

In the centre of the line of Elders Ayn spoke, her voice clear and loud. 'Let all Gather within the Enclave and mourn the loss of our beloved Marcus, Jaibir and father to us all.'

A murmur ran through the crowd before she continued. Robert had only heard the litany twice before, but it was for ever burned in his memory. In all likelihood, he was the only soul here who really understood what it meant.

'Let all Gather within the Enclave to witness the choice of the Key. The Key to wisdom, the Key to life. The Key blessed by the gods and the heart of our power. In the choice of the Key comes the choice of wisdom. Blessed be the choice of the Key for that choice will be our Jaibir and father to us all. He will wield the Key, seek out the Calyx an-Feer and once more regain the secret of the Word of Destruction.'

The Elders spread out to form a circle around the bell with their backs to it. Now Henry spoke. 'Let all those who would be chosen step forward and Stand the Circle. But know only this. Darkness grows in the hearts of those who long for greatness. It is not to be believed that these are worth their own estimation. That is for the Key alone to decide.'

As he finished, a line appeared on the stone floor at his feet. Like an afternoon shadow, the line stretched out and grew until it had formed a perfect circle around the bell.

Then slowly it moved outwards, rippling along the cold stone flags until it stopped only feet from the crowd.

'Come now all those who would Stand. Come to the Circle and let the Key make its choice.'

The crowd waited in expectation. For a moment, nobody moved. Then, slowly, Wilf left his place and came forward until his feet reached the dark line on the floor. Then another man from the other side of the crowd moved. Then a woman to Robert's left – and then Finnlay.

Others were moving forward, but Robert was only vaguely aware – his eyes stayed firmly on his brother. Fear and dread gripped him. He had to get Finnlay off that line. This was not the answer.

But he had no right to stop Finnlay from doing this. It was Finn's choice to make, even as Robert had fought for that same right. Nevertheless, Robert had to try – and now, before the Circle began to move. After that, it would be too late.

He took a step forward but his arm was caught. He attempted to twist away and turned to see who was holding him.

Jenn gazed up at him steadily. 'No.'

The bell rang again. It was too late. Robert turned back to see the elders had moved outside the Circle. The bell began to glow. Twelve sorcerers now Stood the Circle, each facing the pyramid and the radiant bell which hung from its arms. Then, slowly and laboriously, the pyramid of supports dissolved away to nothingness, leaving the bell suspended in the air.

The glow increased, but rather than burn brighter, it fuzzed and shifted shape until the bell had gone. In its place was a sleek black shining orb which glistened like dew in the candle-light. The orb now gave out a faint pulsing hum which the crowd took up in reverent prayer. The cavern echoed with the vibration of the orb and the chanting crowd raised their hands towards the dome above. The pulse beat faster and faster, becoming a single solitary roar.

Then it stopped and silence reigned.

Suddenly, twelve arms of light shot out of the orb to pinpoint each of those Standing the Circle. White faces stunned by the light remained frozen in space as the Key went about its choosing. Time stood still as they waited. Robert could not take his eyes from Finnlay. If he should be chosen . . .

One of the lights died, its object rejected. Then another died and another until all but two remained. Wilf – and Finnlay.

Jenn's fingers dug into Robert's arm, but he was oblivious to the pain. He tensed as Finnlay's face was contorted by some invisible horror. Thoughts, feelings, words flashed across his face and vanished. Then abruptly, the light on him died.

Wilf had been chosen. The Key resumed the shape of the bell and the ceremony was over. Almost as one, the crowd rushed forward to congratulate Wilf. Robert ignored them, unable to take his eyes from Finnlay. His brother had not moved. Robert stepped forward, but before he could get closer, Finnlay turned, pushed through the crowd and ran out.

Music filled the great cavern as a dozen dancers cavorted across the floor, both tired and a little drunk. They were the last of the revellers. The remainder had either retired to their beds or sat slumped in quiet groups around the perimeter quietly talking.

Not yet sleepy, Ayn placed her elbows on the table and gave Henry a smile.

'It's been an interesting couple of days,' he said in sympathy. 'I hope things quieten down for a while after all this.'

'I don't believe you. I think you've actually enjoyed all the fuss Robert and his friends have made.'

Henry shrugged but didn't deny it. 'There've been a few questions raised, I'll admit, and the answers may take some time to find. But that's all the fun of it, isn't it?'

Ayn shook her head. 'I don't know. I think I'm getting

too old for all this. I even did something today I promised myself I'd never do. I asked Robert to Stand. I betrayed his trust.'

Henry raised his eyebrows in a neat white arc. 'Are you sure he trusted you to begin with? From what I can see, apart from his man, Micah, I don't think the Earl of Dunlorn trusts anybody but himself.'

Ayn twisted her hands together, not wanting to agree, but finding it hard not to. She was still raw from her encounter with Robert and her mind simply refused to clear. 'I used to think he did – hoped he did. Oh, I don't know what to think any more.'

'Perhaps,' Henry mused, 'the unexpected death of his wife troubled him more than he showed. After all, Berenice was young and healthy. The shock of that alone would have been enough to change him.'

'You're making the assumption that he has changed.'

'You disagree? Have you spoken to Finnlay? Alone? Robert's not the same man who left Lusara three years ago. That amount of time can change anyone – but Robert more so.'

'Why?' Ayn queried, more curious that she would like to admit.

'Because he's sensitive – to everything that goes on around him. That's part of what makes him a good leader, why he was so effective on Selar's council. Oh, he hides it well but he cannot avoid it. I don't think that's good.'

Ayn paused and looked Henry in the eye. 'I know how I feel about that, but why are you saying it? To me?'

Henry met her gaze without blinking. 'I don't necessarily think we should count on Robert as our friend.'

'Of course he's our friend. Just because he insists on keeping his independence of us doesn't make him an enemy.'

'Not that alone, no.' Henry spread his hands. 'He's never made any secret of his criticism of the Enclave, of our goals and principles. He wanders in here from time to time, talks to some of our finest minds – then goes away contributing nothing more than a few historical theories and the odd refinement to some arcane procedure.'

'You know we can't keep people here against their will. If they feel they really want to live out there, then it's entirely their decision. After all, that's why the Sealing process was developed in the first place. And even if we wanted to, I doubt any of us would be powerful enough to keep Robert here a day longer than he wanted.'

'I appreciate that. It's just that sometimes I think Robert is not so much working to our plan as to one of his own.'

Ayn couldn't help smiling. 'That's funny. Only yesterday I was accusing him of having no plan at all.'

Henry's face showed his surprise. 'What did he say?'

'Nothing.'

'But see, that's my point. He never really says anything to illuminate us on exactly what he's doing – or why. He goes away for three years and hardly says a word about it. Then, of course, he never has told us what the Key said to him when he was what, seven – eight years old?'

'Nine – and don't expect him to tell you now. I don't think he ever will.'

Henry looked away for a moment, then murmured idly, 'Come to think of it, how do we even know the Key really spoke to him at all? Did you hear what it said? Do you have any idea what it was about?'

'No. Nobody does.'

'How do we know he's telling the truth?'

Ayn straightened up in her seat. 'But why would he lie? Not now, but back then, at nine years old? What possible reason could he have had? He didn't know anything about the Enclave back then, hadn't decided he didn't want to join us. Back then it was all a big adventure to him.'

'Granted. But what's stopped him since? Don't you find it odd that in all the years the Enclave has been here, Robert is the first member of one of the Great Houses to have powers in the first place? That he decides at such a young age that he will acknowledge us, but not join us? Why, even his own brother was quick to take the oath. And what's even more worrisome is that Robert is so much stronger than the rest of us. His abilities far outweigh any we've previously seen.

As you've already pointed out, we would have little chance of stopping him if he did turn against us.'

'I fear you're seeing shadows where there are none.' Ayn shook her head, trying to dismiss these ideas before they could take hold. The desire to defend Robert was strong even now. 'Robert is no enemy to us. He's never threatened us in any way.'

Henry shrugged, but he persisted with his point. 'I know how you feel about him, but what bothers me is that, apart from Finnlay, the only other person from a great House with powers who has come through the gate is this girl, Jenn. A girl Robert himself brought to us, and is now taking away. Now – now, we have two of them not bound by the oath – and both powerful people. And really, your shadows aside, what do we know about either of them?'

Morning frost glistened in the hazy sunlight and turned the grass outside a pristine white. Already, though, footprints marred its perfect surface as people went about their day's work. Robert helped Micah saddle the horses, making sure the harnesses were secure against the difficult ride down from the mountains. Fortunately the weather had taken a turn for the better and promised to remain that way for most of the day. By then they would be on safer ground in the gentle valleys east of the Goleth.

Robert put the last pack on to the horse in front of him while Micah did up the straps. Jenn was already mounted up and waiting, her face sombre in the early morning. He couldn't blame her – what did she have to celebrate? Life was becoming more complicated for her as every day went by.

Robert finished with the pack and turned back to the tunnel entrance. Neither Finnlay nor Ayn had come to say goodbye and he couldn't wait any longer. However, fresh in his new role, Wilf approached from the darkness, his brown robes swirling in the gentle breeze. 'I take it you will be back, Robert? For all that we have our differences of opinion, we do value your visits.'

'Yes,' Robert replied dryly, 'I can tell. I wish you the best of luck in your new job, Wilf. I don't envy you.'

'You'd be a fool if you did, considering you as much as turned it down yourself.'

'As to that,' Robert reached up and adjusted a strap on his saddle, 'I can't help thinking that everybody has made a huge assumption. For years I've been badgered to Stand the Circle – but nobody seems to wonder whether the Key would ever choose me. Who's to say it would?'

Wilf opened his mouth, then shut it again quickly. He nodded briefly. 'I wish you a safe journey home, Robert. If the gods are with you, you should get Jenn back to Elita before the snows hit. Do take care of her, won't you?'

'Of course,' Robert nodded. 'I don't suppose you've seen my brother this morning?'

'No. Why?'

'He seemed a little upset about something last night. I half expected him to haul me out of bed in the middle of the night. I can't wait any longer to say goodbye. I tried to find him first thing, but he wasn't in his rooms. When you do see him, tell him I'll be expecting him at Dunlorn for the winter. I believe that was his plan.'

'Of course.'

Robert swung up into his saddle and turned for the Gate. Micah and Jenn followed closely behind as they entered the tunnel and soon they lost the light in the dark forbidding cave. The sandy floor damped the sound of the horses' hooves, which only made it more eerie. They moved slowly in the gloom, Robert unable as yet to make any light. Then a tingle ran over his skin and he knew they had passed through the Gate and would soon be outside.

He raised his hand and with a flick of his wrist, a bright yellow glow spread across the tunnel illuminating their path – and a figure standing in front of them.

'Finnlay! What are you doing there?'

Finnlay's face was a mask of anger. In the conjured light, it seemed overlarge, his eyes smouldering. He stood directly in front of Robert, his jaw stuck out in defiance.

'I just want to know one thing,' he hissed.

'What? Whatever's wrong, Finn?' Robert asked, completely mystified.

'Don't ask stupid questions, Robert! You know very well what's wrong. Just tell me why.'

'I'm sorry, Finn, I don't understand what you want. Why, what?'

Shaking his head as though in pain, Finnlay said, 'Why didn't you say anything? Why didn't you tell me before that the Key had told you never to Stand the Circle?'

*What?* Robert stared at him. He tried to speak, but found his voice wouldn't work. As he struggled for an answer, Finnlay shook his head in disgust and disappointment and betrayal. Without another word, he melted into the shadows.

'Finnlay!' Robert called but the only answer was his own voice echoed back. What was that all about?

'Will he be all right?' Jenn murmured.

Robert turned to see her and Micah watching him closely. He nodded. 'I hope so.'

'Then what's wrong?

He shook his head, 'I don't know – but something strange is happening and I don't understand one bit of it.'

'What's strange?' Jenn's voice was gentle against the stone tunnel. 'If the Key would talk to you, why shouldn't it talk to your brother as well? Perhaps you should have told him before now.'

Robert frowned in the direction Finnlay had gone, his disquiet deepening. 'Should I have said the Key had told me never to Stand the Circle? Well, to be honest, I would have, most certainly. Except for one thing.'

Robert paused. 'That's not what the Key told me at all.'

156

# 7

Micah stood beneath the branches of a golden elm and gazed back at the distant mountains to the west. Black clouds hung ominously above the peaks, edged with a burning red from the dying sunset. There would be snow up there before morning and all trace of their passage from the Goleth would be erased. They'd left just in time. Another few days at the Enclave and they would have been snowed in for the rest of the winter. The gods alone knew what further damage that would have caused.

He glanced back towards the empty hut nestled in the heart of a copse. Smoke trickled from the crumbling chimney, while outside Robert unsaddled and brushed down the horses. Micah had been forbidden any such work because of his injury. However, two days of treatment by the Healers at the Enclave and another four days of rest while they travelled had done much to ease the pain. At least he'd had the sense not to injure his sword arm!

He could hear Jenn calling him back into the hut to change his dressing. She was very diligent in her self-appointed post of journey physician and he did trust her – what he didn't trust was the odd quiet that had grown between the three of them since their departure from the Enclave. His master spoke only when he had to, Jenn answered any questions in a way that forbade further discussion and Micah was left with the dull prospect of talking to himself. With a sigh, he turned and headed back to the hut. Jenn was waiting for him inside, ointments and bandages laid out. He sat down beside her and held out his arm.

As she began removing the old dressing, Micah studied her face. Her dark brows were knitted together in concentration and her lips pursed. Every now and then, she would glance up with those amazing blue eyes – and as quickly look away.

'You're staring, Micah,' she said eventually.

'Sorry,' he replied simply. 'I was just thinking about the Guilde and the way they treated Arlie Baldwyn.'

'Oh? And looking at me makes you automatically think of the Guilde? I'm flattered!'

'Look, you know we've been away a long time. Has that sort of thing become commonplace now? Or was Arlie extremely unlucky?' Micah watched her, hoping the question – and the topic – would be enough to engage her in conversation. This silence was driving him mad.

'And what,' Robert said from the door, 'makes the Guilde less likely to commit an act of torture like that than anyone else?' His arms were laden with saddles which he deposited in a corner. 'Were you really that surprised by it, my friend?'

'Weren't you?' Jenn asked without taking her eyes from her work.

Robert didn't answer – and Micah knew he wouldn't. There was too much history there, too much Robert would never talk about. But Micah did not understand. He continued, 'The Guilde has no mandate to be doing anything of the kind. They're bridge builders, goldsmiths, miners and weavers. Learned men – nothing more. Why do they now wish to be healers?'

'Oh come, Micah,' Robert laughed ironically, 'you know full well the Guilde consider they have a trust given by the gods themselves. A trust to hold and secure the valuable gift of knowledge and learning. They've always guarded that trust jealously. Healing is knowledge. It stands to reason they would want that as well.'

'Are you suggesting that Arlie deserved his punishment?' Jenn asked quietly.

'By the gods, no! But perhaps ... he should have known better than to defy the Guilde.' Robert turned away, his mood abruptly changed. He stirred the fire up a little, but kept his back to them.

Jenn watched him, her expression unreadable. When he said nothing more, she ventured, 'It that it? Is that all you can say?'

'As people keep telling me, things have changed.'

'Oh, yes?' Jenn replied with an arched eyebrow. 'They've changed so much that you're unsurprised to find the Guilde is tightening its grip on Lusara. That soon we won't be able to cut hay or shoe a horse without their permission – and any midwife or healer who so much as looks at a patient runs the risk of losing a hand? Of dying on the trium? Is that why you left the Council? Why you left the country for three years? Because you could see it coming?'

'Jenn,' Micah groaned, holding up his hand in a futile effort to halt her questions. She paid no attention to him, however, and kept her gaze steadily on Robert.

'Not entirely.'

'Then why did you leave?'

Robert turned away from the fire. He didn't look at her, but took a seat close to the flames. 'Because, in my misguided way, I thought perhaps my presence at the capital and my place on the Council was provoking them. I thought that if I removed myself they might relax.'

'Why would your presence provoke them at all? They don't know you're a sorcerer. What did you do to annoy them so much?'

Micah's eyes flitted back and forth between them. He felt like he was watching a fencing match.

'That's a very long story.'

'Of course,' she said dryly.

'And not one that necessarily needs me to tell it. There are plenty of people who know what happened – or think they do. It doesn't really matter. The important thing is that it's an undisputed fact that the Guilde and I do not agree. Since it was unlikely they would pack up and leave Lusara, I thought it best that I did.'

Jenn said nothing to this and merely picked up a jar of ointment. As she began to smear the evil-looking muck on his arm, Micah hissed. It stung!

'Don't worry, the wound is clean,' Jenn said reassuringly.

Micah peered at his arm dubiously. 'And how do you know that?'

'I'm not sure how exactly, but I can see it. It's clean, believe me.'

With a frown, Micah glanced at Robert for confirmation. His master, however, only shook his head in a gesture of complete defeat. He spread his arms wide and in an aggrieved tone, murmured, 'I give up. Will somebody please tell me what is going on here?'

Micah almost smiled and was glad to reply in a like manner, 'It's called medicine, my lord. I told you to attend to your classes more when you were a boy.'

Robert stuck out his jaw. 'I doubt it would have done me much good. There were no classes on solving impossible questions.'

'A pity,' Jenn grunted.

'So tell me,' Robert paused, turning his whole attention on Jenn, 'When did you start Seeing like a Healer? Let me see – first you put that bridge back together, so I suppose that means the Guilde is out of a job. Now you've developed into a Healer, so you can put the Hospices out of work, not to mention the little job you did on my *ayarn* – which could remove the necessity of the Enclave altogether. By that logic, I guess your next move will have to be on the Church – or perhaps even the crown? By the way,' he continued without pausing, 'didn't you want to ask me something?'

'You mean about your inability to take anything seriously, perhaps?' Jenn replied, her head bent to her work. However, Micah could see the corners of her eyes crease up and he knew she was trying not to smile.

Robert persisted, 'Well?'

Jenn finished with the ointment and began winding a new bandage around Micah's arm. 'I don't know why you think I have anything to ask you – unless it's about what happened when we left the Enclave. I suppose I could ask you what that was all about – but it would mean asking you what the

Key really said to you and I doubt you would answer, so I suppose I don't have anything to ask you after all.'

'So you're not curious?' Robert queried lightly.

'Mmm? About what?'

'Elita.'

Jenn froze for just a second, then continued her work without replying.

'Well? I would have thought by now – with only a day's journey to Elita, that you would be full of questions about your home and your father. Unless,' he paused, his eyes narrowing, 'you actually had no intention of going there at all?'

Jenn replied with careful precision, 'I might be entertaining a change of heart.'

'You mean you never meant to go in the first place,' Robert clarified. 'In that case, why did you say you would?'

Jenn's calm momentarily dissipated. 'Because I wanted to prevent all-out war between you and Finnlay. Is that so bad a thing?'

'Finn and I have been at war since he was old enough to hold a sword – and he was a precocious child. That particular discussion would have been no worse than any other we'd had. There was no need . . .'

'Oh really?' Jenn finished tying the last bandage and looked at him directly. 'And what about the night before? For a man who never gets angry, you were doing a damn good job of faking it. After everything else that had happened, I wasn't about to let you fight over me as well!'

Micah opened his mouth to say something, then shut it abruptly. She had a point, though it irked him to admit it. On the other hand, she had, once again, neatly shifted the topic from the one they'd been discussing. Flexing his hand against the constraints of the bandage, he asked quietly, 'So you don't want to go to Elita after all?'

'No.'

'Why not?'

Jenn looked up. 'I don't see any reason to.'

'You mean you don't believe it,' he added.

'Oh please, Micah. Don't you start, too.' Jenn looked exasperated and almost flung her equipment into the bag.

Micah shook his head. 'I only speak out of concern for your welfare. If you don't want to stay at the Enclave then truly, the safest place for you is Elita.'

'Why? Why should I worry about being safe? What difference does it make? I've not worried about it since I left Shan Moss. I can take care of myself and have been doing so all my life. I don't see why I can't continue the same way.'

'No?' Robert murmured. 'And what happens the next time you use your powers, eh?'

'Well, it's simple,' she shrugged indifferently. 'I won't use them.'

'As I recall, that's what you said after the bridge incident. Not that I don't believe your sincerity – it's just that I can't see you refusing to do anything to help somebody in a similar situation. Like now, with Micah's arm. You just used Healer's Sight. Do you think you can stand by and watch somebody die because you don't want to use your powers?'

'A fine point, my lord master sorcerer,' she said with cunning, 'but what difference would it make whether I was wandering the land – or at Elita?'

'The difference is, Jenn,' Robert stood impatiently, 'that you would be safe with Jacob. He'd never let any harm come to you – and you would have the time and space to get used to your powers. Time when nobody would question what you were doing – nor suspect your actions. Believe it or not, you would have more freedom at Elita than you would ever have wandering the country. I can't believe you would be fool enough not to see that.' Without another word, he turned and walked out of the hut.

Micah turned back to Jenn, but she wouldn't meet his gaze. After a minute, he said, 'If I were you, I'd go and talk to him.'

'But you're not me, are you?'

Robert strode into the copse and cast around for more firewood. This whole situation was getting ridiculous. What

162

had happened to his original plan of quietly wandering back to Dunlorn, unnoticed and untroubled? Where had all these damned problems come from? And what the hell was he doing trying to solve them? Everybody had warned him that danger could come from the King or the Guilde, but this? Jenn? Arlie? Finn? Oliver?

The Key.

It had been years since he'd spoken about what the Key had said to him, let alone considered its significance to anyone else. He'd assumed that everyone else had forgotten about that day, nineteen years ago. But he'd been wrong about that too.

So why, in the name of all that was holy, had the Key chosen that moment to lie to Finnlay? What possible purpose could it serve, other than to hurt his brother? Come to think of it, just when did the Key start developing purposes of its own – was it possible that it was something more than a mere tool?

No. He shouldn't have left. He should have stayed at the Enclave, spoken to Finnlay, talked it over with Patric. There had to be a reason for all this.

Robert stopped in his tracks. What was he doing? Wasn't this the very kind of thing he wanted to avoid? No involvement – remember? No involvement, no failure. That was the plan and he must stick to it. The consequences were too terrible to contemplate. But it was so hard to turn his back on them.

'You're an idiot, Robert,' he murmured to the trees. 'You knew this would happen.'

For three years he had travelled knowing the one journey he would never make again was the one that led northwards; home. But then, six weeks ago, the idea had come to him. A cold idea, isolated, but also unshakeable. In quieter moments, and in that haze before he slept each night, it would return to him, plaguing, but each time with an unspoken promise of success. If he stayed away from court, if he refused to involve himself with the Enclave – if he stayed at home – then perhaps he could return to Lusara and cease this wandering life. More importantly, Micah could return to his family, for he would not do so alone. All Robert had to do was remain strong, withstand the pressure that was bound to come. He'd been so sure he could do it.

He began picking up branches, stacking them on his left arm. There was no doubt that Jenn's change of heart had something to do with what she'd witnessed at the Enclave. He couldn't blame her, sorcery was difficult to adjust to. But for her not to return to Elita was simply stupid. There had to be some way to change her mind. Jacob was her only guarantee of safety.

With a sigh, he turned to go back, only to find Jenn standing a little distance away, watching him.

'I'm sorry,' she said after a moment, her voice low. 'I know it's difficult for you. I know you're trying hard not to care and I'm sorry because I know I'm a problem you really don't need.'

All the will drained away from him and he shook his head in defeat. He should be used to her keen perception by this time, but still it came as a rather uncomfortable jab. Problems or no, he had chosen this path and he would have to continue it regardless.

He took in a deep breath and felt his equilibrium return. 'You're not a problem.'

'It's just that I don't see why Jacob would want me back. Not now, after all this time.'

'Oh, Jenny,' Robert couldn't help smiling, 'how could they not want you back?'

She frowned slightly, dropping her gaze. 'It's just that I don't know . . .'

'Come inside,' he said firmly, 'and I'll tell you all about them.'


'Jacob was in his late twenties when he married your mother, Elaine. She was a fair-haired beauty from Cor Adarn, in the north. They'd met at court when Elaine was only about seventeen or eighteen. Her brother Melvin, who was also her guardian, was hoping for a match with King Edward's cousin, but apparently, the moment Jacob and Elaine met, they had eyes only for each other.' Robert paused and leaned forward to stir up the crackling fire. Flames leaped up, making weird shadows on the walls behind them and lighting the faces of Micah and Jenn as they sat listening.

'My father was at court at the time. I remember him telling me years later how angry Melvin was when Jacob approached him for Elaine's hand. Melvin argued, raged and sulked until eventually he realized his sister was determined. Finally he gave his consent and they were married the following summer. Jacob decided to keep out of Melvin's way for a while so they returned to Elita and stayed there for the next two years. During that time, Elaine had her first child, a boy, but he didn't survive his first month. Then, to their joy, a year later she gave birth to a healthy daughter, Bella.'

'Bella?' Jenn breathed. 'Did she survive?'

'She certainly did – although I haven't seen her for about seven years. After she was born, Elaine was advised not to try to have any more children for a while – which she obediently did. But when Bella was about five or so, Elaine had another boy, but this one survived only a few hours. Jacob was so distraught at the prospect of losing his beloved Elaine that the subject of more children was completely forgotten.

'The first time I ever went to Elita was when I was ten. Bella, a year younger than me, took an instant dislike to me and made my life sheer hell.' Robert laughed. 'As you can imagine, my father was unimpressed by my pleas to be allowed to return home. He just told me that I had to learn to deal with that kind of thing. Fortunately, my father was recalled to court after only a few days at Elita and I was allowed to go home. You can thank that lucky incident for the fact that your sister is still alive.'

Robert held out his cup as Micah refilled it with the tangy ale they'd brought from the Enclave. He continued, 'Of course, we didn't know it at the time, but your mother was already carrying another child – you. You were born in the

165

winter. Jacob was delighted – and never expressed any regret that I knew of that you were not a boy. As you can imagine, a son and heir would have meant a great deal to him. Still, he treasured your arrival as though you were the heir to the throne itself. I had occasion to visit Elita a number of times over the next two years but I'm afraid we never met, so I can't regale you with stories of when you were a baby.'

'And what about later? When the Troubles began?'

'Ah, that's different. To be honest, I can't tell you a lot about where your father stood during the Troubles. By that time, I was heavily involved in learning court politics. My father was increasingly involved trying to keep peace between the Houses and I helped him as much as I could. As a result, I had to take on a lot of his responsibilities at home as well. When the Troubles began and escalated to a serious level, I spent most of my time running from one place to the other, trying to mediate between feuding lords. I was returning from one such attempt when I came to Elita, the day after you went missing. As I said before, Jacob was distraught at losing you and your mother fell quite ill. I'm afraid she died a year later. Jacob never really recovered and left much of the running of his lands to Bella, who was a very capable mistress. Despite the ensuing war and the accident Jacob had, Elita managed to survive, with no little thanks to Bella.'

Jenn looked up from the cup in her hands, her eyes suddenly grave. 'What accident?'

'It was at the end of the war. Jacob had thrown himself into repelling Selar – I suppose I should have said before, your family is quite closely related to our royal line, King Edward's, that is. Back four generations, I think. Anyway, loyalty is in Jacob's blood and he drew on all his resources to support Edward. In the final battle at Seluth, Jacob and a small group of his men had cornered what they thought was Selar's private guard. They fought close to a precipice. As each of Jacob's men were overwhelmed, Jacob fought on until his opponent, with a last desperate lunge, pushed him back over the precipice. Jacob fell about thirty feet but somebody found him and got him to safety. They took him home and nursed him back to life, but from that day onwards, his legs have been useless.'

'But that's awful! How can he bear it?'

'I don't know. But he's a man of enormous courage.'

'You seem to know a lot about it. Were you there? Were you the one who helped him?'

At this, Robert's gaze dropped. 'I wish I could say I was, but I was engaged elsewhere.'

'Doing . . . what?'

There was little point in lying to her, even though the truth was known only to a handful of people. 'I was busy saving Selar's life.'

'But . . .' Jenn looked in disbelief at Micah and Robert. 'How could you save his life? Weren't you supposed to be fighting him?'

'Not exactly, no. My father and his men were on the battlefield. I'd been sent to round up some reinforcements. On the way back, as I came close to the battle I crossed a river and there I found a man trapped in the current. He was drowning, so I did the only thing I could do, I dragged him to safety. I'd never met Selar at that point, never even seen him. I didn't even find out until late that night that the man I'd saved in the river was none other than the man who now sits on our throne and who was responsible – in name at least – for my own father's death.'

Jenn stared at him, her mouth open. After a second she came to herself and said, 'So he gave you a seat on his Council as reward for saving his life?'

'It looked that way to some people, but that didn't actually happen for two years. Two years during which I was a prisoner in my own castle. I was spared execution, I think, because I saved his life, but that was all.'

Jenn frowned. 'Execution? Then how did my father survive Selar's reign? Surely if my family were closely related to Selar's predecessor, Selar would want my father removed – and anyone else who could threaten him.'

'He certainly would – and did, in most cases. But Jacob

was no threat to him. He was at that point confined to his bed, never to walk again, with only a daughter to succeed him. Jacob has remained at Elita ever since. His only hope now is to secure the safety of Bella. He ignores Selar and Selar ignores Jacob. They're both content with the situation.'

Robert finished his story and sat back against the wall. It was strange going over all this old history, but somehow telling the story again brought it back to life. He could even remember the laughter in his father's eyes when he had come to complain about how Bella taunted him. And oh, how things would have been different if he'd not stopped at that moment to save the life of a drowning man. Not that he could have done anything different, even if he'd known who that man was. There was a big difference between slaying a man on the field of battle and standing by as the last breaths of life were dragged from him by a raging river. And after all, letting Selar die at that moment would only have changed things for the worse. Selar's forces would still have won that battle, Robert's father would still have died, but instead of the iron-clad hold Selar subsequently placed on Lusara, complete civil war would have broken out. A civil war which would have killed thousands more, and would quite possibly still be raging today.

No. Whichever way he looked at it, saving Selar's life like that had not necessarily been a bad thing. It was just a pity a few others did not see it that way.

Jenn interrupted his thoughts by getting to her feet and bringing more firewood from the pile by the door. 'I'm sorry, but I'm not convinced.'

'About what, in particular?'

'Well,' she said slowly, framing her thoughts, 'I still don't see how we can arrive at Elita and find that my father will even believe it. You never convinced him you thought I'd been taken during the Troubles. My father believes that I am dead. Surely my sudden reappearance all this time later would only stir up bad memories for him. I'm not certain I want to do that to him. If he's reconciled himself to my death, why should I disturb that?'

'It's your right.'

Jenn shook her head, not understanding.

'Your birthright. Just as surely as Bella is his daughter, so are you. Whether you remember it or not, Elita is your home, the home of your family, your ancestors. You have a right to claim it.'

'But it means nothing to me. At the risk of actually agreeing with anything Finnlay says, I would not miss Elita. My father knows nothing of my existence, so he wouldn't miss me.'

Robert looked at her for a moment, wondering how much fear had to do with her reluctance. She didn't look afraid, but he had learned by now that her face could hide almost anything she thought or felt, so he didn't trust it. 'Well, it's your decision. But think about this: if you were in his place, would you want your missing child returned to you?'

It didn't take long. Less than an hour into the morning, the rain began and Jenn was quickly soaked to her skin. Even with the wool cloak and dress Ayn had given her, the cold still seeped into her bones. She tried not to shiver as she rode, but it was difficult. The only warmth came from the horse beneath her as they crossed one gentle hill after another. There was no shelter, no trees, just field after field of cropped hay and ploughed turf. The rain made the countryside look worn, as though summer had sucked up all its vitality.

Jenn could have asked to stop, to try and find some shelter, but she knew that the moment she did, she would be forced to look at Robert, answer the unspoken question in his eyes. She would – but not yet. Not until she'd found some way to refuse that he would accept. So she rode on, cold and wet, in silence. Her mind drifted, going over the story he'd told her last night, then snapping away to safer topics, like the Enclave. When he spoke, she hardly heard him over the rain.

'There's a farm over the next rise. I think we'd better stop for a while and dry out. I don't think this rain's going to last all day.'

Jenn nodded absently, cursing the gods. She said nothing though, merely following behind Micah as they rounded the hill and came down into a neat and wooded valley. The farm buildings were well looked after, but appeared almost deserted as they approached the side of a barn. Robert gestured for them to wait, dismounted and moved quickly and silently between the buildings. He came back after a moment with a grin on his face.

'We'll shelter in the barn. There's no one around. Just an old man and his retainer. The rest have all gone to the market.'

Inside the barn it was warm and filled with sweet-smelling hay. Micah, ignoring his injury, immediately took possession of the horses and, with fists of straw, began to brush them down. Jenn could have helped him but he was happier on his own. She found a seat on the other side of the barn and sat down, folding her arms. Unconsciously, her gaze went to Robert who was busily exploring the building. He glanced at her once, then pulled up a wooden crate and sat down opposite her. He folded his hands and turned his most patient expression on her.

But she was ready for him. 'Doesn't it bother you?'

'Eh?' he murmured, surprised. 'What?'

'Coming back to Lusara knowing how the Guilde feels about you. Aren't you bothered by the things they're doing? Aren't you going to bother them?'

Robert shook his head and gave her a lopsided smile. 'No, I won't bother them – at least, not deliberately.'

'Then, even though you don't ... agree with them, you're content to leave them be.'

'Yes.'

'Why? Why don't you agree with them? Let's face it, there doesn't seem to be much you do agree with – the Enclave, the Guilde, the King – your own brother.' Jenn smiled to take the edge off her tone. 'You're quite an objectionable man, aren't you?'

Robert burst out laughing. She'd known he would and smiled in response. When he finally replied, however, it was not as she was expecting. 'Do you know what the Guilde is, Jenn? Do you know how it came to be?'

The question threw her. She'd never really thought about it. Sober now, she shook her head. 'No. Tell me.'

'Well, believe it or not, the Enclave probably knows more about the birth of the Guilde than they do themselves – mainly because the first sorcerers were members of the Guilde. The Guilde is easily the oldest association in the world, outside of the Church. It was originally formed before the Dawn of Ages, when our world was created out of the ashes of the old. Back then, man knew more, had knowledge far beyond our own and, fearing the cataclysm to come, entrusted a few learned men with that wealth. When the gods battled for supremacy and split the world in two, the only thing that remained was the Guilde. Over the ensuing centuries, the Church and Guilde together rebuilt the world and all that we are now is due to their efforts. The gods blessed the Guilde with their sacred trust and it has never failed in its duty.'

Robert paused and glanced over his shoulder to make sure Micah didn't need any help. Then he continued, but on a completely different tack. 'Do you know what the most valuable thing in the world is, Jenn?'

She kept her eyes on him and replied, 'Freedom.'

He smiled softly. 'All right, the second most valuable thing. Knowledge. It has no price, no peer and can never be taken from one who has it. The Guilde holds knowledge as the most sacred trust – and holds it greedily to itself. It has command of the sciences, of engineering, of reading and writing – everything so important to our survival. But the Guildesmen share it with no one who has not taken their vow. They direct the work and use the rest of us as labourers. That way they retain their hold over us and their power. Somewhere over time, power has become the most import-ant thing to them and, in my opinion, betrays the trust they hold so dear. They intimidate us with their knowledge and

171

enslave us with our ignorance. That's why I don't agree with them. Does that answer your question?'

She had another question. If she was lucky, she could keep him talking – and distracted – long enough for the rain to stop, and then it would be too late. Too late for him to ask if she'd made a decision about Elita.

'How did you know the old man in the farmhouse was alone? Did you speak to him?'

There was less surprise on Robert's face this time, but his smile was not unkind. He knew what she was doing. 'No. I didn't need to. It's something most sorcerers can do occasionally. There are times when you can pick up on the thoughts of others – never a sorcerer, mind. Nothing specific, just absent thoughts when a person is tired. People used to think it was mind-reading but it's nothing like that. I can when I want to. After a while, you learn how to listen for it.'

'But if you . . .' Jenn's voice trailed off as she realized his attention had strayed. Robert turned his head, drawing his brows together. 'What is it?'

He didn't answer but stood immediately and moved across the barn to the huge door. Micah paused in his work and moved to join him. Then, over the pounding rain, she could hear it. Horses. Galloping towards the farm. She could feel the vibrations through her shoes.

Robert pulled the door open a crack and Jenn sneaked up behind him to peer through, just in time to see a band of yelling raiders roar into the farmyard. They kicked open doors and gates, sending panicked animals running. One of the men had a flaming torch which he touched to the thatched roofs as he passed. As they headed for the farmhouse, Robert moved.

'Stay here, Micah. Look after Jenn.' With that, he was through the door and running across the yard. With his sword already drawn, he cut down a raider from his horse, sending the animal galloping off into the rain. Chickens and geese squawked and ran out of the way as Robert reached the second raider. Sullen flames were already rising from the damp thatched roofs, but Jenn could only stand and watch. The barn was untouched and she held on to Micah's arm, knowing that her fingers dug into his flesh, but unable to stop.

By now some of the raiders had turned their attention to Robert. With two men down, and three in the house, there were only another three for him to deal with; they appeared fierce but incompetent swordsmen. Robert moved like lightning, spinning around in the slippery mud to parry each attack against him. His sword flashed up and a man fell, a gaping wound in his side. The second pressed Robert for a moment, but he too soon fell. The third, realizing his mistake early, turned and ran into the house. As he disappeared, Robert waved his hand towards the burning roof and instantly the flames began to die. Seconds later the last of the raiders tore out of the building and leapt on to their horses, their arms full of loot. The torch was tossed on to the roof of the house and then the raiders rode off into the rain.

Micah moved. He grabbed Jenn's arm and together they ran through the mud to the house.

'I told you to stay back!' Robert was inside the building, on his knees beside the old man. The servant lay by the door, his lifeless eyes gazing into heaven.

Jenn twisted out of Micah's grasp and knelt down beside the old man. He was still alive, but his breathing came in grating surges, his eyes shut tight against the pain. Blood seeped from an evil wound in his chest and another on his shoulder. The raiders had cut him down without a thought, just as they had his servant.

'It's too late,' Robert murmured, his voice almost inaudible now. 'He's dying.'

'But can't we do anything?' Jenn reached out and took the old man's hand, but his grip was weak, his flesh cold.

'Yes,' Robert said reluctantly. 'There is something I can do.'

She looked up in time to see him produce his *ayarn*. He gazed at it for a second, and then a warmth seemed to flow

173

from the stone and out across the old man's broken body. Gradually the lines of pain eased from his face and his breathing became more even. Jenn glanced up at Robert but he shook his head.

'I can ease his pain a little. Nothing more.'

Her gaze dropped again to the old man's face and as she watched, he opened his eyes and looked at her. Slowly, a look of breathless awe creased his features and his hand gripped hers hard.

'Blessed Mineah!' he gasped in wonder. 'You have returned to us at last!' With that, he smiled, closed his eyes and let out his last breath. The hand lost its grip in hers and fell to the ground.

Jenn breathed as if for the first time. She hadn't known this man, had never seen him before, but his death felt so real, so personal. He'd been murdered by those raiders. His home destroyed. His family would come back to nothing. She felt his death like a knife in her own heart, sharp and uncompromising.

In front of her, Robert rose to his feet and replaced his sword in its scabbard. When he spoke, his voice was as heavy and as cold as the rain. 'There's nothing we can do for them now. Let's get going.'

Jenn heard his words. She understood. She knew they had to move before either the farmers came back, or the raiders. She appreciated the necessity, felt it in her bones, but she could also hear the stubborn denial in Robert's voice, as though he was calling himself hypocrite with every breath – as though he hated himself for having to say it.

She got to her feet but couldn't look at him. She knew how he felt.

Slowly now, they went back to the barn, collected the horses and resumed their journey.

All day it nagged at the back of her mind. As the rain stopped, as the smell of wet grass rose from the fields around her, as the grey sky rolled on overhead. That old man, his dying breath, Robert's silence, and Micah.

She could feel his gaze on her, but she said nothing. Hour after hour she refused to say anything. And what could she say? What was she supposed to say? What was she supposed to feel? She knew what Robert wanted. The attack on the farm had only concentrated their argument. She would not be safe anywhere but Elita. Damn them – damn them both!

It was the conviction more than anything else. That deep-seated tone of belief in everything they said. And it didn't matter what they were talking about – the Guilde, Elita, even sorcery. She knew nothing, she was the innocent – and at the very same time, she was expected to make some kind of damned decision about the rest of her life!

And of course, they had no idea why she would have a problem. But why would they? Why would Robert and Micah think there was anything strange or odd about taking her back to Elita? Sure, no child taken in the Troubles had ever been seen again and the very fact that she'd been discovered was a cause of some mystery. This ... this kind of thing just didn't happen. She was the child of an innkeeper, raised to the smells of a taproom, the heat of a kitchen. Was she supposed to forget her father? Was she expected to stop loving him? And even though they'd turned her out when he'd died, she had already decided to make her own way in life and had been happy, more or less, with that decision ever since. Then suddenly—

Suddenly, it turns out she is the daughter of an Earl! Suddenly, she has a place in life, a home to go back to, roots she can trace back generations, and at least as far as a kinship with the royal line. Suddenly she has a sister and probably cousins and neighbours as well.

Suddenly she is a completely different person.

Now this sorcery business was hard enough to deal with, and she had real, physical evidence of that. But this? A faceless parent she'd never met – at least not to remember. A sister who would probably not welcome her return. A household who would watch every move she made, waiting for her to slip up, to prove to be an impostor. What if Robert was wrong? What if they really didn't want her at all?

175

No. This was not going to work, no matter what he said. She had no desire to go back to the Enclave, so the best thing by far was for her to slip away during the night, when they were asleep. She'd made her own way in life before and would do so again.

Immediately she began to feel better and turned her attention to the wood they were entering. If she was to make an escape that night, it would be better if she had some proper idea of which direction to go. She might not be able to take the horse – because of the noise – though it would be better if she could because—

Her thoughts came to an abrupt halt. 'Where are we?'

Robert stopped his horse and turned to face her. His eyes were in shadow but she could swear he was almost smiling. 'Why do you ask?'

She couldn't find an answer, she didn't have one. Instead, she glanced around at the tall trees sloping up the hill to her left, the gentle incline on her right going down to a stream. It looked like so many other woods and forests they'd ridden through and yet . . .

Without a word, she swung her leg over the horse and slid down to the soft ground. She'd never considered herself a fanciful person before, but right at this moment it felt like there were other forces at work on her feelings. As though . . . as though something else was controlling her.

'What is it?' Micah asked softly, jumping down beside her. 'Is something wrong?'

She shook her head at him then turned back to Robert, who still sat on his horse, watching her. 'Where are we?'

He turned his gaze to the path they were travelling. 'This wood is called Ballee's. It covers the ridge overlooking a castle and a lake. The castle is called Elita and we'll be there within the hour.'

Jenn was stunned. 'You . . . you liar!' she hissed, taking a furious step towards him. 'You said it was my decision, but all along you meant to bring me here no matter what! All that talk about what I would do . . . and what I would choose . . . and you just decide . . .'

176

'Now, wait,' Robert dismounted and held up his hands to still her anger. 'You have to understand something. You've been Sealed. That places certain restrictions on what you can and can't say to people. But it also protects you to a certain extent. What it cannot do, however, is stop the Guilde from hanging you if you're ever caught!'

'I don't care about the Guilde!' Jenn spat back. 'As far as I'm concerned you can take your sorcery – and Elita. I want nothing more to do with it.'

She paused, struggling to get air into her lungs. He'd betrayed her. The whole thing had been a trap. 'I want nothing more to do with you. Do you hear me? I trusted you – and this is what you do . . .'

'Jenn,' Micah offered, 'you don't understand . . .'

'Leave me alone!' She couldn't look at him – at either of them. With tears of rage blinding her eyes, she turned and ran down the hill towards the stream, then along the river bank until they were far behind her. Only then did she finally stop running.

Think. Think what to do next. Where to go. How to get out of this. Think, dammit—

A noise, there, to her left. What was it? Robert or Micah coming to talk her around? She turned to look but there was nothing there. She took another step forward but the sound came again. Her eyes darted between the trees but she saw nothing. Was it some trick . . .

Another noise, by that tree over there. It had a familiar look to it . . . like she'd seen it before somewhere . . .

The noises merged together, becoming the sound of many horses galloping towards her. She spun around to find a dozen armed men bearing down on her with fearsome menace in their eyes.

She turned to run but her feet would not move. She raised her hands in defence, but they did nothing. She opened her mouth to scream but no sound came out. She took a ragged breath.

Help me—

*NO!*

# 8

Micah didn't say a word. He didn't need to; Robert already knew what he was thinking. It was written all over his guileless face. There was no reproach in those blue eyes, simply an acknowledgment that something had to be done. Not that Micah would ever say anything, he was too loyal for that, but nevertheless, Micah's unwavering sense of justice always prevailed regardless of the odds. Robert knew this, counted on it even as he knew that in some respects, Micah played the part of his conscience, however silently.

With a sigh, he handed the reins of his horse to his friend. Robert knew what he had to do. Somehow he had to prove to Jenn that he was to be trusted. He knew he was right: Elita was the safest place for her, even if it was not for Robert. First he had to convince Jenn to believe him. Then he had to convince her to go to Elita . . . and then he had to convince Jacob that this child was his own daughter.

And it would be all the more difficult because Jacob believed Robert was a traitor and had sworn never to speak to him again.

Robert turned and made his way down the hill towards the stream. His boots sank into the muddy ground, never slipping on the wet grass. Dripping bracken brushed his legs and drops of fresh rain fell from the trees above. Birds had come out after the rain and had already begun their evening chorus. This was a gentle, peaceful wood, and now he had destroyed it.

She would have used it as an excuse. If he'd told Jenn about Jacob's attitude earlier she would only have used it as an excuse not to go to Elita, to save Robert the trouble. So what should he say now? What would she want him to say? Would she even listen?

He reached the stream and headed along the bank, his eyes not on the path, but on the water as it trickled over brown mossy rocks and fallen branches. The air was sweet and cool after the rain, a balm to his misgivings. He'd handled this all so badly. Even from the first moment when he'd told Jenn about sorcery. How the hell was she supposed to understand the danger when he'd hardly told her anything? He was putting her life at risk because he couldn't trust himself to tell her the truth . . .

*Help me!*

*No!*

The scream wrenched him from his thoughts and he sprang into action. He ran forward, tearing along the bank, crashing through brush and bracken. By instinct his hand reached for his sword. Suddenly he burst through the brush and saw her. She was standing alone, her head down, hands over her face. Behind her stood the moss-covered ruins of the old mill. There was no one else around.

'What is it? What's wrong?'

She turned to him, dropping her hands. Her eyes were wide with horror and barely shed tears. She fumbled for words, struggled to speak of the horror. 'I . . . remember it! I remember . . . them taking me. Oh, Robert, it was terrifying. They came so quickly, they didn't even stop. And the old man in the front, on this huge white horse, his face so awful . . .' She gulped in air, trying desperately to shrug off the memory.

Robert strode forward and wrapped his arms around her. She clung to him and gradually she calmed down.

'They came from over there . . . and looked so big . . .' Her voice broke off and she looked up at him. 'It really happened, Robert. I mean, these men really came along here and took me away. I didn't know who they were or why they were chasing me. I just remember being terrified.'

'Do you remember anything after that? Where they took you? What they said? Anything?' If only she could remember, it would be some way to solving a very old mystery.

'No,' she said after a moment, taking a few steps back. 'I

just remember the horses coming towards me and the man in front. He was old, long white hair and . . .' She paused.

'And what?' Robert prompted.

She took a deep breath and wiped her hand over her face. When she looked back at him she was more her usual self, if a little shaken. 'How did you know?'

'Why – I heard you scream, of course. Micah will be following any second, I'm sure . . .' His voice trailed away as she held his gaze.

'But I made no sound, Robert.'

For a second he didn't quite know what to say. Then he glanced over his shoulder to where Micah should be rushing towards them. However, Micah was nowhere to be seen. That meant only one of two things. Either something had happened to Micah and he was unable to come or—

For some strange reason Robert's hands had developed a small tremor. He clenched his fists and it died away. 'You made no sound? No sound at all?'

She shook her head, her voice steady, unlike his. 'I couldn't. I was frozen. I wanted to, I tried to run, but my body wouldn't move.'

'But you did scream?'

'Yes.'

'Sweet Mineah!' Robert breathed. His eyes closed involuntarily. This was incredible! It had always been nothing more than a myth . . .

He opened his eyes again and found she was watching him. Her gaze was patient, as though she expected a reasonable explanation for this as well as everything else. That half-innocent look almost made him laugh. He shook his head slowly. 'You really are amazing, you know that? In an instant, you've just done the one thing that sorcerers have been longing after for centuries. To be able to speak mind to mind.'

Jenn frowned, her dark brows drawn together like storm clouds. 'I'm not sure . . . It might have been one of those things . . .'

'Look, try it again,' he said, his excitement getting the better of him. 'Think a word, just one.'

'All right.'

Robert watched her face for a few long seconds but heard nothing in his head. Not wanting to be disappointed so quickly, he asked her to try again. She did, but still with no effect. Maybe it had just been the memory, maybe because she was re-living that trauma.

'Perhaps you're right,' he murmured. 'It doesn't matter. I doubt the Enclave would take too kindly to it anyway. I think they've had enough shocks for one year.'

Jenn nodded mutely.

'Look, I'm sorry about all this. I never intended to just take you to Jacob. I thought that if I said nothing and got you close enough to see Elita, you might remember something. I never dreamed you'd remember it like this. I know I never really explained it fully, but there are good reasons why I think you're safer with Jacob. I'd still like to show you Elita, but if you really don't want to go then I'll take you to the nearest village, find you a nice inn to work in and I promise you'll never see me again.'

He felt he was rambling and wanted to laugh at his own incompetence, but her grave gaze chilled the thought. He waited for a response, but all he got was silence. With a nod he added, 'Well, think about it. We'll wait with the horses.'

Not knowing what else to say, he nodded again and turned away.

*Robert?*

He froze. Like a feather on a breezeless day, the word drifted into his mind, fluttered briefly and was still. Had he really heard it, or was his imagination finally betraying him? Almost afraid to move, he turned his head until he could see Jenn standing where he had left her. He raised a single eyebrow in question.

Her answer was a smile. Then: *So you can hear me after all.*

He took a single step towards her. 'Your voice is very quiet, though. Is that deliberate?'

*No. I've been shouting at you for the last few minutes but you were so busy apologizing you weren't listening. I'm also shouting at you now. Robert, don't you think it's funny? You always think everything is funny. Why aren't you laughing?*

It was her voice inside his head, as though she were speaking from his memory alone. Each word grew stronger, held more expression. Her prodding irony was not lost on him. He gazed at her a moment longer. 'Why aren't you?'

Almost involuntarily, the smile drifted from her face. She tore her eyes away from his and glanced down at her hands. 'I don't understand why this is happening to me. I'm doing my best, but even I can only take so much change before I start to wonder where I went wrong. Believe it or not, I do trust you. I don't know why I do – but there it is. From what I've seen, you seem to have that effect on most people, so I guess I'm no different there. I don't want to go to Elita at all but—' she broke off, as her hands twisted together. Finally she said, 'I'm beginning to understand why you think it's a good idea.'

'I think perhaps that it would also be a good idea if we kept this new talent of yours a secret for a while. As you say, you've had enough changes for the moment – and you need some time to get used to them.'

She nodded and they began to walk back along the stream. Jenn was silent for a while, then abruptly stopped in her tracks and faced him. 'Just one question though. I appreciate what Henry said about my powers being different and everything, but something doesn't add up here. I mean, if I can speak with my mind – why can you hear me? Shouldn't that mean that you can speak back?'

'I doubt that it works that way, I'm afraid. My powers are just the same as everyone else's.'

'Except that you're so much more powerful. Surely there are things you can do that they can't?'

As it happened, there were, but this was not the time to go into that. He wanted to be able to say she was right, but it would be a lie. He knew because he'd tried it many times

182

before and failed. 'I'm sorry, but at this point in time, you're the only one.'

They climbed up the hill and mounted their horses again. As Robert turned back towards Elita, more soft words drifted into his mind.

*I suppose there have to be a few advantages, Robert. For example, I've just realized that this little skill means that I can actually have an argument with you — but you can't argue back! This could be fun.*

It was the most he could do not to turn and look at her — but there was nothing he could do to stop himself laughing. When Micah asked him why, he sobered a little and replied with a grin, 'I was just having a short discussion with myself, my friend. Then I suddenly realized how futile it was. After all, I can't win, no matter what I say.'

Micah didn't hear it of course, but Robert's mind was suddenly filled with the sound of Jenn's triumphant laughter.

'Well, there it is.'

Jenn sat on her horse and gazed down at the view before her. In the far distance, grey mountains rose in stately majesty, as though keeping a watchful eye on the closer hills. Below them was a shining lake and, jutting out into it, a castle of golden sandstone. A curtain wall stretched wide to the gatehouse on the right and the main keep on the left. Between the walls was a huge courtyard lined with smaller buildings from which curls of smoke rose delicately before being tagged by the wind and blown away. The main keep had another smaller tower on one side and two more on the other, and what looked like a fourth rising behind. Down the valley, half hidden by the wood and the curve of the hills, was a village. Embracing it all was a deep arm of forest going from the edge of the village, around the castle and down to the lake's edge on the other side.

'Well?' Robert asked quietly.

'It's beautiful,' Jenn whispered, not taking her eyes from it.

'Do you remember it?'

'No. But it's still beautiful.'

He said nothing more and she had to turn her head away from the view to see his expression. This was it. After this moment, there would be no going back, no blaming Robert and Micah, no wishing she'd chosen something else. He was truly allowing her to make the decision entirely alone. But a choice was not a choice unless she had genuine options.

'Where else could I go?' she asked, throwing a glance in Micah's direction. 'Where I would be safe – since you feel so strongly about it?'

'I suppose,' Robert said, frowning in thought, 'other than the village option, there is always my mother. She lives at Saint Hilary's, a priory east of Dunlorn, secluded in the mountains. It's cut off for most of the winter, but I don't know if you'd like that very much. I mean, you wouldn't be very free to do what you want. Still, you wouldn't be bothered by the Guilde – although any visible exercise of your powers would bring immediate trial and execution by the Church.'

'Is your mother a sorcerer too?'

'By the gods, no!' Robert laughed. 'And she knows nothing about me or my brother.'

'I see.' It wasn't much, but it was an option. 'Any other suggestions?'

'No other suggestion which would keep you safe from the Guilde, no,' Micah replied, somewhat abruptly. 'I'm sorry, but the fact is that if you kept to your original idea of wandering the country you would only end up getting into more trouble. Then there's your inability, if you'll forgive me, to control speaking your mind when you get annoyed. The Guilde would never bother Lord Jacob at Elita. You could speak your mind and no one would worry about it.'

*If only he knew*, Jenn threw towards Robert but she didn't smile. This was, after all, nothing to smile about.

Oh, well, there was really nothing for it. Whether she liked it or not, she had to admit that Micah and Robert were right. The rest was up to this unknown father of hers.

'Very well. Let's get it over with.'

184

Robert grinned. 'Good. Now you'd better pull up your cloak hood until we get inside. Jacob will need a bit of warning before he actually sees your face.'

As they skirted the water's edge and approached the castle, Jenn's eyes went up to the walls which towered above her, bright and yellow in the setting sun. Their presence had long been detected by the guard which patrolled the top of the wall, so the gates were already open when they arrived.

She followed Robert's horse into the courtyard, keeping her head lowered and allowing her hood to hide her face. She was glad of it. Now that it had finally come to this moment, she wasn't sure she wanted anyone seeing what she was feeling. Her heart began beating loudly in her chest and she had to struggle to control the tremor in her knees as she slid down from her horse. She felt Micah's steadying hand at her shoulder, but for once, she found little comfort in his presence. After all, he would soon leave and she would have to stay here, alone.

'My lord!' a voice close by, accompanied by booted feet on the cobbled courtyard. The man came to a halt before Robert, but Jenn couldn't see anything of him. 'We had not heard you'd returned to Lusara. Is there some problem . . .?'

'No, Neil. Not a problem as such. However, I do need to speak to your mistress. Is she about?'

'Aye, my lord,' the man seemed hesitant. 'Lady Bella is in the hall. I'll tell her you are here. Should I have a boy take your horses, my lord?'

'Um . . . best to wait a moment, Neil.'

'Of course, my lord.'

There were steps beneath her feet and Jenn reached down to lift her skirts. She kept her eyes on the back of Robert's dusty boots as they went indoors. She tried to distract herself by counting the number of scratches and grazes on the worn black leather, wondering how and when each had been gained, but it was a futile gesture. This time her fear had a very solid hold on her and there was little she could do about it. The worse thing was, she couldn't tell if she was more afraid of them rejecting her – or accepting her.

It was darker, but much warmer inside the hall. She could see fresh rushes on the stone floor and patches of muted daylight from windows high on the west wall. There were voices speaking quietly which broke off abruptly. Then a woman's voice, coming closer as she spoke.

'Lord Robert? In the name of the gods, what are you doing here?'

'Hello, Bella,' Robert replied, his voice full of rich warmth and confidence. Jenn couldn't help admiring the way he exuded charm under such awkward circumstances. Though it wasn't much of a welcome . . .

Bella? Her sister?

'You look well,' Robert continued. 'The years have done no disservice to your beauty.'

Jenn was dying to look up, to see that face, but she dared not. Not now – not yet.

'Thank you for the compliment, Robert,' Bella replied shortly, 'but I don't understand what you're doing here.'

'I've come to see you and your father.'

'But you know he . . .'

'Bella,' Robert cut across her, 'it's very important that I speak to you both. I won't trouble you long, but I must have a few moments of your time.'

Bella took a long time answering. Why? Why should there be a problem? If Jacob and Robert were old friends, why wouldn't Jacob want to see him?

'Well, I can't guarantee he'll give you too much time, Robert, but I will take you to him.'

Rushes whispered under her feet as they crossed the hall and through a door at the end. A short corridor sloped down a little and then another door was opened into a much brighter room. In here there was a deep Alusian carpet on the floor and Jenn stared at it in fascination. She'd never actually stood on one before.

'Father,' Bella began, 'you have a visitor.'

'What the . . . Dunlorn? By all that's holy, I told you never . . .'

'Jacob, please wait a moment.' Robert moved forward but

186

Jenn stayed where she was. She could feel Micah behind her, standing close, protective as always.

'I'll do nothing of the kind, Dunlorn!'

'Father, please,' Bella interrupted. 'Robert says he has something important to tell you. Hear him out, I beg you.'

'That's rich coming from you, daughter,' Jacob grunted, but his tone was a little softer. 'Well? Go on.'

'Thank you,' Robert murmured with the same air of confidence he seemed to carry about with him like a shield. 'What I'm about to tell you is difficult to explain, but I ask that you bear with me. As you will probably guess, I've only recently returned to Lusara. I came by way of Aaran and crossed through the forest of Shan Moss before approaching the mountains. It was in the forest that I ... discovered something of great interest to you.'

'And what by Serin's teeth would I want with Shan Moss?'

'Please, Jacob. Hear me out. I didn't realize the significance of what I found until a little later, and then I determined you must know about it – before I even returned to Dunlorn.'

Jenn listened to them, only half hearing the words. Robert was bending the truth a little in order to tell the story and that was entirely understandable. However, there was something else going on here she didn't understand. An undercurrent of mixed emotions coming from both Bella and Jacob. On top of that was the obvious dislike Jacob had for Robert. But why? Wasn't it supposed to be Bella who hated Robert? Surely not her father. That's what Robert had said when he'd told her the story. Unless ...

Of course, he hadn't told her the whole story, had he?

'So what was this discovery, Dunlorn, that made you rush across the country to tell me?'

'Well, it has something to do with the Troubles.'

Jenn couldn't see him, but she could imagine Robert folding his hands together the way he always did when trying to explain something.

'The Troubles?' Bella laughed in disbelief. 'What possible interest could we have in the Troubles?'

187

Robert paused, then replied, 'Very little, I imagine. However, there is someone I would like you to meet.'

He came back to Jenn then and she raised her head enough to see his face. He stood between her and the others in the room and she knew that it was time. He said nothing immediately, only giving her a gentle, encouraging smile, his eyes almost willing her to assume some of his confidence. Then he reached up and pulled the hood back from her face.

'Well,' Jacob demanded from behind Robert. 'Who is it?'

Robert's smile broadened but only Jenn could see it. He controlled it after a second and said, 'This is what I found in Shan Moss. Her name is Jenn and she bears the Mark of the House of Elita.' He stepped aside and Jenn could finally see the rest of the room.

By the fire, seated in a wooden chair with an embroidered back was an old man. His face was creased with deep lines and both his brows and hair were peppered with white. Deep blue eyes stared up at her with mystification while the fingers of his right hand tapped against the armrest in irritation. But behind him—

Bella. Taller and obviously older, Jenn found she was looking up at herself. Although Bella was frowning and her lips were drawn tight, she had the same hair, face and build as Jenn. It was uncanny!

'The Mark of Elita?' Jacob growled after a moment. 'I don't understand. How can she have the Mark . . .' His voice drained away as surely as the colour from his face. 'Did . . . you say her name was Jenn?'

'I did.' Robert took Jenn's hand and led her forward a few steps so Jacob could see her clearly. 'It was the Troubles, you see. She didn't drown – she was taken, just like the others . . .'

'But this is impossible!' Bella snapped. 'This cannot be my sister . . .'

'Your sister?' Jacob frowned, turning his head slowly towards Bella. Then his eyes cleared. 'Not your sister? But of

188

course she is! How can you doubt it? Her face is your own – your mother's!'

He stopped abruptly, realizing what he was saying. 'Your sister – my daughter . . . By the gods! It's true! You're alive. After all these years . . .'

Without even thinking what she was doing, Jenn let her hand slip from Robert's and she knelt down before this old man. His eyes were wide with wonder as they searched her face and she could only imagine what he was feeling at this moment. Suddenly her own fear dissolved like snow on a summer's day. When she spoke, it was with a new, deep calm.

'I don't know you, my lord. I don't remember you at all. I have only Robert's word that the Mark on my shoulder brands me as your daughter. However, if you don't want me here, I can leave and will do so without any word. Robert will take me if you don't want . . .'

'No! Absolutely not. I forbid it!' Jacob's voice rocked the small room, then returned to barely a whisper, 'I just can't believe it, that's all. To find you alive and grown up and . . . Oh, Bella!'

Bella moved to stand beside him, tall and imposing. 'What is this? My sister died. She drowned in the river which flows from the lake. How can she possibly turn up here years later and claim to be your daughter? This is all some scheme Robert has plotted for, I don't know why . . .' She whirled around. 'What are you trying to do to us? You have no right!'

With that, she turned and flew out of the room, leaving a tight, uncomfortable silence.

Robert murmured, 'I'm sorry. I spent so much time convincing Jenn that you would want her here, I never thought how Bella would take it.'

'Don't worry, Robert,' Jacob tore his eyes away from Jenn for a moment. 'Bella will come around. Just give her some time. She's not used to change and I guess the shock has thrown her a bit. Leave her be. Soon she will welcome her sister as much as I do now.'

Jenn looked up at him as he held his hands out to her. She hesitated only a moment before taking them. It felt odd, strange – but also . . . right. She didn't understand why and decided at this moment that it didn't matter. This man was her father – and he did want her back after all.

'I think perhaps,' Jacob continued after a moment, 'it's time we all had a little change in our lives.'

The moon rose in a sky covered with fists of cloud. Only a few determined stars peeked between them but Robert appreciated them anyway. Unable to sleep, he had left his room and climbed high on the westernmost tower of the castle. Now he stood alone, with his hands on the stone battlement, and watched the clouds, trying to guess the next few days' weather. In four, perhaps three days, he would finally be within the walls of Dunlorn. Then his only problems would concern the management of his lands, his studies and the occasional argument with Finnlay.

The castle below him was quiet but for the odd rustle of movement from the host of animals which lived within the walls. The night watch paced along the ramparts but kept their distance from Robert. They knew their master's opinion of him and had no wish to converse with one whom they saw as a traitor. That suited Robert at this particular moment – he had no wish to be disturbed.

Jacob had turned the whole castle upside down in his hurry to announce the return of his lost child. The household had been thrown into chaos as the news had spread and Robert was certain almost every inhabitant of Elita had found reason to pass through the hall to take a look at their master's newfound pride and joy. A few of the older ones remembered Jenn as a baby and their reactions had ranged from stunned incredulity to outright delight. And over all of them, Jacob had laughed, his happiness obvious for all to see.

But it had been Bella who had insisted Robert and Micah stay the night. She hadn't so much as said a word to Jacob about it and Robert suspected she would brook no discussion on the subject. Nevertheless, he did not feel comfortable with the arrangement and determined to leave as early as possible in the morning. He had no desire to play upon any gratitude or duty Jacob would no doubt feel towards him. As far as he was concerned, Jacob owed him nothing.

So why did he feel so restless? Why had he spent two whole hours trying to get to sleep? Why had he come up here, cold and alone, to watch the night sky? Was it possible that after all this time, Robert was beginning to wonder if Jacob had been right all along? That to join Selar's council after the conquest had indeed been an act of treachery to Lusara?

No. Robert sighed and sat down on the cold stone wall. For all that Jacob was an intelligent, honourable man, he had no idea of the truth, of how the whole thing had really begun. Jacob, like everybody else, only saw what had happened and had drawn his own conclusions. None of them had ever bothered to find out how the state of affairs had really come into place. Selar himself had never spoken of it – and with good reason. And Robert had never told the story because it would damage all he'd worked to achieve in the first place.

He looked up at the sky again as the clouds in the east drew together, growing more menacing. It was possible there would be a storm later—

There had been a storm that day, too. That day when Selar had come to see him.

Robert dropped the book and dashed across his study before too much rain could be driven through the swinging shutter. As he reached the window he thrust his arm out into the rain to grab hold of the shutter. Icy needles stung his face, but before he pulled it closed, he caught sight of something in the courtyard below. Two dozen mounted soldiers. He frowned and pulled the shutter closed. Turning back to the fire, he slowly rubbed his hands together, drying them off.

So – his time had come at last.

Two years of imprisonment and finally, soldiers bearing

the royal colours had arrived unannounced at his door. That alone was not a good sign, but for the moment, all he could do was stand before the fire and wait. It wasn't a long wait however. A knock at the door and Robert called out an answer. His bailey, Owen Fitzalan, entered, out of breath and agitated.

'My lord, you have visitors.'

'So I see,' Robert folded his arms. 'Anyone I know?'

'It's the King, my lord!' Owen threw a glance over his shoulder. Footsteps on the stairs beyond the door hastened his words. 'He's brought soldiers, my lord. I fear . . .'

'It's all right, Owen. Find my brother and keep him to his rooms. Tell him that's my order. Then go down and get those men out of the rain.'

Owen frowned, then nodded and took a deep breath. 'If you're sure, my lord? There are not too many of them. Deverin has your men ready . . .'

Robert smiled, though it was an effort. 'No. It's too late for that. If I'd wanted to run, I would have done it two years ago. Just keep Finnlay out of harm's way.'

'Very well, my lord.' Owen bowed and stepped aside as two liveried guards came through the door, followed by a man Robert didn't recognize. Behind them all came Selar. Robert carefully placed his hands behind his back and nodded towards Owen, sending him on his way. Then he turned his attention to the man who was now King of Lusara.

Selar's imposing figure dominated the room. He almost swaggered as he gazed around at the simple furnishings of Robert's study. The guards remained by the door while the other man strode up to Robert, an expression of contempt on his stocky face. A neck, bull-like and heavy, was encased in chain mail, like an obedient dog with a collar. He glared at Robert with sullen intensity, but Robert allowed it to merely wash over him. This man was not the real danger.

'So,' the man began, 'this is the one who would cause us so much trouble, Sire. He's young, little more than a boy. Or is this the younger brother?'

192

'No, this is Dunlorn, Eachern. He's the one.' Selar appeared entirely unconcerned, wandering around and glancing at books and papers scattered across the table which ran down the centre of the room. Robert was relieved he'd put away all his most dangerous papers that morning, although he doubted it would add too much to his current troubles if this man were to discover Robert was a sorcerer – but it never hurt to be careful.

'What's wrong, lad, nothing to say for yourself?' Eachern grunted at Robert. 'Have you no words of respect for your sovereign?'

Robert kept his eyes on Selar and said nothing.

'I'm talking to you, boy!' Eachern bellowed. He reached out and grabbed Robert's shoulder, but Robert anticipated the move and caught the other man's hand in time. With lightning speed, he twisted around until Eachern was pinned with his arm across his back. A little invisible exertion of power was enough to make Eachern's knees buckle beneath him and with a thud he fell to the floor. Robert let go and stood back, his eyes returning to Selar.

'You're an idiot, Eachern,' Selar grunted. 'Get up. Leave us.'

'But, Sire . . .'

'I said, go!'

Eachern climbed to his feet and, with a glare in Robert's direction, stomped out of the room, taking the guards with him. As the door slammed shut behind him, Selar wandered over to the small table by the window on which stood a flask of wine. He poured himself a cup, took a mouthful and turned back to Robert.

'I never thanked you,' he said quietly, 'for saving my life. It didn't seem appropriate at the time and I had other problems to worry about. Still, I'm glad you pulled me out of that river, Dunlorn – even though I dare say you wouldn't have done it if you'd known at the time who I was.'

Robert knew Selar was waiting for a reply so he said nothing. He would need to remember every lesson he'd ever learned from his father to survive this, but it was hard. His stomach was cold, his mouth dry. Silence was definitely best for the moment.

'I see,' Selar nodded, draining his cup. 'So you have nothing to say to me. Unfortunately, I can't leave it at that. I need you to answer a question for me. If I set you free from here, will you raise an army and stand against me?'

The question caught Robert completely by surprise, but he covered it by turning to place another log on the fire.

'You see,' Selar continued, 'I've been told by a number of people I believe I can trust that you are the greatest danger to my throne. It appears the people still hold some affection for your father and, in turn, for you. I'm told that if I were to let you go, within six months you would be leading a rebellion against me. That's something I wish to avoid – for obvious reasons. However, since you did save my life, I felt I at least owed you the opportunity to speak in your own defence.'

Robert gazed into the depths of the fire for a minute, still saying nothing. Then, unable to help himself, he began to laugh.

'I fail to see what you find so amusing!' Selar snapped, slamming his cup down on the table. 'Answer my question, dammit!'

'And what would you do if I said no? Would you actually believe me if I promised never to lead a rebellion against you?' Robert turned, a smile still on his face. 'When you have so many others whispering my treason in your ears? I don't think so. Be honest – you didn't come here to ask me any foolish questions. You came here to see whether you could actually sign my death warrant after I had so inconveniently saved your life. Admit it.'

Selar's eyes lit up with rage. 'How dare you speak to me like that! Whether you like it or not, I am your King and I hold your life in my hands.'

'Then kill me,' Robert replied with a shrug. 'Stop this childish posturing and do the deed.'

'What? Are you eager to die?'

'No,' Robert put his hands behind his back again, calm

194

growing from within, 'merely resigned to it. You made a big mistake, you know, giving me two years to think about it. What do you think I've been doing all this time? Waiting for you to come and rescue me from my prison?'

Selar shook his head slowly and leaned back against the window casement. 'I see my information was correct. You are dangerous – and especially so being only, what, seventeen? You're already as cool as ice, more composed than men twice your age. But I don't believe you. You talk as though you're a man with nothing to lose – and yet you have everything to lose. Even if you don't care about your own life, you have a mother and a brother, not to mention these lands. Are you so courageous with their fate?'

Robert was prepared for this. The trouble was, he was actually enjoying this verbal fencing. What was wrong with him?

He folded his arms across his chest. 'My mother lives at Saint Hilary's, effectively under the protection of the Church, and you'd have to tear the place down in order to get her. I don't doubt you would try it, but do you really want to offend the Church in such a manner so early in your reign? So far they've been tolerant towards you and I think you like it that way.'

'And what about your twelve-year-old brother? Would you consign him to the grave?'

Robert found himself smiling again. 'Finnlay and I are both our father's sons. We are not afraid to face our duty – nor to die by it. If you asked him, I doubt he would say anything different.'

'So you would do nothing to stop me killing him?'

'I would kill you first,' Robert murmured, then glanced up. He held Selar's gaze without flinching. His heart pounded in his chest, but he allowed no sign to show. 'What do you really want from me? Do you want me to provoke you enough to order my execution? Do you want my blessing? What?'

Selar took his time to respond. 'What do you want, Dunlorn?'

Robert pulled in a startled breath. Was the man serious? 'I want you to stop persecuting my people! I want you to stop taking the eldest son from every household and holding them to ransom. I want you to reverse the taxes you've placed on ordinary Lusarans that are driving them further and further into poverty. I want you to stop confiscating land at whim and giving it to your own men. I want you to stop treating this land as though it were a child that needed punishing!'

'What do you know of it? You don't know what you're talking about. You're an innocent in the world of politics and conquest. What I do, I do to keep my throne.'

'And you're doing it so well you've come running to me – a man in prison – to stop me from leading a rebellion. If you were not already in danger, Selar, I would be powerless against you. It's your own ruthlessness that gives me power. If you want to remove me as a danger, then you can do so easily by removing the things that make people rebel!'

'Like you?' Selar tossed back. It wasn't a serious question, but the next one was. 'And would you? Give me your blessing? In public so your supporters could see?'

'Never.'

'Then die and be damned, Dunlorn!' Selar stormed and whirled around for the door. 'I don't need your help!'

'I wasn't offering it,' Robert snapped back. 'I gave it to you once, but you were too stupid to take advantage of it at the time. You don't get a second chance.'

Selar got as far as the door before he paused. Without turning, he said quietly, 'You know, I too am my father's son. Something he taught me was that you should always recognize a unique opportunity when you see one. I did that when I invaded this country of yours, Dunlorn – and what's more, I'm prepared to do it again if I have to.'

He turned slowly. 'In return for your public blessing, Dunlorn, I offer you your life, the lives of your family and people here – and certain concessions along the lines you just mentioned. This is a unique opportunity for you also, and you should not be too quick turning it down.'

Robert listened not only to what Selar said, but to what he didn't say. Could it be possible that his throne was in genuine danger? And not only from those who would support Robert? Was Selar really in so much trouble that he had come here, hoping for something he must have known he would never get? It was incredible, but even as Selar spoke, Robert had no trouble seeing the depth of this opportunity.

He let his hands drop to his sides and walked slowly across the room. He stopped in front of Selar and met his gaze, eye to eye. 'You do need my help, my support – but you will not buy it so cheaply. Nor will I give you my public support until you give me something worth supporting. Anything else would only make people doubt my sincerity and defeat the entire purpose. I'll do it, yes, but only after you have let me help the people. You've already done enough damage for one reign. Give me the power to do some good.'

'But would you use that power against me?' Selar searched Robert's face.

'Not unless you betrayed my trust, no. Unlike some people I could mention, once I make a vow, I never break it. You should remember that if you ever do decide to relieve my brother of his life.'

'Fine words, Dunlorn, but do you mean them?'

Robert took a moment to think about it. He also thought about how close he was to Selar and how easy it would be to kill him at this particular moment. It would be a simple thing to do, to overpower the soldiers downstairs, then gather together his forces and ride towards Marsay with an army at his back. Within weeks he could be crowned King of Lusara and there would be very little left of Selar's conquest for the historians to argue about. So why didn't he do it?

The answer was as simple as the question. Because the only way he could kill Selar was by using sorcery and people would see that – and how long would he keep that throne with everyone knowing he was a sorcerer? Another war

197

would destroy Lusara totally, and Robert had no more claim to the crown than Selar. He would be just as bad as the man he'd replaced. Especially since Robert had no desire whatsoever to be King.

'Yes,' he breathed solemnly. 'I do mean it.'

Selar nodded slowly. 'Very well, Dunlorn, you have a deal. But I swear, you make one move against me and I will destroy you utterly.'

Robert smiled. 'And I make the same vow.'

The moon was lost behind a film of blue cloud and a fine dust of rain began to fall, glistening on the stone ramparts. Robert stared out across the lake, able to see the mountains only in his imagination. It had been eleven years since that talk with Selar, and so much had changed in that time. Strangely, Selar had kept his word and allowed Robert all kinds of influence to help those who'd needed it. In turn, Robert had finally made a public vow of allegiance to Selar and for a while, the whole thing had looked like working. Even more strangely, Robert had found he actually liked the man, and without even realizing it, they had grown closer, becoming friends – good friends. For almost a year, Robert had enjoyed the first happiness since before the Troubles had begun.

But then things changed again – and quickly too. So quickly that he'd never really had any time to stop and work out what to do next. And when Berenice had died . . .

'You've come out without a cloak, Robert.'

He whirled around to find Jenn standing behind him, her face pale in the misty moonlight. 'What are you doing up at this hour?'

She shrugged. 'I'm sorry I startled you, but there's no need to yell at me.'

'I didn't yell. I . . .' he fumbled around for a word, 'I . . .'

'You yelled, Robert. Can we change the subject? This one's exhausted.'

Robert sank back on to his seat with an involuntary chuckle.

'Oh dear. I seem to have disturbed your sombre mood. I apologize again. What were you thinking about?'

'Nothing important.'

'You're lying. You've been standing up here for almost half an hour. I know, I've been watching you.'

'Why?'

'I thought you might jump.'

'Oh?'

'And I wanted to be present when it happened.'

This time he burst out laughing, the dark thoughts of moments ago washed away like cobwebs in the rain.

She waited a moment for his laughter to subside then said, 'You never told me my father hated you. You never said a word.'

'No.'

'Does that mean you won't be able to come back here? Ever?'

'Yes, that's exactly what it means. You'll finally be rid of me for good.'

'I see,' she said firmly, her eyes going out to the lake. 'And you don't mind him thinking of you as a traitor?'

Robert shrugged. 'There's little I can do to change his mind – and what little I could do, I refuse to.'

'Like what?'

'Like waging war on Selar and removing him from the throne.'

'And tomorrow you leave?'

'What's wrong?' he asked lightly. 'Not soon enough for you?'

'Oh, Robert,' she snapped, turning back to him, 'sometimes I could just hit you!'

'Me? What did I do?'

She stared at him for a moment, but, characteristically, he could tell nothing from her expression. Eventually she sighed and said, 'You have no idea, do you?'

'About what?'

'About what I think. About how I feel being left out here, in the middle of nowhere with no means by which to learn any more about these damn powers. By the gods, Robert, you're the only link I have – however tenuous – with the Enclave. What am I supposed to do next?'

She had a point and he felt suitably chastised. Still, from what he'd seen of her abilities so far, it appeared she needed little of the usual training a sorcerer required before becoming adept. At the rate she was going, she would be at master level within the year. On that score, she was probably better off without the training.

'I'm sorry,' he said. 'I'm a fool and I know it. You should be used to that by now. Still, I wouldn't worry about training for the moment. You'll have too much to do here, learning how to be the daughter of an Earl. But you'll get time, eventually. By then you'll be in a position to disappear for a while and go to the Enclave.'

'But I don't know how to get there.'

'Yes you do. You just don't realize it yet. All you need to do is head for the Goleth and your feet will take you the rest of the way. That too is part of the Sealing process.'

'Anything else you haven't mentioned?'

'No.' He shook his head and smiled down at her. For all her brave words, she looked very fragile and vulnerable at this moment, but fool though he was, he was not so stupid as to believe that image. However, his voice was gentle as he said, 'Micah and I will leave before dawn. I don't want to wait around long enough for your father to realize we're still here. Would you pass on my thanks to Bella?'

'You didn't meet Lawrence, though. Bella's husband. He's expecting to see you in the morning, before you leave.'

'Then pass on my apologies to him also. Believe me, Jenn, it's best I leave before dawn.'

She nodded slowly, her eyes not moving from his. *And will you say goodbye to Micah for me? Tell him I'll miss him?*

'Of course.'

She smiled a little and turned to go, then she hesitated. 'You know, you've almost made me wish I'd never said that stupid thing to those Guildesmen to make them come after me. It's been an interesting adventure, but I'm still not sure

I like the consequences. Still, I suppose that's what you get for losing your temper.'

She made it as far as the top of the stairs down to the wall before Robert spoke. 'Jenny?' She stopped and turned back to face him. Once she did, he didn't really know what to say. 'You will be careful, won't you?'

'About as careful as you. Goodbye, Robert.'

The stairs took her away quickly, but before he could even move, a last single thought floated into his mind.

*And I don't know where you got the idea I wanted to be finally rid of you. I never said anything of the kind.*

Micah had the horses saddled and ready for their pre-dawn departure. Robert was already yawning from little more than an hour's sleep. But before he could mount up, Bella appeared out of the darkness and strode across the courtyard towards them.

'I thought you'd do something like this,' she murmured a little acidly.

'Am I so transparent?' Robert replied.

'Sometimes, yes – but then, I suppose I know a different side to you most people don't see.'

'And which one is that?'

'The irritating one.'

'Ah,' Robert grinned. 'Then you will find you have a lot in common with your sister.'

'May I speak to you before you go?' Bella moved away from the horses, Micah and the stable boy who held the animals. 'Tell me honestly. You say she has the Mark of our House. Have you seen it?'

'I have.'

'And you are certain she is my sister?'

'I have no doubts at all. Do you?' Robert studied Bella, afraid to say more.

'Oh, I don't know,' Bella sighed. 'But I do want to apologize for yesterday. I didn't mean to accuse you of anything. It's just that I was so shocked – and I was afraid of what it would mean to father — if there should be some mistake.'

'There's no mistake. And perhaps your apology would be better served if you made it to Jenn.'

Bella frowned and looked up at him. 'There's something that troubles me, however. You insist she was taken during the Troubles? But how? The only children who were taken were boys from the families directly involved in the feuds. My father had no part in that, so why would anyone take his daughter? Who would take her — and why was nothing ever said about it later? And why . . .'

'Why would she turn up, years later, alive and well, when the others have never been seen again? I can't tell you. I doubt we'll ever know. It's so long ago now that even if we did find the person responsible, I doubt they would admit to it — or be able to give you a reason why.'

'No, I suppose not.'

Robert glanced back at Micah then up at the keep. 'I know we've had our differences in the past, Bella, but I want you to do something for me.'

'What?'

'Be kind to her. I don't think she's had much of that in her strange life. She remembers nothing of Elita. She's independent, irritating and intensely curious. She also has an extraordinary ability to take change in her stride. She's very tough but even so, in agreeing to come here, she has made herself vulnerable and she knows it. She'll resist you and try your patience — but all the same, be kind to her, please.'

Bella studied his face for a moment. 'I thought the great Earl of Dunlorn cared for nothing.'

Robert held her gaze. 'Will you?'

She nodded. 'I'll try.'

'Then, goodbye, Bella — and thank you for your hospitality.'

Robert turned and climbed on to his horse. Micah drew alongside him as they rode through the gate. With the castle receding into the distance, the first rays of morning crept over the cloud-shadowed ridge.

'Well, my lord, I suppose it could be worse,' Micah ventured. 'It could be snowing.'

Robert glanced at him and couldn't help smiling. 'Micah, you're a dear and faithful friend, but timing was never your greatest virtue.'

'My lord?'

Robert raised his hand and pointed skywards. 'Look up.'

# 9

Vaughn stood on his balcony and gazed down at the lights of the city. In the early darkness of the winter evening, torches lined the causeway leading to the mount, following the road up until it reached the square below him. Opposite the Guilde Hall, the imposing Basilica was ablaze with orange and surrounded by crowds of city folk, waiting in silence.

The Basilica also waited, lit from inside by a thousand candles. Tall pillars and smooth arches dwarfed the statues of saints atop the door and played counterpoint to the castle wall. Beyond, now in almost complete darkness, the keep stood like a shadow against the sky, a stormcloud of grey stone, silent and uncompromising.

Vaughn grimaced up at the sky as the first few snowflakes drifted down. Of course, it was too much to expect fortune to smile on him all the time. This night had its own advantages, both for his beloved Guilde and for himself. After all, it was not every day one was witness to the funeral of a bishop.

He turned and went back inside where it was warm. Osbert, dressed in his formal bright yellow robes, waited on him. Round and soft. That was always how Vaughn thought of this man, that's how Osbert appeared, but it was far from the truth. Osbert had few real talents but he did have the ability to organize the host who worked for them in secret. Osbert called them his legions and in truth, Vaughn knew very little about them. He didn't want to. All he wanted from them was results.

'I'm beginning to lose patience, Osbert,' Vaughn grunted. He picked up his fur-lined cape and drew it across his shoulders. 'How long am I to wait before you bring me this evidence? All I've had so far are vague reports, suspicions and your assurances that you can get me what I need. If you cannot, why am I wasting my gold?'

'My lord,' Osbert began carefully, 'I did warn you at the outset that it might take some time. The situation is very precarious. My man can't get messages to me every day. He would be suspected. I hope by summer . . .'

'I can't wait until the summer!' Vaughn snapped. 'Have you no idea how important this is? Especially now that Domnhall is finally dead! After all the work we've done, the depth to which we are involved – something like this can easily destroy all our plans. Domnhall is gone, yes, and we have our new law, have the hospices officially under our jurisdiction, but the Church tarries. It could take years for them to pass the work on to us fully. In the meantime, there are demands on our resources that must be recompensed. And if we are to support the King further . . .'

Vaughn didn't finish the sentence. This was not the time to be telling Osbert of their future plans, their future glory. No. First he needed Osbert to complete this one mission.

'I need firm evidence by spring, Osbert. I will wait no longer. Something is going on at Dunwyn. Blair is playing a very dangerous game and I must know what he plans to do. The King must know. Do you understand?'

'Yes, my lord.'

Vaughn nodded. It was time to go; Lewis was waiting for him in the concourse. Together they made their way across the square.

The chant of monks in the quire filled the Basilica with a gentle harmonious glow, like a thick warm carpet on a stone floor. It softened the arches above and the booted feet of those arriving to pay their final respects. Before the altar a priest bowed to the wood-carved image of the Trilogy, famous throughout Lusara for its fine workmanship. Both candles and incense burned and filled the Basilica with a cloying scent of honey and myrrh. They took their familiar places to the left of the quire and sat alone, in the stalls set aside for the Guilde.

Placing his hands on his lap, Vaughn glanced at the dome above and followed its lines down to the altar. He'd never much liked this Church; it was always dark and serious, deliberately trying to invoke the mysterious spirit of the gods. It was pathetic. The Church had long ago lost its connection with the deities. Now it was just an empty tradition, a worthless shell in which the people still held overwhelming faith.

Well, no more.

Tomorrow evening, the clergy would gather within the chapter house and elect the man who would take Domnhall's place. A man who would help his people and join together once more with the Guilde. That at any rate was what Vaughn hoped. Despite the fact that all his plans rested on the outcome of that election, he was powerless to control it.

Vaughn clenched his hands into the soft folds of his robe. He was not sorry Domnhall was dead. For the last thirty years, Domnhall's primacy had blocked every move Vaughn had made to advance the Guilde. But now the time had come for change. Domnhall had been a reformer, trying to bring the Church back to its former glory. But reformer or not, his intransigence had driven a wedge between Church and Guilde.

Yes, time indeed for a change. It was time for the Guilde to rise once more. They had the sacred trust given them by the gods themselves. The trust to care and hold knowledge, to teach and learn, to record and witness. These were not light burdens, but the backbone on which society depended. Without the caretaking of the Guilde, mankind would never have survived the Dawn of Ages, never have passed through the barrier of time, and certainly never have lived through the following thousand years.

Vaughn took a deep calming breath and settled in as much comfort as this bleak place would allow. The only obstacle was tomorrow's synod and the man the Church would choose as the new primate – but no matter what, Vaughn would find a way to ensure success!

As the clergy formed two lines before the altar, Vaughn pondered. He would find a way, no matter what.

Osbert opened the door to the study and Vaughn flew past him. 'By the blood, two hours of that dreary mass – and for what? So we can all sit there and pretend we're sorry Domnhall's no longer with us? Come inside, Lewis, and shut that door!'

He loosened the ties around his throat and snatched the cup of wine Osbert handed him. 'Thank the gods that's the end of him!'

Lewis's sallow face turned to him. 'There are plenty who will miss him.'

'Not nearly so many as he would have liked, I'm sure!' Vaughn snapped. Two hours sitting in the maudlin confines of the Basilica while his hands and feet froze had done nothing to still his agitation. Seeing Hilderic handling the ceremony had only made it worse. Now if he should take the primacy . . .

'Osbert, I have a task for you.'

'Yes, my lord?' Osbert hovered close by the fire, his hands behind his back.

'I need someone inside the chapter house tomorrow night. I must know how the vote goes – who will stand with us and who against.'

'My lord?'

'Don't be a fool, man, you know what I'm talking about,' Vaughn snapped. 'You know the King and I have discussed Domnhall's successor. Selar has made his wishes quite clear to the synod. It is to be either Brome or Quinn. Now I need someone in there to make sure they understand that.'

Osbert shook his head. 'But the only man I have who could get in there without being discovered is Nash and he's on his way out of Marsay tonight.'

'Then stop him! Go, now. I don't care if the election is closed.' Vaughn drained his wine and slammed the cup down on the desk. 'I will know what happens!'

*

The stone floor was cold beneath Rosalind's knees. It made her joints burn, her back ache. She took the pain in, dwelt on it, drowned in it. Fire and ice, agony and isolation. Alone, she prayed.

The Basilica was almost empty now; the last of the court had faded away. The Church guard stood waiting for her to leave before lifting Domnhall's body and taking it away. When they did, they would take her hope with it.

Selar meant to do it. He would start a war with Mayenne. He would tear Lusara apart, bring the Church to its knees, and all because of his desire for bloody revenge. Revenge for being born younger than Tirone, for being favoured by his father and then cast aside when his ailing brother grew stronger. Revenge for having to support Tirone when the barons of Mayenne revolted after their father's death. Revenge for Tirone pushing him out of Mayenne and into Lusara. Revenge for leaving him there to live or die alone, for trying to kill him.

Simple revenge, and yet it would cost the lives of thousands of Lusarans. It would destroy the country her son would one day rule. Dear, sweet, wounded Lusara. In agony. Isolated. Those who saw her pain could do nothing about it. The rest were blind.

And Rosalind saw it all, felt it all, but now that Domnhall was dead, there was no one left to stop it, no voice to rise above the rest. No saviour.

She let her folded hands drop to her sides. Inside her a voice cried out for her to have faith, but she was deaf to its call. Stiffly, she rose to her feet, glanced briefly at the trium then turned around and walked away.

*He fell.*

*Slipping, screaming, tumbling down the slimy riverbank. Icy water sucked away his breath, crashed in on his skull, blinded him, deafened him. Only the old man's triumphant laughter echoed in his mind. Then the pain. The agony of the cold driving into his bones, his clothes full of water, dragging him down, the blade of betrayal slicing the air from his lungs. Inky*

208

darkness swirled around him as the river pushed him along. His mouth opened, filled with freezing poison. He struggled, flailed his arms around, crashed into rocks and logs, his cloak, sword. Nowhere could he find the surface. There was nothing to grasp, nothing but the torrent shoving him further towards hell. Pounding in his ears, pain in his chest. He had to breathe but there was only the water. He was drowning.

Something hit his arm. He could hardly feel it, his flesh was so numb. He stopped moving. His chest ached and he knew he would have to draw breath now. It was time to die.

Then he was moving again and suddenly his head came free of the water. More pain in his arms as something gripped him hard, held his head high. Like a cry, he gasped in real air, coughing and choking – but it was not water and he gulped in again.

There was a voice. Somewhere in the darkness, someone was talking to him. Calm. Comforting. Solid. Strong. He caught hold of the voice, focused on it. Steadily he was dragged forward until he felt a hard surface behind his back. He was lifted up on to the river bank. He lay there, exhausted. In the night, he opened his eyes and saw the stars above, dusted across the sky.

Then the voice again. 'How do you feel? Can you speak?'

He turned his head as a cloak was laid over him. He looked up at the man who had saved his life. But this was no man. This was a boy. Perhaps fifteen or sixteen. Concerned eyes gazed down at him, eyes of a green so deep it was visible even in the darkness.

He nodded and tried to sit up, unable to take his gaze from those eyes. Then suddenly the young face changed, shifted and shimmered and, abruptly, it was Carlan kneeling there beside him. The old man's black eyes laughed at him, his white hair a mockery of the night, the wizened face creased in a triumphant sneer.

'Now I have you! Now you are mine!' the old man screeched . . .

Selar sat bolt upright in bed, gasping in air. For a second he couldn't remember where he was. He turned his head this way and that until his eyes caught the glimmer of pre-dawn light through the window and things shifted back into their familiar places.

His breath steady now, he reached up and pushed hair back from his sweat-drenched face. He leaned over to the table by the bed and grabbed the wine cup which always sat there. But it was empty. Cursing and bone-weary, Selar shoved back the bedclothes and swung his legs over the side of the bed. From there he stumbled to the cabinet by the window and drained the flask of wine which sat there.

Damned nightmare!

There was another flask, this one full. He took that, grabbed a blanket and headed for the window. He pushed the shutter wide open and sank down on the padded seat. Outside a frail mist had settled on the valley and would last until the sun had risen properly. The air was cold, but Selar drank it in, even as it reminded him of his twisted dream.

It wasn't the truth. Just a perversion of it. He'd only been in the river a minute or so before Robert had pulled him out. And Carlan hadn't been there. Not then. Not afterwards. Carlan had only been there to push him into the water.

Selar took another mouthful of the wine, letting the bitter flavour wake his mouth and warm his stomach. He pulled the blanket up around both shoulders but he didn't feel cold. No. He felt empty.

The battle of Seluth, almost fourteen years ago. He'd been looking for Carlan. Just as the battle had edged towards victory, the old man had wandered off. Selar had gone searching for him, wanting to share the triumph with the man who had been instrumental in achieving it. Although it had been Selar's idea to invade Lusara, it had been Carlan who had first pointed out the instability of the warring Houses, the weakness of the King. Without those, Selar would never have dreamed of taking arms against Lusara. She was too strong, always had been.

And he'd found Carlan. By that river. The old man had stood there, his black eyes glinting in the evening light. He'd stood there, held out his grizzled hand and said Selar was now his creature. Like a frightened child, Selar had recoiled, and in response, Carlan had pushed him backwards into the river.

Betrayal. Like all the others, Carlan had betrayed him. All of them had betrayed. All except . . .

But Robert had left. Deserted him. Left him drowning as surely as if he'd walked away from that river all those years ago. He'd gone because he wouldn't break his oath of fealty. Because he wouldn't bend, wouldn't give in to those who battled against his ideals. And Selar had needed him to bend.

Yes, it was best that Robert was gone. Selar was alone now – but alone, no one could stop him.


George, Earl of Kandar and Knight of the Realm, paused by the garden gate, his hand on the latch. In summer this was easily one of the most beautiful places in the castle and even now, in the depths of winter, it still held a certain charm. But it was not the beauty of the garden George had come to see, it was the fur-cloaked presence seated on a bench by the pond.

Surrounded by her ladies, Rosalind glanced up and saw George as he walked through the garden, bowing deeply before her.

'My lord, I thought you were to leave for Kandar this morning.'

'I was, Your Grace, but the King has called a Privy Council meeting for this evening and I must attend. My lands will have to wait a few more days for me.'

She nodded and waved him to take a seat. He noticed the eyes of the other ladies on him for a moment then they turned back to their respective tasks.

'I had not thought you would still enjoy the garden this late in the year. Surely it's too cold?'

Rosalind spread her hands. 'As you can see, we have not yet frozen to death. I feel we spend altogether too much time indoors in winter. Unless we're out riding, we see nothing of the sun and you must agree, it's a fine day to be out.'

'I just hope Your Grace will take no risks with your health,' George murmured, glancing once more at the Queen's ladies. One, a dark-haired beauty of about sixteen, kept glancing at him then looking away in embarrassment.

'Come, my lord,' Rosalind murmured, 'you must have some tale to tell me. I rely on your keen ears to bring me news of my country.' She placed her hands on her lap and regarded him with a steady gaze. There was little vitality in her today, no breeze in her conversation. It was as though she were talking to him only to relieve other thoughts.

George offered her a smile and nodded. 'Well, I've been at court for the past two months. The only story I've heard recently has been about the hermit of Shan Moss.'

'A hermit?'

'Yes. It seems he had a vision. It was towards the end of autumn, I believe. The hermit was once a member of the order at St Cuthbert's and returned there briefly to tell the Abbot his story. He left soon after and nothing has been heard from him since. There is a prophecy, ages old, which tells of a dark angel descending upon the land. He is evil and aims to strike at the very heart of the gods by tearing the Church in two. It appears this hermit had a vision which told him that day had come, that the dark angel was already walking the land and at work to bring the Church down.'

George had assumed the story would entertain her, but rather than smile, Rosalind's eyes grew flinty, her voice a harsh whisper. 'Can it be true? Is this hermit to be believed?'

He hastened to reassure her, 'I know not, my lady. We have many prophecies – sometimes even visions like this do come true. However, I suspect this one is a little over-indulgent. This hermit had lived alone in the forest for twenty years. Who's to say his mind had not become affected by his solitude? I'm sure there's no truth to it.'

'There is much truth to be found in many prophecies, my lord,' Rosalind murmured, her gaze going inward. 'And there is sometimes a truth we may never know about until it's too late.'

He folded his hands in together and ventured another smile. He'd not managed to bring her any cheer at all. It was better that he go now. 'With your leave, Your Grace, I will be on my way. I have some preparations to make before I return home.'

Rosalind nodded her consent and he backed away and out through the garden gate. Turning down the path which led towards the keep, he cursed himself for a fool. He always did when he left her. Cursed himself for going to see her – and for leaving her. But what could he do? She was his sovereign's lady, his Queen. What hope was there in that hopeless situation?

But still he kept going back, and at least she did seem to enjoy his visits. She got precious few. Most of the court ignored her, at times failing even to acknowledge her existence. Her ladies were of the highest born, but that was more out of Selar's duty to their families to find the women places at court than for any concern for his wife's company. Selar himself had as much as admitted to George that he thought his wife an empty-headed child. He'd married her for state reasons, to get an heir that would belong both to Selar and Lusara.

George could not fault Selar's wisdom. That small concession to the old Houses had done much to ensure the peace; even more so when Kenrick was born. The old Houses had long since reconciled themselves to living under Selar's rule, and eventually, under the rule of his son.

But still, George could not help asking of the gods, why had Selar chosen the single brightest jewel in all of Lusara? Why did he have to choose Rosalind?

'Are you done with that yet?' Hilderic demanded, placing his hands squarely on his hips. 'I would like to eat my dinner some time today, if you don't mind.'

Godfrey ignored the Archdeacon's blustering and continued clearing the table of papers, pens and inks in order to make space for the tray Father John was holding. Godfrey could forgive the old man's temper as easily as he could forgive the rain falling. To lose a close friend of many years was bad enough in itself, but that the same man had been your superior and spiritual father made it so much worse.

He completed cleaning up and stood back to allow Father John to lay the tray. As he did so, Godfrey placed himself on a chair opposite Hilderic.

The old man grunted down at the tray then held up his hand. 'Don't go just yet, John. There's something I want to ask you.'

'Yes, Archdeacon?'

Hilderic reached forward and absently poured himself a cup of goat's milk. It was the only thing the healers allowed him to drink these days. 'You were in a better position to see yesterday, in the Basilica. Did the Proctor wear full formal regalia for the service, or was that just my imagination?'

'He did, Archdeacon,' Father John replied with a nod.

Hilderic bent his bushy grey brows together and puffed out his bottom lip. 'Damned cheek! He'll walk straight into the arms of Broleoch for that hypocrisy alone.'

'Was it not intended as a mark of respect?'

'Hah!' Hilderic broke a piece of bread and blew away the crumbs from his lap, 'Vaughn doesn't know the meaning of the word. But never mind. Thank you, John.'

The young priest bowed and left them alone. Godfrey leaned back in his seat and cast a measuring gaze over his colleague's meal. 'Personally, I don't know how you can eat that. Baby's mash and milk of all things!'

'I guess it all depends on how hungry you are.' Hilderic paused to swallow a piece of soft bread. 'Well?'

'Well, what?'

'Don't be an ass, man. How does the count go?'

Godfrey folded his arms across his chest. 'But the election is not for some hours yet, brother. How would I know how the count is? The gods do not favour me with that kind of foresight.'

Lifting his cup to his mouth, Hilderic frowned. 'Are you trying to annoy me – or are you just doing it from habit?'

'Funny thing to ask a priest.'

Hilderic drained his cup and placed it carefully back on the table. He turned a solemn gaze on Godfrey, then nodded slowly. 'Then it's not good, I take it?'

Godfrey lifted one shoulder in a half-hearted shrug. 'It depends on what you define as good. On the one hand we have the old school, the abbots and monks who were never really happy with the changes Domnhall made and would only be too pleased to revert back to their former order. Then there are those who consider themselves moderates and would like to see further but small improvements to our structure – nothing, of course, that would take away any of their autonomy. Then there are the few zealots who believe we should embrace the new order and rejoin our brothers within the Guilde in support of the King. They are happy for the Guilde to take over the hospice work, believing it to be in the best interests of the Church as well as the people. That way they can return to the more contemplative life.'

'And the rest?'

'Isn't that enough?'

'Fortunately, I think you've only scratched the surface.'

Godfrey did smile then, though belatedly. 'I only wish I could. Actually, the vast majority don't seem to have made up their minds yet. We've failed to stop the hospice take-over and few of them have even considered the situation with the raiders. We don't know what Selar plans and so we can't tell them. They're aware of what's been happening since Domnhall died, they just don't appear convinced of anything in particular.'

Hilderic stared in distaste at the remains of his meal then pushed the plate away. Glancing up at Godfrey, he said, 'Our opinions differ, brother. I don't count that as a bad thing. If, by this point, they were already persuaded towards Selar's thinking, then I believe all would surely be lost. That they are still open to argument is at least a point in our favour.'

As Godfrey raised his eyebrows, Hilderic conceded, 'All right, a small point, I admit.'

Standing, Godfrey stretched out his long frame. He laced his hands together and clasped the small wooden trium which hung around his neck from a silver chain his father had given him. 'Actually, my thoughts are less on the election itself and more on what happens afterwards. Suppose we do get our way and neither Brome nor Quinn are elected. What happens then?'

'Not much, I should imagine. Oh, I'm sure Selar will fume and make mighty noises, but what can he do – in reality, I mean? He can't exactly bring the Church down and have us all executed, can he? He's no fool. He knows he'd have a civil war on his hands in no time. There is no way he can afford a direct move against the Church.' Hilderic must have read the sour expression on Godfrey's face. 'What's wrong?'

'I don't know. I just don't like the feel of this. I don't think Selar would take defeat lying down. He waited a long time for Domnhall to die. It's no coincidence he chose this moment to give the hospices to the Guilde. He knew Domnhall was too weak to thwart him. It's obvious Brome and Quinn are essential to his plans. Somehow I just can't see him being philosophical about being beaten again.'

'Surely you're not about to suggest we support the King in the election? For the sake of our own skins?'

Godfrey glanced at the old man, then at the trium in his hand. He shook his head slowly. 'Never that. I just can't help wondering if there is another way out of this. Remember the story about that hermit? About some dark angel tearing the Church apart?'

Hilderic laughed. 'You listen to gossip too much, brother. Besides, Selar has nothing to do with it. He has fair hair, not dark – and before you mention it, Vaughn's is almost white, what there is left of it. I fear that little vision must concern some other dark angel, of which I am sure there are many. Come, let us make our way to the Chapter House.'

Godfrey moved to the door and put his hand on the latch.

'We'll be a little early, but I don't mind. I do want to get a good seat.'

The cold morning air hit Nash's face like a slap and he sucked in a deep breath. A timid sprinkle of rain drifted down, but barely touched him. The atmosphere within the Chapter House had been stifling and more than once he'd had trouble staying awake. The debates had gone on for hours, but Nash, in disguise, had not even been able to get up and walk around for fear of being discovered. As his feet now hit the cobblestones of the small courtyard, he spread his arms and stretched. Vaughn would be breathless to know the outcome of the election, but Nash was in no hurry to tell him.

How much longer would this go on? How many more months was he to abase himself before the Proctor? Oh, Osbert trusted him completely and even Selar had noticed him, requested his attendance at court functions. But Vaughn?

Damn it all! If only he didn't need that pompous idiot – if only he didn't need any of them!

But he did. He needed Vaughn's support, and more especially, his library. Most of all, however, he needed Selar. And he had to be so careful. He could not afford to fail again. He wouldn't have the energy left to try a third time. He must succeed. He would succeed where his father had failed. Five generations was enough to sacrifice on the altar of any ambition, no matter how great the goal.

And he had already come so far. Further than any before him. This time he'd planned properly, taken care of both the Enemy and the Ally. The dangers now were few: all that remained was for him to be patient.

Nash sighed and stilled the warring factions in his mind. There would be time, time to achieve it all, to regain what was lost so long ago.

At the moment, however, it was time to go and tell Vaughn the news.

Nash yawned again and ran his hands through his thick

black hair. Then with a smile, he began walking across the courtyard.

Father John tucked the package of letters under his arm and thanked the courier. Then he turned and made his way quickly across the cloister, trying to dodge the rain. He ducked through the doorway to his master's chambers and scurried along the corridor, wiping a hand over his damp hair as he went. He arrived before the door and pushed it open.

Hilderic stood by the washstand rubbing a linen towel over his face. He glanced up as John entered.

'Archdeacon! The synod is over?'

'As you can see. We've just come out. It's all over. Now I must dress and go and see the King.'

'I will help you, of course. But, surely you must rest first. You've been in there for almost twelve hours. You must be exhausted.'

Hilderic only nodded wearily and let John help him.

'There're letters for you, but they can wait. The courier must have arrived moments before you came out of the synod. He was from my own part of the country and I couldn't help talking to him for a bit.'

'And?'

'Archdeacon?'

'You've obviously got something to tell me.'

John paused and swallowed. Should he tell Hilderic? Would he want to know? Probably. 'Well, the man just told me the most extraordinary story.'

Hilderic raised an eyebrow. 'It didn't concern some dark angel, did it?'

'No, Archdeacon! Actually, it's about a girl – a child, really. You know the Earl of Elita?'

'Before the war, yes. I haven't seen him for years. A good man.'

'Do you remember his daughter? The younger one? I believe he had two.'

'Yes, Bella was the older. She married young Lawrence

Maitland a few years ago. Well, get on with it, boy. The King will want to see me some time this year.'

With a chuckle, John placed the cope over his master's shoulders. 'You won't believe this, but the younger daughter was thought to have drowned in a river when she was about three or four. But apparently she survived. She never drowned at all, but was in fact abducted during the Troubles!'

'The Troubles? How do they know that?'

'Because someone found her — living way on the other side of Lusara. They found her and took her back to her father! Isn't that a miracle, Archdeacon?'

Hilderic paused and pinned John with a steady gaze. 'Do you mean that literally, my son?'

John began to shrug, then stopped himself, 'Well . . . er, I don't know. I suppose it could be.'

Hilderic smiled. 'Yes, I suppose it could almost qualify. And how wonderful for Jacob to have his lost daughter returned — though I suspect it opens up a few questions as to where she's been all this time, and, for that matter, where those other children are. Still, at least one returned is better than none.'

'It certainly is, Archdeacon. But that's not all.'

Pausing by the door, Hilderic turned. 'More?'

John moved around him and opened the door to let him through. 'I thought you might want to know. It's something else the courier told me. Something important. It's only hearsay, of course, but somehow I don't think this is only a rumour.'


'They did what?' Vaughn slammed his hand down on the table and whirled around to face Nash, his dark robes floating after him. The fire chose that moment to spit and crackle. Vaughn took the goblet he held and threw it at the flames, making them sputter and turn bright blue. With two strides he crossed the room and yanked the door handle.

'Lewis! Osbert!' he yelled, then turned back to Nash.

'What the hell does Hilderic think he's playing at, eh? Does he think this is a game?'

Nash kept still, lacing his hands beneath the folds of his robe. 'The Archdeacon had very little to do with it – at least directly. What had been said and done beforehand, however, is anyone's guess.'

'Oh, yes,' Vaughn snapped, 'and I think I can guess very well what that old fool is up to. He thinks we'll all just sit back and take no notice. Does the King know?'

'Archdeacon Hilderic is very probably preparing to go and tell him as we speak.'

'Well, good luck to him!'

Taking a breath, Nash ventured, 'My lord, surely we cannot lose the hospices now?'

Vaughn stood by the door, an inward look on his face. His gaze narrowed for a moment as though he had forgotten Nash was there. Then he looked up and, with a frown, said, 'The hospices have nothing to do with it. No, this is about something far more important. Blast and damnation, but I'll make them pay for this!'

At that moment, Lewis and Osbert appeared at the door, their faces betraying their curiosity, but Vaughn couldn't wait to tell the story. He jerked his hand towards Nash, then reached for his cloak.

'Go ahead, ask him,' he growled. 'Ask him where he thinks we'll all be in a year from now. I'm off to see the King.' He threw his cloak around his shoulders and headed for the door, then paused. 'On second thoughts, Nash, come with me. The King may want to ask you a few questions.'

Nash shook the rain off his cloak and helped the Proctor remove his own. Vaughn had raged and fumed all the way to the castle, but Nash had kept silent, despising the man's inability to control his temper. A pair of guards showed them through the castle and into one antechamber after another. By now, Nash noted, Vaughn had calmed himself considerably and managed to set his expression as though in stone.

They emerged into a round chamber within the great keep itself. To the left a fireplace big enough to roast an ox hosted flames of furnace proportions. Before it was a long ebony table, around which were scattered a number of chairs. There were no tapestries on the walls and only a single window opposite the fireplace, draped with fine Esterian velvet.

Nash took this all in at a glance, then turned his attention to the men within the room. Before him, his back to the door, was Archdeacon Hilderic, Deacon Godfrey at his side. At one end of the table by the fire stood the Earl of Kandar and by him, Duke Tiege Eachern, his kinsman. Duke Donal McGlashen stood on the opposite side of the table with Selar's chancellor, Dai Ingram, together with Earl Payne. At the other end, close by the window, stood the King.

Vaughn and Nash bowed, but Selar barely glanced in their direction. 'Well, Vaughn, I see I don't need to send for you. Was it chance that brought you here so quickly after the Archdeacon — or were you waiting for him to leave the Chapter House before coming?'

'Sire, I was merely curious to know if there had been any word on the election as yet.'

'Yes,' Selar drew the word out, 'I'm sure you were. As it happens, the Archdeacon was just about to tell me the outcome. You were saying, Father?'

Hilderic inclined his head gracefully, 'I was saying, Sire, the synod debated long and hard. I am happy to say we finally lighted upon a man whom we believe to possess the qualities necessary for the Primate of all Lusara.'

'And he is?' Selar prompted softly.

'Aiden McCauly.' Hilderic said the words without expression and they fell flat into the room, like a thunderclap.

Selar raised his eyebrows so slightly the movement was almost lost. For a moment, he said nothing, then he left the window and placed his hands on the back of his chair. 'Aiden McCauly, eh? An interesting choice. A unanimous one?'

'Almost, Sire.'

'I see.' Selar dropped his gaze and nodded. 'And when will his anointing be?'

There was just the slightest hesitation in Hilderic's voice. 'We performed the ceremony immediately after the election. Bishop McCauly is already installed.'

'Already?' Vaughn sputtered. 'No preparations?'

Godfrey murmured, 'We thought it best under the circumstances.'

'And what circumstances were those?'

But Selar raised a hand to silence Vaughn. 'McCauly is already installed as Bishop?'

'Yes, Sire,' Hilderic nodded.

Selar dropped the hand, leaving his eyes on the Archdeacon. After a moment, he nodded again and moved to turn away. 'Very well, you have our leave to go. I'm sure your new Bishop requires your attendance.'

The priests bowed and backed towards the door, making Nash step aside to get out of their way. The doors opened, but Selar stopped them.

'Just a moment, Archdeacon. What was the other thing?'

'Sire?' Hilderic paused, with the smallest glance at Godfrey.

'You said you had two pieces of news for me. I take it McCauly's installation as Bishop was only one. What was the other?'

Godfrey took in a quick breath and spoke over his colleague. 'It was nothing, Sire. Only gossip – a rumour.'

Selar smiled. 'Tell me.'

Hilderic drew himself up and said, 'One of my couriers, Sire, brought me a strange story this morning. It concerns the Earl of Elita.'

Elita! Nash snapped his gaze on the old priest. Elita! What possible . . .

Hilderic continued, 'It appears his daughter, the younger one, Jennifer, was thought drowned as a child.'

'Really? What of it? Has she returned from the dead?'

'You might think so. Apparently . . .'

222

Nash steeled himself against the revelation, dreading it, fearing it, but knowing what it would be.

'Apparently she was in fact taken during the Troubles. She was found living in Shan Moss and has now been returned to her father.'

Nash silently reached back and steadied himself against the wall. Feeling the cool stone against his hand calmed him and he quickly brought his reactions under control. Sure that no one had noticed, he turned his attention back to the King as Hilderic continued his story. There would be time later to consider all the ramifications.

'I'm sure Jacob is a very happy man,' Selar murmured, 'but is that all? It's incredible that one of those children taken during your Troubles has actually been found and returned – but isn't there something else?'

'Yes, Sire. It concerns the person who found her.'

'By the gods, Hilderic,' Selar laughed harshly, 'you take an age to tell a simple story! Get on with it! Who is this extraordinary person?'

'The Earl of Dunlorn, Sire.'

Selar froze. The smile which moments ago looked more like a sneer now crystallized into something entirely different. The entire room was silent as all eyes locked on to the King. Behind them, the fire sputtered and crackled, sending sparks flying. No one moved.

'So he's come back?' Selar whispered. 'Are you sure?'

'I've not seen him with my own eyes, but the report about Elita is reliable. I've no reason to believe the rest of it is untrue.'

Vaughn stormed forward. 'We must do something, Sire. You cannot allow him to . . .'

'I can allow whatever I like, Proctor,' Selar cut across Vaughn, then turned back to Hilderic. 'Do you know where Dunlorn might be now? Is he on his way here, to Marsay?'

'I know no more than I have already told you, Sire.'

Vaughn tried again, 'I can't believe he'd be fool enough to return! And after so long! What can he want? What are his plans? Did he come alone – or with an army? He must be found!'

'On what charge, Proctor?' Selar's tone became icy. 'So far he's done nothing wrong that we know of.'

'Nothing?' Vaughn's voice rose in pitch as his face became suffused with red. 'Need I remind you, Sire, of his crimes before he left?'

Selar raised his hand. 'Those crimes were dealt with at the time. By all means seek him out if you wish – but no man will lay a hand on him without my leave. Is that understood?'

Vaughn's mouth became a set line and he bowed. 'Perfectly, Sire.'

Selar looked around at the others in the room, then back at Hilderic and finally at Nash. There his eyes narrowed a moment before he turned again to the window. His hand came up to dismiss them, but the movement was halted uncompleted. 'Eachern?'

'Yes, Sire?'

'Take a dozen men and go to the Basilica. Arrest Archdeacon McCauly on charges of high treason. Bring him back here and hold him in close confinement.'

'Sire!' Hilderic rushed forward, but Kandar was there before him, his arms barring the way to the King.

'Yes, Archdeacon,' Selar smiled, 'I should have told you before but I have been informed of the most disturbing things about your Aiden McCauly. I had thought not to try him but now, in the light of recent events, I feel it is my duty to do so. In the meantime, I would like you to return to the Basilica and prepare to install Anthony Brome as your new Bishop. I would like him on his throne by nightfall.'

'But Sire! I cannot do that. Bishop McCauly . . .'

'Archdeacon McCauly is a traitor,' Selar snapped, his voice taking on an edge like steel. 'I suggest you look to your own conscience lest I find you guilty of the same crime.'

'If you wish to confine someone, Sire, then take me. But you cannot, must not do this. The Church will . . .'

'Will – what?' Selar moved around the table until he towered above the old man. 'If you and your brethren value

McCauly at all, you'll do as I instruct. I would not like to feel it necessary to execute McCauly so soon after his anointing. It would not be pious. Go now and do it quickly, Archdeacon. You will find it's not so bad once it is over.'

Placing a hand on Hilderic's shoulder, Selar leaned close and murmured, 'You must learn to trust me, brother. I am doing this for the good of the Church and my country. It cannot be good to have a traitor as our Prelate now, can it?'

He straightened up and nodded to Eachern. Steering Hilderic between them, Eachern and Kandar led him away, followed closely by Godfrey. As the doors closed behind them, Selar turned to Vaughn. 'I assume you were coming here in such a rush to warn me, Proctor? I wonder you didn't bother to warn me about Dunlorn's return as well. Or perhaps you didn't know?'

'No, Sire, I did not. If I had known, I would have done something to prevent it.'

'That's as may be,' Selar said quietly, moving towards the door. 'But remember what I told you. You leave Dunlorn alone.'

As he reached the door he paused, glancing at Nash. 'And this, I suppose, was your spy in the synod? You did well, Nash, to go unnoticed like that. Tell me, how was it that the synod did such a foolish thing as to elect the wrong man to the Bishopric? Did they really debate so long? Were my wishes mentioned at all? Was there much opposition?'

'Actually, Sire,' Nash chose his words very carefully, 'there was not so much opposition as you would imagine. In the end, it came down to superstition.'

'Apt for the Church. What superstition?'

'They had all heard that prophecy about a dark angel splitting the Church in two. Unfortunately, both Brome and Quinn have dark hair and they felt it was a bad omen.'

Selar straightened up and glanced over his shoulder at Vaughn. 'Typical! They go over all that for twelve hours, then choose a Prelate based on the colour of his hair! Hah! And they wonder why I interfere! And as for that prophecy? Well, half the country has dark hair – who's to say who this damned dark angel is? It could be you, Nash – or even Vaughn's great friend Dunlorn. He has dark hair, if I recall. Very dark. Attend me tomorrow, Nash. I may have something I want you to do.'

With a bark of ironic laughter, he turned and left them. Slowly the others filtered out of the room leaving Nash waiting on Vaughn. The Proctor stalked off down the hallway. Nash was finally alone.

Someone had found her.

After all these years, someone had found her and taken her home. How had they known who she was? Had they seen her House Mark – or had she finally remembered what had happened to her? No, that couldn't be possible. She had been much too young to remember. The Mark it was, then. And this Dunlorn character must have known enough about the Marks to work out which House she was from. It was just unlucky she managed to find someone who knew what they were looking at.

And what about Dunlorn? Were all those stories true? Was he the threat Vaughn saw? Was there some way he could be a threat to Nash? Well, it was easy to see that he needed to know more about the legendary renegade – and he had just the person for the job.

Yes, and there was a way to see to the girl as well. A way that would make it easy for him to discover how she had developed over the years, without endangering himself. All he would have to do would be to convince Selar – and that should be easy. A word in the right direction, the hint of a possible danger. Yes, no real problem at all—

However, no matter which way he looked at it, no matter how many questions her discovery brought up, there was one thing which circulated in his mind with pounding repetition. She was back. The Ally. Back at home. Back in the game – and that changed everything.

# 10

The closer Finnlay got to Dunlorn, the more his stomach twisted around, the more he wanted to turn around and go back. Not just back to the Enclave, but back in time. Way back to a day when Robert was more than he seemed, when men looked up to him — when Finnlay looked up to him. Back to a time when things made sense.

*Plague not Robert of Dunlorn to Stand the Circle. His place is elsewhere and he has been forbidden to take any path other than his own . . .*

As clear as this crisp winter's day, Finnlay could remember the moment when Robert had revealed his powers, had discovered Finnlay's talents. It was just weeks before Selar had come, when Robert was still a prisoner within Dunlorn. But that hadn't stopped him. Together one night they'd crept out of the castle and travelled across the countryside to the mountains. Robert had risked his life — his liberty — to get Finnlay to the Enclave that first time. Even now he could remember the debates, the arguments that had gone on, the shock that rippled through the Enclave at the discovery that both Douglas brothers were born sorcerers. From that first day, Finnlay knew the truth about Robert's strength, his potential, and it made him proud.

But then Selar had come. With promises and entreaties and the gods knew what else, Selar had taken Robert and bade him betray his country.

A few years later, when Robert had ridden at the head of Selar's armies and defeated invaders from the north, Finnlay was again proud. When Robert had finally defied the Guilde, Finnlay had laughed with delight.

A few precious moments over too many years, and in one stroke, Robert had destroyed them all — with a lie.

For almost twenty years Robert had told them all the same thing. Had insisted, urged them to believe: the Key's message to him was private, personal, and had nothing whatsoever to do with the Enclave.

Finnlay had believed that – why should he not? His brother was not in the habit of lying. At least . . . not until now. Yes, he knew now that Robert had lied all along – hadn't the Key told Finnlay as much?

He pulled his horse off the road and into a muddy field. He paused at the top of a rise and gazed across the moorland. In the distance stood Dunlorn, its ancient grey battlements rising above the heather. The twin hills Room and Borlany flanked the fortress and between them flowed the river Mot. It was a castle built for war, immune to siege and able to withstand any force brought against its walls. Dunlorn had never fallen. Not until now.

So why go back, why follow these people heading towards the castle for the annual festival of Caslemas? Why, when he could still hear those words the Key had whispered to him, should he return to face a brother who had betrayed him – or was it just possible that there was still some hope buried in a heart filled with anger?

More likely it was Patric's prodding. Go home and help Robert: he would never admit it, but he needed Finnlay. It was Finnlay's duty to Robert that mattered now. It didn't matter if he had lied, they were still brothers.

Day after day, week after week. After three months, Finnlay had had enough of bloody Patric. What made it worse was that Patric was right. Finnlay did have a duty to Robert, to Dunlorn—

And maybe, just maybe, if he behaved, if he avoided arguing and kept his temper, somewhere along the line he might actually be able to get the truth out of Robert.

That was the only thing that made Finnlay turn his horse down the hill towards the castle. With all these travellers, it would be quicker going across the moor and through Tar Wood. Not that he was in any hurry, but it was approaching dusk and getting very cold indeed. Almost as a final insult, a few flakes of snow drifted down as he entered the wood—

What was that?

He stopped on the edge of a clearing. There before him were the remains of a cart, a dead horse and a figure seated on a log, draped in a crimson cape. Another horse wandered skittishly on the other side of the clearing, its bridle trailing on the ground and coated with blood.

Finnlay jumped down and dashed to the seated figure. 'Are you all right? What happened?'

The woman turned at his words, drawing her cloak hood back. Her face drained away his words. Dark almond eyes gazed at him amid skin of the softest cream. Her fine nose lifted towards him and her rose lips smiled hesitantly. Framing her face was a shiny halo of honey-gold hair, cascading down one shoulder. She was breathtaking.

She said, 'We were attacked, sir, by a band of robbers. They killed my captain and took my servants. I've been sitting here for an hour, hoping that horse will finally calm down and let me near it. I feared I would spend the night in this forsaken place.'

'I . . .' Finnlay murmured, falling into her gaze. He took in a breath, but all he could think about was his travel-stained clothes, the mud on his boots. He mumbled, 'Allow me to catch your horse, my lady.'

She smiled again and for a second time he found it difficult to remember where he was. With some effort, he stepped back and turned to the horse. It eyed him warily, but made no attempt to run when he moved closer. Slowly and gently he reached out his hand and let the horse take his smell. When it still didn't run, he took hold of the bridle and ran his hands down the horse's flanks. There were no injuries so the blood must belong to the murdered captain. He took the horse back to the lady.

'He's still nervous, so it would be best if you rode my horse instead. It's getting late, but my home is not far. Allow me to offer you Dunlorn's hospitality.'

She stood and favoured him with another smile and his

knees felt decidedly weak. 'You are most generous, sir. Might I know your name?'

Finnlay silently cursed his manners. 'Lord Finnlay Douglas, my lady.'

'Brother to the Earl of Dunlorn?'

'Aye, my lady.'

She laughed. 'Then I am most certainly in safe hands.'

He rode without stopping, except to change horses. After a day and a half, he collapsed for a few hours' sleep in a damp empty hovel. When he woke, he tried to force down some food, but the bread was stale and he had no appetite. He rode again, urgent, exhausted. There was so little time. So very little time. If he should be missed . . .

In the hours before dawn, his horse stumbled and fell. It refused to rise again. Numb with cold, he left it lying in the snow and continued on foot. Long after sunrise, he staggered into a village, paused for his first hot meal, then arranged the purchase of another horse.

With fatigue blurring his vision, he once again took to the road.

The great hall of Dunlorn Castle was one of Robert's favourite rooms, so despite the fact that this was a small gathering, he'd filled it with musicians, tumblers and dancers. Bright candles and a blazing fire shut out the winter night and allowed his guests to enjoy Caslemas Eve in comfort.

Wandering through the hall, Robert passed the musicians and returned to his seat at the table. Everyone else was seated around the fire, clapping their hands to the brisk tempo of lute and pipe. There were a dozen of his friends and their families, and those of his council who lived nearby, people he hadn't seen since he'd come back and those he lived with every day. It was good to hear their laughter – within these walls. Perhaps next year, he might even convince his mother to come and stay for the winter.

A roar of laughter drew his attention and he glanced up

to find Daniel Courtenay approaching from the other end of the hall, his face red with exertion. With a sigh, he sank down on to a chair beside Robert and reached out for a flask of wine. 'It's not polite, you know, to sit apart from your guests.'

'But you all seem to be enjoying yourselves without my help.'

'It's not our enjoyment I'm concerned about, Robert.' Daniel took a deep draught of wine and wiped his mouth on his sleeve. 'This is as much a celebration of your return as anything else. You shouldn't be sitting there feeling guilty you're not out with Deverin's patrol.'

Lord Daniel Courtenay was of an age with Robert and had come to Dunlorn as a page, then as squire during the time of Robert's father. The boys had fought furiously almost from the day they'd met, but over the years had become firm friends. While Robert had been occupied with courtly intrigue and subsequent travelling, Daniel had done his best to avoid court altogether, preferring a quiet life in the country. He had married young and settled down and seemed entirely content with his lot in life.

Though he could never be considered tall, Daniel always gave the impression of being a big man, and years of comfortable living had enhanced his girth to match. His thatch of light brown hair was longer now, but those pale blue eyes still twinkled with a familiar warmth. He turned those eyes on the guests at the other end of the hall, and in particular, on his niece, Amanda.

'She's a pretty girl, isn't she?'

Robert followed his gaze. The lady Amanda was young, fair-haired and possessed of an engaging modesty. She also laughed easily, even if she said very little.

'Yes, she is,' Robert replied evenly.

'Well, whatever you do, don't blame me.' Daniel waved his goblet towards his wife. 'Maud insisted she give you the opportunity to meet her niece. I tried talking her out of it, but you know what she's like.'

Robert smiled into his wine. 'From past experience, yes.'

231

'Maud is such a romantic,' Daniel replied with a straight face. 'She hopes to aid you in achieving the same wedded bliss she and I share.'

Robert nodded slowly and kept his eyes on his friend's face. 'It was a little obvious.'

'Oh, by the gods, don't tell Maud that! I'll never hear the end of it!' Daniel looked shocked for a moment, then burst out laughing. 'At least her heart's in the right place – or so she keeps telling me.'

'It may be, however misguided.'

Daniel's smile faded a little and he paused, fingering the edge of his goblet. 'Is it so misguided, Robert? You're a young man. Do you have no plans to marry again?'

'No.'

'But don't you want an heir? The Douglas House has continued unbroken for the last five hundred years, from father to oldest son. No other House in Lusara can make such a claim. It's almost four years since Berenice died, Robert. Maud may be a little obvious, but she is right. You should marry again.'

Robert slowly folded his hands together. 'I didn't say I wouldn't marry, just that I have no plans to. As you say, I'm still a young man and besides, I have an heir – my brother.'

'But you haven't even seen Finnlay since you came back, have you?'

'No,' Robert lied. 'But that doesn't stop him being my heir.'

'Well, I know you two don't get on, but I have to say in his defence that he's worked hard on your behalf since you've been gone. I know he can be a damned irritating fellow at times, Robert, but perhaps you two can put the past behind you now.'

Could they? It was unlikely – especially after that business with the Key. Robert nodded. 'My friend, the past is always behind me.'

'Good. And you don't have to let on to Maud right away, do you? That you saw through her little scheme? I mean, it will give me a few days of peace, if nothing else.'

With a laugh, Robert spread his arms. 'You mean sacrifice my own peace in favour of yours? Why not? That's what friends are for.'

Daniel smiled and refilled their goblets with the musky red wine. He was silent for a moment, then glanced up. 'Robert, there's something I've been meaning to ask you – well two things, actually. Promise you won't bite my head off?'

Daniel was so apologetic Robert had to chuckle. 'Of course I won't promise.'

'Well,' Daniel paused, 'I couldn't help wondering – if Berenice hadn't died – and in such a strange manner – would you still have left Lusara?'

In a second, Robert's smile drained away. He tried to still the tremor in his voice but it was hard, very hard. 'There was nothing strange in the way my wife died, Daniel. She caught a fever and was not strong enough to overcome it. That's all.'

'But . . . she was with child, wasn't she? I'm sorry, but it's been said that it was the child who killed her.'

'Oh, Daniel, I would have thought you were above believing such rubbish! Certainly, I've heard the stories, however, I also know the truth. I was here when she died.'

'But . . . you were at court.'

Robert clenched his jaw. Should he go on? He'd already said too much, already spoken about the one thing he'd banished from his thoughts. But Daniel wanted to know – needed to know – and Daniel could be trusted. 'I had been at court, yes, but I came here to warn Berenice about my fall from grace with the King, that I would have to leave. I arrived late at night. She was delirious. She died in the early hours.'

'And you left? With no one knowing you'd been here?'

'Yes.' Robert looked away. He'd been so successful over the last three months, so good at avoiding the ghost of Berenice. The ghost that lived in his memory, within these castle walls. But now Daniel had brought it all up, dredged up the vision of her face, beaded in sweat, tormented, dying. And with it, the terrible knowledge . . .

'I'm sorry, Robert.' Daniel murmured.

'What was the other thing you wanted to ask me?'

'It was nothing, really. It's just that we've all heard the story about how you found that girl of Jacob's. Do you really think she was taken during the Troubles?'

Robert sighed and closed his eyes. It was inevitable that someone would ask that particular question. Still, the reminder immediately brought a picture of Jenn to his mind, laughing at him for yelling at her on top of the tower. Robert hadn't heard a word from her – and didn't expect to unless something bad happened. Nevertheless, that didn't stop him worrying about how she was doing.

'I'm sorry, Robert,' Daniel said again, misinterpreting his silence. 'I shouldn't have asked.'

Robert opened his eyes. 'Don't apologize. Yes, I do believe she was taken during the Troubles. But don't ask me why or how, because I don't know.'

'You two don't mind if I interrupt, do you?' Harold Holland lurched across the room, an inebriated grin splashed over his bearded face. He grabbed a chair opposite and fell into it, planting his elbows on the table to support his head. 'I can never resist your parties, Robert. You always did maintain the best cellar in the south.'

'And you always drain it,' Daniel grunted back.

Harold shrugged his massive shoulders. 'It would be churlish of me to decline such gracious hospitality. I expect good wine when I come here, Robert expects me to drink it – a perfect relationship.'

'It's true, Daniel,' Robert chuckled, finally starting to enjoy himself, 'I rely on Harold's taste to tell me how good the wine is. How else would I know . . .'

'Since you never get to drink it, yourself?' Daniel shook his head and with a great flourish, poured a little more of the wine into Robert's cup – ignoring Harold's pleading look.

Harold burped and snatched the flask from Daniel's hand.

Then, still wavering in his seat, he turned a pair of dark, glazed eyes on Robert. 'So now that you've finally come back I suppose we can look forward to things settling down again. I tell you, Robert, Selar's attitude hasn't improved with your absence. He's just as bad now as he was in the first years of his reign, before you went on the council. What do you plan to do first?'

Robert heard Daniel growl at the question he'd not been willing to ask himself. But he was not about to get into this argument, at least, not tonight. Tonight was a celebration and besides, there was something else he had to do. Something much more enjoyable than arguing with Harold.

'Actually,' Robert began with a casual smile, 'I have a very serious duty to perform.'

Harold raised his eyebrows and even Daniel looked puzzled. So much the better. Robert glanced over his shoulder and caught Owen's eye. He nodded and left the hall, returning a few minutes later with a large, cloth-draped bundle in his arms. He brought this to the table and placed it in front of Robert. With a serene face, he turned and left them.

Robert raised his cup to Daniel, unable to control his grin. 'I have been remiss, my friend. As you know, I have been very busy since I returned and as yet, I have not had the opportunity to congratulate you on the birth of your son. I do so now, and wish him long life and happiness.'

Harold joined Robert in the salute and Daniel smiled. Then Robert stood. 'And to mark the occasion, I have for you a small gift.' He removed the cloth covering the bundle. Beneath was a saddle of the finest Lusaran leather, intricately tooled with oak leaves and boars, the signs of Daniel's house.

'Why Robert!' Daniel rose to his feet, his hand hesitantly touching the beautiful present. 'It's magnificent!'

Robert laughed. 'And it will look so fine on the horse that will go with it. One of my best stallions from next year's brood. He'll be broken and trained by the time your son is old enough to ride.'

Daniel's eyes widened. 'No, Robert, that's too much. You're too generous. I can't . . .'

'Oh yes you can. It's not polite, you know, to refuse a friend's gift.' Robert was about to continue when a movement from across the hall caught his eye. It was Owen and he approached in something of a hurry.

'Excuse me, my lord, but there's a late arrival just come in.'

'Oh?' Robert frowned. 'Who?'

Owen folded his long fingers together and smiled. 'Lord Finnlay, my lord – and he's not alone.'

Finnlay had made it as far as the empty guard room when Robert reached him. He was standing close to the fire, his companion cloaked and with her back to him. As Robert approached, Finnlay turned, a flash of indecision on his face followed quickly by a forced smile.

'Robert! There you are! It's good to see you back.'

Robert followed his cue. 'And you've been gone too long, brother.'

'My lady?' Finnlay brought Robert around to meet his companion. 'May I present my brother, Robert Douglas, Earl of Dunlorn. Robert, Lady Valena Cerianne.'

Robert opened his mouth to voice words of welcome, but his breath was taken away by the beauty of the face that greeted him. Her eyes gazed at him, so dark and deep that he felt, for a moment, as though he could almost drown in them. The sensation lasted only a second, but her eyes never left his face.

'You are welcome to Dunlorn, my lady,' Robert managed. He turned to Finnlay – did she have the same effect on him as well?

'Lady Valena's train was attacked by robbers in Tar Wood. She was left stranded.'

'And of course, you were entirely right to bring her here, brother. I'll have my men go through the wood in the morning and see if we can pick up a trail. It shames me to think this happened within the borders of my own lands.'

236

She smiled a little, as though for his benefit only. 'I am in your debt, my lord. It was my own foolishness that caused this tragedy. My captain warned me it was dangerous to travel at this time of the year but I did insist. Now he is dead and I no longer have the benefit of his good advice.'

From her accent she was probably from Alusia, a long way from home. Her eyes seemed to invite his curiosity, but Robert was not so blinded by her beauty as to forget his manners. 'You must be tired and hungry. Owen? Will you organize some supper for Lady Valena and take her up to the east tower. She will be comfortable there.'

'Aye, my lord.'

The lady smiled again and spoke, her voice a soft purr. 'I thank you for your hospitality, my lord. I am most fatigued and will welcome some rest. Lord Finnlay, thank you once again for coming to my rescue.'

Finnlay blushed a little and mumbled his response. As Owen led her away, Robert turned back to his brother. Finnlay took a moment, but eventually met his gaze.

'So, you finally decided to come back,' Robert murmured. 'Was it by choice, or did you get thrown out?'

'Actually,' Finnlay lifted his chin, 'it was Patric who sent me on my way. If it hadn't been for him, I'd probably still be there.'

'Oh? And what did Patric say to change your mind?'

Finnlay's eyes went dark but he didn't look away. 'Some rubbish about how you needed me. Personally, I wasn't convinced.'

'So why did you come?'

'Because I realized that I would never get the truth from you if I didn't. Take it or leave it, Robert.'

The truth? Now that would be nice. If only it was so simple. Still, Robert had to smile. It was so typical of Finnlay to try and bridge the chasm between them in this manner. But – and this was the important part – it appeared Finnlay was prepared to try.

'Very well. I'll take it.'

*

237

'And in the fullness of our devotion, divine Mineah, we ask that you bless us with a fruitful spring, and that we may continue to thrive in the warmth of your love.'

Robert shifted in his seat as Father Colin paused in his prayer and turned to face the congregation. The intimate chapel of Dunlorn was filled to capacity on this day, the most important in the festival of Caslemas. It had already been a long morning, but with mass almost over, the day was by no means finished. There was still the festival by the river, the banquet in the evening.

Once again, Father Colin raised his hands towards the heavens. 'Divine Mineah and blessed Serinleth, we also offer up our thanks for the safe return of our lord and master, whose absence was keenly felt. We ask that you bless him and guide him and keep him safe unto you.'

There was a firm amen from those around Robert and he bowed his head as though in prayer. It was a funny thing, really. This particular part of the religious year was dedicated to the goddess and her powerful works. In recent centuries, however, the ceremony had focused more on the last verified incarnation of Mineah – the one which helped destroy the sorcerers. It was ironic that Father Colin should thank Mineah for the safe return of a sorcerer!

With a final prayer, Father Colin finished the service and Robert rose to leave.

'A lovely service, Robert,' Maud said at his elbow. 'And most appropriate under the circumstances of your welcome return.'

'Why thank you, Maud.' Robert smiled then tensed as Lady Valena joined them. He tried to relax, but every time he saw her, every time she spoke to him, his reaction was always the same.

'Indeed, my lord,' Valena agreed, 'your people hold a great love for you. They are most fortunate you have returned to them.'

She was looking at him again with that same drowning gaze and he found it difficult to respond. As though she knew the effect she was having, she added, 'I sincerely hope

238

their prayers are answered and you will remain with them for a long time. I understand that your brother believes this to be the case?'

Robert forced in a breath and tore his eyes away. Fortunately they landed on Micah, who waited for him by the door. For some reason, Micah was frowning.

'Yes,' Robert replied absently. 'If you ladies will excuse me, I have things I must attend to before this afternoon.'

He waited until they were through the hall and alone before throwing a question at Micah. 'What are you looking glum about? How are things going with your father?'

'Well enough. He doesn't speak to me, but I'm determined to win him round.'

'Good.' Robert nodded; but that wasn't it. Micah was still frowning. 'Anything else?'

Micah glanced over his shoulder. 'That lady – who is she?'

'I told you, Finn found her in trouble and brought her here. I believe she plans to leave tomorrow. Why?'

'I just don't like her.'

'Oh come now, Micah, there's nothing to dislike. Are you not a little jealous that my brother commands most of her attention?'

'Aren't you, my lord?'

Robert paused. He searched Micah's face for some other answer, but came up with nothing. 'Come on. I still have to get changed before I go down and start the festivities.'

Micah said nothing more on the subject and an hour later, changed and rid of his official duties, Robert walked along the wet grass by the river and enjoyed the first bleak rays of sunshine for weeks. He wound his way between stalls selling honey cakes and hot spiced wine. Tumblers performed on a wooden platform erected the day before while peddlers bellowed, selling their wares. Hundreds of people, rugged up against the cold, were out enjoying the spectacle.

Further along the riverbank, Robert saw his brother, unsurprisingly escorting Valena. He tried to avoid them, but it seemed the lady was determined to speak to him.

'This is a most wonderful festival, my lord,' she began,

turning those eyes on him again. 'So many people have travelled so far to see you. For one so greatly loved, I wonder that you left at all.'

Robert tried to smile, but his face felt wooden. 'I fear I am not so loved as you imagine. This is, after all, a festival for Mineah – not me.'

'Still,' Finnlay added, 'it is a good turnout. We even have some sunshine to go with it. Father Colin believes that it's the work of the gods. They're pleased you've finally come home, and are showing it.'

Robert inclined his head for the benefit of Valena. 'I assume you refrained from adding that they might have thought about showing it a few weeks earlier rather than risk half my people freezing to death.'

Valena laughed prettily, her eyes lighting up. 'But you must find so much has changed in your absence. The Guilde spreads its arms across the country. Perhaps one day soon you will find a Guilde Hall somewhere on your own lands?'

'You appear to know a great deal about me, my lady,' Robert replied evenly.

'Nothing more than your reputation, I assure you. Still, I believe you would not welcome a Guilde presence so close.'

Robert began to smile – then stopped. Was she warning him? 'If the Guilde wishes to grace my lands with a Hall then I will not stop them. The real question, however, is would they want to come here?'

The dancing light in Valena's eyes faded and she turned back to Finnlay. 'Your brother retains the skills of courtly debate. I wonder where he practised them.'

'Excuse me, my lord.' Micah stood behind Robert, his face dark and angry. 'Master Ulric and the archers are awaiting you. The crowd is gathered to watch the competition between you and Lord Finnlay. Will you come?'

Robert frowned. Micah was being almost rude. But why? He would have to sort this out – but not now. 'Yes, of course. Finn? Time to display your talents.'

*

240

'I'm sorry, my lord, but my opinion has not changed.' Micah stood close to Robert and handed him another arrow. 'I just don't like the lady.'

Robert took the arrow and slotted it into the string of his bow. The crowd watching the competition cheered his next shot – even before he'd taken aim. Keeping his voice low, Robert asked, 'Is it possible you've met her before?'

'No, my lord. I would have remembered.'

Wouldn't anyone? Robert spread his feet, straightened up and pulled the arrow back. With a practised eye, he took aim on the target and released the string. There was a faint whoosh and a corresponding thud, and the crowd cheered again.

'Another bullseye for his lordship!' Ulric bellowed. 'The score stands all even at twelve shots.'

Robert stepped back to allow Finnlay his next and final shot. He glanced once at Micah, then around at those watching the competition. Daniel was there, cheering him on. Beside him, Valena kept her eyes on Finnlay, almost absorbing his every move. Yes, she was beautiful, and Finn seemed equally taken with her. So what was wrong with Micah?

Finnlay took his shot and the crowd cheered again.

'Thirteen perfect shots for Lord Finnlay!'

Micah handed Robert his last arrow and stood back to give him room. Notching the arrow in the bow, Robert took up position. Again his shoulders tensed for no particular reason. He closed his eyes for a moment and sent his senses out into the crowd. He found nothing in his search and, without thinking, let the arrow loose. He could easily see in his mind where the target was – and instantly cursed himself for a fool. If that arrow should hit its mark—

He felt a push.

The arrow thudded into the target to a disappointed sigh from the audience. Robert opened his eyes to find he'd missed the target by almost a foot – fortunately! However . . .

'By the gods! I'm such an idiot!'

Finnlay came close, his voice a whisper. 'What are you doing, Robert? That shot . . .'

Robert forced a laugh and said loudly for all to hear, 'Well done, brother! I must be getting a little rusty.'

He put his arm around Finn's shoulder's and murmured, 'I should have seen it before, but it's too late now. I have to warn you.' But he never got to finish. Instead, Owen pushed his way through the crowd.

'Forgive me, my lord, Deverin has just returned from his patrol. He needs to see you urgently. He's waiting in the winter parlour.'

Deverin was there, and so was Harold. The big man was sitting by the fire and lurched to his feet almost guiltily when Robert entered. Finnlay and Micah stayed by the door. Robert waved Harold back to his seat and turned to his master at arms. Deverin was almost swaying on his feet, his clothes covered in mud, his face lined with exhaustion.

'Forgive me, my lord, but there's been another raid. Last night.'

'By the gods,' Robert swore, 'where?'

'Nyrac, by Trappers Pond. We came upon them just as they were leaving. Half the village was ablaze, four dead and countless others wounded. The raiders struck just before midnight, killed some cattle and took whatever gold and silver they could find. My men got two of them but they died fighting so I couldn't even ask them any questions.' Deverin paused and ran his knuckles through his muddied beard. 'This is a bad business, my lord.'

'Aye,' Robert nodded. 'And it's getting ridiculous. They're within the borders of my lands but I can't do anything to stop them. I should have been with you last night.'

Finnlay came across the room. 'Do you know how many there were?'

'At least twenty, perhaps more. It was hard to see them in the dark, even with the fires lighting up the sky.'

'Damn it, Robert,' Harold growled, 'what are we supposed

to do? They hit all of us and Selar refuses to lift a finger to help! What are you going to do?'

'Do?' Robert paused, glancing at Finnlay before framing a response. 'Deverin, after the festivities are over tomorrow, you and I will make plans for recruiting more men. I know Owen's objections, but we can't fight this threat with such a small force and it'll get worse once the weather improves. I won't have them attacking my people like this.'

Harold came to his feet again, his face clouded with anger. 'But what about . . .'

Robert stopped him. 'In the meantime, we need to talk, Harold. Tonight, after the banquet. With Daniel, too. We need to co-ordinate our patrols. Perhaps if we work together we can get some results. Will you ask Daniel to join us here tonight?'

'Very well,' Harold grunted. He drew himself in and Robert was in no doubt that Harold planned to have his say later. 'I'll tell him.'

The door slammed shut behind him and Robert turned to Deverin. 'You did well to get so close to them. It's the first time we've so much as seen them. Any other casualties?'

Deverin shrugged. 'A few cuts and scratches. Nothing serious.'

'Good. You go and get some rest. We've a lot of work to do.'

'Yes, my lord.' Deverin turned to go, then paused. His grim face creased into a crooked smile. 'It's good to have you back, my lord.'

As Deverin disappeared, Robert turned back to the fire, staring at the harsh orange glow. How many more people would die before he caught these raiders? And how was he to catch them in the first place? The best way was to go out with every patrol. Then, the next time he got close, he could use his powers to trace them, perhaps even . . .

'Robert?' Finnlay interrupted his thoughts. 'What's going on? What was that business before?'

Instantly Robert snapped back to the present. 'Not here. Let's go up to my study. We don't have much time.'

*

Robert closed the door to his study and raised his hand to set the warning seal. He would have sufficient notice should anyone come up those stairs.

'Well? What's wrong?' Finnlay demanded. 'What were you going to warn me about?'

'Valena.'

'What?' Finnlay stared at him a moment, then turned to pour himself some ale from the table by the window. A little stiffly, he added, 'What about her?'

'She's Malachi.'

The cup slipped from Finnlay's hand and clattered to the ground. He gazed down at it absently then turned back to Robert. 'Are you sure? How did you know?'

'Actually, I didn't – Micah did. I don't suppose I ever told you, Finn, but when I set Micah's Seal, I made sure there was an additional warning frame which would make him very uncomfortable if he were ever in the presence of Malachi. Unfortunately, I was too overcome by the lady's beauty to take much notice of what he said. I admit I felt a little uncomfortable talking to her, but the final straw was that last arrow I fired. Sure I had my eyes closed, but you and I both know I've done that a hundred times and never missed.'

Finnlay was speechless, so it was Micah who asked the important questions.

'So what do we do now? What kind of danger is she? Do you think she knows anything?'

'Not unless Finn's been indiscreet.'

'Me?' Finnlay looked up, shock still pasting his face white. 'I've told her nothing of importance, Robert! How can you even suggest . . .'

Robert laughed. 'Don't get all excited, brother. It wasn't a serious suggestion. As far as I'm concerned, she's done no harm being here and she leaves tomorrow. I suggest you continue your attentions, Finn, so she doesn't realize we know the truth. Actually, I doubt she's found out anything important. If she'd thought either of us were sorcerers, she wouldn't have tried anything herself. As it was, I think she

244

only did it out of mischief. That is, after all, what Malachi means. What concerns me more is what she's doing here in the first place.'

'Well, do any Malachi know who you are?' Finnlay asked, finally getting his mind to tackle the problem.

'Not that I know of. The last time I met a Malachi, I killed him. I didn't give him the opportunity to talk. What about you?'

'Hah! I've never even met a Malachi.'

'That you know of – and let's face it, you didn't know it this time, did you? I think you and I need to do a bit of revision over the next few weeks. In the meantime, while she's still here, see if you can find out a bit more about her. Where she comes from, who her friends are, that kind of thing. I shouldn't need to tell you how dangerous it is for both of us to have her here under this roof. If she should discover anything . . .'

'You wouldn't kill her?' Finnlay demanded, faintly.

Robert paused, but knew what his answer was. With Malachi there was no middle ground, no room for exceptions. 'She's Malachi, Finn, and you know what that means. Let's just make sure she leaves here in perfect ignorance. Keep her away from this room. I've got too many illicit books in here. She'd recognize most of them and know the truth immediately. Tonight, during our meeting, Micah will keep an eye on her. If she does anything, anything at all, I'll trust you to fetch me immediately.'

'Aye, my lord,' Micah smiled grimly. 'It'll be a pleasure.'

Owen had built the fire up in the winter parlour in preparation for the meeting, but in such a small room Robert found the heat stifling and he loosened the throat of his black tunic. Through the closed door he could hear laughter and occasional melodies coming from the hall. All of his people were in there, enjoying the dying hours of the banquet, Valena and her guard, Micah, among them. Silently Robert prayed the Malachi would not provoke him. In these close confines, he would have only one response – and in that moment, he would reveal the secret he'd kept close all these years. His people would desert him, his name would be anathema and his life would be in danger from both Guilde and Church. Not even Selar would protect him — should he want to.

And sorcery would once again become a reality for everyone for the first time in almost a century.

Robert leaned back in his chair and fingered the silver goblet before him. It had been given to his father by King Edward on the day of his ascension. The lip was inlaid with turquoise and on the bowl lay an eagle, its wings spread wide. This same eagle appeared on the Douglas arms, on the ring Robert wore and on the hilt of the sword resting on the table before him. Around the throat of the eagle was inscribed one word: *Fideli*. Faithful.

But faithful to what?

He took in a deep breath and tried to relax. This first winter at home was proving difficult. Yes, there were days when he was glad to be back, but there were many more days when he felt restless and unsettled, unable to concentrate. There was too much unresolved, too many questions he was never likely to find answers to. And now that he was here — and everybody knew it — he was confined within his own castle once more, trapped in a prison of his own making. The rewards of fidelity.

And now Daniel sat at the table opposite him, putting the finishing touches to a schedule of patrols they'd planned together with Harold. Patrols that would hopefully find these raiders, even as they drew Selar's attention with their size. Owen had cautioned him against increasing his army, but in truth, Robert was more concerned with the risk to his people from these raiders than from the King.

'Well,' Daniel placed his pen down and glanced up at Robert, 'I think that should cover us for the next few months. When they get more active with the spring thaws we'll have a better chance of catching them.'

'And if that doesn't work,' Finnlay added, 'then we should return to the idea of setting up a few garrisons. If we can't catch them, then at the very least, we can inhibit their movements.'

Harold slammed his hand down on the table. 'Damn you, you're deliberately missing the point! You must have heard those rumours yourself. There are people who really believe these raids are the work of Tirone. He plans to wreak havoc on us. Why can't you see that?'

Robert shook his head. 'You have no proof of that. Let's face it, these raiders are not so different from the usual bands of robbers Lusara has always suffered from. Yes, they seem more organized, but that doesn't mean they work to a specific plan. Nor do they choose their targets with war in mind. They stay away from towns and hit isolated farms, small villages. There is little to compare with the Troubles and you know it.'

Harold sighed and leaned back in his chair. He scratched his beard then reached out for more wine. 'I suppose these patrols will help. If nothing else, when you go back to court, you will be in a good position to insist Selar does something to aid us.' He grinned. 'Of course, I don't think Vaughn's going to be exactly delighted to see you again. I'd love to see the smirk wiped off his greedy face. I'll see what I can do about arranging a visit to court to coincide with yours, Robert.'

'Don't go making any plans. I won't be going back to court.'

'But how can you do anything from here? You're too far away to exert any real influence! Selar will never take you seriously.'

'I don't intend to exert any influence. I've retired from all that. I told you that when I first came back. I've been away three years and I've decided that what I most want is some peace and quiet. You'll have to look to someone else for help. I don't care any more.'

Harold launched out of his seat, toppling the chair over in the process. 'I don't believe that! Not you, Robert! Not a Douglas, of all people! Hell, your father would turn in his grave to hear you talk like that. You must do something. People depend on you!'

Robert finally turned his gaze on the other man. 'If you feel so strongly about it, why don't you do something yourself? I have no power any more, no position, and despite what you say, no support from the other Houses. I gave all that up when I left. I knew what I was doing, Harold.'

There was a brief knock at the door and Finnlay rose to answer it. It was Deverin, and he whispered something to Finnlay, who frowned and followed him out, closing the door behind him.

Robert tensed. Was it Valena? No, it couldn't be. Micah would have come, not Deverin. Then what was it? Where had Finnlay gone – and why?

Finnlay stood in the corridor and took in a deep breath. It had been so difficult not to voice his agreement with Harold, but he had promised himself and he would keep to that vow no matter what. Finnlay cared, even if Robert didn't. There must be some other way to change Robert's mind.

But: Deverin waited, so Finnlay left the argument behind and took off down the corridor. He avoided the hall completely and arrived at the guard room unseen by any of the guests. It was dark in here, with only a single candle to light the face of the man who greeted him. Finnlay took a few steps forward.

'Is he here?' the man whispered hoarsely. His face was haggard and there were dark lines of exhaustion around his eyes. Mud caked his clothing and his fair hair and he walked with the gait of a man who had spent days in the saddle.

'Please, Finnlay, tell me if he's really here.'

Slowly, Finnlay nodded. 'Robert's here. I'll take you to him.'

He turned back into the corridor, knowing the man would follow him. What was going on? What would Robert say?

Not that it mattered. After his . . . discussion with Harold, Robert was unlikely to be moved by anything this man said. By the gods, how could his brother be so intractable?

There were raised voices coming from within the winter parlour, but Finnlay didn't pause. He pushed the door open and stepped aside to let the other man enter. Robert looked up – then shot to his feet.

'Payne – In the name of the gods, what are you doing here?'

'I'm sorry, Robert,' the young man murmured, his voice weak, 'I had to come . . .'

Fearing Payne would collapse, Finnlay took his arm and led him to a chair, then poured him some wine. Payne drank greedily as Robert pulled up a seat opposite him. The others gathered around, exchanging frowns.

'I can't believe you'd risk something like this,' Robert hissed, pulling a plate of bread and cheese across the table. 'How long have you ridden?'

Payne drained his cup, then put it slowly down on the table. He ignored the food, instead reaching out to touch Robert's shoulder. 'I don't know. Days. It doesn't matter. I had to come. I had to be sure it was true. By the gods, Robert, I'm so glad you're back.'

Robert frowned then glanced up at Finnlay. 'Did anyone see him arrive?'

'Only Deverin. He brought Payne in personally. No one knows he's here.'

'Good.' Robert turned back to Payne. 'Listen, Everard, you've taken a huge risk coming here like this. Is there any chance Selar will find out? You know what will happen to you if he does.'

'It doesn't matter, Robert.' Payne shook his head, his eyes unfocused. 'I had to come to tell you what happened. I didn't dare send a letter.'

'Tell me?' Robert whispered. 'What?'

'Bishop Domnhall died eight days ago. The election afterwards, to replace him . . . was watched. I don't know how. But Selar and Vaughn wanted them to choose Brome or Quinn.' Payne paused and took another mouthful of wine. 'They elected Aiden McCauly though. Do you know him?'

'Not personally,' Robert murmured. 'I've heard he's a good man – a good choice. Go on.'

'He would have been a good Bishop too – except that Selar had him arrested and even now he languishes in the dungeons of Marsay.'

'Serin's blood!' Finnlay swore.

'Selar must be mad!' Harold snapped. 'Arresting an anointed Bishop? On what charge?'

'Treason – what else? Selar has given us no details yet.'

'And he probably won't either.'

Robert held up his hand to silence Harold. 'You rode all this way to tell me this?'

'Yes,' Payne nodded, his eyes fixed on Robert, 'you need to know ... Selar arrested McCauly the moment he heard you'd returned to Lusara.'

It was so subtle, Finnlay almost missed it. Almost missed the way Robert's face changed. He couldn't pinpoint exactly what was different. All he knew was that, despite his protests to the contrary, Robert did care – a very great deal.

Almost more than the news Payne delivered, this revelation came as a shock to Finnlay. For the first time in his life, he'd actually seen past the armour Robert always wore, past the glib humour and offhand remarks. It was all there, in those green eyes – pain, pure and simple. Why hadn't he seen it before?

'Now you must go to court, Robert,' Harold said into the silence. 'You must get McCauly free.'

'No,' Payne insisted. 'That's exactly what you can't do. Vaughn would find some way to get rid of you despite Selar's instructions. Vaughn will stop at nothing to kill you, Robert. That's why I came. To warn you. You have to stay away from Marsay, at the very least until this has blown over. If you don't believe me, then read this. It's a letter from Godfrey. He said you would believe him.'

Robert took the letter but didn't open it. Instead, he rose to his feet and wandered over to the fire. In the silence, Finnlay could almost hear the battle waging inside his brother – he could certainly feel the tension in the room. He stayed where he was, afraid to say anything, but it was Daniel who spoke first.

'It's good advice, Robert. Whatever Selar means by taking McCauly, you cannot help the situation if you go to Marsay now.'

'That's cowardice, Daniel, and you know it!' Harold launched across the room to stand before Robert, his huge frame shadowing the fireplace. 'If you leave Selar to it, he'll go on taking the law and twisting it to his own purposes. Now he's got his own man in the primacy. What will he do next? How much more of Lusara will he destroy before you decide to stop him? Have three years away blunted your honour, Robert? You must go – and now!'

Robert looked up, fixing Harold with that penetrating gaze. He held it for long seconds, then slowly turned to Finnlay. 'And what do you say, brother?'

Finnlay opened his mouth, but the words that came out surprised him. 'You cannot go.'

Robert's eyebrows rose and he almost smiled. 'I'm sorry, Harold, but I've already explained my position. This matter changes nothing.'

Harold's eyes burned. 'Damn you!' he said, and stormed out of the room.

'Daniel?' Robert helped Payne to his feet. 'Will you take Everard to Deverin. Make sure he gets some rest and food before he leaves.'

'Of course.'

As the door closed behind them, Robert picked up the letter and broke the seal. Finnlay waited by the fire, uncertain. Eventually Robert looked up.

'It's incredible. According to Godfrey, the synod's decision was not as simple as it appeared. Apparently they voted against Brome and Quinn because they'd heard that story about the hermit of Shan Moss. Both men have dark hair and they saw that as a sign. I can't help thinking, though, if any man has split the Church in two, it's me.'

'Oh no you don't,' Finnlay came across the room and snatched the letter from Robert's hand. 'Your hair may be dark, Robert, but you didn't force Selar to arrest McCauly. It's not your fault.'

'Payne thinks so, not to mention Godfrey. What is Selar playing at?'

Robert's frown deepened and Finnlay made his decision. 'You may not be able to go to Marsay – but I can.'

'What?'

'No one will know. I can be in and out in a few days. I don't know about you, but I want to know what's going on. Please don't forbid me, Robert.'

Robert took a deep breath and shook his head. Calmly, he took the letter back and folded it up. He turned for the door then paused, his back to Finnlay. 'I have to say, it was good to have you as an ally for a change but I should have known there'd be a price.'

# 11

The hospice stood on the edge of the market square, in the heart of the village of Fenlock and only half a league from Elita. From the chapel door Jenn could see the golden tower of the castle reach high above the trees surrounding the village. Spring had brought a glorious colour to the hamlet and with it, a market of festive gaiety. With the last of the snows melted away, Jenn felt she could finally breathe.

All through the winter she had made this trip with Bella. Every week after Mass, regardless of the weather, her sister had led her through the village to the hospice. They brought food, fresh baked bread, herbs and vegetables from the castle garden, ale from the brewery. Every week, Jenn had visited the sick and poor, the homeless and destitute – and every week Jenn grew closer to them. She learned their names, their families, their hopes and dreams. And sometimes, when nothing more could be done, she knelt beside her sister and prayed for their souls.

It was good work, and necessary. The Church had lost the legal right to run this hospice, but no Guildesman had yet appeared in Fenlock to take charge. Jacob believed they never would. With such a conspicuous display of noble patronage for the hospice, Jacob was determined to show his contempt and defiance of the King. It was a small thing, but Jenn had seen the fire in his eyes as he had spoken. These small rebellions were all that were left to him now. But rebellion or not, for Bella, these visits had another purpose, to teach Jenn about duty.

Bella talked about it as though Jenn had never heard the word before. But of course, with her innkeeper's upbringing, Jenn couldn't possibly know anything about duty! Nevertheless, it had proved, over the entire winter, to be the single most important lesson Bella had tried to instill in her. Oh, the writing and reading and the accounts and the household management and the clothes and the needlework and everything else were very important, but all those were nothing unless Jenn understood her duty!

It had got to the point where Jenn was ready to scream at the very mention of the word. It had developed, in her mind, the shape of a prison. Cold steel bars of Expectation atop walls of stone-carved Duty. The stupid thing was that Jenn was happy to do all this and more, and forget all about the concept of duty: she did it because she loved it.

It had been so difficult to get used to the idea that this was where she belonged. This was her home, her family, her people. This one single place. She had long since stopped waking in the morning wondering where she was today. But she had no time to miss the past, no time for anything other than her lessons. No time to reflect on what she'd done, on how she'd come here – no time even to think about sorcery!

Now that was the really difficult part. Robert had been right, it was so very hard to see those people in the hospice and not help them in some way. Of course, to her knowledge (which, she knew, didn't amount to much) no sorcerer could actively heal anything with the direct use of power. Nevertheless, she did have Healer's Sight and could see, without any effort at all, deep into the heart of a wound, or into the fits of a fever. She knew just what was needed to fix it, but she could say nothing, at least for the time being. At least until she'd learnt enough to be taken seriously by the physicians at the hospice. The good brothers welcomed their visits and were always happy to listen to any suggestion Bella might make, but then Bella had been doing this for years and had gained quite a bit of knowledge along the way. Jenn found it very frustrating, especially as she didn't even know how to do that trick Robert had used, on the old man at the farmstead, to ease someone's pain.

And she'd needed to do that today. Poor Ruth with her tired old body, riddled with evil-smelling polyps and blood-encrusted sores. She'd cried out to the gods to take her, to stop the pain, to let her walk willingly into their arms. But instead, she'd lain there for days, in agony, beyond even sobbing for relief. Jenn had sat with her a long time, holding her hand and saying nothing. She'd tried to shut out the things her senses told her, but it was useless. She sat there and suffered along with Ruth in a way she'd never thought possible. If only she could have reached out. If only she could have eased the lines of pain from Ruth's face. If only she could use her . . .

'Are you going to stand there all day or are you coming into the market with me?'

Jenn whirled around to find Bella standing on the steps beside her, hands on hips. It was a common stance for Bella and one which made Jenn cringe. 'Sorry. I was thinking about Ruth.'

'Well, she's with Mineah now and beyond suffering. Come, we should get moving, otherwise Father will wonder what's happened to us. Look, there's Lawrence.'

Jenn came down the steps beside Bella just as Lawrence pushed his way through the crowd to meet them. As always, Lawrence's gentle brown eyes lit up at the sight of his wife, and as always, Bella smiled in response. He was a lovely man, but one of the best things about him was that Bella always softened in his company.

'I left the horses with the innkeeper at the Boar and Oak, my dear. It's much too crowded here to bring them through. Do you want to leave now or do you want to make some purchases?'

Bella glanced around. 'Well, if you're in no hurry?'

Lawrence bowed with graceful irony. 'I'm at your service, my sweet.'

Jenn stifled a giggle as Bella sniffed and moved on. Following behind, Lawrence paused from time to time and pointed things out to Jenn he knew she would be interested in.

'Now this is a beauty!' He picked up an embroidered

shawl rich in greens and golds. 'By the look of it, it's true Alusian.'

'Aye, my lord, it is indeed.' The woman behind the stall grinned. 'My son did a pilgrimage there last year and brought that back with 'im. 'E brought these other pretties as well.'

Jenn stood beside Lawrence and glanced over the trinkets displayed before her. There was a whalebone jar carved in the design of Alusia's shrine to Mineah, several more shawls, and a small grey stone box, plain and square. Curious, Jenn picked it up and turned it over. It felt warm in her hands and instantly she wanted to buy it.

'What do you want a thing like that for?' Bella demanded, peering over her shoulder. 'It's not even pretty.'

Jenn wrapped her hands around it. 'I think it is.'

'Hah!' Bella turned away, giving Jenn the brief opportunity to pay for the box. Lawrence gave her a quick smile and they turned to follow Bella through the crowd. Suddenly a hand reached out and grabbed Jenn's shoulder.

'It's you, isn't it!'

Jenn shrank back from the hideous face that leered down at her. The man was huge. He wore rags which hung loose from his body and his eyes bore the gleam of madness. 'It was you, you lying little whore . . .'

'Let her go!' Lawrence bellowed, launching towards the man. He struggled for a moment before he could finally release the man's hold on Jenn.

'No!' The man roared, 'I'll kill her! It's all her fault!' He flailed around with his arms, knocking people aside. By now the crowd had parted around the man as he continued to spit curses. Jenn remained frozen to the spot, with Lawrence standing protectively between them.

He roared again and dived to get past Lawrence, who stood firm against the bigger man. Then the crowd came to their rescue. Strong hands pulled the man back and although he struggled, they kept their hold. He continued raging against them until suddenly Bella moved forward, her voice cool and soothing.

'Stop it, Joseph. That's enough. You've scared her plenty, now leave it alone. You've done your job. Go home.'

Joseph stared at her with glazed eyes which abruptly filled with tears. 'But my lovely Tali, my lady. She's dead, you know. She died because of that whore . . .'

'Enough,' Bella murmured again. 'Leave it, Joseph. You can do no good now. Go home.'

With a nod from Bella, the men holding him led him away, but even as he went, Jenn could hear his mutterings. The crowd dispersed and went back to their normal business and immediately Lawrence turned around to Jenn.

'Are you all right?'

She nodded, her eyes still on the retreating men. 'Who was that? What did he mean? Why did he call me . . .'

'Pay no attention to him, Jennifer,' Bella replied crisply. 'He's quite mad. I doubt he'll bother you again.'

'But who is he? I want to know.'

Bella sighed. 'You wouldn't remember him; you were too young. Still, I suppose you should know. His name is Joseph Yates. His wife Tali was your nurse. When you disappeared by the river you were in her care.'

'And everybody blamed her for my death?'

'Everybody shunned her, no one would take her in, nor even speak to her. Then one day she was found dead in the forest. Joseph has been a little unbalanced ever since. I suppose now that he knows you've returned, it just makes it so much harder for him.'

Jenn closed her eyes. A weight like stone sat on her chest and she breathed deep to ease it. She'd never thought of the wider consequences of her abduction, or the effects it had had on other people. If only she could help Joseph in some way, but she couldn't. He was beyond her help. She couldn't even tell him why she'd been taken.

'Come,' Lawrence murmured, putting his arm around her shoulders, 'I think it's time we were getting home.'

Jenn nodded, then looked down at the little stone box in her hands. Lawrence followed her gaze. 'Oh no! It's broken!'

It was true. Somewhere in the scuffle with Joseph, Jenn

had gripped the box so hard in her hands that its delicate stone sides had cracked in two. She held one in each hand then, with a shrug, put them into her pocket. 'This is becoming a habit.'

'What?'

'Nothing. Let's go.'

They made their way through the crowd to the Boar and Oak where Lawrence retrieved their horses. He held Jenn's as she mounted, but the moment she got up on to the horse, a strange feeling washed over her, like cold water.

Someone was watching her.

Instantly she looked around at the passing villagers and at first she saw nothing. Then—

There, a face in the crowd – but as soon as she saw it, the face disappeared. All Jenn was left with was the memory of a pair of hazel eyes and a deep feeling of disquiet.

Jacob sat in the long walled garden in the shade of a yew tree his great-grandfather had planted. It had been a symbol of peace between two brothers who had fought for years. On the day the eldest had ascended the throne, the younger had planted this tree and had sworn from that day on allegiance to the crown of the Earls of Elita. The tree had flourished and grown, tall and proud. Such could not be said, however, for the House it sheltered. Fate or the gods themselves had decreed that the Ross family should fade and perhaps even die. Without a son to take his name forward, Jacob had only his daughters to follow him, and one of those had been married for seven years without issue. As for the other?

Despite his sombre mood, Jacob still could not help smiling when he thought of his Jennifer. After so many years, so much pain and anguish . . . If only Elaine had lived to see it. If she could only have known her child still lived, she might have had the strength to live herself. But it was not to be. Jennifer was back, that was the important thing. All the rest were only memories of things he could not change.

258

But it was the past and its memories which kept him in the garden today. Jacob glanced across the grass. Latham Campbell had travelled a long way to see Jacob, and all because of the past. Old and worn, Campbell was still a man to be reckoned with. And he'd seen a lot of tragedy in his life, not the least of which was the loss of his son and heir in the final battle against Selar, at Nanmoor. The very same battle in which Jacob had almost died.

Campbell sat on a bench, his lean legs stretched out before him. With almost forced patience, he kept his hands together and gazed up at the yew branches high above. There, celebrating the first weeks of spring, a pair of finches prepared to nest. In a musing voice, Campbell finally spoke. 'You're not telling me what an old fool I am, Jacob. Is it because you feel pity for me?'

Jacob shook his head slowly. 'No. You're no fool, Latham – unless you've changed a lot over the years. You follow your heart just as you should.'

'Even now? After all these years?'

'Even now.'

Campbell nodded and threw Jacob a wry glance. 'But you do feel pity for me?'

'I feel you are a man searching for some small ray of hope. If that is pity . . .' Jacob shrugged and left the sentence unfinished.

Abruptly Campbell stood and began pacing up and down the path in front of Jacob. The rose border at his feet had yet to bloom, but the tiny green leaves trembled with his every step. 'Where are they? What can be keeping them?'

Jacob was about to reply when sounds from the courtyard beyond the wall told him the waiting was over. Moments later, the garden gate opened and Bella walked through, followed by Jennifer. He waved them over, then turned his attention to Campbell. The old man had stopped his pacing and was now staring openly at Jacob's younger daughter.

Jacob introduced them, adding, 'He's come a long way, Jennifer. Baron Campbell would like to ask you a few questions.'

Jennifer's wide blue eyes seemed dark in the sunshine and a brief smile flashed across her face. 'What kind of questions?'

Campbell indicated the bench under the tree. 'Please sit down. I'm sorry I've done this so abruptly, child, but I came here as soon as I could – as soon as I heard. I live on the other side of Lusara, you see, and with the winter being harsh, I couldn't make the journey earlier. These old bones won't do the riding they once did. Please, do sit.'

Jennifer glanced once at Jacob and for a moment, she looked quite nervous. He smiled reassurance to her as she sank to the bench. Bella waited beside him. From the expression on her face, Jacob felt she had a pretty good idea of what this was about.

'What would you like to ask me?'

Campbell stood before her and twisted his hands together. 'I've heard the story about how you were abducted – and how you were found again and brought home. I need to know . . .' He paused, fighting for his words.

In response, Jennifer smiled up at him then reached out and took his hand. 'Go on, my lord. What do you need to know?'

Jacob couldn't take his eyes from them. It was incredible. Campbell, until now worn and tired from his journey and almost reeking anguish, visibly relaxed at the touch of Jennifer's hand. He looked down into her eyes. Jacob could only guess what he saw there, but whatever it was produced a sad smile. With a sigh, Campbell sank down onto the bench beside her.

'I need to know . . . if you remember anything about the men who took you. I realize you were very young but – do you remember anything? Who they were? Where they took you? Did they ever say why? Would you know them if you saw them again? Did you ever see any . . . others?'

'Others?' Jennifer murmured with a frown. Then abruptly, her eyes widened. 'You lost someone? In the Troubles?'

'My grandson, Keith. He was abducted two months after you. He was barely three years old. His father was killed fighting Selar and I just thought ... I hoped you might be able to tell me something – anything that might shed some light on his fate. Did you never see any other children? Any others with a House Mark?'

'I remember very little, I'm afraid. Just the moment when they came through the forest. I don't even remember them taking me away, just the moment when they came. There were perhaps a dozen men, armed and mounted. I do remember the old man in front rode a white horse.'

'But what about afterwards? Do you remember anything after that?'

Jacob spoke up. 'Come, Latham – she was four years old. How much could she remember after thirteen years?'

Campbell met his gaze for a long moment, then stood and began pacing up and down again. 'I'm sorry, Jacob. I don't mean to lay my troubles at your door. But you must appreciate that your daughter represents something we'd always thought impossible. All our children were abducted, with never a word of ransom. Taken from us as though they were no more than cattle! The spoils of war – only there was no war. And we never knew who took them or where they went. They just disappeared, Jacob! And now this child of yours has been returned. You can't blame me for wondering if my grandson is still alive somewhere in Lusara with no memory of who he is. What if he's ...'

Campbell was working himself up but it was Jennifer who stood and stopped his pacing. Again she took his hand. 'I can offer you little comfort, my lord. I never saw any other children and I only remember my home in Shan Moss as though I'd lived there for ever. I am sorry my return has brought back these memories for you.'

'Oh, child, I don't blame you. Rather I thank the miracle that placed Dunlorn in your path. If it hadn't been for him, you too would still be lost.'

There it was, that name again. Jacob had done his best to forget that he owed so much to the traitor.

As though Campbell had read Jacob's thoughts, he caught himself up and threw an apologetic glance in his direction.

Then Campbell turned back to Jennifer. 'Forgive me. I realize I'm asking the impossible of you. But I had to try. Still, just answer one more question for me. When Dunlorn found you, how was it that he saw your House Mark? Did he see it right away – or did he recognize you first?'

For some reason, Jacob had never asked her this question himself. Now that it was spoken, he burned with curiosity to know. He leaned forward in his chair and held his breath in anticipation.

Jennifer, as though feeling eyes upon her, stepped back and folded her hands beneath her gown. 'It was an accident that Robert saw it at all. We were riding through the mountains and my horse stumbled. I fell and slid down a slope. When Robert and Micah reached me, the shoulder of my dress had torn and revealed the Mark.'

Although she said this in exactly the same way she had answered all Campbell's questions, for some strange reason, Jacob knew she was lying. He couldn't pinpoint how he knew – nor which part was a lie – but nonetheless, his daughter was most definitely not telling the truth.

But why? Why would she lie about it? Unless ... had the traitor done something to her? Had he ...

No! Dunlorn might be many things but he would not take advantage of an innocent child like Jennifer. Despite his many faults, Dunlorn, within certain bounds, was a man of honour.

Nevertheless, what was Jennifer hiding?

With the last remaining shreds of sunlight draining across the floor of the stillroom, Jenn put down her work and began to light some candles. They would have to stop work soon and go down for supper. Baron Campbell would be there and he was sure to ask more questions. Jenn sighed. There was nothing she could do about it. There was no way around the fact that every mention of Robert's name would only make her father more unhappy.

'What are you sighing about?' Bella murmured, her

attention focused on the embroidery in her hands. 'You're not still upset about that incident with Joseph, are you?'

Jenn brought a candle over and set it on the table. 'I feel very sorry for him. Are you sure there's nothing I can do?'

'Short of bringing his wife back to life, no.'

'But perhaps if I talked to him, explained what happened.' Jenn sank down on her stool but didn't pick up her work again. Instead she kept her eyes on her sister. She'd had almost four months to get used to Bella and her abrupt, sometimes harsh manner, four months during which Jenn had almost given up hope that Bella would ever like her. Unfortunately, though, Bella was still her teacher and Jenn had to rely on her knowledge.

'Perhaps if I . . .'

Bella glanced up. 'You're not about to suggest I write a letter to Dunlorn, are you?'

'What makes you say that?'

'I'm not stupid, Jennifer. I know you're worried about Campbell and wondering if there's some way you can help him find his grandson. I know you – you want to help everybody – like Joseph. Robert is the next logical step in the search. However, if your discovery was such an accident, I doubt Robert would be any help to Campbell and I don't think Father would appreciate you suggesting it.'

Jenn watched her for a moment, saw the frown of concentration on Bella's face, the thin line of her lips. She had that *look* – the one which would brook no discussion. Bella always got that look whenever Robert's name came up.

'I'm sorry, Bella, but I don't understand why you don't like Robert. I mean, I know why Father won't have his name spoken, but you? Why? What did he ever do to you?'

Bella turned sharply at this, her work forgotten. 'Don't use that tone with me! This has nothing to do with whether I like Dunlorn or not. Nor is Father's opinion of great concern here. The simple truth is, that despite the fact that Dunlorn rescued you and brought you back here, he is not the hero you seem to think he is. Oh, I know you've heard all the stories, but there is a lot about that man you don't know. Things you would rather not know.'

Jenn's heart leapt to her mouth. Could Bella possibly know the truth – the real truth about Robert? If so, how did she know? Robert had never mentioned it, but then, Robert hadn't told her many things.

She clasped her hands together and took a calming breath. 'What kind of things?'

'Even the greatest of heroes have a dark side to their nature, Jennifer, and Dunlorn is no exception. All the world knows of his public exploits, but there are some deeds that were always kept quiet for one reason or another. I admit that he and I have never been friends, but I must not take only Father's thoughts into account, but also those stories which are kept secret. Stories which show his true nature.'

'What stories? And do you know – for certain – if they are true? I mean, have you ever asked him?'

'I hadn't seen him for years before he came here with you. But I swear he would deny none of them if you asked him. I wonder, did he ever tell you how he saved Selar's life? How he could have let the man die, but didn't?'

Jenn hardly dared take in a breath of relief. 'Yes he did.'

'Then did he ever tell you about the day Selar came to see him, two years after the conquest? The day when Robert sold his honour for the sake of his freedom. Did he mention how he alienated the Guilde so much that Selar had to throw him off the council? That Robert deliberately flouted sacred Guilde law in order to gain possession of a small piece of land?'

Bella paused then added, 'Did he ever tell you how he killed his wife?'

'What?' Jenn froze in the act of reaching for her needlework. She wanted to laugh at the suggestion, but Bella's eyes held no humour.

'It was no coincidence that he left the country only days after she died. Oh, I know he'd been removed from the council, but men have lost their position before and not run away. But Berenice died so soon after and what very few

264

people know is that he stopped at Dunlorn before he left —
and she died that night.'

'How do you know about it?'

'That's unimportant.'

'But it doesn't mean he killed her.'

'No? Then why did he leave? Ask yourself that. Why did
Robert leave Lusara?'

There was an owl in the woods beyond the castle wall. Every
night Jenn listened to it call and hoped it would fly down
into the little garden, but it never did. Instead, there was
only a faint haunting echo drifting across the warm spring
evening and high up to the battlements of Elita. Jenn paused
as she crossed the empty courtyard and turned her head this
way and that to track its direction. It was now the only living
reminder of her previous life in the forest.

At Shan Moss she would often leave the crowded inn and
head out into the cool forest. Even in winter there was a
peace and serenity to be found among the trees, the hills
and valleys. Over the years she had got to know it very well
and now, living in this castle, with all her new advantages,
she missed that gentle harmony. She longed to reach out
and touch the rough bark and feel the damp-moulded leaves
beneath her feet. There in the forest, there were no demands,
no obligations — and no questions.

She continued across the courtyard towards the garden,
but her feet moved slowly, held back by the weight of her
thoughts.

An endless stream of questions, one following the other in
an almost random collection. How was she to develop her
powers? Who were the men who had abducted her? Why
had they? Why was she the only one ever found?

Had Robert really killed his wife?

Jenn paused with her hand on the gate latch. In the dark,
her flesh was almost invisible. But if she reached out with
her senses just a little, she could see it quite clearly. The
hand of a sorcerer.

No. It was impossible. Robert was a soldier, experienced

in battle, but he was also a man who had exiled himself rather than break his oath to a King. There was no way a man of such honour would murder his own wife.

But how do you know, a voice inside her asked. How can you be sure about anything with that man? He confides in no one. Trusts no one. So why trust him? Why believe in him? He's a powerful sorcerer, capable of almost anything. All those who knew Robert well trusted him – and hated themselves for doing so.

So what on earth was there in him that made her so sure?

Actually, she smiled, it was easier to focus on what wasn't in him. Greed. Lust for power. Selfishness. Sure, he had his own obscure reasons, but he had refused time and again to take on the leadership of the Enclave, a position which would surely give him more power than he could dream of. And he could easily have allowed Selar to die – or killed him at a later time.

Yes, there were so many ways Robert could have allowed himself to be overtaken by evil, even to the point of abandoning her to either the Guilde or the Enclave. But he had chosen the way of good. Every time.

There were answers to be found. But there was another, deeper answer. One which was more difficult to pinpoint. One which she had seen many times in his eyes. That ... what was it? Sorrow? Pain? Is that what she saw? If so, why did no one else ever see it? Perhaps other people saw only what they wanted to – and they didn't want to see Robert vulnerable.

Jenn reached out again and pulled down the latch. With a click, the gate swung wide and a rush of spring scents wafted towards her. She breathed in deep – and paused.

Someone was watching her. Just like at the market, she could feel eyes upon her. But she was alone. Surely alone.

Carefully she turned and scanned the dark shadows of the courtyard, the stable against the north wall, the kitchens to the east, the guard house by the gate. Nothing. A dog sniffed around the blacksmith's anvil and ignored Jenn completely. There was nothing there. So what was this feeling?

Taking a deep breath, Jenn began to reach out with her senses, not even sure she was doing it the right way, seeking out further as though her hands spread across the dark courtyard, feeling every cobblestone, every crack and pebble. She felt cold and disembodied as she pushed out until—

'Who's there?' she murmured, her voice trembling. 'Why are you hiding?'

From the shadows of the stables, a figure emerged. It was a woman. She came forward slowly, spreading her arms wide in a gesture of peace. 'I'm sorry, my lady. I didn't mean to frighten you.'

Jenn waited until the woman came close. 'I wasn't afraid. I want to know why you were hiding.'

The woman's face was near now, but this time Jenn ignored the darkness and looked at her with sorcerer's sight. Hazel eyes and dull blonde hair. A squarish face more handsome than pretty, with a small mouth held together as though in disappointment. There was something vaguely familiar about her.

'Who are you?'

Abruptly the woman dropped her servile manner and chuckled. 'I suppose I shouldn't be surprised you don't remember me. You had so much to think about when we last met, and it was quite a while ago.'

'What is your name?'

'I will tell you willingly, but you must never repeat it – not in full. I am Fiona Ferris. My mother is Ayn and my father was Marcus. You may recall we met shortly after he died. Do you remember me now?'

Jenn took a step back. 'You were at the . . .'

'Exactly.' Fiona cut her off with a wave of her hand. 'But you know you mustn't say the word. Not ever. Even if you know no one can hear you, which can never be guaranteed in a place like this.'

'But Robert and Finnlay said it all the time.'

'Well, Finnlay is no surprise. He was always disobedient. Robert should know better.' With a glance back towards the guardhouse, Fiona drew Jenn close to the garden wall. 'It's not a good idea for us to be seen talking here for too long, so I'll make this brief.'

'Why are you here? Has something happened?'

'If you'll just stop asking stupid questions for a moment, I'll tell you. I was sent by the elders. I would have come sooner but there was the winter. Anyway, I'm here now – and believe it or not, entirely at your service.'

Jenn shook her head, still not understanding. 'But why?'

'Why do you think? To teach you! I'm quite qualified, you know. Adept for three years. I don't have the skills of my father but I have been teaching for a long time. I think I can be of some help to you. By the look of that scan you just did, I was right to come.'

'But you said you were sent.'

'I volunteered,' Fiona smiled, but not pleasantly. 'I know why you chose to leave us, but frankly, I don't care about all that. What is important to me – and the elders – is that you are trained properly. If you're to be any use to anyone – even yourself – you need training. Robert should never have deserted you all the way out here.'

'He didn't . . .'

'Look, I don't have time to argue. If we're found together now, before I've arranged things, it will ruin everything. I just wanted to make sure you weren't going to throw me out once you recognized me.'

'But what if I don't want any training?'

Fiona paused. 'Do you? Speak now if you don't.'

Jenn took a deep breath. 'Yes, I suppose I do. But how . . .'

'Don't worry about that. Just trust me. I know what I'm doing. Unlike some people I could mention, I've not spent my whole life living in a cave – or a forest.' Fiona began walking away, raising her hand in farewell. 'You will see me again. Goodnight.'

Jenn watched her go, disappear into the shadows. She tried, but her powers seemed to fail her this time and she lost all sight of the woman.

So, they had sent her a teacher. And why? So she would return to them and do . . . whatever it was they wanted. Still, having Fiona around could be helpful and if nothing else, she would be able to answer a few questions.

Jenn turned and headed through the garden gate. She took the first path on her left, which skirted the wall lined with lemon trees. A gust of wind rustled the leaves of the old yew tree in the corner and pulled some clouds free of the pale moon. Not much, but enough for her to see the figure of the old man seated beneath the yew branches. He looked up as she approached, so she took a deep breath and put aside her thoughts of the Enclave. Baron Campbell waited for her, waited to ask more of his questions. But Jenn had questions of her own.

'I wasn't sure you would come,' Campbell murmured in greeting. 'I know it's a little late and a girl like you should be fast asleep by now. Thank you.'

Jenn shrugged. 'It's not so late and besides, Bella and Lawrence are still awake. There's candlelight from their window.'

Campbell nodded. 'So, tell me. Do you think if I asked Dunlorn, would he help me?'

Taking a seat beside him, Jenn folded her hands together and placed them carefully on her lap. 'I don't see how he can. As I told you, he only discovered my identity by accident. He would have to have a lot more accidents in order to find your grandson. That doesn't mean he wouldn't have any ideas. The only way you'll know is if you ask him. But tell me what happened when your grandson was taken. I know very little of the Troubles. Where I grew up it was hardly ever discussed and these days my father prefers to think of other things.'

'He was never really involved with the Troubles anyway. He was too isolated out here and although he knew just about everybody involved, Jacob was always the kind of man who kept to himself. When the fighting began, he thought it best not to take sides.' Campbell glanced across at Jenn, then reached up and ran both hands over his tired face.

'You know,' he continued, 'I had almost passed the stage of thinking about the Troubles, but since I heard about you,

I've thought of little else. Like the day I heard about the first battle between the Houses of Butchart and Payne. Oh, they'd long had a feud over some silly thing, but suddenly they faced each other on Cadden Field. Twenty-seven men were killed that day alone, and many more wounded. Both Butchart and Payne survived to accuse each other of evil practices on the battlefield. The rest is history.'

Jenn leaned forward until she could see his weathered face in the filmy moonlight. His eyes were in shadow now, but even so, they seemed to look into the distance as he remembered those times. 'It's a history I barely know. What happened after that first battle? How did the Troubles get so bad that Selar felt confident invading?'

Campbell eyed her sideways. 'If that first battle had been allowed to die down, then Selar would have had no chance at all. As it was, peace never got a chance. Early the following year, Payne's people were ambushed by men wearing Ramsay colours. The Randalls, traditional enemies of the Ramsays', told Payne who was responsible. Payne turned on Ramsay, but because they were allied to the Kendalls there were now five Houses involved in the fighting. I remember the arguments and recriminations, the challenges and the duels. Somewhere in there, the Earl of Caskie tried to calm things down, but unfortunately bringing the Houses together only erupted in fighting and Payne was killed over the meeting table. His son, the older brother of the present Earl, Everard, swore that it was all a plot and gave his oath to wipe out the entire Caskie House. From that point on, we were virtually lost.'

'But what about King Edward? Did he do nothing?'

'Edward was weak. He threw blame about like it was seed corn in a ploughed field – no mind about where it landed. The Houses very quickly lost faith in his judgement and so did he. Two years before, his Queen had died, leaving him with no heir. With the succession in doubt, his power base dried up and he was left isolated. There was very little he could do. However, not all the Houses were involved in the feuds. The exceptions were few. Your own house of Ross and those of Maine and Douglas.'

'Douglas? Dunlorn?'

'Aye. Robert's father, Trevor, was a great man in his time. He travelled from one side of the country to the other doing what Edward should have done. Somehow, he managed to keep faith with all of the Houses – and his courage is still remembered.'

'So what happened in the end? How did Selar manage to invade?'

Campbell shrugged. 'He waited. Over a period of three years, the Troubles escalated to the point where almost every major House in Lusara had a blood feud with at least two others. No trust, no friends. Allies one day became enemies the next. Selar crossed the border, fought a few minor skirmishes and was well advanced before any House could mobilize their forces. Since they were already divided, it took months to get them all to work together. There were two major battles, the first at Nanmoor and the second at Seluth. That's where my son was killed, where Trevor died, and where your father received his wounds. King Edward also died on the battlefield. Selar was crowned at the Basilica in Marsay eight months after he crossed the border.'

Jenn tried to absorb all this. So much division and hatred had cost Lusara its identity. In a flash the truth of it came home to her. She and her country had both lost their identity at the same time, in the same way.

'So,' she breathed, glancing up at Campbell, 'what happened to your grandson? How did the abductions begin, or were they just part of the Troubles?'

Campbell folded his arms. 'At the time we were in no doubt that they were part of the Troubles. I don't remember who was taken first, but Blair's son was definitely taken early on. It's difficult to say. There were so many raids and ambushes and battles – so many people were killed, innocent people. At first it was hard to put the disappearance of one or two children down to any single thing. That was until young Peter McGlashen was taken, in broad daylight. A dozen or so armed and mounted men swarmed down on a caravan taking him and his mother to visit her uncle. They killed the guard, left the mother and women and took young Peter. He was two years old. His parents waited in vain for a ransom demand, but none came. It was much the same story with my grandson. With all of them.'

'But,' Jenn began slowly, and very carefully, 'I was the only girl taken. Why? It doesn't make any sense. All the other Houses were in some way connected with the Troubles. Even yours. But you said my father was never a part of it – and even if they were only taking heirs, I am the younger of two daughters. I was of no value to anyone. Why me?'

Campbell turned his head and looked at her for a long moment. 'I guess it depends on what the purpose was – in the first place, I mean. If it was to get ransom, then yes, taking you meant nothing. But if there was some other reason?'

'But what?' Jenn insisted.

'Well,' Campbell searched around for an answer, 'perhaps all those children taken were from Houses directly influential on the one responsible. Perhaps they were all enemies. Perhaps the man behind it all originally meant to return you to your homes, but never got around to it, or died on the battlefield fighting Selar. I wish I knew.'

'So do I.' Jenn glanced up again at the light on the tower. It was getting very late, and if she didn't go in now she would be missed.

'I don't think Robert can help you. I'm sorry.'

'I understand, lass,' Campbell stood and offered her his arm. 'But you needn't worry. I have no false hopes – well, not many. At this late stage, all I can do is try. If I did not, I would never be able to sleep at night. As it is . . .'

Jenn smiled and took his arm. Together, they went back into the castle.

Fiona appeared two days later, in the company of Bella. The moment Jenn saw her, she began to wonder if it had been such a good idea to agree after all. Bella introduced her as a teacher to take Bella's place when she and Lawrence left for the summer. Fiona, along with Father Brian, was to continue Jenn's interrupted education. There was still so much to learn if she was to take her place in the society to which she belonged. Fiona said nothing as Bella rattled on then finally, after much justification, Bella left them alone. The moment the door was closed behind her, Fiona moved. She stood close to the oak panelling and kept her ear there for a moment. Then, without a word, she waved her hand over the lock and turned an expectant face on Jenn.

'We can talk safely now. I've just put a warning on the door. I'll teach you how. It won't keep anybody out, but you'll always know when somebody's approaching. I warn you though, don't try to open a door that you know has a warning put there by somebody else. You'll get a nasty shock.'

Jenn got up from her seat and crossed the solar. With a frown she said, 'But you didn't use your *ayarn*. Don't you need one?'

'I did. Every sorcerer uses an *ayarn* every time they practise. Except you, of course. For the rest of us mere mortals, it's dangerous not to.'

'But shouldn't I need an *ayarn* in order to learn the things you have to teach me?'

'Look, I don't know any more about what kind of powers you have than you do, so please don't ask me. For the moment and until we know more, I will teach you as though you were using one. It's the best I can do.'

Jenn nodded, feeling like she was being swept along on the tide of Fiona's eagerness. She moved away a little, wanting to slow this down. 'I still don't understand how you got here – or why Bella employed you. How did you do that?'

Fiona just shrugged and moved through the room, glancing at things here and there. 'I have references from other places I've worked.'

'But I thought you were a teacher back at the . . .'

'I do that every winter. In the summer, I'm a Seeker.'

'Like Finnlay?'

Fiona laughed. 'Nobody's a Seeker like Finn. That's like saying all sorcerers are like his brother!'

'But that's what you do?'

'Yes. All sorcerers can do it to some extent. You'll learn that as well. Each day I'll teach you a little more, along with your proper lessons. Otherwise your sister will wonder why you still know nothing about the world.'

Jenn nodded and sank back on to her seat. Fiona continued to move around the room, but Jenn didn't take her eyes off her. She wore a plain gown of grey wool over a white shift and while not rich, the colours suited Fiona's colouring and made her, in the warm daylight, almost pretty. Her eyes were alight with intelligence and energy, as though she had a thousand things she was determined to get done every single day. A formidable presence. She would be about Finnlay's age, but bore none of the trappings of marriage or children. Was that why she had volunteered?

Curious, Jenn asked, 'Do you like being a Seeker? Do you enjoy travelling the countryside looking for others?'

Fiona bent down to study an enamel pot by the fireplace. 'I am a Seeker – so liking it is not a question.'

'But you're not married?'

'No. And before you ask, I have no desire to be.'

'Why not?'

At this Fiona stopped her exploring. 'Two reasons. Firstly, our brethren no longer practise arranged marriages as they do outside. They did once, before the cave community existed, for reasons lost to us over time. Once it was all very magical and wound up in ancient scripture, a process called Bonding. Nobody had a choice at all. But as I said, we no longer practise that and nobody would know how to go about it anyway. I expect with your family connections, you'll have as little choice as we once did.'

'What has my family to do with it?'

Fiona laughed. 'You're the daughter of an Earl, Jenn! Think about it! One of the last remnants of the old royal

274

line. How much choice do you expect? Your father would like an heir and your sister has so far failed to produce one.'

Jenn swallowed at that, unable to really take it in for the moment. 'And the second reason you aren't married?'

The hazel eyes glinted back. 'The man I would marry would never ask me.'

'Oh.'

'Yes, exactly. And there's your first lesson. Don't ask a question unless you're ready for the answer. Now, to begin,' Fiona was about to continue when she broke off, her head tilting sideways as though listening for something. 'Somebody's coming.'

Without moving, she waved her hand in the air and, in her mind, Jenn felt a tiny click. Seconds later the door opened and a servant appeared summoning her downstairs to her father – urgently.

By the time she arrived in his study at the end of the great hall, Bella was already there, along with Lawrence and Campbell. Her father sat in his usual chair by the now empty fireplace. As she entered, he looked up, his face dark and deeply lined.

'Jennifer! Come in, child, close to me. I have some news. I've just received a letter. The courier arrived moments ago, from the King. It's the first I've received since I retired here after Seluth. He writes to congratulate me on the return of my lost daughter and . . .'

'Come on, Father,' Bella pressed, 'what else does it say?'

'Jennifer has been summoned to present herself at court,' Jacob replied flatly.

'What?' Bella breathed.

'By the gods!' Campbell sank into a chair by the window.

Bella moved across the room. 'Father, you can't let her go. You know what he will do. He's already imprisoned Bishop McCauly on trumped-up charges of treason. We are of the old royal line. He will see Jennifer as a threat to his position. You can't let her go!'

Jacob shook his head at her pleas then reached out and

took Jenn's hand in his. 'That's exactly why I must let her go, Bella. You know I don't have the power to stop him.'

'But . . .'

'You'll go with her. In a week. You'll take care of her and bring her back safely. You and Lawrence.'

He paused, turning his gaze on Jenn. She said nothing, merely tried to still the rising tide of fear which threatened to overwhelm her.

Jacob nodded slowly. 'May the gods protect us. The monster wants to meet my child!'

# 12

Godfrey emerged from the dark corridor and paused to allow his eyes to adjust to the spring sunshine. The courtyard was glaring but it was much warmer than the dungeon where McCauly now lived, and nowhere near as damp.

As he walked across the cobblestones, Hilderic was waiting for him by the inner gate, his hands clasped together in what should have been pious patience, but was more likely to be the exact opposite.

'Well, how is he?' Hilderic demanded.

'Keep your voice low, Brother,' Godfrey murmured, eyeing the guards closest to them. They wouldn't be able to hear but that was no reason to take any risk. 'He's well enough. The Queen visits him almost every day, bringing him fresh linen, books and such. He's a little thinner I suppose, but that's to be expected.'

Hilderic frowned and shook his head. 'I thank the gods at least that Selar finally allowed a visit. To keep him confined there without even the Sacraments as comfort is a barbarity below even the King. Did McCauly say anything?'

Godfrey sighed. 'He said we were to do nothing to gain his release. He refuses to be the instrument of the Church's destruction. Instead he wants us to be united behind Brome – even if Brome is the King's voice.'

'But that's . . .'

'I know, brother, I know.'

'By the gods,' Hilderic hissed, 'if only we had some help.'

'I know what you're thinking,' Godfrey said. 'I wouldn't suggest you go looking for help in that direction.'

Hilderic frowned. 'Why? What have you done?'

'Nothing, Brother.' Godfrey murmured.

The older man opened his mouth, then shut it briskly. He

took in a deep breath and drew himself up to his full height. 'You'll pay for that lie, Brother.'

'I already have.'

'And what makes you so certain he won't come?'

'I know him. We used to spar together.'

'Spar? But you know nothing of swordsmanship.'

Godfrey shrugged slightly. 'It wasn't that kind of sparring.'

Hilderic shook his head, obviously furious. 'You had no right, Godfrey! No right at all. If Dunlorn . . .'

Instantly Godfrey raised his hand to silence the older man. The guards might not be close, but it was a foregone conclusion that they'd been instructed to report any mention of Robert's name — especially by the clergy!

He took Hilderic's arm and led him through the outer gate and towards the Basilica. 'We should discuss this in private, Brother.' Hilderic was still fuming, so Godfrey increased his pace. The old man stumbled and almost fell. Fortunately, he was caught before he could hit the ground. Caught by a pair of dirty hands, wrapped in rags.

'Are you all right, Father?' the stranger murmured with concern.

Hilderic steadied himself and shot Godfrey an angry frown. 'Yes, thank you. Deacon Godfrey was not paying as much attention as he should.'

Godfrey rolled his eyes and was about to help Hilderic on his way when he paused to look again at the stranger. The man was his own height, but obviously a beggar. His clothes were filthy and shredded with years of wear. The man's face was grimy, making the lines around his eyes deep and dark. But it was his eyes which made Godfrey pause. There was something very familiar about those eyes.

As though the man could read his thoughts, he dropped his gaze. 'Do you have any news of His Grace, Bishop McCauly?'

Godfrey blinked. Why did this man seem so familiar? Even the voice . . . 'Father McCauly is well, my son. I have just seen him. But you should be careful being so close to

278

the castle gates, otherwise they might throw you in a cell with him.'

'A poor beggar might suffer a worse fate, Father,' the stranger replied, keeping his eyes downcast.

Still none the wiser, Godfrey took Hilderic's arm once more. 'Thank you for your timely help, my son, and remember my words of warning.'

The beggar bowed and Godfrey moved on. What did it matter who the beggar was anyway? Right now, there were much more important things to consider – like how to commit treason and get McCauly free.

So . . . that was Deacon Godfrey, Robert's old friend. A man close to the leadership of the Church. A man who knew enough to warn Robert not to approach Marsay. And the old priest? Obviously Archdeacon Hilderic. And Godfrey had just seen McCauly. So much the better.

Finnlay melted into the shadows of the Basilica. Godfrey was right. A beggar attracted too much attention in this kind of environment. Time for a change of disguise – and for that matter, time to go and find Murdoch.

It took him little more than half an hour to get from the castle to the other side of town. He paused in an empty alley only long enough to adjust his clothing and then set out to find the tailor's shop. Although he'd never spent a great deal of time in the capital, Finnlay knew Marsay well enough to find the street without too much trouble. It was down at the bottom of the mount, inside the city wall but close to the river which surrounded the city. On this warm spring day, Finnlay found the rising smell of shops and carters, animals and taverns almost overpowering and it was with some relief that he ducked into the doorway of the tailor's premises. It was darker in here, and smelt of oiled wool. It took a moment for his eyes to adjust and when they did, he saw Murdoch attending a customer.

'I shall be with you in a moment, sir,' Murdoch smiled without a flicker of recognition.

Finnlay nodded and moved to wander around the tiny

establishment. Folds of soft Alusian silk lay on a bench by one wall, surrounded by bolts of rough woven hessian.

'What are you doing here?'

Finnlay turned around and, seeing that they were alone, shrugged. 'What do you think?'

Murdoch shook his head. 'You might have warned me you were coming. I nearly had heart failure when you walked through that door. Come upstairs. We can talk there.'

With the shop door closed for the afternoon, Murdoch led Finnlay up the steep narrow staircase to the upper floor. Once there, he poured them both some ale, then moved to stand by the little window which looked down into the street.

'Are you waiting for someone?' Finnlay asked, pulling off his filthy cloak.

'Yes. He's just coming up the street. Wait here while I let him in.'

Murdoch was gone only a few minutes and when he returned, he brought with him a stranger. Finnlay stood to meet him while Murdoch closed the door and put a warning on it.

'Unless I'm mistaken,' the stranger began, moving forward, 'you are Finnlay Douglas. We've not met, but I've heard about you. I'm John Ballan.'

'There's no point in being discreet, John,' Murdoch laughed, pouring him a mug of ale. 'Finnlay will find out everything there is about you, whether you like it or not. He's that kind of sorcerer.'

'Thank you, Murdoch,' Finnlay replied flatly. 'And just what is it that I will find out eventually?'

'This is Father John Ballan, Finn, secretary to Archdeacon Hilderic. You've never met before because John has made only one visit to the caves. He entered holy orders as a young man and spent his life working here on our – and the Church's behalf. Now don't look shocked, Finn. It doesn't do you justice.'

Finnlay took in a deep breath and sat down. 'An amazing coincidence. I just met your superior.'

'Really? Where?'

'Coming out of the dungeons. Godfrey had been to see McCauly.'

Murdoch's face went white. 'What in the name of the gods were you doing there? Have you no idea how dangerous it is? On top of that, Godfrey and your brother were good friends – there's a good chance he could have recognized you!'

With a shrug, Finnlay replied, 'He came close. I had to give him a nudge to shake him off. He's probably forgotten all about me by now.'

Murdoch sank on to a chair by the table, shaking his head in disbelief. 'You're a fool, Finn. What were you doing?'

'Trying to find out about McCauly.'

'But that's what I'm here for, to pass on that kind of information to the others.'

'Yes, well, I'm not living in the caves at the moment. I'm back at home.'

The room fell silent. Finnlay sighed and waved his hands at the two men. 'Well, go on and ask.'

'You're back at home?' John murmured. 'With your brother?'

'Yes, that's right. Cosy, isn't it?'

'I must know something. Godfrey wrote your brother a letter in secret. Is there a chance that the letter asked your brother to do something about McCauly?'

'No, quite the opposite. He warned Robert to stay away.'

'And will he?'

Finnlay drained his ale and reached for the jug. 'My brother is determined to remain completely uninvolved with everything except the management of his estates. I've no doubt he'd very much like to do something about McCauly, but I think we all know that the moment he tried, we'd have a civil war on our hands. Have you got any food, Murdoch? I'm starving.'

Murdoch rose and opened a cupboard. He produced half a cold chicken and some bread, which he handed to Finnlay.

281

With a frown he said, 'But I felt sure that when Robert chose not to Stand the Circle . . .'

Finnlay interrupted, 'So what's happening here? Are there any moves to free McCauly? Is the Church standing behind him?'

'The Church,' John replied, 'is split – just as that prophecy foretold. There are no real moves planned, but that doesn't mean things will stay that way. At the moment it's a waiting game. I fear a lot of it depends on this new man at court.'

'What new man?'

John glanced at Murdoch. 'It's taken some months, but effectively he's replaced your brother as Selar's closest friend. His name is Samdon Nash – and he's a member of the Guilde.'

'Ye gods!' Finnlay breathed. 'Is he Vaughn's pet? Is this another move by the proctor?'

'No, I don't think so,' replied Murdoch. 'They've grown close. I think it's only a matter of time before Selar appoints Nash to the council. You should try and get a look at him while you're here, for future reference.'

'Very well. But why do you think his presence has such a bearing on McCauly?'

Murdoch stood and refilled their mugs from the jug of ale. He returned to the window and gazed down at the street below. 'You never spent much time at court, did you? A few quick visits when Robert was on the council.'

'I came for a couple of weeks, one summer . . .'

'Still, you were never around much. You forget how much the King needed your brother. Not just his work and support, but also his friendship. Selar's a lonely man, in a foreign country, surrounded by enemies and blood-sucking supporters. People like Vaughn and Tiege Eachern are not friends, but tools to use as he chooses. Once Robert left, there was a big hole in Selar's life and now it's been filled by Nash. When Robert was around we could breathe easy, but not so with this man. I have a very bad feeling about him, Finn. I don't like him at all.'

'Have you scanned him? He's not Malachi, is he?'

'No, nothing like that. I don't get that close to him. John sees him more than I do.'

Finnlay glanced across at the priest. The young man lifted his shoulders, but obviously had nothing to contribute. 'It is possible, though, isn't it? I mean, if he's Malachi, he may have found a way to screen it, so that we can't tell.'

'Finnlay,' Murdoch smiled, 'not all evil men are necessarily Malachi. I'm just saying that Nash is a man we should keep our eyes on, that's all.'

'I see.' Finnlay emptied his cup once more and turned away from the window. 'Well, I have to get going. I can only stay in town a couple of days and there is still a bit I have to do.'

'Before you go,' John raised his hand, 'is it true about the Ross girl? About how you found her? Is she really as powerful as they say?'

'Yes, it's all true. Why?'

'It's just that there's a story going around within the cave community, that is, that your brother knew where she was all along – and knew about her powers. That he might have had something to do with her abduction in the first place – because of her powers.'

'What?' Finnlay burst out laughing. 'Well, I've heard some things in my time but that really beats the lot! Robert? Abduct a child during the Troubles? My brother? The man who is so honour-bound that he won't stand against the King because of an oath? You must be kidding!'

'Well, you must admit that it's a little strange.'

'Nothing strange about it, Father John!' Finnlay laughed again. 'I know – I was there when it all happened. Every bit of it. Think about it. If he really wanted her for some reason, would he just return her to her damned father? Wouldn't he spirit her away somewhere? And for what purpose? Robert has no need of her powers – he already has more than he knows what to do with. Sometimes I wonder what the Enclave is thinking about!'

'Finn . . .'

'Oh, forget it, Murdoch. No one can hear me and you

283

know it. Saying that word is no more damning than anything
else we've said here. Look, I must go. I'll drop in before I
leave Marsay. Anything else you can tell me about this Nash
fellow will be welcome.'

Murdoch waved his hand towards the door then added,
'Please, Finn – be careful.'

The courtyard was filled with sunlight and the heat of a
dozen men sparring with sword and mace. The crash of steel
and occasional cries of triumph or encouragement echoed
around the grey sandstone walls and melted into the cloudy
sky above. All around the perimeter servants and lords done
with fighting towelled themselves dry and watched the
continuing conflicts.

Nash had not fought today, although he had for the last
two. This morning he waited on the King with a jewelled
goblet of wine and a slip of snowy white linen. He stood in
the doorway of the pavilion, erected for the sole purpose of
giving Selar somewhere from which to watch this event
when he wasn't taking part. In the centre of the courtyard,
Selar sparred with Kandar. Although Nash knew the Earl to
be a fine swordsman, he could see George was not perform-
ing at his best. More than once Selar was able to slip through
his guard to nick the point of his sword against Kandar's
gleaming chain mail.

'Deep thoughts?' a sensuous voice murmured in his ear.
'Do you envy the young Earl and how close he is to your
dear friend? Do you not wish to be so close to him yourself?'

Nash smiled, knowing she couldn't see the expression.
'Your obscene suggestions do not do you justice, my dear.
You would be wise to keep them to yourself.'

'I can't help it. Just seeing the way you watch them puts
these thoughts into my head. For all your fine talk of power,
is there not something else you want? Is there no other
reason why you share every waking moment with the King?'

Languidly, Nash placed the cup of wine on the small table
by his elbow and turned to look at her. Her face was

composed with serious concern but her eyes danced and reflected hints of sunlight. She slowly smiled.

'And are you going to tell me that you are suddenly jealous?' Nash murmured. 'After all this time?'

'Jealous? No. But Samdon, you know I don't trust you. I've told you a thousand times. After five years, you should know I mean what I say.'

Nash stepped forward and she backed away further into the shadows of the pavilion. 'Perhaps you would like to leave me. Is that it? Do you want to return to your brothers and sisters? Do you miss the Malachi so much? Do you regret leaving their narrow ambition for the sake of my grand one?' He laughed and bent his head to kiss her smooth white throat. 'Ah, Valena, if only you would leave me. Then you wouldn't be such a distraction to me.'

She laughed and moved closer, breathing close to his ear. 'Yes, I'm so much of a distraction that the moment I return you ignore me. I've been back two weeks and you haven't even asked me about my trip, not even to ask if I had a good Caslemas.'

Nash gazed down at her and noted every curve and line of her beautiful face. His hand came up and delicately traced the edge of her bodice where it met her flesh. Automatically, he sent his senses out into the courtyard, but the King was still fighting and no one was paying Nash any attention at all. He smiled again. 'I assumed, my dear, that if there was anything terribly important, you would come to me immediately.'

'Then you assume too much on my part. Returning in itself was important, don't you think?'

He couldn't help but laugh. She was so very good at this. So skilled in the fine art of seduction. No wonder the Malachi wanted her back. Without doubt she was one of their finest – but that was also the reason why he wanted her. Because he appreciated her much more than they ever could.

'So then, what did you find out about our renegade Earl?

Is he planning treason? Is he any threat to Selar – and therefore to us?'

Valena gently removed his hand from her breast and stepped back a little. Her face lost that enticing smile and instead became immediately more practical. 'I think he's a spent cause. He's weary of the fight and has no desire to be involved with it again. He'll stay at home, I promise you. As far as he is concerned, your position is secure.'

'But?' Nash queried with a raised eyebrow.

'He has a younger brother, Finnlay. I don't know that it's important, but he does have an interest in the history of sorcery.'

'Really?' Nash breathed. 'And do you think he has any power?'

'No. He's just an interested amateur. Besides, I thought you picked up all the possible candidates years ago. At least, that's what you told me. Can you have missed anyone?'

'No,' Nash shook his head, 'I spent five years scanning Lusara before I even began taking them. I know I collected every child with powers from a major House who was born at the time. There may be others since then, but they don't matter. My father's instructions were quite clear. It is this generation that is the most dangerous. Any following are of no consequence.'

Nash broke off and glanced over his shoulder. 'You'd better leave. He's coming in for refreshment and I don't want him to see you. Not yet.'

'I'll wait for you tonight,' she murmured in farewell, once more in her most sensuous voice.

She was gone just as Selar strode into the pavilion, tossing his sword on a chair and sweeping up the goblet of wine Nash held out. Following close on his heels were Vaughn and Osbert.

'Forgive me, Sire,' Vaughn began with little flourish, 'I must speak with you.'

'What is it?' Selar frowned, appearing entirely dis-interested.

'That matter we spoke of some weeks ago?'

'What matter?'

'Evidence, Sire.' Vaughn smiled. 'I have it.'

It was not so much the abrupt appearance of Vaughn that caught Rosalind's attention, but the sudden exit from the pavilion, the abandonment of sparring practice for the day. Younger knights continued to work in the centre of the yard, but Selar and his favourites disappeared through the doorway below her open balcony without even a word of explanation.

Not that Selar needed to explain anything. He was, after all, the King and could do what he liked. Even if it meant locking up a properly anointed Bishop! No matter that he'd committed no crime...

'Forgive me, Your Grace.' A quiet voice interrupted her thoughts. 'Do you expect the King to return to the yard today?'

Rosalind turned slowly. Her ladies were not so close to her that they could hear every word of this conversation. They stood by the door apparently ignoring Rosalind and the priest now standing before her. Godfrey waited with his hands clasped patiently together, his eyebrows raised slightly as though in perpetual surprise. He neither smiled nor grimaced, but rather gazed at her openly, begging a trust she could only dare to believe.

'It is ... possible,' Rosalind replied after a moment, keeping her voice clearly audible, 'he may return. I'm not sure. Was there something...?'

She swallowed carefully and tried not to appear nervous. She'd not spoken alone with this man since that night when she'd stolen out of the castle to warn him of Vaughn's plans with the hospices.

Godfrey seemed to sense her agitation and smiled gently. 'I was hoping to beg for another audience with Bishop McCauly ... I mean, Archdeacon McCauly.'

Rosalind couldn't hide a little smile at the deliberate mistake. It appeared there was a small joke they could share between them, even with the ladies present. 'Of course,

Deacon. I'm sure the King would listen to your petition. I'm also sure that the Archdeacon would be grateful for another visit.'

'I was hoping to bring him the Sacraments, Your Grace. If I could perhaps convince the King to allow me to celebrate Mass in the cell each week . . .' Godfrey's voice trailed off, dropping to merely a whisper, then, 'Please – you will let me know if you think McCauly is in any immediate danger, won't you?'

Rosalind's eyes snapped to the women by the door. They were chatting between themselves, but very aware of Rosalind's guest. 'But what danger?' she stammered, turning her attention back to Godfrey.

'From the King,' Godfrey replied quickly. 'If you hear anything at all, please find a way to let me know. I don't know if I can do anything – but I can at least try.'

Would Selar actually try to kill McCauly while in prison? It didn't seem possible – and yet . . . Rosalind breathed deeply and nodded. 'Of course, Deacon. I promise.'

'I've waited too long for this, Vaughn. You told me this would only take a few weeks!' Selar splashed more water on his face, then took the towel from Nash's hands and moved over to the fire. The King's chamber was quite chilly and Nash put another log on to the small blaze.

'The situation has been very delicate, Sire,' Vaughn insisted. 'More delicate than we realized in the beginning. If we pushed too hard they might have known what was happening.'

Selar tossed the towel away and folded his arms. 'Very well, tell me. What is Blair planning? What is your evidence?'

'A letter, Sire, from Blair to one of his neighbours. They have already set up garrisons around Dunwyn and further afield. By the summer they will cordon the area off and allow no admittance to anyone. After that, having gained support from the rest of the country, they plan to march against you.'

Selar nodded slowly. 'And how did you get your hands on this letter? Was it your spy? Who is he?'

'Roy Seaton, Sire.'

'Seaton? That worm?' Selar sank into a chair. 'All right, who else?'

Vaughn, as though given a breath of life, took a step forward. 'Galbraith of Lonley, Lord Eshton and his brother Clarence, Kitson, Knollys and Lacy. There are others Seaton has mentioned in previous communications. I have them noted down.'

'I should hope so. Anyone else I should know about?'

Vaughn laced his hands together and rested them against his yellow surplice. 'One, Sire. Oliver Sinclair, Duke of Haddon.'

Selar sat forward with a start. 'Haddon? You can't be serious!'

When Vaughn didn't answer, Selar sprang to his feet and strode to the door. 'Bates! Get Eachern and Kandar up here immediately!'

As the door shut again, Selar paced back to the fireplace. He was silent a moment, then glanced not at Vaughn but at Nash. 'How long a ride is it to Dunwyn from here?'

'About five days at forced march, Sire. Less if there are horses to change.'

'Five days.' Selar thought again. Then to Vaughn, 'Is there any chance Blair knows about Seaton?'

'None, Sire. Seaton is still enmeshed, along with the others. They think to catch you unawares.'

'Then he won't be expecting me to send a force down to meet him in the middle of spring, will he?'

Kandar and Eachern arrived and were quickly apprised of the news. Selar's orders flew about the room like angry hornets. Eachern was to lead a force of the King's own men, five hundred strong, supported by Vaughn's Guilde guard of two hundred. They were to leave at dawn the following day.

'And remember, Eachern, I want Blair and Haddon alive. I want them to stand trial and I want them to pay. No man breaks his oath to me without suffering for it! Do you understand? As for the rest, I don't care what you do with them – but I do care to hear there is nothing left of Dunwyn by the time you leave. Go.'

The room emptied, leaving Nash alone with Selar.

'Open those damned curtains will you? It's too hot in here.'

Nash quietly did as he was bid, then on impulse, brought the jug of wine over to refill Selar's cup.

'It's been three years,' Selar murmured.

'Sire?'

'Three years – and what happens only moments after he gets back? His damned uncle gets himself embroiled in treason! You never met Dunlorn, did you?'

'He left before I came to court.'

'But you've heard stories?'

'Who has not?'

Selar gave a bark of ironic laughter. 'Robert, for one.' He reached for the wine and refilled his cup again. For a moment he gazed into the dark liquid, then gently placed it on the table. 'There are many stories – and many lies. But the truth is that I removed Dunlorn from the council more for his own safety than anything else.'

'I understand, Sire.'

'Do you?' Turning a piercing grey gaze on him, Selar shook his head. 'No, I don't think you can.'

'There she is.'

'Where?'

'Just passing through the gate, do you see?'

'Oh yes. And who are the others?'

'The raven-haired woman beside her is her sister, Bella, and the man riding in front is Bella's husband, Lord Lawrence Maitland, a wealthy but minor baron. It's a small train, of course, half a dozen guards and a couple of servants. I suppose they hope to keep a low profile while they're here.'

'It won't do them any good.'

Nash turned away from the window and gazed down at Valena. She wore a shift of the finest gauze silk in a gentle cream colour which set off the honey-gold of her hair to perfection. He reached out and swept a strand of it away from her face and bent to kiss her. This time, however, she made no move to encourage him.

'Are you certain that's her?' Valena murmured, her eyes still on the city below.

'I'd know her face anywhere,' Nash replied.

'She has no aura.'

Nash turned back to the window. 'Of course not. Her powers are still submerged. Hell, I put enough effort into it. When they do develop you'll be able to Seek her regardless of where she is. Hopefully, though, we'll be able to postpone that moment for as long as possible.'

Valena nodded absently and left him by the window. Without a word, she picked up a gown of deep blue and slipped it over her head.

'What's wrong?' Nash asked softly without approaching her.

'Nothing.'

Nash glanced once more out of the window, then sat down on the padded bench. 'Tell me.'

Valena began lacing up her gown but didn't look at him. 'You got Selar to order her here, didn't you? You suggested she might be a threat to his throne if she managed to produce a male heir.'

'Yes. What of it?'

'Why? I thought you said it was too soon for her part in all this. So why did you want her here? What do you plan to do with her now that she's so close?'

Nash ventured a chuckle. 'What are you worried about? That I'll want her to replace you?'

Valena stamped her foot, managing, despite her frown, to still look exquisite. 'Stop it, Samdon. Just tell me the truth. Why do you want her here? Is she a danger to us? Tell me, dammit!'

Nash rose to his feet and crossed the room, 'Don't push me too far, Valena. I've warned you before.'

She pouted and dropped her chin. 'Oh? And what will

you do to me? You're not going to use that old threat of killing me with the Word of Destruction, are you?'

'I could.'

'Rubbish! You don't even know what it is. If you did, we wouldn't be going through this ridiculous charade. Now stop this silly game and tell me what you're going to do.'

'I plan to do nothing when she gets here. I just want to get a look at her. That's all.' Nash backed off. His anger wasn't real, but one day, despite her beauty and other talents, she would push him too far. And then, Word of Destruction or no, he would kill her.

Valena took in a breath and continued dressing. 'Perhaps I should have a quiet chat with her.'

'No!' Nash snapped, then smiled to soften his words. 'You're to stay away from her, my dear. Do you understand? I don't want you anywhere near her. You're too overpowering and too damned dangerous by far.'

Valena decided to make it a joke. 'Now you're trying to flatter me.'

'I'm serious. I didn't put all that effort into getting Selar to invite her here just so you could ruin it. I will observe her from a distance and speak to her when the moment is right. I can find out what we need without you getting involved.'

The laughter died in her voice and she looked up at him with dark, serious eyes. 'You are sure about all this, aren't you? Sure of what your father and grandfather taught you? There's no mistake?'

'None,' he replied with certainty. 'The only mistake was the battle of Alusia. If it hadn't been for our loss there, this would all have happened two hundred years ago. As it is, the delay has proved useful. So much has been lost since then, we are the only ones who know anything about it. I need you to promise me you will behave.'

She nodded. 'I promise.' Then the sparkle returned to her eyes and she lifted her head to kiss him languorously. 'I hope, though, you don't mean that too literally.'

As always her kiss was sweet and, as always, he found it difficult to remember why he'd been angry with her. Even

292

though a part of him knew she did it deliberately, it didn't dim the power she had over him. He stood back to allow her to finish dressing. 'We must hurry. We have to get young Keith on his way before the armies get too far ahead of him. They've already got the morning's head start.'

In a swirl of velvet, Valena donned her cloak and together they left the tower and descended to the stables. There the young man waited patiently for them, dressed for his journey.

'Good morning, master.'

'Good morning, Keith,' Nash began easily. There was no one else about so he quickly checked the saddlebags on the waiting horse. 'You know what you have to do?'

'Yes, master. I'm to stay behind the army until it reaches Dunwyn and then take the place of one of the soldiers when the battle is joined.'

'And then?' Valena murmured.

'I'm to kill both Blair and Haddon, if possible without revealing myself.'

Valena smiled and turned to Nash. 'I told you he was ready.'

'And of course I believed you, my dear. Keith, show me your shoulder.'

'What?' Valena took a step forward. 'You're not going to do that here! What if someone sees you?'

Nash laughed. 'What can they see? Besides, I dare not send him off to Dunwyn without setting this afresh.' Without another word, Nash reached up and placed his hand over the faint Mark on the young man's shoulder. Seconds later he removed it and the shoulder was clean.

'By the gods, you are arrogant!' Valena murmured, then abruptly laughed. 'You are such a good servant to Selar. Not only do you supply him with raiders that he can blame on his brother, but you also happily remove his two greatest enemies. All without him knowing about it!'

Nash had to purse his lips not to smile. He turned to Keith. 'Time for you to go.'

'Yes, master.' Keith mounted the horse and rode out through the courtyard.

Valena moved close to Nash, her voice dark and sultry. 'I'm sure his father would have been proud of him – if he were alive.'

'Well, his grandfather's alive – and I don't think he'd be proud one little bit. Baron Campbell is a good friend of Blair's. Personally, I think there's a touching irony to all this. Somehow, I think it fits.'

'If you're so pleased,' Valena added, 'I suppose you don't mind accompanying me through the town. I would at least like to get a look at the girl, since you won't let me near her. I promise to behave myself. If we hurry we can be out in the street as she passes by.'

Nash gave in gracefully. 'Why not?'

Finnlay left Murdoch's shop for the last time and headed back along the street to the hostelry to collect his horse. It had certainly been an interesting few days, but he was glad to be going home. And there was so much he had to tell Robert – not that he would be that interested. Tales of intrigue, rescue plots and dawn troop movements were of no concern to Robert these days. About the only thing Finnlay could report that would get Robert's attention was the fact that Selar had no intention of doing anything at all about these roving bandits that were plaguing the land. Small bands of inconsequential raiders meant nothing to Selar – even if they did fire the gossip of almost every tavern in the capital. Whether Selar was concerned about them or not, the people were and they didn't understand why the King refused to do anything about them.

His horse was saddled and ready for him, but the street was too crowded to mount up just yet. So Finnlay led it through the back alleys towards the gate. He paused at the entrance to the main thoroughfare, which was even more crowded. With a sigh, he glanced up at the sky and the dark threatening clouds which hung there. It would pour down before the day was out. He sighed again and went to turn into the main street, then paused and instantly shrank back into the shadows.

There, walking along the crowded street was that man, Nash. Dressed in grey, with only his silver badge of office denoting his rank in the Guilde. His face was lean and angular and sported a finely trimmed beard of black hair. He was neither ugly nor handsome, but remarkably unremarkable. However, the same could not be said for the woman with the most exquisite face Finnlay had ever seen who strolled beside him.

Valena!

They were greeted at the keep by the castle chatelaine and shown to rooms high in the south wall, overlooking the river. From her window Jenn gazed into the distance, trying to imagine what the ocean looked like, but there were only thick grey clouds tumbling across the horizon and no sign of any sea. With the early glow of sunset behind her the green valley looked flat and intransigent.

'Well, it's better than I expected,' Bella remarked firmly, entering through the open door. 'These rooms are comfortable, but not sumptuous. Anything more and I would have been seriously worried.'

'You're always worried,' Jenn murmured before she could stop herself. Instantly she regretted it and cast an apologetic glance over her shoulder. Before her sister could respond, she added, 'Why is it good?'

'Because it means Selar intends to pay no particular attention to us – or rather, to you. It's not flattering, but much safer this way, trust me.' Bella ran a finger along the stone lintel above the fireplace and the small wooden table in the corner.

'If I'm so unimportant, why am I here?'

'There is a big difference between being important and being a threat. Just be glad you're only one of those things.'

'If I had to choose, I'd rather be important than be a threat,' Jenn offered with an attempt at humour. 'At least we'd get better rooms.'

'Don't be stupid!' Bella snapped back. 'We've been over this a hundred times! Our position is very precarious and you know it. The only reason why our House was allowed to survive Selar's conquest was because Father was incapable of being any threat to the throne. Have you absorbed none of the history Father Brian has taught you? Don't you know that a monarch always rids himself of any rival family line? That's what makes his position so secure – there is no alternative. We've remained secure because Father never produced a son who could be supported as a rival King. I have ... no children of my own, sister, but you are another matter entirely.'

Jenn's light mood dissipated completely before Bella's onslaught. In a pale voice she asked, 'But who would marry me? With my background? Without a husband or son, I'm no more a threat than Father.'

Bella almost smiled – almost. 'And that's exactly what we want Selar to see. You need to show him that you have no interest in politics – in fact, it would almost be worth your hinting an interest in taking the veil. Anything to make him believe that we are best left well alone.'

With a final glance around the room, Bella nodded. 'I expect you to do your best for all our sakes. This will not be an easy month, but I warn you, be careful of what you say to these people. Trust no one. You know none of these people, nor where their loyalties lie. Create the façade, Jennifer – it's supposed to be something you're good at. Oh, and while we're on the subject – do your best not to mention Dunlorn while we're here. He's not exactly held in high regard any more and I don't want people thinking there is some kind of alliance between our Houses. I'll be across the hall if you need anything.'

Bella closed the door behind her and Jenn slumped against the wall. Feeling the cold stone through her sleeve did nothing to reawaken the delight she'd felt when they'd first arrived in this extraordinary city. She should be pleased to be here, and would have been, if not for Bella's words. How had life become so dangerous?

An icy sick feeling seeped into her stomach and she tried to breathe deeply as Fiona had taught her. One of several exercises designed to ease fear – despite the fact that Jenn still refused to admit aloud that she ever felt any. These days, it was getting harder to convince herself, let alone anyone else, and for all her robust enthusiasm, Fiona had done little to help. Oh sure, Jenn had learned how to set a warning, but could not under any circumstances do anything that resembled the light Fiona could produce from her *ayarn*. Fiona insisted that it was too early to be making any assumptions, but deep down inside, Jenn knew there was really very little the Adept could teach her. As yet, Fiona had not recognized the full extent of Jenn's abilities – much less the fact that Jenn could speak directly into Robert's mind.

Robert.

With a sigh Jenn tossed off her cloak and turned back to the window. The evening sky had grown darker now and in the distance a rumble of thunder beckoned a storm.

In this place, Robert was the enemy. To these people, his name alone was dangerous. But they would ask her about him, that much was certain. And what would she say? What could she say? Could she tell them they were all wrong, that Robert could be trusted above even the King they all served?

Hah! They would laugh at her, and immediately assume she was his ally, that her House could be condemned along with his.

But how was he? Had he survived his first winter at home? Was he still resolved to his future?

Once again, Jenn turned her face full to the window and focused her thoughts with as much care and precision as she could manage. Finely now, as Fiona had taught her to work. Focus and concentrate. Gather the power from within. Gather and send it out, like a beacon in the twilight. Send it out as far as possible. Make it strong and clear. Harness the energy inside to do something Fiona knew nothing about. Push hard . . .

*Can you hear me?* she called. *Can you hear my words? How I wish that you could.*

297

... and for the briefest, tiniest moment, she felt something. Not a word, nor even a thought as such ... but something ... involuntary, surprised, even shocked. An echo of a thought in response to her call to Robert, like a pale shadow cast on a hazy day. Could it be him? Could he have possibly heard her so far away?

She opened her mind and let her thoughts float on a cool and inviting sea, not even daring to breathe in case she missed his response. But there was nothing and the moment had passed. Disappointed, she tore her eyes away from the sky and chided herself for being such a fool.

Unfortunately, Nash was not alone when it happened. Instead he was with Vaughn and Osbert – and Vaughn was not happy.

'He is evil, I tell you, to his very core!' Vaughn bellowed. 'I will have him destroyed if it takes my last breath!'

Osbert raised his hands in a vain attempt to calm Vaughn. 'My lord, we have plenty of time to catch Dunlorn. Sooner or later he will show his hand. If there is any evidence of his collusion with Blair, then we will find it. At the moment, however, Dunlorn's inaction merely looks like further support of the King, and how can there be evil in that?'

Vaughn bounced to his feet, his eyes red with fury. 'Don't try to tell me what I know! That man is a ...' he gasped, then finished, 'he is evil and I will not justify my reasons further. Get close to the King, Nash, and bring Dunlorn down. That's an order!'

Nash bowed and backed away to the door. Silently he slipped out, took two steps along the empty corridor and stopped.

That touch. Who could it have been? Valena? Another Malachi? Who?

There was only one way to find out. Tonight he would have to find a quiet place and scan the entire city from top to bottom. Somewhere within the walls of Marsay was a sorcerer of extraordinary power. He would have to find them. He must.

# 13

The clouds on the horizon glowed gold with the coming dawn. The fine misty rain which had plagued Robert all night had lifted and left his men in peace long enough to complete the ride home. They were all tired. Even the horses, spelled on alternating nights, were now showing the strain of these fruitless vigils. But what else was he to do? The raids had not let up with the onset of spring, they had in fact increased in number. Even with the help of his neighbours, no further contact with the raiders had been achieved, let alone their defeat.

It was so frustrating. This was all he had left to do, the only action he could allow himself to perform. If only he could do more . . .

No. Now was not the time to waver – especially with Finnlay due back from court this evening. Now, more than ever, Robert had to remain firm. To become involved again would only guarantee disaster.

A pale watery sunrise greeted them as they rode through the gates of Dunlorn. Robert dismounted and left orders with Deverin that there would be no patrol that night. The men needed more than a few hours' rest now and, raiders or no, they deserved it. He climbed the stone steps to the great hall. Bone-weary and almost asleep on his feet, Robert very nearly missed the pair of muddy boots lying by the glowing hearth. The feet they belonged to were stretched out from the foot of a tall-backed chair.

'Finn?'

His brother jerked upright, his eyes glazed with sleep. 'Ah, Robert, you're back. Good. I was just resting my eyes. Wanted to speak to you before I went to bed.'

'Did you ride all night?' Robert came around and sank

into a chair opposite. Owen appeared and offered him breakfast, but his appetite had long since departed. As Owen left with a frown, Robert turned back to Finnlay. 'What was the hurry? I wasn't expecting you until tonight.'

'Got sick of riding, really,' Finnlay mumbled, rubbing his hands over his face. 'Had an interesting time, though.'

'And McCauly?' Robert asked without pausing. 'He's still in one piece?'

'He's fine. Still in prison, but he's fine.'

'But no chance of getting him out?'

'Not that Murdoch can see.'

'Well, if there's nothing urgent, you can tell me all about it tonight, after we've both had some sleep.'

Finnlay shook his head and looked up with red eyes. 'I don't know whether you'd call it urgent, Robert, but I saw Valena – in the company of a Guilde man who's become Selar's most trusted friend.'

'What?' Robert hardly had the energy to react, but that didn't stop the chill that ran down his spine. 'A Malachi – so close to the king? Are you sure?'

'Saw her with my own eyes, Robert. I'm hardly going to forget a face like that, am I? They were not ten feet from me – and no, she didn't see me. I only saw her as I was leaving Marsay, so I can't tell you anything more. It's . . .'

Finnlay broke off with a frown of pain. He shook his head again then glanced up in apology. 'Sorry, my head hurts with all that riding.'

Robert stood. Finnlay was more than tired, he was unwell. 'You look about as bad as I feel. Come on, I'll help you up to bed. We can talk about this later.'

He reached out and took Finnlay's arm, drawing him to his feet. Finnlay swayed and almost fell, murmuring apologies again. Robert put Finnlay's arm around his shoulders and almost carried him up the stairs. All the way up, Finn kept mumbling something about Murdoch and a priest but Robert could make no sense of it. By the time Finnlay was in bed, the murmuring had stopped and Robert left him to sleep.

*

Micah took the supper tray from Owen and made his way up the stairs just as the last light filtered through the hall windows. He moved silently along the corridor and paused before Robert's study. The door was open, but he still knocked.

'Come in, Micah, put that down and take a look at this.' Robert was leaning over the long table which ran down the centre of the room. As usual it was strewn with papers and books and it was at one of these that he now pointed. 'I'd forgotten all about it. You remember when I bought it? In Budlandi? I meant to show it to Finnlay when he came back from the Enclave but he ran off to Marsay and now he's sick in bed . . .'

'My lord?' Micah stayed back from the table and waited. 'I have something I need to tell you.'

'What is it?' Robert murmured, absently.

Micah just waited. He had to. There was no way he was going to make this confession unless his master was looking at him. It was hard enough as it was, without doing it like a coward.

'Well?' Robert prompted, then turned slowly. Reading Micah's sombre expression, he straightened up. 'All right, out with it. What have you done?'

Now that the moment had come, Micah found it difficult to find the right words. He took several breaths but none of them really filled his chest. In a last-ditch effort, he swallowed and pulled back his shoulders. His father always said it was good for courage and now was the time to try it.

'My lord,' he began, 'I received a letter today – the latest in a series over the last few months. It was from . . .' Micah paused, glancing over his shoulder to the door.

Robert took the unspoken suggestion, closed the door and put a warning on it. 'Go on. Who has been writing so regularly to you?'

'Jenn.'

Robert's eyebrows shot up. 'Oh? And have you been replying?'

'Aye, my lord.'

'And?'

'My lord?' Micah frowned.

'Was there something else?' Robert replied, the hint of a smile creasing the corners of his eyes. 'Did you expect I'd have some objection to your writing to her?'

'You don't?'

'Of course not!' Robert laughed. 'Why would I? I assume you've worked out some way to keep your correspondence out of Jacob's sight, or Bella's for that matter.'

'We have, my lord.'

'So what's the problem?'

Micah shook his head. Even after all these years, there were some days when Robert's responses still surprised him. He was so sure Robert would have a problem with his writing to Jenn that he'd spent all day trying to gather up the courage to tell him. Then, to get such a reaction? Sometimes it was a lot worse to think about a problem than deal with it.

'I'm sorry, my lord. I thought, after what you'd said about keeping her away from the Enclave and everything . . .'

'And when did you become the Enclave, my friend? I know she's fond of you. Why shouldn't you write to her? Actually, I'm glad. I'm not exactly in a position to keep in contact. Besides, I'm not sure she'd welcome it.'

'Actually, my lord, that is part of the reason why I told you now. As I said, I got a letter from her today and she mentioned something she wanted me to discuss with you. She's been doing some research about the Troubles. In particular, about the abductions. Apparently, Baron Campbell went to see her, asking if she could help in finding his grandson, Keith.'

Micah quickly outlined that meeting, then added, 'Based on the theory that there was one person behind the abductions, she decided to try and find some motive. Assuming that each child was taken in order to secure the loyalty or services of each House struck, she mapped out all the relative alliances and positions. Then she applied that to the list of children taken.'

'Very diligent of her,' Robert murmured lightly, but Micah knew his interest was caught.

'The thing is – there is no pattern. There is no way all those children taken could have helped any one man.'

'So it wasn't one man; all along we'd assumed the opposite. I don't understand why she was looking.'

'She also wrote to all the Houses concerned, asking for descriptions of the bandits. Each abduction was performed in exactly the same manner, and in each of them, the leader was an old man who rode a white horse.'

Robert stared at him, frozen to the spot. Outside, a gentle wind rattled against the shutters and made the candlelight flicker and jump. Micah held his breath and waited. All this made no sense to him but given enough time, Robert was sure to make some connection. He had to. This was too important.

Slowly, Robert moved, taking one, then two steps towards the window. 'There is no way that several culprits could exactly copy the manner of abduction – so therefore, it must be one man. The times and distances make it possible. But if there was no motive tied in with the Troubles – then why?'

He fell silent again for a moment, then suddenly turned to face Micah. 'Oh no! Don't tell me Patric was right all along!'

'About what?'

Robert gave an ironic smile. 'Just as a sideline, don't you think it's amusing that despite the fact that she's so far away, she still manages to catch me out? My own fault, really. No, to get back to the point, Patric was very enthusiastic about one of his pet theories the last time I was at the Enclave, before we went away. He said that it was too much of a coincidence that Douglas was the only major House ever to produce a sorcerer – and two in the one family. He said that there had to be more, but that because our Seekers never looked for them, they were never found.'

'And you were only found because of that accident you had.' Micah nodded.

'And I brought Finnlay into the fold when I realized he

had talent too, exactly. So what if there were more – but somebody found out and took them during the Troubles? Who would look for them? By the gods, the Troubles must have seemed like a gift from heaven. But that doesn't get us any closer to finding them – or the person responsible – unless . . .' he paused and turned back to face Micah, 'unless it's been there all along but we've been blind to it.'

Micah frowned, not understanding for a moment. Then it hit him. 'Malachi?'

Robert nodded, but as quickly shook his head, 'No. I can't see how they'd just leave Jenn to live in a tavern in the middle of nowhere. There must be some other explanation, some other reason someone would want to gather them up.'

'And their purpose?'

'As children, I don't know. But as adults? As adults, they would be far more use. Hell! I was a fool to believe Jenn would be safe at Elita!'

Micah knew where this was heading and raised his hands to forestall it. 'My lord, Jenn did say you would react like this. She told me to tell you she is perfectly safe. She has developed certain defences and will know if anyone comes to her with . . . evil intentions. But there was something else.'

'There's more?'

'She's been ordered to present herself at court. She will be there by now.'

For the first time in his life, Micah saw the colour drain completely from his master's face. It was not a comforting sight, and it brought a chill to his stomach.

'What does Selar want with her? Why would he need to see her? I . . .' Robert turned away and walked to the fireplace where kindling had been set. He remained very still for a moment, then abruptly swept his left arm out in a gesture of frustration. The kindling exploded into flame and Micah jumped back. What was this? Anger? From Robert?

'I'm sorry,' Robert murmured after a moment.

Micah took a few steps forward and said softly, 'You knew it wasn't going to be easy. You just have to hold on.'

'While people around me are hurt? I just sit back and

304

watch it all happen, Micah?' Robert whispered. 'Is that what I've chosen? Is that my destiny? To be witness to it all, knowing I can do nothing to stop it? That when I tried to, I failed . . .'

'If you could, would you change your mind?'

'By the gods, Micah, I don't know! It's at times like this that I miss my father. He never managed to get into this kind of trouble.'

'If you will forgive me, my lord,' Micah smiled a little, 'much as I loved and respected your father, he was not the man you are.'

Robert turned at this with a sad laugh. 'As I said, he never got into this kind of trouble. Well, I've got nobody but myself to blame. And I'm not completely powerless. There're still those damned raiders to tackle.'

'Yes, indeed. Of course, they'd make life a lot easier if they didn't always seem to appear one step ahead of us – or behind us.' Micah was glad to change the subject.

Robert nodded and headed back for his wine, then stopped with the cup halfway to his mouth. 'You know, Micah, for the son of a farmer you can be pretty clever sometimes.'

'My lord?'

Robert drained the cup and thumped it down on the table. 'Call Deverin and have him gather a dozen of his best men – on fresh horses, mind. We're going out again – and this time, I know exactly where to look for these damned raiders!'

This was not the first time Robert had had to work discreetly. There were sixteen men to manage, plus Deverin, who had refused to stay behind. Twelve men on horseback, each making his own share of noise, and Robert had to use his powers to muffle the sounds of them all without drawing any attention to what he was doing. Micah knew, of course, and expertly shielded Robert from any casual glances. With luck, the men would be concentrating on their work too much to notice how quietly they were travelling.

They headed east, in the opposite direction and half an hour behind the other squad Robert had ordered out as an afterthought. If this didn't work, by sending out another party he would get a second crack at it.

'Are you sure you know where we're going, my lord?' Micah murmured, as soft as dew.

'Positive,' Robert nodded, his *ayarn* clutched firmly in his left hand. 'We scouted Wenlay Copse last night. Where better for them to hide than the last place we looked? Don't worry, my friend, they'll be there.'

The wind had risen by the time they neared their destination. As a kind of compensation, however, the moon also chose that moment to disappear behind a bank of heavy cloud. The darkness was complete, making Robert's task that much easier. He halted his men halfway up the rise of the moor and gathered them together.

'Listen carefully. It's my guess the raiders are camped in the copse below on the other side of this hill. We have to move slowly and in complete silence. Half of you will take the east side, the other half, the west. Come down as far as you dare without giving the alarm. Stop and wait for my signal. By now most of them will be asleep, as I'm sure you all wish you were. Still, there's bound to be a guard so I want you to wait until I've removed him before you strike. Good luck.'

In one movement, his men turned their horses and continued up the hill, splitting into two groups just short of the crest, then disappearing over the top. Micah waited beside Robert until they were gone, then said, 'What are you going to do? How far can they get without being seen?'

'Not far, I'm afraid. Come on, we have very little time.' He led Micah around the hill until they could see the edge of the copse. They were close enough to hear the trickle of water in the brook running into the valley. 'This will do. Leave the horses here.'

My but it would be useful to have Jenn's little trick of speaking mind to mind. It was just this sort of occasion that would benefit immensely. He dropped to the ground and felt Micah beside him. Together, they crawled through the heather, making no sound at all. Then, only thirty feet away, Robert stopped again and drew out his *ayarn*.

'Are you . . .' Micah whispered.

'Yes,' Robert replied, 'I'm going to try the biggest mask I've ever attempted. I need you to keep watch for that sentry.'

Micah turned his gaze out towards the copse, leaving Robert to focus on the stone in his hand. From here he could easily see the faint glow of dying camp fires between the trees. This was the place indeed.

He closed his eyes and took in a deep breath. Like most masks, he would have to do this without letting the *ayarn* glow. It was complicated, but not impossible. He let his thoughts calm and still, then, he reached deep inside and bullied up the power he required. He gathered it together in a single narrow beam, sent it through the *ayarn* and out into the wilderness. The stone obediently kept the beam rigid and tight, leaving him the freedom to direct it where he would. He spread it out in a sheet of blankness big enough to cover both sloping sides of the copse. Further and further he went, his senses stretching distances he'd never thought possible. Beneath the mask he could feel the heartbeats of each of his men, almost see their faces in the dark. Then . . .

'By the gods!' he whispered, 'there's a Malachi down there!'

Again he pushed further, until the circle was complete. All sides of the copse were now covered by the mask and anyone looking up from the camp would see nothing but the heather-covered hill. It would hold long enough for them to attack. Hopefully, the sleeping Malachi would remain ignorant of it as well.

'Right,' Robert breathed, 'let's go.'

At a crouch he ran down the slope to the edge of the brook and with the last of his energy, sent his senses out far enough to identify the sentry. He was only a few feet away, sitting with his back to a tree – dozing.

Robert glanced at Micah and waved him around to the

other side where the horses stood. However, while men might be fooled by a mask, the animals were oblivious to it. They heard the approaching men and stamped their feet in response. With jingling bridles and rattling bits, they produced enough noise to bring the sentry to his feet, before Robert could reach him.

'Alarm!' he cried – then gasped as Robert's dagger hit him in the chest. He fell to the ground with a thud, but the damage was done.

'Next time, we hit the horses first!' Robert grunted, then put his fingers to his lips and sent out a mighty whistle. He released the mask and instantly his men charged down the hill, yelling their battle cry. The pounding of horses on the moorland roused the rest of the camp and suddenly there were men flying everywhere, swords raised.

Robert darted through the trees swinging his sword left and right. He had to find that Malachi, and fast. The clash of swords echoed through the copse as men and horses screamed in the night. Half the camp fires were kicked out by men trying to hide, while the other half were burning brighter than ever. The wind stepped up, gusting with fervour through the tree tops above and sending a haze of dust through the camp.

Robert ran between the trees, searching for the Malachi. He reached the edge of the copse where the valley dropped away below. He was about to turn when a movement on his left stopped him. A sharp prod against his senses supplied the answer. A man, racing down the slope towards some scattered horses – the Malachi!

In a flash, Robert was after him, scrambling down the slope in a shower of rocks and stone. He came to the bottom in a neat roll but the man was already mounted and off. Without stopping, Robert jumped on the nearest horse and tore off after him.

Keeping his body low, Robert spurred his horse on, gradually gaining on his quarry. He drew level, then ducked as a sword came flying towards his face. The hit was wild, missing by inches, but Robert retaliated with a quickly aimed swing of his own. He heard a cry of pain and the horse stumbled but managed to keep going.

Side by side they galloped across the moor and through another wood. Robert ducked below branches as he sped along while hanging leaves slapped his face at every turn. Still he pursued, swinging out with his sword at every opportunity. They left the wood and sped across flat land, their horses slowing with exhaustion.

Suddenly the ground dropped below them and his quarry fell from his horse, tumbling down the slope into the darkness. Instantly, Robert jumped down and clambered after him, but by the time he got there, the man had his sword drawn and was ready.

'Who are you?' Robert demanded, parrying the first blow. Almost instinctively, his powers awoke and he swung his sword again with twice the force.

His opponent staggered back, his face creased in surprise. 'You? Dunlorn?' The shock lasted only a second and the Malachi lunged again, only this time he brought his own powers to bear. In a flash his sword glowed bright, blinding in the night. He swung with bitter determination, but Robert was ready. As their swords clashed, Robert's blade caught its own fire, drowning out his opponent.

Furious, the Malachi spun around. Robert took the opportunity and lunged forward, embedding his sword in the man's side. Slowly the Malachi crumpled to the ground. As the sword fell from his fingers, Robert thudded to his knees.

'Who are you?' he demanded of the dying man. 'Tell me, dammit! Who are you?'

A gurgle of air and a brief sigh were his only answers. Deflated in his victory, Robert sat back on his heels and caught his breath. Then, wearily, he climbed to his feet. With a last glance at the dead man, he shook his head and made his way up the slope to the horses. He mounted up and turned back to Wenlay Copse.

All was quiet when he returned. The fires had been rekindled, making the area almost as bright as day. Deverin had already begun the task of assembling the dead raiders while Micah was seeing to the wounded.

'Any survivors?' Robert asked, sliding down from his horse.

'I'm afraid not, my lord. They all fought to the death – like demons.' He finished tying the bandage around Alard Bain's arm then got up from his seat. From the look on his face, Robert knew that something was wrong. 'There's something you should see.'

Micah led him to the other side of the copse. There, close by a dwindling fire, lay the body of a raider. A huge gash in his arm and belly had spelled the end of his young life. Micah crouched down beside the youth and, with a glance back at the other men, murmured, 'I didn't think you would want the others to know about this, my lord. The gods know I wish I didn't.'

He reached down and drew back the cloth covering the young man's shoulder. Robert dropped to his knees to see the Mark clearly lit by the dying embers so close by.

'By the gods! This is not the work of Malachi – this is . . .' Robert ran out of words. He closed his eyes for a moment, trying to blot out the reality of it all. Then he nodded slowly and looked down again at the dead boy.

'You do recognize him?'

'Aye, by the mass, I do. He's Peter McGlashen – the House Mark is very clear.'

'But what was he doing . . .'

'He was one of the first taken during the Troubles, Micah, and I have no idea what he's doing with this lot. Did you examine the others?'

'Yes. I found him first, then checked the rest when I realized.'

Robert nodded. 'You did well to keep him apart from the others. I'll have Deverin get him back to Dunlorn somehow, in secret. I want to give him a proper burial in my chapel. He doesn't belong with these bandits, no matter what happened to him!'

He stood and began walking back, but Micah called after him, 'Are you going to tell the Duke?'

'No!' Robert bellowed and continued towards the firelight.

Robert balanced the tray on one hand, tucked the scrolls under his arm and with the other hand reached out and opened the door to Finnlay's room. His brother, lying flat on the bed and covered in a jumble of rugs and papers, turned his head and sighed.

'Oh, not more food. I swear that doctor thinks my illness is born of starvation!'

Robert grinned and placed the tray down. 'Well, don't blame me. I'm only following orders.'

'And brought by the very hand of the lord himself! I am honoured.' Finnlay elbowed himself up until his back rested against the pillows. 'Or rather, I should be.'

'I see your temper hasn't improved,' Robert murmured equably. He pushed aside some of the papers and perched on the end of the bed. 'Still, you look a lot better today. How do you feel?'

'After a week stuck in here? You really want an answer to that?'

'Then you're definitely getting better. Good. Here, I thought I'd bring these in as well. No use you sitting here getting too idle.'

'Why didn't you tell me earlier that you'd brought all these books back from your travels? There's a few here that people at the Enclave would kill to get a look at. Then again, I suppose that's why you didn't tell me.'

'Believe it or not, there was no deliberate intention on my part. You were never around long enough to show you. It's your own fault.'

Finnlay shook his head and turned away from the manuscripts. 'I don't know, Robert. None of this other business makes any sense. Why would the Malachi abduct all those children and then leave Jenn in Shan Moss? I agree that despite that fellow you killed, none of this is anything like the Malachi activity we're used to. They've never resorted to raids like this on ordinary folk. They've always concentrated on us – on trying to find the Key!'

'Unless they've suddenly changed tactics.' Robert shrugged. After a week, he'd come no closer to an answer himself. It was more worrying to think of Valena operating so close to the King.

Finnlay was silent for a moment, then he sighed, 'Look, I've been thinking . . .'

'Oh, dear.'

Finnlay raised his hand, 'What I said to you, back at the Enclave – I had no right. I just want to say I'm sorry.'

Robert sat back a little and raised his eyebrows. 'What's brought this on?'

'Nothing in particular. I don't understand why you kept the Key's words to you a secret, but I can accept it. I won't mention it again.'

Robert turned away, unable to meet that steady gaze. He stood slowly and poured them both a cup of ale from the tray. Handing one to Finnlay, Robert took his and wandered over to the window. This was unexpected. That Finn should now, after all these years, virtually set him free was a welcome but nonetheless unsettling surprise. That it should concern the Key was even more unsettling. Perhaps it was time for the truth after all, or at least the part of the truth he could get away with revealing. Yes, Finnlay deserved that much, if nothing else.

He took a deep breath, but kept his eyes on the purple fields of heather high on the moor. 'I appreciate how difficult it was to say that. I also appreciate how you felt at the time. It must have been very hard to find out that I'd been lying to you all these years when I told you that the Key's words to me had nothing to do with the Enclave. It must have been quite a shock. It was to me.'

The fever had slowed Finnlay's reactions, but not so much that he could miss the hesitation in Robert's voice. Robert could hear the breath of suspicion in Finnlay's single question. 'What do you mean?'

Robert dropped his head and shook it slightly. After

almost twenty years, he found it very difficult to even think the thoughts, let alone speak them aloud. 'I mean I was shocked that the Key had told you a lie.'

Silence.

After a moment, Robert finally turned his head to find his brother staring at him with incredulity ... and something that looked a little bit like pride. Robert shrugged. 'It's true. I couldn't answer you that day because I couldn't grasp what you'd said. I found it impossible to believe that the Key would deliberately tell you something which I knew was untrue. I still can't work out why it did. It doesn't make any sense.'

An ironic smile drifted across Finnlay's pale face and even made it up to his eyes. 'Sense? Hah! But just go back a little. Am I still fevered or are you actually trying to tell me that when the Key spoke to you all those years ago it didn't forbid you to Stand the Circle?'

Robert nodded.

Finnlay took in a breath and held it for a few seconds, then abruptly let it out noisily. 'Well! If I hadn't heard it myself I wouldn't have believed it. You don't know how much ...'

'Oh, believe me, I do,' Robert interrupted, moving to the end of the bed again.

'But why did the Key lie to me in the first place? Up till now we'd always assumed it could only tell the truth – that it was merely a receptacle of information, or a guide at the very least. Now it seems it has the ability to think for itself. Except ... Except that you've known about that all along.' He knitted his brows together. 'Forgive me, Robert, but what did it tell you?'

Robert smiled faintly. This was definitely the hard part. He drained his cup of ale and balanced it on a flat part of the bed. Resuming his perch once more he laced his hands together in a patient gesture. 'Actually, to be brutally honest, I can't tell you.'

As Finnlay began to protest, Robert held up his hands. 'No. I mean that literally – I can't actually tell you. I can't speak the words out loud, I can't hint as to their meaning, I can't even tell you the general subject. I physically cannot tell you. And, forgive me, but even if I could, I wouldn't.'

'Why?'

'Because,' Robert paused, choosing the only part of the truth he dared speak, 'because there's a very good reason why the Key won't let me. I know that's difficult to understand, but if you look at it from my perspective it does make sense. The Key told me something very . . . dangerous. I don't know why it told me, of all people, but nonetheless, knowing what it is, I would rather no one else knew it.'

A slow smile lit Finnlay's face. 'By the gods, Robert, you really are one of a kind. But tell me, if I asked you a direct question, would you be able to answer it?'

'I might.'

'Take pity on me, Robert. I've nothing else to do and I'm bored stupid. Indulge me.'

Robert chuckled. 'Very well.'

Finnlay began, pursing his lips in thought. 'I shall assume you will refrain from hitting me as I'm sick in bed – but tell me, this secret the Key imparted to you – did it tell you where the Calyx is hidden?'

'By the gods, no!' Robert laughed.

'All right then, I accept your explanation. Out of respect for your wishes, I will enquire no further.'

'Heaven save us!' Robert laughed again, 'you're suffering a relapse. You've finally developed a sense of humour!'

'Don't pick on me, Robert, I'm sick.'

'Oh, and you think that makes a difference? You know the saying, Finn: the best time to kick a dog is when it's down.'

'Yes, yes, all right,' Finnlay grumbled, but he couldn't disguise the smile on his face. 'By the way, did you read that passage about Bonding? Where is it?'

He rifled through the papers until he came up with the right manuscript. He spread it out and ran a finger down the script until he reached the point he was looking for. 'Yes, that's it. You know how we'd always assumed the Budlandi lost the meaning of Bonding centuries before the formation of the Enclave? Well, it turns out we were the ones who lost it, back in the first days of the Enclave. Remember they had a fire which destroyed most of the library they brought from Bu? Well, the whole thing was listed down in there. The reasons, pairings – everything. Only a few of them still exist.'

'But Bonding was just their way of arranging marriages, Finn. What has it to do with us?'

'Where's your curiosity? I thought you were a historian. Listen. I'll have to translate as I go, but ... um ... Yes, *To the blessed god of thunder and rain be given the right to Bond together these two, whose mutual tenets will remain undivided to the end of their days. Theirs will be a ... er ... happy and fulfilled union* – or something like that – *and once joined as such will be indivisible by any mortal. Those whom the gods have chosen are Bonded from birth and must by all faiths and determinations, fulfil their destiny together. For those who are Bonded will be no other.*'

Finnlay glanced up. 'Sorry about the translation. I'll do a proper one once that doctor lets me out of this bed. By the sound of it, Bonding was meant to continue even if we knew nothing about it. Perhaps you and Berenice were Bonded ...'

Robert couldn't sit there any longer. He got up without a word and strode to the door.

'Robert? Wait!' Finnlay climbed out of bed and stumbled across the room. 'What did I say?'

How could Robert explain? How could he even broach the subject? Keeping his thoughts reined in tight, he shook his head sharply.

'Please, Robert,' Finnlay put his hand on the door, blocking Robert's exit. 'Tell me what's wrong.'

Slowly, painfully slowly, Robert turned his head until he met Finnlay's gaze. 'There's nothing wrong, Finn. Go back to bed.'

But Finnlay wouldn't let him go. 'There's something you're not telling me. What is it? Is it about Berenice? About Bonding? What ...'

His voice trailed off, and abruptly, Finnlay took in a sharp breath. Silently, Robert willed him to forget it but didn't dare reach out and push the thought away. Finnlay would sense the interference. But he could not – must not – put the pieces together!

This day, the gods were not with Robert.

'You *were* Bonded to Berenice!' Finnlay breathed, his eyes widening in shock. 'That's what the Key told you, isn't it? But how can that be dangerous?'

That was enough. Robert snatched Finnlay's hand away from the door and spun him around. Without pausing, he propelled him back to the bed. 'You're still delirious, Finn. I'm sorry but I can't discuss this further with you.'

But Finnlay struggled, 'Stop it, Robert! All right, I know you can't tell me – but why? Why don't you ever speak about Berenice? Ever? You refuse to marry again, even to get an heir. Why? Is it because you were Bonded? Is it because she died? Is this the dangerous thing? Was there something else the Key told you? Please, Robert, tell me what happened!'

'No!'

Finnlay's eyes flared with anger and he did something entirely foolish. He grabbed Robert's arm and focused all his meagre powers to hold Robert still. Like swatting a fly, Robert unleashed his own powers and slapped Finnlay backwards on to the bed. Instantly he regretted it. Where had his control gone? All those years schooling himself and now, just like that, he'd come so close to losing control of the demon!

Robert clenched his fists and took in a harsh breath. 'You want to know, do you? You think if I tell you, if I talk about it, then it will all go away. Well it won't, Finn. Not ever.'

Now there was no anger in Finnlay's voice, in his eyes. There was nothing but calm, and perhaps even pity. 'Did the Key name Berenice?'

'Of course not!' Robert snapped back, then paused. That was the closest he'd ever got to speaking about any part of the Key's message.

'Then how do you know it meant Berenice?' Finnlay crept

316

forward, pressing his advantage. 'Why won't you tell me what happened?'

Robert closed his eyes and straightened up. He was drained, of energy, of will, even of desire to keep the truth from Finnlay. This had gone too far and now there was only one way to stop it. For ever.

He opened his eyes to find Finnlay watching him carefully. Slowly and with painful precision, Robert began to speak. 'When I got back here, she was already ill with a fever. She was drenched in sweat and crying out with the pain. The doctors could do nothing for her so, believing I could help, I sent them away for a few minutes. We were alone but she didn't know me. She didn't recognize me. She just held her belly and cried out for the child she carried. I wanted so much to help her, to comfort her, so I took her hand, brought out my *ayarn* and reached forward to ease her pain. I sent my senses out, touched her and the child. For a moment it worked. Then something seemed to take hold of the power and twist it around. I couldn't control it and before I knew it, Berenice screamed and died in my arms.'

Robert took in a deep breath, his eyes still on Finnlay. 'I killed her, brother. I killed my own wife.'

The chapel bell rang twice, paused, then rang a third time. Its baleful sound echoed across the sandstone cloister and floated up to the abbey church beyond. Within the square, a tall oak spread its branches to caress the cloister roof and cover the grass below with shade. A brick well stood in one corner of the square, capped by a wooden lid now littered with a fine sprinkling of dust.

Lady Margaret Douglas gazed down on the cloister from her room above and watched as a novice approached the well and began drawing water. From up here, it looked like Sister Helen, with her long, fine fingers and square set shoulders. She wore the habit of the House, grey robe and black mantle, with the white veil of the novice. Against the shaded backdrop, the veil looked almost luminous as it caught the sunshine, a halo of soft linen. Margaret looked

317

away and up over the top of the church to where the peaks of the surrounding cliffs rose towards the mountains. The air was clear and fine up here, so far from town or village. When Saint Hilary had founded the abbey more than two hundred years ago it had been her wish to separate the order from the daily trials of ordinary life. For the first fifty years that wish had proved hard to fulfil, with the abbey completely cut off for almost all of the winter months. Hilary had died an ancient woman of eighty, her bones resting under the altar of the church, and since then a small but strong community had grown up around the abbey. They were still cut off and most definitely separated from the rest of the world, but there was less of a struggle to survive. Saint Hilary's was isolated, remote and very peaceful: the perfect retreat for a widow unable or perhaps just unwilling to cast aside her mourning.

A flicker of movement on the ridge above caught Margaret's eye and she watched it for a moment as it came closer and separated into the shape of two riders. As they came down the steep slope Margaret found she could recognize at least one by the flaming red hair which floated around in the sunlight. The other man could therefore be only one person. She waited a little longer, then turned and made her way downstairs to the reception room.

After a few minutes, the door opened and Margaret smiled. 'Heavens, Robert! Two visits in less than a month! What can you be thinking of?'

Her son moved forward and took both her hands in his. He leaned down and kissed her cheek, his face cold from the ride. 'I thought you might be missing me.'

'And Micah!' Margaret took a step forward. 'How are you? I haven't seen you since you got back. Are you pleased to be home, or is it a little dull after the exotic climes of the last few years?'

Micah bowed over her hand. 'You are looking radiant as ever, Lady Margaret.'

Margaret shot a glance at her son. 'He's learned to be courtly, Robert! What have you two been up to?'

318

Robert took her hand and tucked it in the crook of his arm, then led her through the door and out into the sunshine. 'I do my best but there are some things I just have no control over. Unfortunately, Micah is one of them.'

A quiet chuckle from behind told Margaret that Micah followed them. She glanced aside at Robert. Her eldest son appeared to have weathered winter without harm. He looked well, if not necessarily happy. Every time she saw him, however, it struck her how much he looked like his father. More than a handspan taller than she, Robert sported the same wavy dark hair which occasionally glinted with auburn in the light of a summer sunset. His brow was clear and graced with the same level eyebrows which were so expressive of his moods. Robert had even inherited his father's green eyes, though a darker hue. His straight nose and wide, generous mouth gave way to a firm jaw and when laughing, made her think that Trevor did indeed live on in his son.

And there was something else Robert had inherited: his father's charm. Or was it charisma? Something both men had in full measure, Robert perhaps even more. It was a quality that made people trust and believe in him, made him an easy hero to worship. A quality that made him attractive in more ways than one. But, unlike his father, Robert had always remained completely unaware of the effect he had on other people.

Yes, he was handsome, this son of hers – handsome enough to make even a few of the novices notice when he came to visit. However, not knowing him as Margaret did, there were a few things they did miss. Like the way there was no spring in his step any more, nor any glint of genuine delight in his sea green eyes. Robert put on a good performance, but mothers are not so easily fooled.

'You know, Robert,' she said after a moment, 'my sisters here are very disturbed by your constant visits. It took days for them to get over the last one.'

For a moment, Robert looked a little startled and she had to smile. He had a dry enough wit himself and was therefore surprised when someone else used it on him.

He grinned. 'Afraid they'll throw you out, mother? I'm surprised they haven't already.'

'I'll thank you not to cast aspersions on my character. I'm your mother, show some respect.'

They took a path along the garden edge which wound between hedges of lavender and rosemary then up to the potters' kiln on the other side. From there Margaret could see her favourite panorama of the mountains and the narrow valley in which the abbey lay.

'This is a nice spot, isn't it?' Robert said, gazing out at the view.

Margaret let go his arm and sat down on a tree stump which still clung tenaciously to the rocky ground. 'You say that every time you come up here. Forgive me, my dear, but is there a specific reason you came? Not that I'm complaining, I just wondered. Is anything wrong?'

Robert glanced over his shoulder at her, then at Micah, who dusted off a neighbouring tree stump for himself. 'I thought I'd let you know how Finnlay was.'

'You're not bored, are you?' Margaret couldn't help herself. There was always something about Robert's detached calm which encouraged her to prod him. She knew Finnlay felt the same way about Robert, but he saw it more as a challenge.

'Bored, mother?' Robert raised his eyebrows in mock horror. 'Never. I came to tell you how your younger son is. Duty, mother, duty.'

Margaret nodded, but smiled nonetheless. 'And how is Finnlay?'

'Much better. He's up and about now, even if he does still need rest. But that's what you get for riding off to Marsay in the spring rains.'

Margaret felt her good mood dissipate as quickly as frost on a hot day. 'He went to Marsay?'

Robert shrugged. 'There was little I could do to stop him, short of forbidding him.'

'Then you should have.' Margaret stood and clasped her hands together in a gesture designed to encourage patience.

'I know we're far from everything up here, but we do hear what happens, at least within the Church. We know all about Bishop McCauly and that fool Brome. Saint Hilary's is afire with gossip about it. I should have thought you'd have more sense than to allow your brother to go walking into a mire like that. Why, anything could have happened.'

Robert turned and gazed down on her with easy reassurance. 'Mother, he was all right. Finnlay just went to find out for himself how bad things really were. No one knew he was there. You don't need to worry.'

'Worry?' Margaret almost laughed at the suggestion. 'Ever since the day I decided to come here and leave you two alone at Dunlorn I have worried about you. And you have given me cause – not least because at times, I thought you would actually kill each other. But I was determined to leave you to your own lives. But worry? Why should I worry, Robert? After all the things you've done, the places you've wandered, the Kings you have upset, why on earth should I worry?'

Robert laughed and wrapped his arms around her, planting a kiss on her forehead. 'Oh, mother. What would I do without you?'

Margaret drew back from him with a slightly acerbic smile, 'I can give you a list, if you like. And don't give me that worldly, comforting smile, Robert. Neither you nor your brother can be trusted – Micah will support me on this, won't you?'

'I wouldn't dare contradict you, my lady.'

With a glance at the young man, Margaret returned to her tree stump. She wasn't really angry, nor even irritated. The simple fact that Robert had allowed Finnlay to go to Marsay told her that her sons were finally on reasonable speaking terms. For the moment, that was enough. Clasping her hands together on her lap, she asked, 'So how are things at home?'

'Why don't you come back with me and see for yourself?'

'I can't, Robert. You know why.' Margaret gazed at her

son for a moment, wondering if there was some other reason why he had come all the way up here to see her.

'But you do have a life there. You could make one. It's your home, mother.'

'No. Not without your father. You have no idea how bad it was for the first few weeks after he died. As much as I wanted to be with you while you were imprisoned there, I was so glad I didn't have to be in that place without Trevor. I beg you to understand. Without your father, I have only a half life left. Part of me died with him and the remaining part is better off here at the abbey, where I can at least teach a few meagre skills to the novices and postulates. I dare not even take the veil because I cannot give myself fully to the service of the gods. You two don't need me around and you know it. Please, don't ask me again.'

Robert's eyes remained glued to hers for a moment, then he looked away. 'Do you remember the day you met my father?'

'As clearly as I'm seeing you. Why?'

'Do you remember what you thought when you saw him? The very first thing that came to your mind?'

Margaret couldn't miss the uncharacteristic intensity in her son's gaze, but she didn't flinch. 'Yes, I remember.'

'What?'

She shrugged. 'He's the one.'

Robert's eyebrows rose in surprise. That particular expression had always made him look a little vulnerable, and this time was no different. 'And you never doubted it? Afterwards? When you got to know him?'

'I only became more certain – I still am to this day. Robert, what's this about? Are you thinking of marrying again? Have you met someone?'

Her son shook his head and a gust of breeze tossed a strand of hair across his eyes. He reached up and brushed it away. 'No. Nothing like that. Sorry. It's just something Finn and I were discussing.'

'To do with what?'

322

'Just some old manuscripts he was reading. History. Nothing more. Forget it.'

She was tempted to do as he suggested, but for the life of her she couldn't make the connection between her meeting Trevor and some historical manuscript. However, there was no point in questioning him any further. Once Robert decided not to talk about something, there was no changing his mind.

'My lord.'

Micah interrupted her thoughts and she looked up. The young man with the flaming red hair was standing and pointing out along the valley. Racing towards them across the gently sloping fields was a rider. The horse beneath him was exhausted and galloped unsteadily. As it crept towards them she could see white foam about its mouth and a layer of sweat on its hide. Whoever it was, he was in a big hurry.

'Can you see who it is?' Micah murmured moving to stand beside Robert and Margaret.

Robert shook his head. 'No. But it looks important.'

The lay workers who tilled the land of the abbey had stopped work to watch the rider pass by. A few had gathered before the gate and were ready when the horse came to a stumbling halt. Barely waiting for them to take its head, the rider jumped down and, receiving instructions, ran through the gate and up the steps towards the garden.

Margaret glanced at her son, then turned to where the steps came out behind the lavender hedge. Moments later the man appeared, dust and mud smeared over his clothes while an empty scabbard swung idly at his side. He caught sight of them and rushed over with what seemed the last of his strength. He took one look at Robert and sank to his knees.

'My lord,' he gasped air in ragged breaths, 'I have ridden long and hard with most grave news.'

Margaret found her hands clutch together against the words she most feared. McCauly. Something must have happened.

Robert, with more steadiness than she, moved a step

forward. 'Calmly now, man. Get some air into your lungs first, then tell me.'

'Sad tidings, my lord,' the man seemed unable to lift his head. 'I come to tell you of a treacherous battle – and that your uncle, His Grace the Duke of Haddon, is dead.'

# 14

'Well, I must say, Jenny, that it's all been very quiet so far,' Lawrence smiled as he accompanied her into the shady garden. 'Perhaps Bella's fears will turn out to be unfounded.'

'Perhaps,' Jenn replied absently, glancing at the others in the garden. It may have seemed quiet to Lawrence, but after two weeks in Marsay, Jenn had discovered the court was a hive of all sorts of activity, some of which was obvious and some of which was almost invisible. For example, there was the Dowager Duchess of Coily, whose son was in love with one of the Queen's ladies, but the Duchess disapproved of the match and so the lovers had to meet in secret. It appeared that all the court, with the exception of Her Grace, knew about it. There seemed no end to the amount of gossip which passed from one group to another. Just when Jenn had thought she'd heard the latest, another piece would fall into her lap. Not that she eavesdropped as such, but it was difficult to be unaware of the web of intrigue.

Lawrence was a better guide than Bella. He was easygoing and knew quite a few of the people at court. He'd spent a lot of time there off and on over the years and continued to keep in contact. He escorted Jenn with all the deference of a knight accompanying a Queen and at times had Jenn laughing with his chivalrous manner, as though it were a private joke between them. It was Lawrence alone who had made those first few days bearable. Especially now with the news about Robert's uncle. Jenn longed to leave court, go to Dunlorn, but what could she do? Robert had lost his uncle and nothing would ever change that.

As Lawrence led her to a quiet bench by the pond, Jenn caught sight of the Queen surrounded by a small group of ladies but, like everyone else at court, she hardly glanced in

Jenn's direction. There was a well-dressed man sitting close by Rosalind and they seemed to be deep in conversation, but at this distance, Jenn could only guess what they talked about.

She'd met the Queen officially on the evening of their second day. The Queen had been polite, welcomed her to court, but said nothing more. Jenn had been glad of the easy escape. She was not altogether sure of what she could possibly say to a Queen. Of Selar she had seen almost nothing, only glimpsed him once at the end of the room. The tall fair-haired man had barely noticed her presence, but that did nothing to alleviate Jenn's disquiet.

After a few moments of silence, Lawrence said, 'I wanted to talk to you about Bella. Principally to ask you to be patient.'

Jenn glanced aside at him. 'What makes you think I'm not?'

'Oh, nothing really,' Lawrence gave her a companionable smile. 'It's just that sometimes your face gives you away. When you first arrived at Elita I could hardly begin to know what you were thinking. Now it's not so difficult.'

'I do my best,' she murmured, dropping her head, 'but patience is not my strong point.'

'Oh, don't take it as a criticism, Jenny,' Lawrence patted her arm, 'I meant only to suggest that you give her a little more time. Your sudden arrival has caused a huge change in her life.'

'I know, Lawrence,' Jenn nodded. 'I promise I'll try.'

'Good.' He smiled, then froze as his eyes focused on something behind her. In a more conspiratorial voice he added, 'Have your best curtsey ready, Jenny dear. I think the King is finally making his move.'

Jenn's eyes widened, but she had enough self-control to stop herself from spinning around in her seat to see. When she did move, she took her cue from Lawrence, standing as he did and turning around to drop to a low curtsey. Remembering Bella's admonitions on the subject, she remained down, staring at a pair of silver-trimmed grey boots for some minutes. Then a distinctly superior and slightly amused voice bade her rise.

'So, this is Jacob's child. Stand up straight, girl, and let me take a look at you.'

Jenn let her eyes rise only as far as the emerald pendant which hung around Selar's throat. Her heart was beating wildly and she didn't dare open her mouth to say a word.

'Yes. You have the look of Ross about you.' Then impatiently, 'Oh, cease this demure behaviour, child, and look me in the eye!'

Jenn was only marginally aware of Lawrence beside her and the man who stood beside the King. She lifted her eyes to meet Selar's, while trying desperately to get some control over her heartbeat.

The face that greeted her was not quite what she'd expected. He was older than she'd thought, about forty-five, tall and solid. His grey eyes were narrowed and topped with fair brows which were brought together as if in deep thought. An aquiline nose rested above a fine-lipped mouth set at the moment somewhere between a grin and a sneer – it was difficult to decide which. His finely modulated voice erred on the quiet side, as though he knew he would be heard regardless of how he spoke. His bearing was that of a man who was accustomed to power, and who knew how to use it.

So this was Robert's great and closest friend. Or had been.

Selar spoke again. 'I'm pleased you were able to accept my invitation to court. It had occurred to me that because of your rather odd upbringing you might enjoy a spring in Marsay.'

Jenn noted the pause and realized he expected her to say something. She opened her mouth and some words came out. 'Yes, thank you, Sire.'

The King leaned a little closer to her. 'I suppose your father was quite surprised to find you were still alive after all these years. You must have had quite a few stories to tell him.'

'Yes, Sire.'

'And do you like our beautiful city?'

Jenn swallowed and tried to stop her throat from going dry. 'Yes, Sire.'

Selar straightened up, but the grim smile never left his face. 'Yes, I hope you do enjoy your stay with us, my lady, and perhaps while you're here, we may even be able to find you a husband. I'm sure your father would not object.'

He turned to the man on his left. 'Remind me to look into it, will you, Nash?'

'Certainly, Sire.'

Jenn shot a glance at him, but he only smiled gently and she turned her attention back to the King. Selar moved as if he would turn away, but paused. Slowly the smile drifted from his face. 'It would be injudicious of me not to enquire about your erstwhile rescuer, Dunlorn. It was he, was it not, who so conveniently found you and returned you to Elita?'

Not content with merely beating madly, Jenn's heart now leapt to her mouth. 'Yes, Sire.'

'A hero to your father, no doubt – but of course, I was forgetting; your father thinks Dunlorn is a traitor, doesn't he?'

Jenn couldn't reply. It was impossible to guess how far this questioning would go, and there were so many things she didn't dare say. If only Selar would forget all about Robert, stop asking her about him, just move on. She wanted to reach out and push him on his way.

As though in response to her silent plea, Selar gave a low chuckle. 'A word of advice, child. See no more of Robert Douglas, Earl of Dunlorn and now Duke of Haddon. I'm sure your father will appreciate the wisdom of it, even if you don't. Lawrence.' Selar nodded to them both, then, with Nash at his side, walked away. Jenn watched him pass by the Queen with only the slightest inclination of his head, then he left the garden.

Beside her, Lawrence let out a noisy sigh. 'And I pray to the gods that will be the last of it. You did well. Jacob will be proud.'

'Proud?' Jenn's eyes stayed on the Queen's little group,

who were glancing in her direction. 'Of what? Of the fact that I didn't disgrace him?'

Lawrence laughed quietly. 'Come, I think we should go and report to your sister. With any luck, Bella will relax a little after this. I'm just glad she wasn't with us. She doesn't like Selar at all. She's always blamed him for Jacob's accident. Come.'

With his hand on her elbow, Lawrence firmly led Jenn back to their rooms.

Rosalind left the garden with Kandar and her ladies trailing behind. She couldn't get any closer to Selar. Even if she'd asked about McCauly, Selar wouldn't tell her anything. Her questions would only irritate him and there was every chance he would then refuse to let her visit McCauly in the future. So how else to serve the Bishop? How could she tell if Selar intended him harm?

Kandar? Would he be able to do something? He was Selar's cousin, after all. Selar wouldn't suspect him of having any other motives for asking about McCauly – and Selar was more likely to tell his own cousin the truth of his intentions. Yes, that was it. The best way. The only way. And then she could get a message to Godfrey.

But how was she to ask such a thing of George? Directly, with her ladies listening and watching everyone she spoke to? Or indirectly – and have him completely misunderstand her questions?

Then he would ask Selar who would immediately know who was really asking the question . . . and . . . and . . .

What was the point? None of them were in a position to get McCauly free. Even Godfrey had refrained from making such a promise. For Rosalind to try anything so obvious would show her hand and achieve nothing. All she could really do was wait and listen. Patience.

Patience and hope.

It wasn't much, but it was a world better than nothing at all.

\*

'But Sire, I beg you to reconsider. You've already signed the warrant; all that's left is to assign a date for execution. It would be unwise to wait any longer.'

Nash watched Vaughn work himself up into a sweat with yet another appeal to the King. Vaughn was so explosive these days, Nash wondered how Selar put up with him. As always, the King merely nodded with an ironic smile which was, to Nash's eyes, extremely insulting. Vaughn was oblivious to it, though, and continued on regardless.

'If Blair is allowed to live, then there is no doubt he will be a figure others will seek to support. If he . . .'

'Did I say I was going to let Blair live?' Selar stood and walked the length of the empty council table. 'I merely said I was not ready to fix a date. I want to make him sweat a little. His wife and son are still in custody. As long as we have them, Blair and whatever supporters he has left will keep their places. I expect I will make a decision some time next week. Oh, and while we're on the subject, I thought I told you I wanted both Blair and Haddon alive. Why do I have only one prisoner?'

Vaughn shrugged indifferently. 'An unfortunate accident, Sire. Haddon would not surrender and fought with the intention of not being taken. I have questioned the soldier who killed him and the man appears to have had little choice.'

'Nevertheless,' Selar nodded, 'I want that man punished. Not severely, mind, just a reminder that I prefer my orders obeyed — even if he did do me a favour by removing Haddon.'

'Yes, Sire. And about Dunlorn?'

'What of him?'

'Surely it's time to send a deputation to him, to find out what his involvement with his uncle was? He must have known about the treachery beforehand. If he is implicated, he too must be punished.'

'Must?' Selar spat the word out. 'When I want to know anything about Dunlorn, I'll ask! Not before.'

'But Sire, you cannot go on protecting him like this. With

McCauly and Blair incarcerated, Dunlorn would have no trouble gaining support from the people to march against you, if only to secure their release.'

Selar's voice dropped low. 'I told you once before, Proctor. Dunlorn will never stand against me, you understand? Never. I have made the decision to leave him be, much as I did with Jacob Ross, ten years ago. Let them both stew. They cannot and will not harm me and they are better left to quietly rot, out of sight and mind of the sympathetic people. Dunlorn's inaction will quickly drain away any support he might have had on his return, and as to his involvement with Blair? We have no proof that he knew anything about it. I'm satisfied with that and I expect you to be, too. Do I make myself clear?'

Vaughn puffed himself up, setting his jaw at a solid angle. 'Yes, Sire.'

As Vaughn bowed and left, Selar glanced down the table at Nash. 'He gets himself in such a tangle, the fool. I'd respect him more if he could learn to control that ridiculous temper of his.'

Nash risked a smile. 'You would not be alone there, Sire.'

Selar drew a chair out from the table. Sinking on to it, he sighed, 'I wouldn't bother putting up with him if I didn't still need the support of the Guilde. Is there any chance that Osbert is in a position to replace him?'

'Not as yet, no.'

'A pity,' Selar grunted.

Nash laced his fingers together, 'Can I ask you a question?'

'Certainly.'

'Why do you still protect Dunlorn? Oh, I appreciate that you don't want to make a direct move on him, especially so soon after his uncle's death. You don't want a martyr on your hands. But I guess there is more to it.'

Selar nodded slowly and cast his gaze down to his hands. 'There is, Sam, much more.'

Nash waited a while, knowing that Selar would eventually say more if he were given the time.

'Vaughn and the others continue to assume that I still feel

I owe Dunlorn my life,' Selar continued after a moment. 'Perhaps in some way I do, but my actions aren't motivated by emotion. I can't tell you why I removed him from the council – but suffice to say that the moment Dunlorn left Marsay things changed quite dramatically. You must understand how formidable an opponent he was. While he stood beside me, I enjoyed watching him in action, the way he demolished any opposing argument. But it was never going to last for ever. I think both of us knew it. He was certainly useful at the time.'

'And still is.'

Selar smiled a little. 'While Vaughn rages against my intractability over Dunlorn, he's not berating me about anything else. And who knows when I'll need a conveniently placed scapegoat?'

Selar stood abruptly and stretched. 'No. Things are better as they are. I would rather Robert stay out of my way than face the prospect of opposing him again. Besides, Vaughn is way too sensitive on the subject. He claims he has good reason but refuses to say what. I think Robert has lost any desire to do battle again. He has no more will to lead than your average sheep. Regardless of what Vaughn says or thinks, Robert swore an oath to me. I know for a fact that he would rather die than break that oath. He once warned me that if I ever struck at his family he would destroy me. Well, by killing his dear uncle, I've done just that, but I've heard not a peep from Dunlorn. As I say, Robert is a spent force. By the way,' Selar came around the table and ushered Nash through the open doorway, 'what do you make of Jacob's little brat?'

Nash raised an eyebrow. 'She's pretty enough, though she doesn't seem to have anything useful to say for herself. I suppose your intimidating presence might have had something to do with it.'

Selar laughed and clapped him on the shoulder. 'As it should. I'll leave the rest up to you – after all, it was your idea to bring her here in the first place. You find out if she's as thick as she seems, or if she's genuinely intent on taking the veil. One way or the other, we have to get her a husband, someone I can trust. We need to do it before Jacob can. Talk to her, get her confidence – but whatever you do, make sure that sister of hers is not around. I swear that woman has a tongue sharper than my sword!'

Nash smiled and laughed along with Selar. Certainly he would talk to her. By all means; what else could he do but obey the command of the King?

The night was silent and still. Even the city was quiet now, wrapped up in a peaceful slumber that was undoubtedly far from innocent. With only the church bell to strike the hour, Nash settled into his favourite seat by the window and closed his eyes.

Five times over the last few weeks he had tried this, yet every attempt to find the rogue sorcerer had failed. But rather than still his fears, this absence of discovery merely deepened his concern. Could it be possible that there was someone he'd missed? Had his carefully planned efforts to neutralize the Enemy failed, that now, with the Ally so close, the Enemy had surfaced?

It was inconceivable – and yet, not entirely impossible. There was a small chance that he'd not found all of the children born at that time.

But no. That touch had come from someone very powerful indeed. Why, even Nash had not been so strong at eighteen years of age.

Then, it wasn't the Enemy. It was someone else. But who?

Nash took in a deep breath and held it hard in his chest. He brought his hands together and touched the blood-red garnet ring he always wore on his left hand. He focused, still and silent. His breathing stopped, his thoughts faded. Dark and strong, he sent his senses out into the city.

There was Valena, asleep in her little house not far from the Guilde Hall. Her aura was so bright, so familiar, he could see her as clear as day. There were others too, Vaughn, Osbert, his brothers in the Guilde Hall. Then further out, down the sharp slope of the mount, towards the river.

Thousands of tiny, sleeping auras, powerless, impotent and fruitless. These were different to sorcerers; they were pale, lifeless, almost invisible except to the practised eye. He moved on again, down to the river. Down to the cold water. Around the wall and back up towards the castle. More and more of them, all unaware of his sensitive touch. The King, councillors, courtiers. All there. All except—

His eyes snapped open. No! It wasn't possible! Not after all his work. She couldn't have done it alone!

But she had. It was obvious now – painfully obvious. That touch he'd felt the first night she was here. It was her – the Ally. Somehow, despite all his efforts, she had developed her powers independently of him and now he had no control over her at all!

Nash leapt out of his seat and stormed across the room, but he wasn't going anywhere; he was filled with the sudden energy of a man who senses danger. Real, living, blood-swirling danger. Abruptly he stopped his pacing and glanced down at the ring on his hand. Unbidden, laughter welled up inside him and he shook his head in bizarre delight.

So, it would be a much greater challenge. But then, he always knew she would not be easy to turn. But she was the Ally and there was nothing she could do about that. The best part was: now he knew the Enemy was out of it!

With that comforting thought, Nash threw off his clothes and fell into bed. He went to sleep with a smile on his face.

Jenn wandered along the corridor quite alone. Bella had finally allowed her out on her own, but Jenn was not interested in seeking any other company. Peace was all she wanted right now. There were still another two weeks before they could safely leave Marsay. Two long, dreary and tense weeks. Two more weeks where Jenn would have to watch every word, every gesture. Two weeks during which any small thing could go hopelessly wrong. The King had spoken to her now and seemed content to leave her alone, but what did that mean? Had he finished with her? Was she just supposed to sit around waiting for him to find a convenient husband as he'd said?

What was the point in caring about it all? She was powerless to stop him, powerless to do anything other than what she was told. More surely than if she'd been imprisoned, she was trapped. Completely and utterly. Trapped in a life at odds with everything she'd ever expected.

The corridor was lined with windows on one side which let pools of bright sunlight dapple the wooden floor. Along the other side were doors; at the end, the passage turned sharply left. As she rounded the corner, however, the sound of voices ahead made her pause. With a hand against the stone wall, she stretched her head forward to see who was speaking. Two ladies of wealth and rank, judging by their dress, were wandering backwards and forwards before a bay window, while a third, older woman sat on the cushioned seat. Jenn would have continued past them, but something in their tone of voice made her pause. She took a step back to make sure they wouldn't see her and waited.

'. . . and it was such a shambles, Frances, I can't tell you. You should have been there.'

'I wish I had.'

'There was the King, dressed to outshine any lord in the garden, and he makes a specific effort to go and speak to her. And what does she say?

'What did she say?' an older voice murmured.

'Nothing! Or almost nothing – just yes, Sire, and no, Sire. But can you believe it? Singled out by the King for private conversation and she can hardly utter a word!'

'I doubt you'd have the same problem, Hettie.'

'No, I would not. But then, I don't have a background as . . . colourful as hers.'

'Nicely put.'

'But really, what can she be thinking of, presenting herself at court like this? Does she think to find a husband this late in life? She must be eighteen or nineteen. And who would have her?'

'Well, she is heiress to Elita.'

'Yes, but she has no eye for fashion, wears unsuitable colours and has no manners to speak of. Honestly, I don't know what people think of sometimes. Surely that grim sister of hers should have taken her in hand.'

'Maybe she can't bear to. I'm not sure I would welcome a sister back into the family like that – especially after all the things she must have got up to.'

'Yes! I can just imagine.'

'I'm sure you can.'

'It's barbaric, thinking she can just come back into noble society as though she'd had a normal upbringing. I've heard she spent most of her childhood serving tables in a tavern!'

'I've heard that's not all she served . . .'

Jenn didn't wait to hear any more. She turned and ran blindly back down the corridor. She had to get out of here, out of this whole feeble, rotten place. Without looking, she tore down the stairs and through the doors at the bottom. Suddenly she was in sunshine – the central courtyard of the castle. She stopped for a moment, her heart pounding, then set off again towards the castle gates. Beyond stood the Basilica, tall and peaceful in the afternoon. Breathless, she reached the huge bronze door and pushed it open.

It was darker in here, even with the sunlight streaming through the stained glass windows above. She rushed forward, then paused and continued at a more sombre pace. The building was almost empty of people and its cool shadows and high domed roof enfolded her like a comforting embrace. Her breathing quietened and she reached the altar steps in a daze of conflicting emotions. Above her, suspended high on the wall, hung the trium, symbol of the eternally interwoven gods. Mineah, Serinleth and the evil Broleoch.

Without thinking, Jenn sank to her knees, her eyes remaining on the trium. She tried to form a prayer to Mineah, but no words would come. It seemed even her thoughts had lost their freedom.

'She knows the prayer is offered, even if you don't know what to say.'

Jenn started at the quiet voice behind her and turned

336

slowly to find a young priest waiting with his hands folded beneath his surplice. He continued, 'That's the way it works, you see. The inspiration of faith comes not from the mind but the heart. Mineah knows that. She knows that it is at times when people most need her that they can hardly find the strength to ask for salvation. The words are not important.'

His voice was soft and calm, his manner gentle. He watched her with the eyes of a priest, not a lord or a King. He demanded nothing of her, not even a response.

She glanced back at the trium. 'So why do we pray?'

'Why do we speak? When we pray we communicate as much with ourselves as we do with the gods. Sometimes, the only way we know how we truly feel is if we voice a prayer.'

'And I can do neither,' Jenn murmured, her head dropping. Slowly she got to her feet and turned to face him.

'I did say sometimes, my child. The most important thing is that you put your faith in her.'

Jenn shrugged, meeting his gaze. 'I used to put my faith in myself, Father. Now I feel I have none left to give to anyone.'

He said nothing for a moment, then held out his hand to her. As she took it, he led her away from the altar and down the south nave. Then he spoke again, his voice even quieter than before.

'I know it is difficult to believe at times like this, but you are not alone. Even if it seems that all those who love you have deserted you.'

'It's not that, Father, it's just that . . .'

He stopped walking and waited for her to continue.

'I . . . have no place any more. I've lost so much that . . . but I shouldn't complain, really. I mean I found my father, my home and everything. But . . . but there's no freedom! Everywhere I turn they're there, pushing me. Nothing I was before matters now. Nothing I did. I shouldn't complain; I know I have so much now but . . .' she paused, her eyes searching through the shadows of the basilica as though for answers. 'I just don't know who I am any more.'

Despairing, she looked back at the priest. He responded with a gentle smile. 'Yes you do. You know exactly who you are. You've not changed, you've just taken on more than you can absorb in a short time. You'll sort it out, sooner or later, and when that happens, you'll wonder why you had a problem in the first place.'

'But there are problems now, Father,' Jenn protested, but he held up his hand and touched it to her lips.

'You are not alone, Jenn, believe me.'

She started back from him, but he didn't let go of her hand. Jenn? How had he known who she was? Why had he called her that?

He must have seen the shock in her face. He said quietly, 'I believe we have a mutual friend. Finnlay?'

Jenn said nothing, but allowed him to lead her back along the nave towards the door. He continued, 'I am Father John Ballan, my lady. If you have any need of me at all, I am always here. If you need to send for me, just ask for Archdeacon Hilderic's secretary. You are not alone, my child, and never will be.'

He stopped at the door and reached up to trace the figure of the trium on her forehead in blessing. Then with a last quiet smile he was gone.

She meandered down the steps, not even bothering to look back. Not alone? How? Inside her head she was alone – and even if Robert could speak to her, over this distance she was still alone. It was all very good saying that but . . .

'Good afternoon, my lady. Have you been to see our lovely Basilica?'

Jenn turned swiftly at the voice. It was that Guildesman who had been with the King. Nash. He strode up to her with a smile. 'It is an enchanting building, is it not? Full of fine works and those glorious windows. We are very proud of it here in Marsay.'

Jenn gathered together what little self-determination she had left and formed a polite response. 'Yes indeed, you have every reason to be.'

'Some of us within the Guilde are in fact a little jealous.

Our Guilde Hall is rich, of course, but does not have the same soaring splendour of the Basilica. I would show you inside the Hall, but as you know, it is open only to those who have accepted the sacred trust.'

'Of course,' Jenn nodded. Why was he bothering to talk to her – and so pleasantly? Had he been sent by the King?

'Do you walk back to the castle, my lady? Will you allow me to escort you?' Nash bowed slightly and they began walking up the hill towards the gates. 'I imagine you have found things to be quite different here in the capital. It must seem so crowded after your months in the peace of Elita.'

She glanced aside at him. 'Do you know Elita?'

'I passed by once, many years ago,' he replied. 'A breathtaking place with those mountains in the distance. On a clear day I should think you would be able to see for leagues.'

'You can. I fell in love with it the moment I saw it.' Despite her concerns, she found it very easy to converse with this man.

'And have you had the opportunity to get to know it well since?'

'Not really. There's not been the time with all I've had to learn. I look forward to the days when I can ride out and explore the hills and moors. So far I've only seen them from the castle tower.'

Nash nodded. 'You will forgive me, my lady, but you realize there has been much talk of your surprise return to your father. We all assumed that those children taken during the Troubles were long lost. It seems a miracle that you were found at all. Is it true that you remember nothing of your previous life at Elita?'

Jenn wanted to be nice, wanted to reply in the same pleasant tone, but all she could hear were those women in her head and their spiteful comments. And for all this man's courteous manner, he was still a member of the Guilde and very close to the King. She said, 'I remember nothing at all. It came as a complete surprise to me when I was told of my true heritage. It took me some time to really believe it.'

'And now? I've heard some mention of your private devotions. Are you planning a life in the Church?'

Scrambling now, Jenn grasped at the first words that presented themselves. 'I . . . haven't decided yet though I confess the life does appeal to me. I have spent too many years wandering and I long for the kind of peace that can be found only within the cloister. Of course, I must wait a little. I have so much learning to catch up on and I am not anxious to leave my father so soon after I have returned.'

Now where the hell did that come from?

'Of course.' Nash nodded and gave her a generous smile. He was quite open and disarming. 'Forgive me, my lady, but you are wary of me, are you not?'

Jenn shot a surprised glance at him, but it seemed he didn't require an answer.

'You are understandably cautious, I know. You wonder if I will report what you say to the King.'

'Well . . .' Jenn paused, unsure whether to admit the truth or not. There seemed little point in evading it. 'I know you are close to the King. I cannot help wondering why he wanted me here.'

Nash laughed, but not unkindly. 'You are tactful, my lady. You have no need to be. I'm sure your friends have explained the reasons behind your visit. You should take no personal offence, nor have you any reason to be afraid. The King means you no harm.'

Jenn looked into his eyes and saw only honesty there, a directness not common among the others at court. It was hard not to like him. She smiled hesitantly. 'I would never suggest that. But you must know, all this is very new to me.'

'Of course,' Nash smiled again.

They had now reached the inner courtyard, where a crowd of people surrounded a party of riders about to embark towards the hills for the afternoon. Nash glanced at them, then turned back to Jenn. 'It would be a great pity if, while you were here, you were not allowed to explore the hills around Marsay, my lady. Do you think your sister would allow me to take you out – perhaps tomorrow?'

'I . . .' Jenn fumbled. She would love to go out, but with Nash? An Alderman of the Guilde?

'Ah, Nash! There you are!'

They turned as no less a person than Proctor Vaughn approached with long strides. 'The King is asking for you, Nash—' he broke off when his eyes landed on Jenn. She blushed under his scrutiny and dropped her gaze.

'Lady Jennifer, I believe,' Vaughn murmured. 'I must take this opportunity to welcome you to court – and back to the land of the living.'

Vaughn bowed, but for some reason Jenn couldn't define, she felt a wave of disquiet brush over her senses. She'd not felt anything like this when speaking to the King and tried to put it down to the awful reputation of this man. He was, after all, Robert's greatest enemy and she was on her guard. Her whole body tensed as if she were about to be attacked.

She looked up to find him smiling with what he probably thought was warmth, but it looked more like a grimace.

'I have been meaning to speak to you, my lady, since I heard of your arrival. Your story interested me. A remarkable rescue. I wonder that His Grace thought to return you to your father so long after your disappearance, but I'm sure he thought it was the noble thing to do. Tell me,' he added, dropping the smile a little, 'did he tell you what his plans were?'

Jenn stared into those bleak cold eyes and her disquiet intensified. It was so like the pressure of the Enclave council, but darker, more menacing, like a cavernous sewer. Was it coming from Vaughn? From someone else in the courtyard?

But Vaughn was waiting for an answer. She pretended to misunderstand. 'His Grace, my lord Proctor?'

'The Duke of Haddon – of course you would know him as Dunlorn, my apologies. Well?'

'My lord?'

'What do you know of his plans, child?' Vaughn bellowed. People turned to look at them—

And deep inside her, the seeds of panic began to grow. They were all watching her, waiting for her to do or say something wrong. Something that would get her into trouble – or Robert. She was way out of her depth. If only she could just run, run away from all of them.

'I understand your reluctance, my lady,' Vaughn continued, his tone now sickly and soothing. 'But you do yourself no service by not answering. You must know Dunlorn is a traitor. Would you put your own loyalties beside his? You must tell me when he plans to come to Marsay. I know he will. I just want to know when.'

Frantically, Jenn struggled for words, for something that would not incriminate Robert. 'He ... His Grace said nothing about coming to Marsay. He said only that he would stay at Dunlorn.'

'You're lying!' Vaughn spat and snatched her hand. 'He has tainted you with his evil and now you take his side. Tell me, girl! Tell me the truth!'

Jenn gasped as he crushed her hand. She tried to pull away, but he was much too strong for her. He would have her trapped, imprisoned until she told him what he wanted to hear. He wouldn't let her go until she said something, anything, that would put Robert into a worse prison. But how could she? Would she lie to get away from this man? To rid herself of the mouldering evil which seeped into her senses with such icy determination?

Yes! Anything – she would do anything to get away. Now. For ever. Get away from these hateful people, their lies, their deceit, their hatred and fear. Her fear. Her senses screamed for release. Yes. She would say anything at all, even ... even...

Betray Robert?

By the gods! What was she doing!

Jenn tore in a breath and stared at the man who held her hand so tight. She saw his narrow eyes, his gaunt face, his deep and forbidding hatred of the one man who had had the courage and strength to defy him. Then she saw him again, as he really was. Petty, greedy, vengeful. When the winds of time swept him away, there would be nothing left

342

of his lust for power, nothing left of him. Just the memory of his evil, twisted mind.

Like a wall tumbling down in her head, all the fears and desperation of the last few weeks and months dropped away. All that remained was a cold, vicious anger.

Deliberately she allowed her eyes to well up with tears. She returned his gaze hesitantly, allowed her voice to tremble just a little. 'Forgive me, my lord. I did not mean to appear disobedient.'

As she said this, she reached out with her senses, through his clammy flesh. Something Fiona had talked about. Push, gently at first. Then harder. Push his thoughts away from her, away from Robert.

'I'm sorry, but His Grace spoke only of his wish to return to his home. I believe he plans to remain there. He has no desire to return to court.' Believe me, she pushed harder. Forget about this. Leave me be.

She held his gaze for a moment longer, then abruptly the pressure, the disquiet vanished. Jenn almost sighed with relief.

Vaughn raised an eyebrow and released her hand. When he spoke, it was as though he was entirely pleased with what she'd said. 'Very well, my lady. I sincerely hope you enjoy the remainder of your visit. Nash, see Lady Jennifer to her rooms before you go on to the King.'

Vaughn turned and strode away and it was all Jenn could do not to laugh triumphantly. But she was not out of danger yet. She turned back to Nash. 'Thank you for your courtesy, sir. But please, do not let me keep you from your duty to the King. I can find my rooms alone. I would enjoy riding out with you tomorrow if my sister agrees.'

Nash raised his eyebrows and for a second looked as though he were about to ask her something. Then the expression changed and he smiled. 'I shall seek her permission tonight, then.' He bowed with a flourish, then left her.

She desperately wanted to run; her exhilaration was hard to contain, but she managed a demure walk inside and through the corridors to the last staircase. Then, with a laugh, she bounded up as fast as her skirts would allow and skipped along to the door of her room. She stuck her head inside and finding it empty, strode across the hallway and rapped hard against the door of Bella and Lawrence's room. She heard a call to enter and marched in.

Bella was seated at the table writing a letter while Lawrence was midway through a heavy book.

'Good, you're both here,' Jenn said with a quick smile. 'I think it's time we quit this charade and went home. If you like, I'll get Addie to run down and let our guard know. If we're quick about it we can be gone in the morning.'

'What,' Bella lifted her head from the letter, 'have you gone mad? We can't just leave here. We've not stayed our allotted time. The King...'

'The King couldn't care less about me and even if he does, he knows where he can find me. I think we should go.' Jenn grinned, feeling better than she had in a long time. There was a lot to be said for getting angry, especially when that anger was directed at your own self-pity and fear.

'But we can't leave,' Bella insisted.

'Look, if the King really wants to make sure I stay, we'll find out soon enough,' she pointed out.

Lawrence moved across the room in his usual quiet way. 'Look, Jenny, I think you're being a little hasty here.'

'No, Lawrence, I'm not. I know exactly what I'm doing. We've played this game long enough, this business about keeping our heads low because we're so afraid of what might happen. Believe me, Selar sees no threat in me, no threat that can't be solved by marrying me off. I've had enough of apologizing for my return – of apologizing for my House. It took me thirteen years to come back to it and I'm damned if I'm going to be ashamed of my name now! Let's get packing.'

'But Jenny,' Lawrence tried once more.

'And while we're at it,' she stopped him with a blistering smile, 'I'd rather you didn't call me Jenny. Jenn or Jennifer will do just fine.'

She turned and started back out of the door, flinging a final comment over her shoulder. 'Let me know if you need any help packing.'

Moonlight danced on the waters of the Vitala like so many glow-worms in the night. A gentle breeze wafted across the valley and through the window of Nash's room. He turned his face into it, let it caress his cheek, brush the hair across his eyes.

Selar had laughed. He'd laughed at her audacity. He'd laughed and said, let her go. He'd laughed.

Of necessity, Nash had laughed with him, knowing that there was nothing he could do to stop her. Not this time.

By the blood, he had been so close! She'd walked alongside him, so near he could have touched her. He'd taken his time, knowing that his work could not be rushed, and believing she would stay in Marsay for the full month but no, she was gone.

Valena was waiting for him, expecting him to come to her rooms. She would want to know what had happened, but just at this moment, he had lost all appetite for her cloying affections. He needed to do some serious thinking. He'd come a long way over the last year, so far that he'd attained the kind of close friendship with Selar that he required. But it was not close enough yet, or he would have been able to stop Jenn from leaving.

Casually, like the touch of the breeze, he sent his senses out into the night. Now that he had met her, he should be able to find her, Seek her wherever she was. But he felt nothing, just like this afternoon.

Oh, she'd handled Vaughn so skilfully. Nash had made a simple attempt to reach out and touch her shielding, but he'd failed completely. All he could See of her was her absence. Yes, she was powerful indeed, just as he'd always been told.

He picked up the ancient manuscript left forgotten on the window seat and stared at the tight scrawl and crushed italics. The language was old Saelic, unknown in modern times. There were not a dozen scholars within the Guilde who could have read this scrap – and even fewer who would understand a single word of its meaning. But Nash could.

*Let her live not nor be not alone. For she will be the guiding light against the Angel of Darkness. She is the light of hope and that which will break us. We strive for her life even as she for our destruction. She is the last of her line. All ends and begins with her. Cherish and rejoice in her and be joined together with her for all eternity.*

Nash gazed out the window once more as a pale breath of cloud drifted across the moon. He let the paper fall to the ground and the cool breeze touch his face once more.

Jennifer Ross. The Ally. He must either take her – or destroy her.

So be it.

# 15

Finnlay swung his legs out over the corner of the staircase and settled on to the cold stone step. With his back against the pillar he folded his arms and continued watching the scene in the stableyard below. Robert and Deverin were practising with sword and dagger – at least, Deverin was practising. It was anybody's guess what Robert was doing. Finnlay's brother had always been something of a natural with the sword. As a young man he'd had some fine teachers but, one by one, Robert had surpassed them all and had then made a point of passing what he knew on to Finnlay. However, there were a few moves Robert was now making on Deverin that Finnlay had never seen before. Even more unsettling was the single-minded method Robert had employed against his opponent the moment they'd taken up the weapons.

Rather than stretch and warm up a little with the usual easy parries, today Robert had launched an all-out attack, sending Deverin skittering across the cobblestones and up against the feedshed wall. Robert had taken a step back to allow Deverin more room to move, then immediately re-opened the assault. Deverin was obviously trying his best, but as steel rang out against steel it was already very clear who the victor would be.

Finnlay heard a soft footfall on the doorstep behind him.

'Good morning, Micah,' he murmured, not taking his eyes from the action.

Micah plumped himself down beside Finnlay. 'He's no better, then?'

'No.'

'I'd hoped that with your lady mother's return to Dunlorn

he would begin to come out of it. It seems I was overly hopeful.'

'We all were, Micah. Any other suggestions?'

Micah only shook his head. Then he said, 'What do you think he'll do now?'

'You mean about claiming his inheritance? Nothing. By now I'm sure Selar will have confiscated all of Oliver's lands. The only thing left is the title, which even the King can't take. But if you asked him, I'm sure Robert would say he'd rather have his uncle back than be addressed as the Duke of Haddon.'

'He can't decline it, can he?' Micah said.

'Nor would he, if only out of respect for Oliver. No, in that matter at least, he has no say.'

'Like everything else, you mean.'

Finnlay glanced aside at him. 'You're worried about him. Me too. I've never seen him like this, not even after father died, or Berenice. He's closed in completely, hardly says a word to anyone, and when he does it's obviously forced. Hell, I just don't know what to do.'

There was another sound behind them and Finnlay turned to see a familiar friendly face beaming down on him. 'Why, Daniel! Whatever are you doing here?'

'Just passing. Thought I'd drop in and pay my respects.' With a rustle of garments, Daniel squatted down on the other side of Finnlay, balancing himself with a hand against the pillar. He was silent a moment, watching the swordplay, then he grimaced as Robert pushed Deverin back from a clinch. 'Robert's fighting like a demon. What's got into him?'

Finnlay couldn't find an answer and just shrugged. Daniel continued, 'Your letter said he was depressed, but this? This isn't depression, Finn, this is fury. He looks every inch a man who is preparing for war.'

Finnlay turned his head slowly and gazed at his brother's old friend. 'Is that your considered opinion?'

'Most certainly it is. Look at him. He's anticipating every move his opponent makes and is there before. He makes no outward attempt to end the match, but gives Deverin every opportunity to find a break. Robert's testing himself, making sure there are no flaws in either his offence or defence. Yes, that's exactly what he's doing.' Daniel glanced across at Finnlay, then Micah. 'What's wrong? What did I say?'

Finnlay looked at him. 'Nothing, Daniel, nothing. Have you any suggestions as to how to break him out of it? You've known him a long time.'

'And you're his brother, Finnlay. Have you tried talking to him? Trying to get him to talk? You can't work out how to fix it if you don't know what the problem is.'

'Isn't it obvious what the problem is? He's been like this ever since word reached us about Oliver. Robert came back here, shouted some orders about the nightly patrols, then shut himself in his study for two days. Not even Micah could get in. It takes no prizes to guess what he's thinking.'

'Oh?' Daniel twisted around, 'and what would that be?'

Finnlay almost smiled. There was such a rich choice – from Oliver to McCauly. Not to mention the revelation about Berenice. That bothered him more than anything.

But Finnlay said nothing of this and instead replied, 'Come on, you know what Robert is like about blaming himself. He saw Oliver days after he arrived back in Lusara. Robert's bound to be thinking that if he'd just done something at the time, then Oliver would be alive today.'

'Possibly. Then again, you don't know for certain. I mean, I think there's more to this mood than pure self-recrimination. This goes way down deep. Like I said, you really have to talk to him.'

With a sigh, Finnlay climbed to his feet. The others also stood. 'Talking to my big brother about anything serious has always been difficult,' Finnlay said. 'Right now it's impossible. He won't talk to me, Micah or even mother. If you don't believe me, try for yourself. Go ahead, try. Maybe you can get some sense out of him.'

Finnlay gestured towards Robert who, with fine beads of sweat glistening on his forehead, had finally stopped the match and was even now handing his sword to a waiting boy and towelling his face dry. Daniel smoothed down his jerkin and trotted down the steps to the stableyard. He waited until Robert had finished with the towel, then took a couple of steps forward. Finnlay remained above with Micah, watching everything.

Robert glanced at Daniel, then looked quickly away.

'How are you, Robert?' Daniel asked tentatively.

'Fine,' Robert grunted, 'you?'

'Fine, fine.' Daniel hesitated and glanced up at Finnlay. Turning back to Robert, he dropped his voice a little. 'I was truly sorry to hear about your uncle. He was a good and brave man.'

'Thank you.' Robert nodded and began walking away, but Daniel took a few steps after him.

'Robert?'

Pausing in his stride, Robert turned slowly, seemingly unaware of Finnlay and Micah on the steps above.

'Robert, do you want to talk?'

For a split second, Robert's eyes flashed brilliant green, but all he said was, 'No.' Moments later he had disappeared around the corner of the feedshed, leaving Daniel standing alone in the stableyard.

Finnlay and Micah came down the steps to join him.

'I warned you,' Finnlay said without triumph.

'Do you really think he would?' Daniel asked in a voice full of awe. 'Do you think he would actually go to war against Selar?'

'You were the one suggesting it, Daniel, not me.'

Daniel turned and faced Finnlay square-on. In his eyes was something very much akin to fear. 'Yes, but you know him better than I do. Do you think he would?'

Finnlay didn't reply immediately, but turned a steady gaze on Micah. Slowly, the younger man shook his head, a silent message in his eyes. Almost imperceptibly, Finnlay nodded, then gave Daniel a half-smile of comfort the way he had seen his brother do on many tense occasions. 'Sure he would! That's why I was so pleased to see you, Daniel – you can be a great help. Come, let me tell you how.'

Placing his arm around the laughing Daniel, Finnlay took him indoors.

Margaret touched the wick of one candle to that of another and as the flickering flame grew strong, she placed it carefully on the tray before the altar. As an afterthought, she picked up a third candle, mouthed a silent prayer and stood it beside the others. Then with a final glance at the trium above, she knelt on the chapel floor and bowed her head. Despite the memories it engendered, it was comforting to once again kneel before the altar of Dunlorn's tiny chapel. If only she were here for another reason.

A scrape of leather on stone behind her made her lift her head. She turned slowly, but she already knew who it was.

'Robert?'

He was in darkness, standing the shadows. He didn't reply.

'Please, Robert. Come closer. You mustn't allow this to beat you.'

He turned to go.

'Robert, I beg you. I've lost both husband and brother to that man. Do you think I don't know how you feel?' She stood, but did not walk towards him.

He paused. She waited. Finally he spoke, his dead voice barely echoing through the stone chamber.

'I'm glad you've come home, mother.'

She blinked and he was gone.

Finnlay read as he climbed the stairs to Robert's study. The manuscript was one his brother had brought back, but Finnlay had found it only that morning, lying among the forgotten papers on Robert's table. The script was difficult to decipher and contained sentences made up of both letters and numbers, which he couldn't begin to understand. Nevertheless, he couldn't put it down and tried instead to find where it fitted into the growing bank of information on sorcery they had collected. At this rate Finnlay would have to schedule a visit to the Enclave to try and match up this new material with what was held in the library there. Somehow, something here must have a bearing on where the Calyx lay hidden. Although he'd said little about it, finding the Calyx was still in the forefront of his thoughts, and these days it was good to have something to distract him. Perhaps finding the Calyx could even help Robert. After all, if it could free the Enclave, then surely it could also free him?

Without looking up, he entered the study and made his way directly to the table where Robert kept his notes. He placed the manuscript on a clear space to one side, then cast around for the other related stuff, but as he looked up he realized he was not alone as he had supposed. Robert sat in the window embrasure opposite him, gazing out, unaware, it seemed, of Finnlay's presence.

With a frown, Finnlay tried to measure this countenance with the fury Daniel saw, but it was impossible. Robert was neither angry nor sad. He was ... nothing. His face was a blank, and Finnlay was tempted for a moment to shout at Robert just to get a response. However, he opted for a different tack and sent his senses out to try and register Robert's presence. But even there he failed. Either Robert was shielding himself, or Finnlay's meagre powers were fading. He knew which was more likely.

He turned back to his notes. He was about to pick up a heavy, leather-bound book from Semsay when Robert spoke – the first time without prompting since Oliver had died.

'I was about to commend you on your restraint. It seems I was hasty.'

'Pardon?'

'No shouting, no pleading, no tantrums. I'm impressed.' Robert's voice was a monotone, his face barely moving.

Finnlay didn't know how to respond to this, but he knew he must. 'Thank you.'

'But you couldn't stay away from my books, could you?' Robert turned his head slowly and looked at Finnlay with empty eyes.

'No. Why should I? I don't understand what's wrong with

you, Robert, but I refuse to go down with you. I for one intend to keep working.'

'Life goes on?' There was not even the hint of a smile in Robert's sardonic tone. 'Fine. Go ahead. Don't let me stop you.'

Finnlay pulled in his bottom lip, then without another word picked up the papers he needed and headed for the door. However, before he could leave, Robert flung a final message after him, his voice low with an almost feral warning.

'And if you go writing letters about me to my friends – or enemies – again, I'll make you very sorry.'

Finnlay fled, running down the stairs till he got to the bottom. For a moment he stood there, gulping in air. How long was this to go on? What did he have to do? And he did have to do something. Robert was his brother. No matter their past differences, Finnlay just could not leave Robert to drown alone. The consequences were too awful to contemplate.

Micah paused outside the door to his master's study, a tray balanced on one hand. Had a warning been placed on the door or was it safe to enter? Having no powers of his own, Micah could only guess. He cursed inwardly that the gods had placed him in the service of such a man as Dunlorn, without giving him the power to help him when he most needed it. And he could do nothing but wait for Robert to emerge from this on his own. Until then, Micah would not give up. He would serve Robert, regardless of whether Robert thought he wanted serving or not.

Reaching out with his free hand, Micah pushed down the latch. The door opened without any trouble and he entered the room, looking for Robert amidst the jumble of furniture, books and papers which littered the room. Even by normal standards the room was a mess. And there was Robert by the fire. Dressed in his customary black, his body stretched out on one chair with his feet resting on the arm of another. He appeared to be asleep.

Micah studied him for a moment, placed the tray down on a table close by. With a glance at the fire to make sure it would not die out, he headed for the door.

'Micah?'

'Yes, my lord?' Micah spun around, trying not to sound over-eager.

Robert opened his eyes and regarded him across the room. He was silent for a long minute, then he said, 'They're all worried, aren't they?'

Micah nodded.

'Tell them not to, will you?'

'Of course, but if I may ask, why should we not worry?'

'Because I'm not worth the trouble. Trust me.'

Micah measured the tone of his master's voice, then took a step forward. 'I do,' he replied simply. 'I always have.'

Robert's eyes latched on to him. Micah was unable to move under that penetrating gaze, but after only a few moments his master looked away. 'Well, perhaps that was your first mistake.'

Micah wanted to retort, but kept his head. 'I think perhaps you need to go away for a while. I think you need to go and visit . . .'

'No.'

'But she . . .'

'No,' Robert turned back to Micah with dull eyes. 'I can't and that's all there is to it.'

Micah's heart sank once more. He turned to go, but as he approached the door, Finnlay came sailing through, his arms full of tightly rolled manuscripts.

'Ah, Micah, there you are! I've been looking for you!' Finnlay smiled breezily. 'I found something that might interest you.'

As though Robert were not even in the room, Finnlay began clearing a space on the big table and dumped his armload of scrolls. He rustled through them then picked a single one out, unrolled it and weighted it down with the nearest things to hand, an ink stand and a compass.

'Now,' he continued glancing up to make sure Micah was

standing close by, 'remember how you were asking about the palace of Bu? And whether it had really been built by sorcerers a thousand years ago? Well, look at this. It's a detailed drawing done of the palace by a historian some seven hundred years ago. I knew I had it somewhere, but it took me till this morning to find it. Here on the west face, see that marking there? It's a hieroglyph depicting an underground tunnel. The tunnel goes from the desert here right under the palace to the central domed area. The really interesting thing is that this tunnel was carved out of solid rock.'

Micah stared down at the drawing on the table, then shot a glance back to his master. Robert had returned to his reclined position, his eyes closed once again. Turning back to Finnlay, he saw that the younger lord was, despite his casual manner, extremely aware of what his brother was doing. Finnlay's eyes appealed for help; it seemed he had a plan.

'Solid rock? What's so amazing about that?' Micah asked, hoping that it was the right question. From the brief glint in Finnlay's eye, it was.

'Nothing really – except that the tunnel is over five hundred feet long and according to this drawing, its walls are as smooth as ice.'

Despite the main purpose behind this discussion, Micah found he was genuinely intrigued. His eyes dropped to the drawing again. 'What does this mean, here? I can't read this language.'

'I'm not exactly fluent in it myself. That says "door to the inner soul" – I assume some kind of royal inner chamber.'

'Who was the historian? Did any text accompany the drawing?'

'If there was, it's long lost. I got this from a monk in Sethlien about five years ago.'

Robert's quiet voice filled the silence. 'Cordor.'

Finnlay paused, glanced over his shoulder and, with a nod, acknowledged the correction. 'Cordor it was. Anyway, the monk had been going through his library and was about to throw all this stuff out – fortunately I was able to help him get rid of it. He had no idea what it all was, again, fortunately. Tell me, when you visited the palace ruins, did you see any sign of this tunnel? If this drawing is accurate, it just about proves that there had to be some kind of arcane work done on the building at its inception. It could confirm that Bu was indeed a home of sorcerers – and possibly the place where the Key was created!'

A scuffle of feet and furniture behind them warned them of Robert's approach. They parted as he came between them. He reached forward and with a swift movement which almost dislodged the ink well, he turned the drawing around until it was upside down. He planted his finger on the place where the tunnel seemed to end. 'This is an above-ground causeway, not a tunnel, and it goes across the east face, not the west. Its walls are covered in faded hand paintings of ochre on bare rock which show no signs of fading. You bought the drawing from the monk who was glad to get rid of it because he feared it was blasphemous and would condemn him to an eternity of flames. And,' Robert paused for effect, 'he knew exactly what it was.'

There had been no anger in Robert's monologue, merely a purposeful crispness. Micah glanced at Finnlay, hoping he knew what to do next. So far it seemed the plan was working.

Finnlay did know. 'Oh, really? Well, if you're such an expert, brother, what does this mean?' He reached across the table and brought forward another, smaller sheet of vellum, illuminated down one side with gold, reds and blues. 'As far as I can make out, it clearly mentions the Calyx, and the fact that it was kept in a building on the other side of what we now know as Marsay.'

It was nicely done, but Robert was no fool and didn't immediately take the bait. He paid no attention to the paper Finnlay held; instead watching his brother with a mixture of suspicion and cunning. 'The Calyx? That's quite a coincidence.'

Finnlay shrugged without rancour. 'Coincidence or not, read it and tell me I'm wrong. I dare you.'

For a brief second, Micah thought he'd seen the barest shadow of a smile flash beneath Robert's features. It was too quick to pinpoint and was immediately overwritten by a frown as Robert took the paper from Finnlay's hand. 'Fine, have it your own way.'

Micah tensed as the silence grew. He shot a questioning glance in Finnlay's direction and received a steady look as confirmation. But was this all just a ruse or had Finnlay actually found some information as to the whereabouts of the Calyx? To his knowledge, there were only two other documents which told of the Calyx, its value and its relationship to the Key, but neither said anything about where it was. Micah knew: he'd read them both. He'd not understood them, but he had read them.

Finally Robert spoke. 'You would do better spending the time practising your Saelic grammar, Finnlay. A more accurate translation of this would be, "from Kennis Town the Calyx was brought, in humble procession to lie within the walls of Thraxis's home, in the shadow of Omaysis. There he wished it to lie safe until the day when man would know how to use it. The Great Marklord placed it well within safe keeping, locked from eyes who would abuse its power."'

Robert glanced up. 'Kennis Town is on the other side of Marsay, Finnlay. It didn't go there, it came from there.'

A slow smile spread across Finnlay's face. 'Then all I need to do is find out what this Omaysis place is and I can find the Calyx.'

Robert shook his head, not taking his eyes from his brother. 'You're missing the point, Finn. Certainly this document mentions the Calyx – and I appreciate how your pulse must be pounding with enthusiasm – but it also mentions the Marklord having taken it. We know he lived long before the Calyx was created. This document must be a forgery.'

Micah's heart sank as he heard those words, but strangely, Finnlay began to laugh quietly. Robert looked as if he would take offence but instead, his gaze narrowed and shifted back to the paper in his hand. He placed it down on the table and in the blink of an eye produced his *ayarn* and held it out. On touching the paper, the amazing little stone began to glow softly – and Robert gazed up at Finnlay with genuine amazement.

'Where in the name of the gods did you get this?'

'Actually, I didn't – you did. In one of those books you brought back.'

'But I've never seen it before.'

'Not surprising. You see, I had a little accident this morning. I dropped that big heavy book from Semsay and split the binding. Rather than risk you wringing my neck, I took it upstairs and tried to mend it. As I peeled off the leather to get a better hold of it, I found a corner of this page stuck between the binding and the back. It was difficult, but eventually I freed it.'

Robert nodded. 'Then worked out this ridiculous charade in order to get me to take a look at it?'

Finnlay shrugged. 'Hell, you don't need to tell me my Saelic grammar stinks.'

With a slow nod, Robert glanced at Micah. 'Did you know about this?'

'No, my lord.'

'Then I guess you have yourself the genuine article – and a surprising one at that. It mentions both Amar Thraxis and the Marklord together with the Calyx. I suppose that throws most Enclave learning to the winds. We'd always believed Thraxis was of a later era. Of course, to my mind, the most amazing thing is the connection between the Marklord and the Calyx. It opens up a whole realm of possibilities.'

Micah took a careful look at the page on the table. 'Forgive my ignorance but who is Amar Thraxis? And this Marklord? I think I have heard you mention him, but remind me.'

'Amar Thraxis was, we think, a member of the first order of the Guilde. He wasn't very important as such, but he seems to have moved around a lot. His title suggests quite a low ranking, but since we have no access to Guilde records we really don't know anything solid about him. He apparently wrote a few books, but I've never seen them. Popular belief has it that he had a hand in creating the Calyx.' Robert paused with his fingers gently touching the ancient parchment. 'The Marklord, according to tradition, is the man who, by some process we know nothing about, created the House Marks. It has always been considered a remarkable achievement, but his original purpose has been lost along with his method. All we have left of him is the occasional literary mention and our persistent birthmarks. He was always understood to have achieved this work three hundred years before our earliest records of Thraxis.'

Finnlay took a few steps away from the table, deep in thought. Quietly he said, 'There must be a reference somewhere about this place called Omaysis. The name doesn't sound familiar but if we could just track it down . . .'

Robert struck the table with the flat of his hand, making the inkwell jump. 'By all that's holy, Finn, will you please stop leaping from one point to the other and pay attention! Very few things in life are achieved by perpetually taking short cuts.'

'But Robert . . .'

'Look!' Robert almost shouted, but his anger was more noisy than real. 'The answer is right under your nose.'

He thrust the page at Finnlay and waited for his brother to scan its contents again. When Finnlay looked up, obviously mystified, Robert reached over and tapped his finger on the left hand side. 'The illumination, Finn. Look at the pictures. They're not there just for decoration, you know. Look at the top, a horse caravan travelling over flat land. Below that a man with a trium held towards the heavens, and at the bottom of the page, two mountains, one with a strangely familiar peak.'

'By the gods!' Finnlay breathed. 'It can't possibly have been right in front of us all along.'

Micah couldn't stand the suspense. 'What mountains? Where?'

'Nanmoor,' Finnlay said.

359

'It's that small mountain range we skirted on our way to Elita, Micah. Remember I tried to point it out, but there was a low mist and the peaks were virtually invisible.'

'But . . .' Finnlay almost trembled, 'I never really thought this was . . . This was just,' he paused, glancing at his brother, 'oh, never mind. I'll get packing. Thanks, Robert.'

Finnlay started for the door, but his brother stopped him. 'I don't think so.'

'What?' Finnlay turned around. 'What's wrong now? You're always complaining you never get any peace when I'm around. I'm doing you a favour. I'll only be gone a couple of days.'

'Peace?' Robert murmured as though it were a private joke. To lighten it he added, 'How much peace do you think I would get with Mother here day after day, telling me off for letting you go out alone in these troubled times? It was bad enough when you went to Marsay.'

'What was bad enough?' Lady Margaret stood in the doorway and glanced at both of her sons.

With a subtle movement, Robert slid the important page under a pile of innocuous ones. 'Finnlay was just complaining of being bored, Mother. It seems I don't give him enough work. He wants to travel north for a few days.'

'Oh really? Where to?'

'Not Marsay, Mother,' Finnlay smiled to hide his sudden discomfort. With a warning glance towards Robert, he added, 'I'll be back before you know.'

'I'm sorry, Finn,' Margaret placed a hand on his arm, 'but I don't find that at all comforting. I can only think of what happened the last time Robert allowed you to leave Dunlorn alone.'

'Oh,' Robert said casually, coming towards them, 'did I imply he was going alone? No, sorry, I don't trust him, Mother. I will be accompanying him – so you can worry about both of us at the same time. Concentrate your efforts, as it were. However, Micah will stay and look after you, so you won't have to worry about him, too.'

Lady Margaret looked as if she was about to hit him.

360

However, she had obviously noticed the sudden change in her eldest son, so she just lifted her chin, shooting a glance in Micah's direction as though for confirmation. 'I suppose I had better postpone my visit to Saint Hilary's, then. Somebody should stay here and look after things. By the way, I just came up to tell you Daniel sent a message over to say he wouldn't be coming tomorrow after all. Well, I'll leave you to it.'

As she disappeared down the steps, Finnlay shut the door behind her. With a wave of his hand, he put a warning on it, then turned slowly back to his brother.

However, Micah spoke before Finnlay could say another word. 'I don't think I should stay behind, my lord.' No, definitely not. Especially after the way Robert had behaved since his uncle's death. This was hardly the time for Micah to let him go off on his own.

Robert's reply was short, but the hard glint in his eyes had vanished. 'I need you here, Micah, I'm sorry. Go and spend more time with your father, my friend. Finnlay will keep an eye out for me, won't you, brother?'

Finnlay swallowed, hardly moving, 'You're serious about this?'

'I am.' Robert nodded. 'I meant what I said – I don't trust you.'

Finnlay's face creased in a broad smile, 'For once, dear brother, I can honestly say I'm glad to hear it.'

It had felt too easy, Finnlay acknowledged. For just a few minutes there, he'd thought Robert had finally come out of his shell, but after three hard days in the saddle, Robert had hardly spoken. Sure, he mentioned the weather, their path and where they might obtain bread and firewood, but his tone was always eerily cold and empty. By dusk as they reached the edge of a small forest, Finnlay was ready to scream.

'We'll go in to the wood,' Robert spoke suddenly. 'It'll be easier to find shelter unobserved than out here in the fields.'

Once he got over the shock of hearing another voice,

Finnlay turned his horse to follow Robert, replying, 'I don't see that it makes a difference if we're seen. What harm can it do?'

'Surely you can't be serious, Finn.' Robert glanced at him. 'Do you really think Selar would be happy if he thought I was wandering the countryside?'

'But you're not doing anything wrong.'

'You mean apart from trying to find a sorcerer's symbol of enormous power? Believe me, it wouldn't take even that much to make them alarmed.'

Finnlay thought for a moment then glanced sideways at Robert. 'Do you think Mother knows?'

This brought a sharp answering look from his brother. 'I don't know.'

'We can't keep it hidden from her for ever, you know. I mean, it was all right while she was at Saint Hilary's, but now she's returned for good?'

Robert kept his eyes firmly fixed on the path ahead. 'Hell, Finn, I don't know. You know how she feels about the Church and everything. How am I supposed to tell her that not only one, but both of her sons are mixed up in sorcery. She'd never understand. We'll just have to be more careful. I'll see what I can do about fixing a permanent warning on the door to my study, then make sure we never discuss anything dangerous outside of there. Apart from that, we can only hope.'

They stopped and set up camp in the shelter of an ancient oak, lighting a modest fire to ward off the cool night air and the wolves they could hear howling in the distance. After they'd eaten, Finnlay settled down with his back against his saddle and watched his brother solemnly. This apparent change seemed to last for only short periods. Outside that, Robert continued to withdraw into himself, unwilling to talk about anything. Finnlay decided to take a gamble.

'I don't think you should go on blaming yourself over Oliver.'

Robert started and glanced up. 'What?'

'It wasn't your fault. He would have known the danger, but that's what he chose. You can't blame yourself for ever.'

'You think that's what this is? Guilt?' Robert laughed, but with a bitter edge. 'I can assure you, brother, that this has nothing to do with guilt.'

'But you . . .'

'You've changed your tune, Finn. A few months ago you were trying to convince me to join Oliver and support him, that it would be my fault if he failed. Well, now he's dead, do you think I'm going to believe that the blame doesn't lie with me? Please, brother, try and be consistent, if nothing else. If you don't mind, I'd rather not discuss it further. Here, let me have another look at that page. I suppose you actually believe we'll find the Calyx at Omaysis?'

Finnlay sighed and shook his head. Another change of mood. 'We might. I think it's worth trying, don't you? After all, this is the first time we've found any trace of where the Calyx was hidden. I'd be a fool if I didn't make the attempt.'

'And is that all this was?'

'No.' There was no point in denying the truth. Robert had obviously suspected all along. 'But I didn't really think we'd be able to find this place – I had no idea where Omaysis was. I just thought it would be another obscure reference we'd never be able to understand. However, I do believe we'll find the Calyx one day.'

Robert shook his head, reached forward and stirred up the fire. 'Do you? I don't.'

'Oh?' Finnlay asked, startled. 'Why not?'

'I think it was lost deliberately.' Robert replied, his eyes going dull once more. 'I think we'll never find it – because we were never meant to have it.'

The ground rose steeply along the path they'd chosen. It was not the easiest road but it was the quickest. They skirted a ridge which brought them eventually to the foot of what they now called Omaysis. The peak rose to a stately height above them, mighty, although not as mighty as many in the Goleth range. Around the base of the mountain were rocky cliffs separated by burgeoning streams which tumbled down the slope to the valley below. A long blanket of forest wrapped itself around the base of the mountain and followed the streams down, growing stronger and more dense as it gained a hold on the lush valley.

They traversed the mountainside heading for the cliffs. It was tough going and they soon gave up riding the horses, leading them in single file instead.

'This is ridiculous, you know,' Robert called over his shoulder. 'We have no idea what we're looking for.'

'Well, you might not,' Finnlay called back, 'but I remember hearing something once about caves under those cliffs. Maybe somebody once built a house in there?'

'Why build a house in a cave?' Robert threw back with a little of his old humour.

They paused on a rocky outcrop about halfway up the first line of cliffs. Robert frowned up at the massif above, then down at the drop below. In the distance was a small village which lay beside the water course as it hooked and twined its way between the hills.

'All right then, a dwelling of some kind,' Finnlay replied.

'That's all very well and good, but we're assuming this house or whatever is still standing. Who's to say it wasn't destroyed by later generations? Or swept away in a flood, or burned down – or merely crumbled away over the centuries?'

'Then why are you here if you think this is so hopeless?' Finnlay led the way down to where he could see an easy ledge into the cliffs.

'It doesn't matter why I'm here. Be content that I am. Careful there.'

They reached the ledge and tied up the horses. Then, with Finnlay leading the way, they edged along the cliff wall, making use of any handhold they would find, even those as little as a stringy root or a fist of clay. Finnlay made his way to a cluster of bushes which clung tenaciously to the side of the cliff. Water came out below them, but its source was not the cliff above. There must be a cave of some sort behind it.

He pressed the branches away from the stone. There,

barely wide enough for a man to get through sideways, was a narrow fissure, seven, maybe eight feet tall.

'Can you sense anything on the other side?' Finnlay murmured, barely able to contain his excitement.

'Yes. It opens out and goes back quite a way.' Robert glanced at him with a sardonic smile. 'Not much of a front door, though.'

Taking a careful hold of the bush, Finnlay squeezed himself into the fissure. Rocks and stones pressed hard against his face, but he continued on until with a gasp, he stumbled through and down a short slope. Robert followed behind, almost immediately lighting up his *ayarn*. The cave was just high enough to stand in and sloped down on the left into the darkness. Before them were two more fissures, one which was almost horizontal and barely big enough for a rabbit to squeeze through. The other was quite big enough for a man.

Robert led the way this time, keeping his *ayarn* held out in front of him. Finnlay followed, scraping both hands and knees in his haste to move on. At the end of the second fissure was another cave, this one smaller than the last.

Finnlay looked around for any signs of human passage, but the rocks were swept clean. 'An old water course,' he murmured then stopped. 'Robert, do you think it's possible, since this place is so close to Elita – could there be any references to it in Jacob's library?'

Robert continued along the walls, running his hand down the smooth surface in search of the next opening. 'You should have thought of that before we climbed in here.'

'But if we don't find anything it would be a good place to look next. Do you think if we ask him? If we made some plausible excuse . . .'

Robert stopped in front of another fissure running at an angle away from the sandy floor. He reached up and pulled himself into the opening, taking the light with him. In the sudden darkness, Finnlay caught his answer. 'You try asking him, Finn. I can't go near the place. Look, do you think we can complete one step on this ladder before we leap to the next?'

'Right, coming,' Finnlay called and climbed in after him. He continued, 'Are you sure Jacob won't receive you? Surely he's softened a bit since you took Jenn back.'

'She's not there, remember? She's in Marsay,' Robert's voice echoed around the next cave, 'visiting Selar.'

Finnlay jumped down from the fissure and landed beside Robert. 'I know but . . .'

'For the love of the gods, Finn!' Robert groaned, 'Will you please, just this once, take no for an answer? I said I can't go near the place. Isn't that enough for you?'

Finnlay watched him for a moment, forgetting why they were there. Robert was gazing up at the cave roof, oblivious to his scrutiny. The mood had changed again, without warning, and despite his weary tone, there was an edge to Robert's voice that hadn't been there before. Was he worried about what would happen to Jenn in Marsay? Perhaps it was time to tell him.

He took a deep breath and said, 'You know they sent her a teacher?'

'Sent who a teacher?' Robert continued, searching the cave. 'Am I here on my own? Are you just going to stand there all day?'

'The Enclave sent Jenn a teacher. Fiona. She left on the first day of spring. Jenn must have learnt something by the time she left for Marsay, Robert. She'll be all right.'

'What?' Robert paused and turned, his body stiff.

Finnlay hastened to explain. 'Fiona volunteered. She's a good teacher, really. I don't think she has anything to prove to you, Robert. Not any more.'

Robert took a step forward. His eyes were alight with burning fury. 'After all I did to protect Jenn, you and those . . . those *idiots* deliberately go against her wishes and send her a teacher. I've a good mind to . . .'

'What?' Finnlay mumbled, suddenly afraid.

'Nothing.' Robert shook his head, the light in his eyes dying. 'And you wonder why I don't trust you.'

He turned back to the tunnel and resumed pulling the rocks clear. Finnlay stumbled forward. 'Robert, please, I'm sorry . . .'

'It's too late for apologies. You swore your oath and now you must keep to it. Look on the bright side, Finn – we've finally got something in common.'

Finnlay sank to his knees beside his brother and blindly pulled at the rocks barring their way. All these years he'd been so sure that one day Robert would come around to Enclave thinking, that basically their goals were the same. It would be just a matter of time before Robert would take the oath himself, and then there would be no conflict. But that conflict went so much deeper, and Finnlay had allied himself with the one organization that Robert would never bless. The gulf between them would never close; it would only grow bigger over time.

Right now, Finnlay felt every tiny bit of that divide.

Robert pulled the last of the rocks away and stepped into the narrow opening. Finnlay followed without watching where he was going. He slipped and fell, but as Robert helped him up, his eyes were transfixed by the sight that greeted him. A door. Solid, man-made, and alone on the opposite wall.

Finnlay scrambled to his feet. 'This is it! It must be.'

'Wait!' Robert joined him only inches from the door. 'If this is the right place, then there may well be some kind of sorcery at play here. Remember what that manuscript said – kept in safekeeping? The Calyx is hardly going to be just sitting here waiting for us to come and collect it.'

Without another word he brought his *ayarn* up and studied the door for a full minute. Then, taking a quick breath, he pressed his palm flat to the surface. The door swung inwards, scraping against the sandy floor. More cautiously now, Finnlay moved forward, raising his own light high in the air. As they crept further into the room, features began to take form and shape. The cave had obviously been a dwelling of some kind.

'Look, a table and chairs.'

'Upset, though,' Robert added, taking the left side of the wide room. 'If I didn't know any better, I'd say the place had been vacated in a hurry. But a long time ago – look at the dust.'

Cobwebs were strung across every angle in a thick sticky mess. Along the walls here and there were roots from some determined plants growing through tiny cracks from the rocks outside. Debris both human and natural covered the floor, mats, cooking utensils, rabbit dung and the dry skeleton of a small bird. An ancient mustiness hung in the air; when they stood still, no sound could be heard but their breathing.

'This is incredible!' Finnlay whispered. 'Do you think this might have been a kind of community like the Enclave? And why haven't we heard about it before? Where did the people go? Could this really have been the place where Thraxis hid the Calyx? Where the Marklord himself once walked?'

'You know . . .' Robert's voice broke off as he stared down at a broken stool at his feet. 'Something's been bothering me about that script. Why would the Marklord have anything to do with the Calyx? And why would he be mentioned in the same document as Amar Thraxis? Unless . . . unless Thraxis *was* the Marklord.'

'Robert, I don't think . . .'

'No, wait.' Robert held up his hand. 'Think about it. It is possible. We have so little to go on, the assumptions that were made centuries ago were based on much less information than we now have. What if those assumptions have always been wrong? What if Thraxis was the Marklord – and did make the Calyx. The Calyx was always purported to be for the use of sorcerers, so that would mean,' Robert's face lit up with inspiration, 'there is a correlation between the House Marks and sorcery.'

Finnlay was about to object, but suddenly found that a lot of untidy pieces fell together in his mind. There was no firm, solid way of proving his brother was right but alternatively, there was no way to prove he was wrong. It was an incredible leap of logic, but it had the ring of truth to it.

He nodded. 'Of course, that doesn't answer the question about the three hundred years' difference between the two. However, all we need is the Calyx and we'll know for sure.'

They began a methodical search of the room, disturbing dust and cobwebs alike. There were shelves towards the back of the room, behind which was what looked like a secret niche, but, it was empty. Another smaller room led off at the end, but that proved equally disappointing.

Finnlay came back into the larger room frowning. 'Maybe there are more rooms to this place. Deeper within the mountain. Like the Enclave, this could be just the surface of a whole village.'

'Yes.' Robert straightened up and tilted his head back to look at the ceiling. Then he said in a whisper, 'Unless we're going about this the wrong way.'

'What do you mean?'

'That manuscript said, "kept safe from those who would abuse its power". But who exactly would that be? It couldn't be sorcerers because the Calyx is supposed to be a tool only we can use.'

'Evil sorcerers, then.'

'Perhaps,' Robert glanced at him. 'But think of it this way: if you wanted to keep something safe from people who would abuse it, how would you do it?'

Finnlay grinned. 'I'd leave it lying around somewhere in your study.'

Robert acknowledged the dig with a lopsided smile of his own. 'Anywhere else?'

Finnlay thought about it for a minute, trying to put himself in Thraxis's place. Then he looked up, 'If I had sufficient power available, I would disguise it as something completely harmless – and then leave it lying around in your study.'

This time Robert actually laughed. With a nod he said, 'Dim your light for a minute. I want to try something.'

Finnlay did as he was told, allowing the glow from his *ayarn* to die until it was barely visible in his hand. Robert's light vanished as he lifted the stone until it lay level with his eyes. Hardly able to see in the engulfing darkness, Finnlay instead allowed his senses to float in the hope that he could discern what his brother was doing. He didn't dare speak.

Robert kept the stone in front of him for a few minutes, then slowly stretched his arm out and turned a full circle on the spot. As he began a second turn a single brilliant beam shot out of the *ayarn* and landed on a spot in the far corner.

Finnlay held his breath and gently made his way across the room to where the beam stopped. Once he'd marked the place, Robert abruptly converted the beam back to its normal light and joined him.

'What did you do?' Finnlay asked.

'A variation on the same thing the Key does to choose a leader. I merely focused in on the properties of the Key and hoped it would seek out a like aura. Of course, I began with the assumption that there is some similarity between the Key and the Calyx, but it does appear to have worked.'

'Well, I don't see that it was so successful,' Finnlay bent down and pointed, 'all it found was a broken jug.'

Robert crouched down beside him, frowning for a moment. Then he flashed a smile at his brother. 'Oh really?' He reached forward, touched his *ayarn* to the jug—

And it was suddenly replaced by a long solid metal object about the length of his hand.

'What the . . .!'

Robert reached forward and picked it up. 'It seems you and Amar Thraxis think along the same lines – a disturbing concept.'

'But . . . that's not the Calyx,' Finnlay stood, his heart beating loud enough to hear, 'is it?'

Robert shook his head. 'I don't know what it is.' The object was tubular, with two circular nodules at one end. A pair of fine silver wires hung from the other with bands of intricate design running the whole length of the rod. 'It could be anything – even a piece of the Calyx. All we know for certain is that it's important. Why bother hiding it in such a manner if it wasn't?'

'Well it's definitely not a part of the Key, so I suppose we must assume you're right about there being some affinity between the Key and the Calyx. Hard to imagine, considering the Key is only five hundred years old while the Calyx is over a thousand.'

Robert nodded and tucked the object inside his doublet. Then he turned and led the way out of the room.

As Finnlay followed through the door, he noticed another fissure to his left. With a brief word, he began to make his way through it. It angled down sharply but he laboured on, determined to exhaust every possibility.

Robert didn't object, following him as he passed through one cave after another. The fissures died out and were replaced by narrow tunnels carved out by water over the aeons. They dropped quite a distance until finally Robert called a halt.

'That's enough for one day. Let's make camp in the forest and try again tomorrow.'

Finnlay didn't want to give up, but he nodded, seeing the sense. He glanced back the way they'd come and gave a nervous laugh. 'I only hope we can find a way out of here.'

'There's no need,' Robert said with confidence, 'This tunnel here leads to one of those streams. We'll get a bit wet, but it'll be easier going outside than back through there.'

Finnlay agreed and followed his brother. The tunnel narrowed as they moved towards the surface of the cliff, the dirt beneath their feet turning to mud, covering their ankles with icy water. Finnlay tried to stifle his disappointment and sort out the questions Robert's discovery brought up. There were so many problems associated with finding the Calyx that his concentration was wholly diverted. As a result, he didn't see the danger until it was too late. All he saw was Robert silhouetted against the daylight, framed by the tunnel walls. Then, a split second later, he heard a splash and Robert vanished.

# 16

Bella had argued from the moment they'd left Marsay right up until this morning, when Jenn and Lawrence had left her at Maitland Manor. From that moment onwards, there'd been the most blissful silence, with only the occasional subdued comment from Lawrence. It was a triumph for Jenn, and despite the small knot of guilt nagging in the pit of her stomach, she remained sure of her decision. After all, Selar hadn't stopped them leaving, had he?

But it was so lovely to be back in familiar lands. Still some hours from Elita, Jenn could already see the mountains she loved, the hills and valleys, green and windswept. With the late afternoon shadows drawing across the road, she travelled alongside Lawrence, for once entirely content. When they finally arrived at Elita, Lawrence would return to Bella and Jenn would see nothing more of them until the first autumn leaves began to fall. By then Bella might have calmed down, perhaps even accepted the return of her sister.

Either way, Jenn refused to go back to their old habits. Yes, Bella did have a lot to teach her, and Jenn was eager to learn, but not to lose herself again in trying to be the sister Bella wanted. She was not content to bow her head and say nothing, to follow along without question – to pretend that her past did not exist. Jenn was prepared to try, but in the end, Bella would just have to learn to accept her as she was, for what little time they had left. In a year, perhaps less, Selar would find a husband for her, and then the last of her freedom would be gone. And there was still so much she had to do . . .

. . . *Robert.*

As if in a dream, the forest around her faded, the gusty winds died away. Her vision swam and suddenly she was falling into a whirlpool of swirling darkness. Pain hovered at the edge of her awareness, black and breathtaking. She struggled against the dizziness, against the pain in her chest, when suddenly her vision cleared and she blinked against the sunshine.

Robert was in trouble. In pain. Close by.

With a crushing certainty in her heart, Jenn shot a glance at Lawrence, but fortunately he'd noticed nothing. Furtively, she closed her eyes a moment and cast out with her senses. If Robert was close by there was a chance that she might be able to Seek him. She didn't know what she was doing, but the urgent compulsion in her head pushed her. Robert was in trouble and she had to do something.

Her senses spread out through the forest around them, forward at first between the tall pine and spruce, downhill towards the river. There . . .

She could almost see him as her eyes opened in shock. She had to get to him – and fast, but how? She could hardly tell Lawrence the truth, let alone the guards. No, she would need help to get to Robert, but Lawrence would have to do. Now all she had to do was convince him.

She brought her horse to a stop, letting the others go by. Lawrence turned his horse until he faced her. 'What's wrong?'

'I want to go though the forest. The others can go along the road.'

'I'm sure they can, but I can't very well let you go off on your own. I know we're close to home, but your father would kill me if I let anything happen to you. Come along now. You can come out this way for a ride tomorrow.'

'No, Lawrence,' Jenn said firmly. 'I need to do this now. Let the others go on ahead – you can come with me.'

Frowning, Lawrence glanced through the trees she had indicated. 'I really don't see . . .'

Jenn held up her hand, gently trying to exert a feather-light influence on his attitude. 'Please, Lawrence.'

He gave in easily. 'Very well.' Calling instructions to the waiting guards, Lawrence followed her into the forest.

373

Jenn didn't bother wondering how she was going to explain this later. If she was wrong, it wouldn't matter. If she was right – well, maybe no one would ask how she'd known Robert was there.

They travelled in silence as the forest around them thickened. The ground dropped away and Jenn could hear running water. She urged her horse on, desperate, even though the compulsion had gone.

The trees came to an abrupt end as she reached the stream bank. The sharp drop to the water was matched by a similar rocky bank on the other side. Ferns and bracken lined the bank in huge clumps, reaching down to the water in a glory of greens and golds. Lawrence murmured something about finding an easier place to cross, but Jenn hardly heard him. Instead her eyes searched desperately for some sign of Robert. He had to be here. There was no sign of anything downstream, so Jenn turned her horse upstream, guiding it carefully along the rising bank. Above her, the stream cascaded down huge boulders in the hillside, carving a path through the forest that was aeons old.

After a few minutes, however, not even the horse could manage the treacherous path. Lawrence said they should go back to the road, but Jenn ignored him and jumped from her horse. Her skirt caught on the bracken but she struggled on, more certain every minute that Robert was here somewhere. She was getting close – but where was he?

A flash of colour, there! A thin line of cobalt blue tangled between some rocks. Jenn shouted and crashed down the bank into the water. She staggered against the cold, the current tugged at her clothing, but she waded forward, dauntless. She stumbled and fell, but her hand reached out and grabbed hold of the blue cloth. Struggling, she dragged herself forward, pulling hard. Her other hand stretched out and finally touched flesh and bone. Robert! Caught between the rocks, face down in the water. Without hesitating, she dragged his head up. Blood ran from a wound on his forehead and down the side of his lifeless face.

She turned to call Lawrence again but found him wading

374

through the water behind her. Turning back to Robert, she put her fingers on his throat. He was still alive. Heart pounding with relief, she held him and waited for Lawrence.

Exhausted and heartsick, Finnlay eventually returned to the horses. He'd followed every avenue down from the tunnel mouth to the edge of the forest and had still found no sign of his brother. He'd tried calling out and then, desperate, he'd fallen in an effort to reach what might have been a promising stream. Now, bruised and aching in every muscle, he collected the horses and made a steady trek down the mountainside, unwilling to even think about what had happened to Robert.

Taking this safer path meant that it took him more than an hour to reach the forest below the cliff. Leading the horses through the undergrowth, he finally found the major watercourse leading from the mountain. Slowly and deliberately he followed it down. Robert had to be down here somewhere. Alive. He couldn't have died, not like this – not Robert, of all people.

But it was getting dark. Clouds rolled across the sunset and a brisk wind whipped around his sodden clothing. Shivering, Finnlay continued on, unwilling to stop. Finally the sun sank, leaving only haunting fingers of red streaming across the sky. He stopped and sat down to rest. He tied the horses to a rock and brought out his *ayarn*. He'd tried this three times already up on the mountain but had sensed nothing of his brother. That could mean only one of two things. Either Robert was unconscious – or he was dead. Perhaps by now he might have woken up and Finnlay would be able to Seek him out.

He closed his eyes and concentrated solely on Robert. In his hands, the stone began to glow and grow warm. He sent out his mind along the river downstream from where he sat. He searched and searched but found . . . nothing.

Finnlay opened his eyes, but couldn't see the dusk-lit river bank before him. All he could see was that moment when Robert had slipped and fallen down the cliff.

'Don't move!'

He froze as the voice behind him warned again, 'Stay right where you are! Did you see that, Florric? That thing in his hand?'

'Aye, Raymon, I did.'

The bracken around Finnlay rustled as the men moved closer. He started to turn around, but the first man shouted again, 'I said keep still, sorcerer! I have my bow on ye. But I'd rather not kill ye myself.'

'No,' said Florric with a grim laugh, 'We'll leave that to the judges. They'll love this! A real live sorcerer. Come on.'

A hand landed on Finnlay's shoulder. 'Look,' he began in his friendliest tones, 'I don't know what you saw but I can easily explain . . .'

'I said don't move!'

Finnlay felt a breath of air brush past his ear then a crashing pain in his head. He fell forward on to the rocks and everything went black.

Robert floated on a sea of gentle blue, gazing up at a sky of deep azure. The water was warm, and so very soft. Like down, it caressed his skin, sank deep into his weary muscles, into his very soul. Calm. He'd never felt so calm. Was this real peace? Was this what it felt like? With the gentle motion of the sea rocking his body in time with his heart, he had no desire to move. The water lapped into his mouth but it was sweet, like honey. He drank mouthfuls of it, the flavour exploding on his tongue in a thousand tiny spirals. Where was this place? Was this death?

A cry reached his ears and something dark moved across the sky. He followed the black dart as it hovered and dived, climbed and soared. An eagle. A black eagle. His eagle. It swooped over him again and again, but it never threatened, only accompanied, like some faithful guide in this beautiful dreamworld. Peace, it seemed to say. Peace and calm. Trust. All will be well.

Robert opened his eyes. The sky was gone. Now there was

376

a vaulted ceiling, darkened, candlelit. The shadows from a fire flickered across the arches, vanished into the corners. He was in a bed, somewhere. Warm, comfortable, quiet. But where?

The smell of herbs to his left and he turned his head. A table, bowls, jars, bandages. Was he injured? Further on now, there, the fireplace, a portrait above it, hanging from the golden sandstone wall, the face unfamiliar. Beside the fire another small table, a chair, with a woman seated, reading . . .

Jenn?

She was turned towards him, but her eyes were intent on her book. A candle stood on the table beside her, leaving one side of her face in soft shadow. She was frowning, her fine brows drawn together in puzzlement. Her lips were parted, her tongue caught on her upper teeth. Deep concentration. But oh, how she had changed!

She wore a simple red gown, no jewellery. Her thick dark hair was plaited and fell over one shoulder, past her waist. Candlelight danced across her skin, making her eyes sparkle. She looked older and taller and different and quite, quite beautiful.

Mesmerized, Robert watched her, noting every tiny movement she made. Soon though, her eyes darted to him and back to her book − then she paused. She glanced at him again and seeing he was awake, she sprang out of her chair, dropping the book to the floor.

'You're awake!' she cried, her smile pure sunshine. 'How do you feel?'

Robert struggled to form some words. His mouth felt like lead. 'What happened?'

'What happened?' she laughed. 'You mean you don't remember? I was hoping you could tell me.'

'Have I been ill?'

'You had some kind of accident. You hit your head and almost drowned. You've been lying there unconscious for the last twelve hours. It will be dawn soon. Don't you remember what happened?'

Robert shook his head, still unable to look away from her. 'No. How did I get here?'

'I found you. Lawrence helped me bring you back. Are you hungry? I have some bread and cheese here, and wine.'

She leapt up and brought a tray back to him. He pushed himself up a bit and immediately felt sharp stabbing pains in his shoulder and hip, bruises on his legs and a searing ache in his left wrist. He raised his hand to find it heavily bandaged.

'Where's my *ayarn*?'

'Don't worry.' Jenn laid the tray on his lap. 'I removed it when no one was looking. I put it under your right sleeve.'

She pulled off a piece of bread and put it in his mouth. She tore off another lump but he took it from her. 'I'm not an invalid.'

She said nothing but sat on the side of the bed and watched him. Between mouthfuls he said, 'How did you find me?'

'I don't really know how it happened. We were coming back, riding past the forest, and suddenly I had the feeling that something had happened to you. When I tried Seeking you, I found you lying in a river, unconscious and injured. Lawrence helped me bring you back.'

Robert paused with a piece of cheese halfway to his mouth. 'You found me? While I was unconscious?'

'Yes. Why?'

'Well, strictly speaking, that's not supposed to be possible.'

'Well nobody told me I couldn't do it, so I tried. Why, can you?'

'There's been the odd occasion, yes.'

She shook her head. 'One of these days, Robert Douglas, you and I are going to have to sit down and have a very long talk.'

Robert had to smile, though it hurt. 'What did you tell Lawrence?'

'Nothing. I just persuaded him to help me.'

'By logic alone?'

Her eyes darted away. 'Not entirely, no.'

'That was an awful risk to take.'

'I didn't have a choice.' With a shrug, she poured him some wine, held the cup out. 'Are you sure you don't remember anything?'

He tried, but there was nothing there. Nothing that could account for him being in a forest this close to Elita. But he did remember something. 'I shouldn't be here. Your father will want me gone.'

'Yes,' Jenn replied gently, 'when you're better. Tell me, do you feel all right? I mean apart from your injuries?'

There was an intensity in her gaze that hadn't been there a moment ago. To please her, he searched within, but again came up with nothing. Everything seemed to be wiped clean, fresh, like his own personal Dawn of Ages.

'I feel fine, Jenn. Why do you ask?'

The intensity disappeared and she smiled again. 'It doesn't matter.'

She stood and took the tray away. 'I think you should try and get some more sleep. Perhaps in the morning you'll remember what happened to you.'

'But I'm not really tired,' Robert protested. He didn't want her to leave yet.

'Well, would you like some more wine?'

'Thank you.'

She sat on the edge of the bed again and refilled his cup. What was it about her that was so different? This was not the poor homeless waif he'd brought to Elita almost six months ago.

'Tell me,' he began quietly, 'do you miss your wandering?'

'Honestly? Yes, I do.' Jenn folded her hands on her lap and gazed down at her fingers. 'There are days when I wish I could just take a horse and go. Sometimes I even believe I'll do it. I lost my freedom, Robert, and that was always very precious to me. I know that's not what you intended, bringing me here, and I guess I didn't think much about it either, but I lost it all the same.'

'But how much freedom did you have before, living in Shan Moss?'

'At the inn? A great deal.' A warm smile lit her eyes as she glanced up at him. 'My father was a good man. He never beat me – even though I deserved it sometimes. I used to slip out at night, when the inn was busy and I should have been working. I'd go into the forest and climb a particular tree. I tried to see as far down the trade road as I could. I kept wondering what the world was like away from the forest. What did the ocean look like, mountains, fields of wheat and corn. I longed to see more, but I never wanted to leave home, my father. When he died . . .'

'What happened?'

She looked away, frowning. 'His nephew came and took over the inn. He said I was too young to stay there. He sent me to a cousin's farm on the other side of the forest. She took me in but she had a dozen children of her own and didn't really want me. Life was . . . hard, for a while. That summer the crops failed and her husband got very drunk. In the morning, he threw me out with nothing more than a few coppers and a loaf of bread. I didn't go back.'

Robert kept silent, entranced by her story. No wonder she'd not wanted to come to Elita. She must have been so afraid they wouldn't want her – or would reject her because of her past.

'I didn't really know what to do, where to go. I wandered for a few days, then came upon a village. I asked at the inn if they had work and they gave it to me. For months I stayed there. It almost felt like home, with all the people coming and going. Then one day, a storyteller came. He held the whole inn in raptures as he told his stories. At the end, they gave him money and he moved on. I thought, that's what I can do. Travel and tell stories, collect stories. So free. I never dreamed I would meet one of those legends, become part of a story myself.'

Very carefully, Robert asked, 'And are you sorry you did? Sorry you came here?'

At this she gazed at him with sparkling eyes, 'No, Robert.

I'm not sorry. There are other things besides freedom, aren't there? You can hardly disagree with me.'

'No,' he said, 'I can't.'

'And he doesn't remember anything about what happened?'

'Not so far, but he will, I'm sure.' Jenn came around the table and poured Jacob some more ale. She tried not to frown at the glaring light which swept through the study windows, but it was hard. That's what you get for sitting up all night. At least Robert had slept again and should be feeling much better this afternoon.

Jacob ignored the ale in front of him and instead caught her hand, forcing her to meet his eyes. 'He can't stay here long.'

'I know, Father.' What did he want from her? Did he want her to prove to him that she felt no loyalty to Robert? Did he want her to turn Robert out, regardless of his injuries? 'Please don't worry. He won't stay a moment longer than he has to. He's quite aware of how you feel about him.'

Jacob released her hand and glowered down the table. 'It has nothing to do with how I feel about him. After your abrupt departure from court, I'm more concerned about how this will appear to the King! He must be watching both our Houses very closely. What is he going to say when he finds out Dunlorn's been here? You must learn to appreciate the finer points of your actions, Jennifer. You endanger not only yourself, but others.'

'But it's all very innocent, Father. Robert had an accident and we helped. Surely even the King cannot take exception to that.'

'How do you know?' Jacob said. 'What makes you so sure it is innocent? You don't know what Dunlorn was doing in that forest, and he claims he cannot remember. I've not survived this long in a dangerous world to be such a fool, even where you're concerned. I realize you feel you owe him something but I must look to your safety, child. If Dunlorn has any honour left, he will agree with me.'

Jenn wanted to protest. She wanted to tell her father the

depths to which Robert's honour went, but she couldn't. After all these years, he was never going to change his mind. What Jacob really wanted was to know was that he could trust her.

'Of course, Father,' she murmured, hating herself even as she deliberately lied. 'I'm sorry. I'll make sure he leaves the moment he can climb on to a horse. He won't come back, I promise.'

Finnlay had no idea what time it was, or how long he'd been in the cell. It never looked any different: dark, damp, with an overpowering stench of rats and rotting mould. A tiny sliver of light came from under the door, stretched across the hay-strewn floor. Smoky light came through a window high above on his right, little more than a foot wide, but it led only to the corridor and not outside.

All this time they'd left him alone, afraid of him, afraid even to interrogate him. What terror his mistake had engendered – by the gods – what had he done?

He crouched on the floor, wrapped his arms around his body and tried to stop shaking with the cold. At least, he wanted it to be the cold. He couldn't afford fear. Not now.

His hands were like ice; the chains around his wrists and ankles cut into flesh and bone. The pain in his head was sharp and when he moved he could feel dried blood flake away from his skin. He was thirsty, but in this damp cell, the thought of drinking only made his stomach churn.

They had taken his *ayarn* and without it, his senses were blind.

Not the best way to end a life.

Finnlay forced out a laugh, tried to see all this in the same ironic way Robert would ... But it was useless. Robert was dead, and Finnlay had killed him.

A clank of metal against wood and the door swung wide, flooding the cell with light. Finnlay screwed up his eyes as two men entered, their swords drawn and pointed at his chest. A third man followed and put a bowl of water by Finnlay's feet.

'So, how do you feel now, sorcerer?' the man grunted. Cold, black eyes stared out of a face pitted with scars from some childhood disease. There was contempt and hatred in that gaze, and some fear, too. 'Want to confess your crimes?'

Finnlay remained crouched in his corner. There was no need to provoke these people further. Their ingrained fear was already enough to make them want an excuse to kill him on the spot. 'I have nothing to confess. As I tried to tell those men in the woods, I'm not a sorcerer.'

'Tell that to the judges!' the man spat. 'They'll be here in two days to try you. You have until then to repent. We have a priest standing by when you want him.'

'But I have nothing to confess . . .'

'Then perhaps you need a little encouragement,' the sergeant waved his hand and one of the guards moved forward, his sword aimed at Finnlay's face. With the smallest flick, the sword point slashed Finnlay's right cheek, down to his chin. The pain burned like fire, but Finnlay refused to cry out.

'I think it's time you told us who you are. What were you doing in that forest? Where do you come from?'

Finnlay scrambled to his feet, his heart pounding loud enough to hear. They must not find out his name – ever!

'Come, sorcerer! Your name! Who are you?' Suddenly the sergeant lashed out and hit Finnlay across the face. Finnlay stumbled against his chains and fell back to the wall. Before he could even get his breath, the sergeant hit him again, this time in the stomach. As Finnlay doubled over, fighting for air, the sergeant came close, his breath foul in the dank cell. 'Not so powerful after all, are you?'

'I . . . tell you,' Finnlay gasped, trying to stand up straight again, 'I'm not a sorcerer.'

The sergeant grabbed Finnlay's hair, pulled his head back until his neck was stretched tight. 'Say that once more, sorcerer, and I'll cut your throat here and now! I don't really care about waiting for the judges. I know how those Guilde fanatics feel about you people – but me? I'd rather rid the world of you personally. We don't want your lying, evil ways

383

here. Do you understand? Dark Angel you may be, but I'm not going to let you out of here unless you're either already dead or going to the stake.'

With a jerk, the sergeant shoved Finnlay's head back against the wall and moved away. 'Chain him to the wall. We don't want him to get any ideas about escaping, do we?'

The guards grabbed him then, pushing him back against the wall. He could feel the blood trickling down his throat, making his muddy shirt wet. As they pulled up his right hand however, the sergeant lunged forward. 'What's that?' he said as he grabbed the ring from Finnlay's finger.

'Where did you get this? A black eagle on a silver mount. I'm sure I've seen that before somewhere.'

'I found it,' Finnlay replied quickly.

'Oh, really,' the sergeant sneered, 'then you won't mind if I take it and find out who it really belongs to. It's a valuable ring, like your clothes. Rich. Perhaps you didn't find it. Perhaps you stole it – from a dead man.'

The sergeant laughed then, and together with the guards, moved back out of the cell. The door clanged shut, but it was only as the echo died away that Finnlay noticed the other feeling, the one that crept up on his senses like a shadow in the night. Blind without his *ayarn* he might be, but this sensation required no special talent. Not since he and Robert had worked on it a few weeks ago. There was a Malachi nearby, no doubt about it.

His chains clanging around him, Finnlay settled back down to the floor. His hands began to shake again – and this time it *was* with fear.

It was almost sunset by the time Jenn took the doctor up. Robert was still asleep when they went in, but woke immediately. Jenn helped him sit up and for a moment ignored the nagging doubt in her heart. There would be time to explore that later.

'This is Doctor Wishart,' she began. 'He's come up from the hospice to see you.'

384

Robert glanced at her, then nodded to the old man. 'We've met before, Doctor, have we not?

'Your Grace is kind to remember,' Wishart murmured, his rheumy eyes giving away nothing. 'And how does Your Grace feel this evening?'

'Evening already? Well, I feel a little stiff, but I think I could get up.'

Wishart nodded, reaching out to touch the bruise on Robert's forehead. 'I think perhaps Your Grace's wounds are a little more serious than they seem at the moment. You will have trouble walking, and that knock to your head will make you dizzy if you try. I recommend two weeks' bed rest, Your Grace. No less. Do you remember how it happened?'

Jenn quickly moved to the end of the bed and threw Robert a warning glance. *Tell him you fell from your horse. Nothing more.*

'My horse stumbled, Doctor. I must have fallen and hit my head.'

'I see,' Wishart murmured, probing his shoulder. He straightened up and turned to Jenn. 'The herbs you are giving him will do for the moment, and I suggest a poultice for the shoulder, my lady. Other than that, he just needs to stay in bed. I'll call back in three days, but do let me know if there are any further problems.'

Jenn nodded and showed him to the door. When she came back, Robert was watching her with a mixture of confusion and annoyance. She had to smile.

'You're enjoying this.'

'How ungenerous!' she laughed and sat beside him. 'After everything I've done for you.'

'Look, I can't stay in bed for two weeks. I feel fine.'

'I know. Actually, I'm afraid the old doctor was being a little over-cautious. Your injuries aren't that bad at all. You've not broken anything, although riding is going to be painful for a while. Nevertheless, you do need some rest, at least for a couple of days. How do you know Doctor Wishart?'

Robert flexed his wrist and his expression immediately became shuttered. 'He tended my wife once.'

'Oh.' So that was how Bella had known. By the gods – it couldn't be true!

Abruptly she got up and brought back his supper tray. She sat it on the bed in front of him. As he began eating, she continued watching him. He was still very pale and the normal lustre in his eyes was gone. That just made it worse. But he didn't seem to feel anything. He behaved normally, as though nothing was wrong. Had he forgotten about his uncle, or did Robert really have that much control? If so, why could she see the pain – there, inside him, like a disease?

Jenn sighed. 'Perhaps we'd better concentrate on what happened to you yesterday. Do you remember the forest at all? Do you know why you were there?'

'I don't remember any forest,' Robert frowned, 'nor a river.'

'Well, do you know what this is?' She reached under the bed and brought forth the item wrapped in scarlet cloth. 'I found this inside your doublet. I couldn't recognize it so I hid it along with your *ayarn*. I didn't want to take any more chances.'

She unwrapped the silver object and held it up for Robert to see. He frowned again and the wound on his forehead grew dark red. He closed his eyes for a second, then hissed in a breath.

'Finnlay!' He struggled to sit up but she held him back.

'What about him? Was he with you?'

'Yes. We were up on the mountain, investigating the caves. I fell, must have gone down the cliff. He must be looking for me even now. By the gods, he'll be frantic. I've got to . . .'

'No. I'll send some people out to look for him. If he saw you fall, he'd be combing the river. Just wait here.' Before she could move however, the door burst open and Fiona stood there, her face white with shock.

'Jenn, I've been looking for you! I've just heard the most disturbing news.'

'What? What's happened?'

Fiona darted a glance at Robert, then closed the door quickly, waving her hand to set the warning. 'It's Finnlay. He's been arrested on charges of sorcery.'

Now Robert did get out of bed, and Jenn did nothing to stop him. Instead she pressed Fiona for more details. 'How did it happen?'

'He was in the forest. Two woodsmen saw some bright light coming from his hand. Going from the description, it sounds like Finnlay. Was he with you, Robert?'

'Aye, he was. Jenn, I need the rest of my clothes. I have to get Finn out of there.'

Her heart racing, Jenn nodded slowly. 'Yes, of course.'

'But you can't go anywhere like this,' Fiona cried. 'You're not fit even to ride!'

Robert ignored her protest and reached for the doublet Jenn handed him. 'Where are they keeping Finnlay?'

Fiona hesitated, looking from Robert to Jenn and back.

'Tell him,' Jenn murmured, 'you can't stop him and you know it.' With that, she turned and pulled open a chest sitting by the opposite wall. Quickly she rummaged through the old clothes, coming up with something in dark colours.

'Finnlay's in a village called Kilphedir, in the heart of the forest. You'll never find it on your own.'

'Robert's not going alone,' Jenn added. 'I'm going with him. Fiona, you'll have to help us. I can get horses saddled and waiting outside the garden wall, but I need you to do a mask. The guard will see us leaving otherwise. Robert can't manage one and I've yet to learn.'

'You have no idea what you're doing!' Fiona insisted. 'You've never done anything like this before. What if you're missed. What will your father say?'

'We don't have time for this,' Robert said, pulling on his boots.

No, they didn't. Jenn tossed the old clothes over her shoulder and turned to face Fiona. 'It will be much worse if you're missed. You're the stranger here – they will assume you had something to do with it. If you stay here, you can provide an excuse for me. I've gone to bed with a headache. I stayed up too many hours looking after this renegade. My father will believe you. Trust me. Please, Fiona, Finnlay's in danger. We must help.'

Slowly the resistance died in Fiona's eyes. 'Very well,' she said.

The night was clear and a thousand stars glittered above like diamonds in the sky. A cool breathless breeze floated across the lake and up to the ridge where Robert paused long enough to make sure they weren't being followed. But the valley was empty and he turned his horse for the downward slope. Jenn rode behind him, dressed like a stable boy, her hair bound up beneath a cloth cap. On the surface she looked tiny, young and vulnerable, but the way her eyes shimmered determination, he wasn't fooled.

Robert gave the horse its head as it clambered down the rocky incline. The pain in his hip was bad and likely to get worse. How could he help Finnlay like this? If only he hadn't slipped and fallen down that damned cliff. If only he hadn't gone on that stupid venture in the first place. If only Oliver hadn't been such a fool!

Yes, he remembered now. Everything, right down to the last agonizing, blistering detail. But he couldn't worry about it now. Now he had to concentrate on rescuing Finnlay and find a way out of this awful mess.

'Are you all right?' Jenn asked, bringing her horse alongside his.

'Why do you keep asking me that?' Robert snapped.

'I'm sorry.'

'And don't apologize!' Robert kicked his horse and cantered off. He assumed she followed. For more than an hour they rode in silence, keeping mainly to the trees where they lined the contours of the gentle hills. After that however, Robert had to call a halt, to walk the horses for a bit. He tried shifting in his saddle to ease the pain, but stopped when he realized Jenn was watching him. She said nothing, only rode behind him, the spare horse beside her.

He gave up trying to stop the pain, instead focusing his mind on the real problem at hand. 'How well do you know Kilphedir?'

'I don't,' Jenn replied quietly, as though she'd rather not talk at all. 'I haven't been allowed to stray far from Elita – at least, not until we went to Marsay.'

'Then why did you insist on coming along?' Robert demanded without pausing. 'Do you even know where it is?'

There was no reply at first. Then Jenn drew her horse alongside his, reached out and caught his bridle. She brought both of them to a halt and fixed him with a steady gaze. She paused as though trying to find the right words, but he had no time for this. 'We have to keep moving.'

'Robert,' Jenn began without anger, 'If you don't stop fighting me, I'm going to hit you.'

'You? Hit me?' It was absurd, and without meaning to, Robert burst out laughing. Jenn watched him gravely, saying nothing. 'You don't need to. Come, let's move on. You can tell me about your trip to Marsay.'

They continued on, but Jenn was unusually silent. Was she still angry with him? 'Well? Did you enjoy yourself in our lovely capital?'

'Not really,' Jenn murmured. 'There's nothing much to tell. I met a lot of people who stared at me like I was some monster. Some people were very kind, others not. I met the Queen.'

Robert shot a glance at her, half-afraid to ask. 'And the King?'

'Yes. But he was more interested in what you were doing – and in finding me a suitable husband.'

Of course he would. There's no way Selar would ignore a potential threat like Jenn. Not when his own son was still a small child. 'Did you meet anyone else I know?'

At this she turned a flinty gaze on him, clearly visible in the starlight. 'I met your dear friend Vaughn. He was most insistent that I tell him your future plans.'

Robert frowned. There was something very brittle in her voice, something she wasn't telling him. 'What did you say?'

*I told him you were determined to stay at Dunlorn. Liar!*

With a chuckle, Robert shook his head. 'Well, it's nice to know some things haven't changed. Is that all? Nothing else?'

'No. Nothing. Listen, have you any idea what we're going to do when we get to Kilphedir? We can't exactly just walk in and take Finnlay home, can we?'

'No. However, I can't make any real plans until I see the place, find out where they're holding him. What bothers me more is whether Finnlay is trying to escape. Without a horse he won't get very far. They'll just pick him up again and assume his guilt – if they haven't already. Damn, I should have been watching where I was putting my feet. If I hadn't fallen, none of this would have happened!'

Robert paused long enough to shoot a grin at Jenn, 'But no, you're right, I don't have time for self-recrimination. We need to keep to the point. What else can you tell me about this village?'

Jenn gazed heavenwards in silent appeal. Eventually she replied, 'About five hundred inhabitants. Surrounded on all sides by the forest. The road goes through east to west. Actually, you might have seen it from the cliffs.'

'I think I did,' Robert said. But what was Finnlay doing now? Would he try to escape? 'Jenn, tell me, do you think you could try talking to Finn? Warn him to stay where he is?'

'I don't know. It's worth a go.' Jenn stopped her horse and in the dim light he could just make out the pale oval of her face with her eyes nothing more than dark shadows. She frowned. 'What should I say? The shorter the message, the better chance I have of getting through to him.'

'How about: "idiot"?'

She smiled. *All right, idiot.*

'Not me,' he growled in mock anger, 'Finnlay!'

*Sorry, sometimes I get you confused.*

She was silent for a moment, then, on the very edges of his awareness, he heard a whisper. He couldn't make out the words, but he knew it was her voice. As it melted away she glanced up. 'I don't know if it worked. I just told him to wait because we were on our way. However, unless you've told him about my little trick, he'll probably just think he's going mad.'

Robert nodded and turned his horse back to the path. 'He won't be the first one.'

'Do you think they know who he is?' Jenn asked out of the darkness.

'He won't tell them.'

'But if they find out anyway? What will happen then?'

Robert had already thought about this, was trying hard not to, in fact. 'His name will be anathema. He will be hunted from one end of the country to the other. If he's ever caught, he'll be executed immediately. On top of that, there'll be stories about sorcerers everywhere. Suspicion will be rampant. It's what we've always tried to avoid.'

'And what about you? Will they assume you're guilty too?'

'Probably. I'll worry about that when I get to it. Now all we have to do is rescue my brother without getting caught ourselves.'

Woods became hills, which in turn became woods again. After two hours they finally reached the edge of the forest and paused on the bank of the river.

'This is where I found you – further up, though.'

The water was black, deep and very fast. 'Is there a better place to cross?'

'Not without going upstream for an hour or so. We can't afford the time, can we? The moon will be up soon.'

Without a word, Robert turned his horse down the bank. It stumbled and splashed into the water. His knees were drenched and the cold bit at his wounds. The current was violent, but it only increased his urgency. There was so little of the night left to get Finn out and away before they could be found, before Jenn could get home safely.

The horse clambered up the opposite bank and Robert turned to watch Jenn. She led the spare horse, but with both animals being pushed together by the current, they stumbled, threatening to throw her into the water. The horses reared and screamed in panic.

'Let the other horse go!' Robert cried, already heading back into the river. Without pausing, he reached inside for the power to steady the animals, to stop her from being dragged downriver. He tried – but there was nothing. No powers! That blow to his head . . .

'Jenn, hold on!' he bellowed, crashing into the water. Turn your horse into the current. Be careful.

She let go the reins of the spare horse and turned into the force. Immediately her horse righted itself and gradually she made her way towards Robert. The moment she was up on the bank, he splashed forward and caught the other animal. His wrist screamed agony as he pulled the leather, but he didn't stop. Seconds later they made it to the bank, the animals panting with the exertion. They were wet, but fortunately the night wasn't too cold.

Jenn was squeezing out the water from the edges of her cloak. She glanced up at him with a bemused smile. 'You know, Robert, life is never dull when you're around.'

'Really?' Robert laughed. 'I suppose that's why you missed me so much. Come on, let's get moving.'

# 17

They picked up the pace again, cantering to get warm. By
the time they grew close, Robert was in considerable pain.
The forest drew close around them as they stopped in a
scrubby clearing where dots of starlight appeared through
the branches above. Robert swung his leg over the back of
the horse and tried to ease himself down to the ground. As
his bad leg hit the forest floor, however, it buckled beneath
him and he fell hard. Jenn jumped down and rushed to his
side.

'Robert, you're a damned fool – and I'm a bigger fool for
letting you do this. Come on.' She put her arm under his
shoulders and dragged him to the base of the nearest tree,
resting his back against the trunk. She darted to her horse
and returned with a small pouch.

'Why is it people like you always think they're indestruc-
tible?' She rummaged around in the pouch and brought out
a small flask. 'Listen, you know that thing you did? With the
old man – the way you stopped his pain? Can you do that
on yourself?'

Robert couldn't help smiling. She was so brisk, so efficient.
She ordered him about like he was a child and didn't give it
a second thought. Unlike almost everybody he'd ever met,
she wasn't afraid of him, hadn't even shrunk back from him
when he'd snapped at her.

'No,' he replied, 'it can't be directed inwards.'

'Then can you teach me how to do it?'

'We don't have time.'

'Very well,' Jenn said evenly, 'you'll just have to drink
this.'

She held out the bottle to him. He took it and swallowed

a mouthful of the most sickly, bitter, revolting mixture he'd ever tasted.

'Ah!' he gasped, 'what is that?

'Punishment,' she replied flatly. 'In a couple of minutes the pain will start to go. It should last a few hours, long enough to get Finnlay out. After that, you'll just have to suffer.'

She turned away long enough to put the bottle back in the pouch, then sat on the ground beside him. She stared at the branches above, up at the stars, then across the clearing to where the village lay hidden by the trees.

'I want to tell you,' she said softly, 'how sorry I was to hear about your uncle. It was a terrible thing to happen.'

And just like that, it all came back. It was amazing how swiftly he could remember, how long it took him to forget. And there was so much he had to forget. It had been easy the last few hours, with something else to do.

'Robert?' Jenn murmured and waited for him to look up. 'You don't realize it. You can't see it because you're so close to it. But I can see that . . . you're dying.'

Robert forced a laugh. 'What? But you said my injuries weren't serious! Have you poisoned me?'

She didn't smile in return. She just shook her head and reached forward, placing her hand on his chest, close to his heart. 'You're dying in here. As each day goes by and you continue to struggle with yourself, another part of you dies. Soon there won't be anything left. You're dying, Robert, believe me; I can see it. The worst thing is, there's only one way you can stop it. You must do something.'

Her eyes locked on to his and he suddenly found it difficult to breathe. How could she see so clearly what others were blind to? How could she know so much about the demon?

The realization took his breath away – and knocked him hard enough to push everything back down, deep inside. With a grim smile now, he answered her. 'I can't . . . do anything, Jenny. It's not as simple as you think. There's so much you don't know. It's just not possible.'

394

Jenn frowned, unmoved by his evasive response. 'Does it have anything to do with what the Key told you? Is that what's holding you back?'

Robert's heart stopped. 'What makes you say that?'

'Does it?'

The compulsion to tell her was enormous, but he couldn't tell whether it was coming from her or himself. He took a breath and said, 'Yes.'

She held his gaze for a long time then glanced away briefly. When she turned back, it was with a frown. 'You may have failed before, but does that guarantee you'll fail again? Have you always mastered everything the first time you tried? Are you really that clever? Robert, I'm not telling you what to do. I'd never dream of it. All I know is that if you're to survive, you must act. Withdrawing from life is not the answer. You know what I'm saying is true, don't you?'

Her eyes remained on him, unwavering but also strangely uncertain. It was as though she had the ability to see deep inside him to a place he was blind to himself. How could she see so much?

What else would she see – what else could he dare let her see?

Above, the trees rustled with the wind, reminding him it was time to go, but for just a moment, he stayed there, watching her, unwilling to move and destroy these few strange moments of peace. Her face, so young and yet so old, held none of the insistent pressure of all the others; instead, she merely voiced what his own heart kept telling him. Yet she did it with care, as though she were afraid of hurting him.

With his eyes still on hers, he took her hand from his chest and gently raised it to his lips. Her skin was cool soft. She didn't pull away.

'Come on,' he murmured, 'let's go and get my wayward brother free.'

She helped him up and he found that noxious mixture had done its work. The pain in his leg and hip was almost gone, certainly enough to get over the next few hurdles.

With Jenn following close, he worked his way through the trees. The forest came to an end and they took shelter behind a huge oak. From there they could see the village, almost a town.

Now, were his powers still gone, or had his head wound healed enough now? There was only one way he would know. He pushed down carefully. Yes, there was something stirring, but he couldn't hold it, control it. He couldn't sense anything further than the other side of the tree.

Swearing silently, he glanced at Jenn standing at his shoulder. 'Can you sense where he is?'

*Just a second.*

Robert waited, wishing he didn't have to rely on her this way.

*He's in a building by the church wall. Can you see the tower? We'll have to go down the main street to get to it. There seem to be a lot of people around.*

Yes, there were. 'I'd say word has already got out about the capture of a sorcerer. People will travel leagues to see the trial. Still, it could be useful to us.'

*You mean they won't notice two more strangers?*

'One more – you'll stay here. Help me get this bandage off my wrist. I can't use the *ayarn* in my right hand.' He didn't dare tell her he could hardly use his powers at all.

She reached out and unwound the dressing, glancing up at him with raised eyebrows. *I'm to stay here, am I? Safely out of the way?*

'That's right.'

*And how are you going to stop me?*

Robert snatched his hand away from her and tore the rest of the bandage off. 'I'll tie you to this tree if I have to!'

*Stop shouting.*

'I'm not shouting, I'm whispering.'

*No, Robert. I mean you don't need to whisper either.*

But he didn't have time for this. He turned away and with his *ayarn* in his left hand, he sent his senses out into the village. Yes, there was Finnlay, still in his cell – along with a number of guards. Damn! Still, there was no way around it . . .

*Robert, I heard you. Back at the river. You told me to turn my horse into the current – but you didn't say it aloud. You can speak back to me now.*

Robert froze. Slowly he turned back to face her. Hardly daring to hope, he gripped his *ayarn* tight and formed a single word. With as much force as his wounded body could muster, he sent it towards her.

*Jenny?*

Her answer was a brilliant smile.

*By the gods! I can do it too!*

*Yes! Fun isn't it? Perhaps in future you'll learn to listen to me. Now, before you get carried away, I suggest we move on.*

Laughing his submission, Robert turned and stepped into the street. She was right – he couldn't stop her.

The church was small with a high wooden tower and a graveyard full of inky-black shapes. Robert led Jenn, crouched low until they gained the church wall. Feeling stronger by the minute, Robert kept his senses alert, feeling for anyone who might cross their path. The village was already patrolled by woodsmen and farmers wearing swords. Unaccustomed to such arms, these men challenged every soul who passed by them, whether friend or stranger. The whole village seemed on edge with such a dangerous prisoner. Robert felt it was his duty to ease that strain, relieve them of the burden.

He glanced down at Jenn, crouched beside him. Her blue eyes were wide as she kept watch on the graveyard, the street beyond. The moon had yet to appear, but it was only a matter of a few minutes.

*Robert, are you sure we can get Finnlay out? I know I'm new to this but that building looks like a proper guardhouse. I think he's in some kind of cellar.*

*He is. There're also at least a dozen guards in there with him. Can you sense them?*

*No.*

It was amazing. It was getting easier every time he did it. It was possible he didn't even need to use his *ayarn* any more – but then, he hadn't the first time, had he?

Standing, he gave Jenn a lift up on to the wall. As she jumped down, he climbed over and landed beside her. Before them was a small courtyard and a large gate to their left, leading back to the street. Quickly now, they crossed the courtyard to a heavy wooden door. Robert was about to attack the lock when his senses warned him of someone approaching. They were in the shadows but the man would soon see them.

*Damn! A guard! Keep still and I'll try a mask. I don't know if I can do one big enough to cover us both.*

*Don't worry.*

Robert was quick, but not yet strong enough. The guard came towards the door and stopped in his tracks. 'You! Boy! What are you doing in here?'

Jenn instantly left Robert's side, turning the guard away from him. At that moment, the moon rose, flooding the courtyard with ghostly blue light. Jenn backed away from the guard. 'I just wanted to see the sorcerer . . . that's all.'

'Well, you can't. Get out! Go on, boy, leave before I lock you up!'

Jenn turned and ran down towards the gate. As she disappeared, the guard shook his head and continued his patrol, never even looking in Robert's direction.

*Jenny?*

*Has he gone yet?*

*Yes, but you'll have to be quick and quiet. If he catches you coming back, he'll throw you in with Finnlay.*

*Coming.*

He turned his attention back to the lock. She reached his side as a faint click echoed across the courtyard.

*You never told me you could do that!*

A lopsided smile brushed across his face as he pulled the door open. *There're a lot of things I never told you.*

They stepped inside, closing the door behind them. Robert was faced with a short, darkened passageway running from left to right. It was empty. He reached out and placed his hand flat on the wall opposite him, sending his senses along its surface, first one way then the other. *There's a guard room down that way. Four – no, five men. Can you sense them?*

*No.*

*Focus on the door at the end, then imagine what the room inside might look like. Now, close your eyes and let your senses pick up their breathing, their heartbeats. You don't need to push hard – just let it drift.*

*Yes! I have them.*

*Good – keep an eye on them.*

*What if they come out?*

Robert grinned in the darkness. *Then we'll just have to be a little more imaginative.*

He took his hand from the wall and pointed to his right. They moved silently down the passage until they came to a corner. The passage continued further into the building, while a staircase led down to their right. There was only one small problem. The passage up here was full of guards, and downstairs there were another two.

Robert grabbed Jenn and pulled her back into the shadows. *I knew I shouldn't have let you come!*

*Oh, stop being a baby! Look – they're going that way. There must be another guard room down the end. They must have been doing a patrol along the corridor. You know, to keep people like us out.*

*People like you, you mean. Have you no respect? All right, they've gone for now, but the ones downstairs are still there, outside Finn's cell. Come on.*

Swiftly and silently they crept down the stairs, pausing a few from the bottom. Finnlay felt so close now, Robert could almost reach out and touch him. He glanced up and saw a small window in the stone wall, barred both across and down, not that it was big enough for anything but a rabbit to climb through.

*Yes*, Jenn grinned in the yellow lamplight. *He's in there, isn't he? This is easy!*

*With two guards standing watch over the prisoner?* She

must be joking. Still, there was only one way out of this. He pulled her down on to the stairs, low and out of the light from above. *I want to you promise me something.*

*What?*

*That you'll never tell anyone what I'm about to do. I mean no one at all.*

*I promise.*

Robert nodded, knowing the movement was lost in the gloom. As it happened, he wasn't even sure he was up to this in his currently depleted state. However, short of killing the guards – and the noise that would cause – he didn't have a choice. So, focusing on his *ayarn*, he slowed and stopped his breathing, then let his concentration hone in on a single point in his mind. As soon as he felt it secure, he took a mental dimensional step sideways. His body shuddered with the exertion, but the working held and he moved down the last few stairs, around the corner. The guards were standing there chatting, but they didn't see him. Good. It worked.

Walking slowly, Robert held his breath as he approached them. Already waves of exhaustion swept over him. This was so much harder than a simple mask, one of the reasons why it was forbidden. A mask of blankness was a simple trick. Making yourself completely invisible while you moved was another thing entirely.

Silently, Robert came to a stop before the two men. He raised both hands and in a single movement, knocked them unconscious. He scrambled to catch them both and slid them to the ground without making a noise. He couldn't do it all and released his illusion with a brief snap.

Without wasting time, he grabbed the cell keys from the guard at his feet and glanced back at Jenn. She was watching him, her eyes wide. However, her thoughts were completely silent. It was just as well – how could he explain to her why he was so adept at the forbidden side of the art?

The key slipped into the lock but made a horrible noise as he turned it. He pushed the door open and almost laughed at the surprise on Finnlay's face. He looked relatively uninjured, apart from the scar on his cheek.

'Robert! You're alive!' Finnlay beamed.

'We don't have much time,' Robert replied, reaching up for the manacles. Swiftly, he freed Finnlay and together they dashed out of the cell and back to the stairs. Finnlay almost bolted with fright when he saw Jenn, but fortunately didn't waste time asking questions.

*Robert, I think the guards are moving. We have to hurry!*

They got halfway up the stairs when Jenn pulled on Robert's sleeve. *What happens when they wake up? When they see Finn's gone?*

Robert glanced down at Jenn and almost answered her verbally, but stopped himself just in time. *They'll be after us.*

*And if they don't see he's gone?*

There were questions Robert wanted to ask her, but there was no time. All he said was, *Can you do it?*

'What are we waiting for?' Finnlay hovered, frowning at both of them.

Robert nodded and quickly sent his senses out to the two guard rooms. They were moving, but not in this direction. At least, not yet. They had a few minutes, no more.

'Jenn's going to try something, Finn. I'll go back and lock the cell door.'

It took him seconds and he left the keys where he found them. When he got back to the stairs, Jenn was standing in front of Finnlay, her hands holding his face. She was gazing at his brother with such intensity that Robert couldn't move. Then he couldn't help it, he had to see what she was doing. He stretched up to the window into Finnlay's cell. There was little light, just enough to see a shape take form, shimmer and fade. Within a second, it reappeared, more solid, crouched on the floor, bound hand and foot with chains. A perfect replica of Finnlay, wounds and all. It was incredible!

*How long will it last?*

Jenn dropped her hands from Finnlay's face and shrugged. *Just long enough for them to be sure he was rescued by sorcerers.*

'Let's get out of here.'

They sneaked up the stairs, but now the guards were moving. As they crept across the passage towards the door,

Robert heard two guards come out and walk towards them. He didn't wait to see if Jenn's illusion had worked. Instead, he pulled the outside door open and ushered them through.

The guard was nowhere to be seen and they ran across the courtyard, climbing the fence in seconds. Robert paused there to listen for the alarm, but all was quiet. With a grin at his brother, he turned and led them back to the horses.

'We did it!' Jenn laughed, climbing on to her horse.

'Yes,' Robert grinned, easing his tiring body into the saddle, 'but we still have to get away.'

Finnlay stood and stared at both of them, 'How the hell did you do it? By the gods, I thought I was dead – that you were dead! And what's Jenn doing here?'

'Finn,' Robert said, 'get on your horse and let's go. I'll tell you all about it as we ride.'

Robert gave him a carefully edited version of his rescue, leaving out the new skill he'd acquired that night – and his illusion. Unfortunately, that didn't answer all Finnlay's questions.

'I have to tell you, Robert – I knew you were coming. At first I thought I was dreaming or hearing things, but just suddenly, out of the blue, I heard this voice tell me to wait and that someone was coming. It was eerie. Then when that damned door opened and you stood there . . .' Finnlay shook his head, his utter bewilderment totally visible in the glowing moonlight.

'Perhaps you have a guardian angel,' Jenn murmured lightly. 'Not wishing to change the subject, but what are you going to do now? Did they find out who you were?'

'No, but they have my ring. It's only a matter of time before they know. There's something else. I won't say I'm positive, but I think there was a Malachi in that village. Even without an *ayarn* I could still sense that hideous aura.'

'What did it feel like?' Jenn asked suddenly.

Finnlay frowned. 'Like the outside edge of a bad headache, only worse.'

'But evil? Really horrible?'

'No. Not like that. Why?'

'No reason.'

Robert wanted to ask Jenn more, but she clearly didn't want to discuss it further. 'It makes sense,' he said. 'If a Malachi was nearby and heard a sorcerer had been captured, he would come running. If they find out who you are though, that makes it much worse. I guess it was too much to hope for, getting away without a scratch. Still, at least you have somewhere to go.'

'The Enclave. Great!'

'What's wrong, brother?' Robert chuckled. 'I thought you loved the place. We'll take Jenn back to Elita, then continue on. There're a few things I want to discuss with Ayn and the others anyway. But we'll have to move quickly. It won't take them long to realize you've escaped and once they do, we'll have to be well clear of the area.'

They rode in silence for the next couple of hours, pushing the horses and their own strength to the limits, but as they crested the last hill, with the dark shadow of the castle huddled in the valley before them, Robert paused. Determined now, he turned to Jenn. 'You didn't tell me everything about your encounter with Vaughn. Was it so terrible?'

She was silent for a minute then replied, 'He really hates you, you know? With every fibre of his being. He would do anything to destroy you. I'm sure he's been at the King to arrest you and tie you in with your uncle.'

'Of course. What else?'

'I . . .' She struggled, obviously not wanting to tell him. 'I felt something. Really evil. It was like that pressure from the council, but much worse. I just wanted to run and hide.'

By the gods! 'Who was it?'

Jenn met his gaze, suddenly wary. 'I don't know . . . but I think it might have been Vaughn.'

Finnlay's mouth dropped open, 'Vaughn? With powers? Are you sure?'

She glanced uneasily between them, 'No. Not certain – but there was something . . . well, ominous about him. Maybe it was just his hatred. I can't be sure. However, this

'. . . evil was coming from someone there – someone at court. I wondered if it might be Malachi.'

'Sweet Mineah!' Finnlay breathed. 'If Vaughn's got powers, then . . . Could it have been Valena?'

Robert shook his head, 'No. Jenn's been Sealed, Finn. A Malachi would have no influence on her at all. Jenn wouldn't even sense it. If this was a kind of pressure, then it couldn't be Malachi.'

'Well, did you ever sense anything like that from Vaughn when you were at court? Could you have missed it? It hardly seems possible.'

Robert studied Jenn's face for a moment, then looked at his brother. 'Until tonight, I would have said the same. But these days it seems anything is possible – but not, however, probable. Jenn isn't certain it was Vaughn. Was it just the one occasion? Was there anyone else it could have been?'

'Yes, but I don't know who,' she said out aloud. Silently she added, *But there was a moment, the night I arrived at Marsay. I tried to call you and for a second I thought you'd heard me. Did you?*

*No.*

She smiled slightly. 'I don't know. Perhaps it was just Vaughn's hatred of you. He's really twisted, you know. What did you ever do to him to make him hate you so much?'

*You had to ask, didn't you?* Robert sighed. 'He's got his reasons. I'm sure everyone just thinks he's demented.'

Finnlay turned to him quizzically. 'So? What did you do?'

'He found out.'

'Found out what?'

'Use your imagination, Finn. Vaughn found out I'm a sorcerer, but he can't say or do anything about it.'

'What?' Finnlay coughed.

'You Sealed him, didn't you?' Jenn added, beginning to laugh. 'Oh, what an evil, cruel – and appropriate – revenge!'

'Oh, it wasn't revenge,' Robert replied lightly.

Finnlay held up his hands, 'But how did he find out? When did all this happen?'

Robert took a breath, not sure he wanted Finnlay to know.

404

'He found out because I told him and I told him because he had already become suspicious of another sorcerer who was only visiting court. I didn't dare let him further his investigations, so I made out that it was all my doing and told him. Then before he could say a word, I Sealed him and now he has to live with the secret, unable to say a word to anyone, no matter how much he wants to.'

Jenn laughed again, but Finnlay only glowered.

'Who were you protecting, Robert?'

With a sigh, Robert turned his horse back towards Elita. 'Who do you think, Finnlay? Come on, we have to get Jenn back before she's missed. While we're at it, we'd better concoct a story for my sudden disappearance from Elita.'

Jenn glanced over her shoulder to the suddenly silent Finnlay, 'Don't worry. I think I have just the thing.'

Robert left Finnlay in the shelter of the woods behind the castle and took Jenn back alone. Before they could get too close, Jenn pulled up her horse. 'I can go on alone from here. There's no need to risk someone seeing you. It will ruin Finnlay's story.'

Robert nodded. 'You'll have to be very careful. Don't do any practising for a while. It'll take some time for the furore over Finnlay's disappearance to die down. Until it does, we're all in danger. In the meantime, I'll do some research. See if I can find out more about this mindspeech. Maybe with both of us doing it we can reach across a bigger distance.'

She nodded, 'Perhaps.' *You know you can't come back here, don't you? Father won't allow it.*

*Yes, I know.*

*Will you?*

Robert smiled. *Yes.*

She nodded then turned her horse and rode off into the darkness.

# 18

Nash galloped his horse through the castle gates and right into the stables. He jumped down, threw the reins to a stable boy and ran across the courtyard. He turned swiftly through a side door and along the short passage, then out into the open again and across the grass to the tower Selar had granted him. Without pausing, he took the stairs two at a time, arriving breathless at the top landing. The door before him was closed, but that didn't stop him. He jammed his hand down on the latch and shoved the door open. It crashed back against the wall as he strode through into the room.

'Why the hell didn't you tell me Finnlay Douglas was a sorcerer?' Nash bellowed, slamming the door behind him.

Valena sprang up from her seat by the window, her face white with shock. 'What are you talking about? Finnlay? When did . . .'

Nash hissed in a breath, 'I've just had word from the judges sent to a village called Kilphedir. A man had been arrested on charges of sorcery – the first in a century. From the description and his signet ring, that man must be Finnlay Douglas. Don't tell me you didn't know.'

'But I didn't!' Valena frowned, picking up the book she'd dropped. 'I sensed nothing from him at all.'

'By the gods, woman, you were at Dunlorn for three days! How in hell could you miss it? You're a trained Malachi! You were taught at an early age to sense the aura of a strange sorcerer. You should have noticed him. Why didn't you?'

'Well, perhaps there was nothing to notice,' Valena snapped back. 'You're assuming these charges are founded on truth. For all we know it could be some big misunderstanding. The witnesses could have been drunk – or just lying! Why do you assume that I was wrong?'

'Because, my dear,' Nash dropped his voice and moved closer, 'the prisoner escaped without leaving any trace. He got past two dozen guards and a cell locked from the outside. How could he be anything but a sorcerer?'

Valena sank back on to her seat, her hands gripping the book so hard her knuckles went white. 'He escaped? Have they caught him?'

'No.'

Her voice was a pale whisper. 'But he couldn't be. I would have known. I would have sensed something.'

'Not if he already knew you were Malachi. He could have shielded himself once he discovered you. His aura would have appeared entirely normal to you.'

'Then why didn't he kill me?' Valena looked at him, her eyes dark and angry. 'Why did he let me leave if he knew what I was? You're taking this too far, Nash. You're trying to see around corners. Finnlay couldn't have known.'

Nash shook his head and snatched a flask of wine from the table. His throat was parched after his long ride. He drained the flask and thumped it back on the table. 'Perhaps he knew and perhaps he didn't. The point is, you didn't sense him.'

'But Sam,' Valena began, but he cut her off.

'That's not the worst of it. This village where they were holding him, Kilphedir, is no more than three hours' ride from Elita.'

'By the gods,' Valena breathed. 'Then that could mean . . .'

'That I was wrong all along. Finnlay Douglas could be the Enemy. What else would he be doing so close to her home? How else could he be strong enough to shield himself from you, such a powerful Malachi? How strong is he to escape from a prison in that manner?' Nash fought to control his desire to panic. If he had been wrong all this time and the Enemy was still out there, so powerful, so acquainted with Elita, then all his efforts of fourteen years ago had been for nothing. The danger was still there. Alive and uncontrolled!

407

If he couldn't contain this problem, then everything was once again thrown into doubt, as it had been for centuries.

He took a deep breath and slowed his racing heart. All might not yet be lost. From Valena's description, Finnlay Douglas didn't appear to be any real threat to anyone. And if he had no idea of the history he was fighting, then that would play to Nash's advantage. Very well, then. Back to the game.

He turned back to Valena to find her exquisite face had regained its colour. 'We must find him,' she announced without preamble.

'Yes,' Nash nodded, heading for the door.

'Where are you going?'

'I have to see the King – and Vaughn. I have to convince them to send me south to investigate this matter. Apparently the last civilian seen near the prison was a young boy. I have to find him. In the meantime, you gather our men together. Send Lisson down to Elita to ask a few questions in the village. Have the others out looking for Douglas. We have to find him – and kill him.'

Vaughn wavered unsteadily on his feet and reached out a hand to the chair Selar was seated in. As he slowly regained his composure, he opened his mouth, capable only of voicing a whisper. 'Finnlay Douglas? Are you sure, Nash?'

The young Alderman held up the letter from the judges in Kilphedir. 'I can only go by the description of the ring, my lord. A black eagle on a silver background.'

'That's Finnlay,' Selar grunted. 'Robert's ring is gold, as the heir. I saw both rings together, that summer when the brothers were here at the same time.'

'But,' Vaughn stammered, hardly able to believe what Nash was saying, 'are you sure it isn't . . . Dunlorn?'

'That's enough, Proctor,' Selar snapped. He stood and turned away to the fireplace. Vaughn watched him, saw the lines on his face deepen, the sudden shadow around his eyes.

'Sorcery,' Selar murmured. 'Again. Why? Why now?'

The question was obviously directed at Nash and for a

moment Vaughn fumed. It had taken the young man so little time to gain the King's trust, become his closest confidant. It was impossible to believe Nash still gave Vaughn his full loyalty. With the favour of a King behind you, what might you not aspire to?

He would have to do something about Nash one day. But not yet. There was still a lot of use in him.

Nash folded the paper into three and put his hands behind his back. Patiently, he tried to address Selar's question. 'We cannot be sure it is sorcery, Sire. At the moment, all we have is a garbled report from the judges Governor Osbert sent. There are two witnesses to the original offence, but whether they will swear under oath is another matter.'

'And what of the boy caught near the prison? Has he been found?'

'I don't know, Sire. Perhaps.'

Selar turned around. 'And perhaps he helped this sorcerer to escape! Have you thought of that? Was he alone – or was there an old man with him?'

Vaughn took a step back at Selar's unbridled anger. This was unlike him. Did he feel the same way about sorcery that Vaughn did? He hoped so.

'Sire, if you will permit me?' Vaughn began carefully. 'I will send Osbert down to this village as soon as he returns to Marsay tomorrow. This matter is obviously too weighty for the judges. Osbert can investigate the matter fully, ask your questions, find out the real truth.'

Selar was nodding, but Nash looked like he wanted to say something. Vaughn decided this once to exercise the upper hand. 'I will also send Nash down now, if you have no immediate need of him, Sire. I'm sure he will be most diligent in his efforts, won't you, Nash?'

Stiffening, Nash bowed obedience. 'Yes, my lord. As you wish.'

There, that will teach him who rules the Guilde! Perhaps a few days in the saddle will bring him to heel. And with any luck, he might just be able to prove that Finnlay was a sorcerer.

By the gods! Two of them! In the same family! And no one had known. All these years and no one ever suspected the evil buried within their ranks. Well, perhaps Finnlay was lost to him but there was a way to catch the brother yet!

It rained all the way from Marsay. Steady, solid, depressing rain. The road was bogged with mud, the bridge at Merrin washed away. It was insolent, determined and perverse, the kind of rain that falls towards the end of summer when people have begun to believe the good weather will last all year, the kind that destroys crops only weeks before harvest.

Nash loved it.

The roads were empty, fresh horses available and riding with his hood up meant no one saw his face as he travelled south. No one would remember him, or the questions he asked. Nobody would glance out and see the stranger passing through. Perfect anonymity.

But it didn't last. By the time he met Lisson in Fenlock village, the downpour was little more than a light mist, floating up from the valley lake. They met in the tavern on the corner of the market square, the Boar and Oak. Nash took a seat by the fire, facing the door. There was no reason to suspect she might come in here, but why take the chance?

He took off his cloak and ordered ale for them both. Then, feeling every league of the last three days, he put his elbows on the table and waited for Lisson. The young man spoke quietly and easily, as though they were having a polite conversation about nothing of particular importance. Just as he'd been trained to do.

'There's already been a lot of talk, master. They think this fellow might even be that Angel of Darkness the hermit spoke about last year. There is some fear and a lot of curiosity. None of them have ever experienced sorcery and find it more interesting than terrifying.'

'I'll remember that,' Nash murmured as two large jugs of ale landed on the table. He paid for them and glanced around casually, making sure no one would hear or pay them any attention. 'Go on.'

'I believe there was some activity up at the castle on the day the man was captured. An injured lord was brought in. They nursed him, the doctor here saw him. It was His Grace of Haddon.'

'Robert Douglas?' Nash murmured, amazed.

'Yes, master.'

'Is he still there?'

'No, master. He left the following night.'

'Alone?'

'Yes, master.'

This was most strange. Had the brothers been together? If so, what had they been doing? Why had Haddon left so suddenly if he was injured? Very strange indeed.

Nash took a deep swallow of his ale then stood. 'Stay here for a few more days and see what else you can find out. I'm going to take a room and clean myself up. I have a lady to see.'

It was impossible to miss the guarded looks he got riding into the forecourt of Elita. People stopped in their work and stared at him, at his Guilde robes. In their eyes, Nash could see the loyalty to their rebel Earl, the last dregs of a forgotten era. They didn't want the Guilde here, on his land – they didn't want Nash.

All the same, the bailey, Neil Hogarth, treated him with deference, showing him into the hall, providing him with wine as he waited. What were they all thinking, these silent watchful people? Did they wonder if he came to herald a new era? One they would loathe and despise? The rule of the Guilde?

He could have laughed. If only they knew. What would they say of the war Selar planned? Would they remain loyal to the House of Ross if Selar convinced them his brother in Mayenne was a real, imminent threat? Would they desert their lord to go and fight alongside Selar, the man they hated?

Yes, they would. All of them – and that was the beauty of it. In one swift stroke, Selar would finally unite all the old

Houses with the new, combined together against a common enemy. History had proven the axiom. And Selar would never know that he'd helped to destroy all he'd worked to achieve. Not until it was too late.

'My lord will see you now,' Neil announced from the other end of the hall. Nash placed his cup on the long table and followed him through a door and down a short passage. A door at the end was opened for him and he entered a room rich in furnishings and colour – and something else.

She was there, standing behind her father's chair. Long dark hair, shining and free. A black gown enhanced her colouring, made her eyes glow such a deep blue. Her hands were folded together in patience, or perhaps to prevent them twisting as he'd seen her do at court. By the gods, she was lovely!

'You will forgive me, my lord,' Nash began with a bow towards Elita's Earl. 'I apologize for arriving unannounced, but I have been sent by the King.'

'To what purpose?' Jacob replied, waving him to a seat.

Nash smiled thanks, noting the rug which covered the old lord's crippled legs. No more fighting for this ancient soldier. 'I have been instructed to investigate the events at the village of Kilphedir.'

'So why come here?'

He knew she was watching him, felt every flicker of her eyes, but he kept his attention on Jacob. 'You know the events in question?'

'I have heard rumours.'

'Then you will know that the man arrested is believed to be Lord Finnlay Douglas.'

Jacob said nothing to this. He just sat there and waited for Nash to continue. Very well. 'I believe his brother, the Duke of Haddon was here at Elita the same night?'

'What of it?'

'Are the two events not connected?'

'How can they be?'

Nash frowned. Was he missing something? Jacob didn't appear to be lying, or even trying to hide something. What was going on? 'Surely it cannot be a coincidence that the younger brother is arrested on charges of sorcery while at the same time, the elder is here nearby, recovering from injuries.'

'Your information is impressive, Alderman, but incomplete. Finnlay Douglas is dead.'

Nash scrambled to find the flaw, the slip of a lie, but Jacob was telling the truth. 'Have you seen the body?'

At this, Jacob shook his head. 'No. My daughter did.'

Now Nash did turn his gaze on her. She was watching him steadily, with only a suggestion of wariness. He needed to be very careful here. He couldn't risk alienating her, but still he needed some answers. 'How did you see it, my lady?'

She looked to her father before answering. 'I nursed His Grace through the worst of his injuries. It was only the evening of the second day before he regained his memory. He'd had a blow to the head, you see. Both he and his brother had been exploring the cliffs the day before. Finnlay slipped and fell before his eyes. His Grace went in search of him and fell too.'

'How did he get here?'

'I was returning from Marsay and passing through the forest. I heard a cry and rushed to help. His Grace was injured and dazed. He quickly became unconscious, so I was unable to find out what had happened. I brought him back here and treated his wounds.'

'And when he remembered his brother's fall, he left? Alone?'

There was silence. Jacob darted a glance to his daughter and gave a sharp shake of his head. 'No, my daughter left with him.'

'I was concerned about him travelling so far with his injuries barely healed. We took a spare horse, hoping Finnlay would be well enough to ride. We ... found him at the bottom of the cliff, his body broken and bloody. He was tangled amongst some rocks in the river, face down. Dead.'

Oh, it was a good lie. So good he could almost believe it.

413

So convincing was her storytelling that he was tempted for a moment to wonder if it was true. But she hadn't finished.

'I helped His Grace take the body from the water and put it on the spare horse. We rode back towards Elita but I left him at the edge of the woods. He returned home to bury his brother.' She turned away, bent to the small fire. Her father reached out and brushed the hair away from her face, a touching gesture. Jacob believed her.

Nash stood and wandered over to the window, taking the time to sort out his thoughts. Was she lying? He just couldn't tell. But if it was the truth, then that meant that Finnlay Douglas was not the Enemy. So who was the man who'd escaped so skilfully?

And why had he been wearing Finnlay's ring?

'I'm sorry to make you retell the story, my lady,' Nash murmured, trying to keep his voice under control. 'It must have been most upsetting to find the young man like that. Did you know him well?'

'I'd never met him,' she replied, once again beside her father. 'I only knew him from what His Grace told me.'

'As he brought you from Shan Moss to Elita? Of course. Tell me, was Finnlay wearing his signet ring when you found him?'

'I . . . don't know. I didn't look. Why?'

So innocent, so demure, so wounded. He wanted to kiss her! 'And you know nothing of the man charged in Kilphedir? Nothing about sorcery?'

'Sorcery?' She laughed – and he had her! 'Why would I know anything about sorcery?'

Yes! There it was. The perfect lie. As perfect as all the others she'd told him, except that this was one he knew about. She knew all about sorcery, he'd felt her power at Marsay, had felt her resist his pushing and probing. She was lying now, just as immaculately as she'd done before.

But why? To protect Finnlay? That had to be it. So Finnlay had escaped and she had gone out to meet him, with horses – and his brother.

Yes, that was it. Desperately he wanted to push her again,

414

try her strength against his, but he didn't dare. If she sensed it she would know it was him and it was much too early for that little discovery. Still, he couldn't resist a little Malachi-like mischief.

'I wonder, my lord, that you allowed your daughter out at such a time of night. And with a man you regard as a traitor.'

'My feelings for Robert, Alderman, are none of your business. And before you protest, I did not give Jennifer my permission to go. She slipped away, believing she was doing the right thing.'

'But such behaviour? From a high-born lady?'

As though to deliberately irritate Nash, Jacob smiled. He reached out and took his daughter's hand. 'You must understand, Alderman. My daughter has had a very ... unusual childhood. Some habits learned are hard to break. Nevertheless, I am very proud of her.'

'Yes, of course. You have every reason to be.' Nash smiled genuinely. She was indeed worthy of pride – but not for the reasons Jacob believed in. 'I will take my leave of you, my lord, my lady. I have other inquiries I need to make. Thank you for your time.'

He bowed to them both and left the room with the memory of her face lingering in his eyes. So formidable, so delightful – and so very dangerous. It would have been pointless trying to push her, she could still resist him as she had before. No. He would have to drag the truth from someone else. Someone else who'd been there, in the forest. Someone unable to resist him.

Robert Douglas.

As the door closed behind Nash, Jenn tried to pull her hand from Jacob's strong grasp, but he wouldn't let go. Instead, he dragged her down until her eyes were level with his.

'Understand, Daughter! You will never see Dunlorn again! Do you hear me? Never!'

'But Father, he's done nothing wrong...'

'You cannot be my daughter and give time to that man as

well. I don't care if he did return you to me: that is my debt to repay as I please. But you will do as I say. You will vow never to see or speak to him again. Promise!'

Jenn struggled to find words, struggled for time, for space to convince him, but ten years had done more damage than she could repair in a few short months. To Jacob, Robert was trouble. A traitor of the worst kind, a man who had forsaken his country for the glory of serving a usurping King. A King who could easily and happily wipe out her entire House, destroy them as he'd destroyed Lusara. Unless she agreed, Robert's treachery would become hers.

By the gods, what could she say? Robert had said he'd come back and when he did, Jenn would see him, would speak to him. She had to . . .

But it was hopeless. With a heart like lead, Jenn dropped her head and fought back tears. 'Yes, Father. I promise.'

# 19

Patric paced up and down before the gate, ignoring the chilly evening and the brittle wind sweeping across the mountain. Despite the cold, Ayn and Henry kept watch with him, both waiting for the same thing. The arrival of Robert and Finnlay.

But what could be keeping them? More than four hours now since the signal that they were on their way up and there was still no sign of them. But nothing could have happened, the sentries would see. They'd send word, go and help.

Damn it, where were they?

He could go out. Through the gate. Travel along the path down the Goleth. He'd done it before. Once, in daylight. But now it was dusk and without a torch he'd lose his way, probably fall over the bluff, and his crumpled battered body would be found months later, picked over by carrion and rodents, worms slithering out of his eye sockets. No. Best to stay within the gate.

Patric turned back to the tunnel once again, but this time there was something moving within the gloom. Two figures, followed by weary horses. But something was very wrong. Finnlay came forward, his arm under Robert's shoulders. As they emerged from the darkness, he stumbled and Robert gasped.

He was obviously injured, and feverish too. His face was deathly pale and shiny with perspiration. A huge purpling bruise swelled his right temple. Even those sea-green eyes were dull and lustreless, as though the colour had been washed out of them by an icy winter's rain.

'What's happened?' Ayn cried, moving quickly despite her age.

Patric sprang to support Robert and glanced at Finnlay for an answer.

'We had some trouble. It's a very long story.'

'Trouble?' Ayn said, 'what kind of . . . No. That can wait. Robert needs to be in bed – now! Patric, help me get him inside.'

Ayn washed her hands in the old wooden bowl she kept by the bed and dried them on a scrap of linen. Then she took the pestle and mortar, gave the pungent mix inside one more turn, then transferred it to the bandage.

Robert didn't stir as she redressed the wound on his shoulder. His eyes were closed, his face almost serene, but for the lines of pain etched around his eyes. Pain from riding hard for five days with such injuries. He'd passed out almost as soon as they'd laid him in his bed and he'd not woken since.

'Will he survive?' Henry asked from the door.

Ayn finished applying the poultice and straightened up. 'Of course he'll survive. Robert's too strong to let a few bruises and a fever kill him. He's much too stubborn.'

'Then it's mostly fatigue?'

'Yes,' Ayn replied more confidently than she felt. There were times when having Healer's Sight gave her no comfort at all. If only she could be sure she was treating all Robert's wounds.

'Ayn,' Henry spoke gently, laying his hand on her shoulder, 'the council convenes again in an hour. If Robert does not awaken soon, we may have to make the decision without him.'

'We will make no decisions until we've heard what he has to say, Henry,' Ayn snapped. 'You'll only make it worse.'

'How much worse can it be? Finnlay was caught, probably identified. This is the greatest catastrophe of the last century.'

'Is it?' Ayn grunted, gazing down at Robert's bruised face. 'I'm not so sure.'

'Ayn,' Henry whispered, 'the time is approaching when you will have to decide where your loyalties lie.'

*

418

'You don't understand, Patric. He's worse. Much worse than he used to be.'

Patric glanced once at Finnlay then resumed climbing the frail ladder. This part of the library was unused and mostly forgotten, and consequently, extraordinarily dusty. He sneezed three times in quick succession and almost fell.

'What do you mean, worse?'

'You should have seen him after Oliver was killed. He hasn't really been the same since. His moods change from one second to the next. Half the time I don't know whether to take him seriously or not.'

'That never worried you before.'

Finnlay leaned back against a long narrow bench. 'But something's changed. I don't know what. Even his friend Daniel was worried. He tried to convince me Robert had decided to go to war against Selar.'

'What?' Patric started. The ladder began to waver against the high shelf and he gripped it with both hands. Steady again, he glanced back down at Finnlay, 'Do you agree?'

'I don't know what to think. Micah is sure Robert would never break his oath to Selar.'

'No, I suppose not.' Patric turned his attention to the rows of scrolls laid out on the top shelf of the library. He was sure the book was up here ... somewhere. In a worn black leather tube. Yes, there it was.

He leaned forward and coaxed the tube out with his fingertips. He almost lost hold of it, but then it fell into his hand and he began retracing his steps down the ladder. He jumped the last two to the floor and moved around Finnlay to the empty bench. It lay the length of the dark cave, by law, lit only by enclosed oil lamps. Blackened streaks marked the roof and the old double door was grimy with oil smoke. Hardly anyone came to this part of the old library now, partly because it was buried in the deepest part of the caves, and partly because there were few Enclave scholars who could read Saelic, Giffron and the other obscure old languages these books embodied.

Patric laid the leather tube down carefully. Finnlay was

watching him, the shadow of exhaustion almost gone from his eyes, although the scar was still healing: a permanent reminder of his personal misfortune.

'And so Robert has been like this – all the time?'

'Except for the night they got me out of prison. For a while he was his old happy, cynical self. Before that and on the whole journey here, he's hardly said a word to me. Hell, I know he was injured – but this? Tell me what's going on, Patric. He's my brother and I can't reach him!'

'Perhaps he doesn't want to be reached,' Patric murmured. He pulled up a high stool and settled on to it. 'It's as though fate is conspiring against his wish to retire. All these things playing on him, those raiders, the Malachi, McCauly's arrest, your uncle – everything. All forcing him to act, to do something.'

'Well, it hasn't done any good, has it? Besides, Robert can't be pressured into anything: I know, I've spent years trying.'

'Yes,' Patric frowned, 'but tell me, what was so different about the night of your rescue? Was Robert just pleased to get you out, or was there something else? Did you argue at all?'

There was almost a smile on Finnlay's face now. 'Not me, no. But I tell you, Jenn has his measure. She doesn't let him get away with anything. And there was something strange going on, an understanding maybe. Like they'd been working together like that for years.'

Really? Now that was interesting – but it would also have to wait until Robert woke up, which hopefully would be soon. Two days' sleep should have worked wonders.

'So,' Patric continued, carefully taking the scroll out of its case, 'what are you going to do now?'

'Now?' Finnlay laughed, but without humour. 'I have no idea.'

'Well, I could make a suggestion.'

'What?'

'Yes, what?' They both whirled around to find Robert standing in the doorway. The bruises had faded, his colour had returned and there was a familiar light in his eyes. Even in this gloom he looked much better.

'Well?' Robert added, 'I would really like to hear your suggestion.'

'I . . .' Patric stammered. 'When did you wake up? I looked in on you half an hour ago and you were still out.'

'And so you came all the way down here so I had to limp down those stairs to find you. Then, of course, I'll have to get all the way back up. Thank you.' Robert glanced up at the shelves of books lining every wall of the ancient cave, then back at Finnlay. He moved into the room, keeping his eyes on his brother.

'I didn't tell anybody, Robert,' Finnlay murmured. 'Only . . . Patric.'

'I know, Finn. But wait a moment.' With that, Robert raised his left hand, his voluminous white shirt a blur in the lamp light. Suddenly the huge double doors creaked, then slammed shut with a bang.

Patric gasped, 'How did you do that?'

But Robert was still looking at Finnlay. Without a word, Finnlay reached inside his doublet and pulled forth a cloth-bound object, crimson and heavy. He placed it in Robert's hand and turned away.

'Can I see it?' Patric couldn't help himself.

Robert nodded and placed it down on the bench. Instantly Patric tore the cloth away and examined the silver rod.

'Well? What do you make of it?'

'It's hand crafted,' Patric replied, returning to his seat. 'Very fine work. It looks like silver, but I suspect there's some copper in there. It has that colour. I'd say these wires are supposed, to be attached to something but the knobs on the end look like handles to me. At a guess, I'd say that it's a part of something bigger, like the hilt of a sword. Perhaps it's part of the Calyx – or maybe part of something that was used for ceremonial purposes. Remember that book I was reading about Bonding? There's a chapter in there about the ceremonial tools.'

'Was this mentioned?'

'I don't know, but I can check.' Patric put the rod back down and spread the scroll out on the bench. Finnlay held one end and Robert the other. He did a quick scan to start, then began again, his finger moving slowly down the vellum. 'No. Nothing. I was certain there would be something here.'

'Well,' Finnlay ventured, 'perhaps we're looking in the wrong place. It might not be a ceremonial tool. After all, the Calyx was only mentioned once like that. At all other times, it is referred to as an object of great value and purpose.'

Patric had to smile. 'I don't recall any index mentioning a chapter of that name.' He glanced back at Robert and began to roll the vellum back up. 'I take it you don't want the council to know about this. Is there any particular reason I should know about?'

'I'll explain later,' Robert replied, turning around to take a look at the library again. 'I haven't been down here for years. Not since that night when you tried to convince me there was a connection between the House Marks and sorcery. At the time I thought you were bored stupid and just inventing theories to keep yourself busy.'

'And now?'

Robert glanced at him evasively. 'I still don't understand how you came to the conclusion in the first place. The House Marks have been around so long now, most people ignore them completely. There's never been any proof that there is a link with sorcery. Quite the opposite, in fact. However,' Robert paused, his hand reaching up to lift the tassel from a scroll, 'if we assumed from the beginning that the Marklord invented the Marks for a reason, then it might just make sense.'

'Forgive me, brother,' Finnlay said, 'but I don't follow your logic. How can that make sense?'

'Well,' Robert turned around with a grin, more like his old self than Patric had dared hope, 'perhaps he wanted to identify several families in perpetuity in order to keep track of their offspring. It might have nothing to do with sorcery, but only property.'

422

Finnlay shook his head. 'By why keep track? Why would you want to?'

But Patric had an answer. He darted around the bench and brushed his hair from his eyes. 'Wait. If we assume for a moment that there is a connection between the Marks and sorcery – then the Marks would be a good means by which to ensure the Bondings.'

'What?' Robert looked startled for a moment, then burst out laughing. 'Oh, I do like coming here, Pat! You've always got something new for me. It's such a delight listening to you. You're the only person I know who can conjure a complete theory of our history out of thin air!'

Still laughing, Robert bent to examine a shelf of bound books, but Patric wasn't so easily put off. 'Tell me, is Jenn still showing all the signs of enormous power?'

'Yes. Why?'

Patric hardly knew why he'd asked the question. There was something there, nagging at the back of his mind, and he had no choice but to pursue it. 'It makes sense to me. Remember, Bonding was a very important part of our history at one time. No marriages were performed unless the couples were Bonded. We know the Marklord worked with the earliest sorcerers, so why shouldn't he create something like the House Marks? If Bonding was so vital, he'd want to make sure it continued, regardless of what happened. I know we lost a lot of our lore when the Enclave was founded and the rest of this library burned to ashes, but that doesn't necessarily mean Bonding no longer exists. After all, we don't know what the Marks are for and yet they continue to persist in each generation.'

'But,' Finnlay objected, 'we don't even know what Bonding is. Who's to say it wasn't just a symbolic ceremony like betrothal is today.'

'There's nothing symbolic about betrothal, Finnlay,' Patric argued. 'In law it's considered just as binding as marriage. There is a deeper meaning and function than simple ceremony. It was designed to join the incumbents together when they were too young to marry, to bind their families

423

together. A firm promise and contract for the future. Bonding could easily be the arcane equivalent, designed to make sure that two particular people would marry.'

'Except for one thing,' Robert pointed out. 'We're just assuming there's a connection between the Marks and sorcery because we're assuming that Thraxis and the Mark-lord are the same person – and that Thraxis created the Calyx specifically for sorcerers. We're completely ignoring the three hundred years between them and basing one assumption on another without proof for any of it. The silver rod we found by accident is no guarantee that we are on the right track to find the Calyx – and we don't even know that Thraxis put in it that damned cave. But even it if was all true – even if the Marklord did create the Marks to keep track of offspring, there's no suggestion that he had anything to do with Bonding. That's an ancient sorcerers' tradition we know almost nothing about. The Marks still persist today, as does sorcery, but Bonding doesn't. If you were right, Bonding would have no choice but to exist. Everyone with a House Mark would be a sorcerer and every sorcerer alive would be Bonded.'

'Perhaps some are,' Patric murmured, the words tumbling forward without thought. 'Or rather, only those sorcerers with House Marks. I think you and Jenn are Bonded.'

Robert froze. His eyes grew flinty, his breathing was silent. Only the flickering oil lamp showed any signs of movement.

In the silence, Patric gathered his courage together and put forward his evidence. 'Let's look at it objectively. You help this girl out, save her from the Guilde. Next thing, it turns out she's got talents. Before you can blink an eye, she's split your *ayarn* then, just as you're trying to work out what it all means, she puts the *ayarn* back together. Something happened there, Robert. Something important. Now you tell me she's still growing in power and I suspect, doing things you aren't even telling me about. Even Finnlay noticed some deeper level of communication between you and Jenn. I've only just seen it, the pattern going through all this. That business with your *ayarn* set and completed the Bonding, just as though it had been a proper ritual. You both have House Marks, you're the two most powerful sorcerers in the land – you have to be Bonded.'

As Robert's face grew dark, Finnlay moved forward, suddenly nervous. He raised his hand. 'Patric, I don't think you should . . .'

'No,' Robert murmured, coming forward slowly, 'I don't think you should continue either.'

'But you can't close your eyes to the truth, Robert. Can all this be a coincidence? You said her powers are growing. Is there anything else you haven't told me? Anything that would prove that I'm wrong? Please, go ahead. You know how I love to be set straight.'

'Patric!' Finnlay snapped, 'stop it. That's enough.'

'More than enough.' Robert met Patric's gaze for a long time, but there was no menace there. Only something deeper, like sorrow, but Patric couldn't be sure.

Robert picked up the silver rod and tucked it in his belt. His voice heavy and weary, he said, 'I was right: you spend too much time buried in your books. You know nothing about life outside, and so everything seems to have these neat little patterns to them – patterns you love to create. We know almost nothing about Bonding. "Setting"? "Completing"? How would you know? What if I hadn't been there when she came through that forest? What if we'd never met? What if it had been Finnlay who'd tried Sealing her? How can Bonding still work under these kinds of conditions, and what's the point of it anyway – especially after all these years? There is no history of sorcery in either my family or Jenn's. How can the Marks and sorcery possibly be connected? I tell you, Patric, you don't know what you're talking about.'

Patric took in a swift breath and moved closer to Robert, more certain now than ever before. 'I may not know, Robert, but you do.'

Robert's head jerked up – then Finnlay stepped between them. 'Patric, I told you that was enough. Leave it alone.'

'Why are you protecting him?'

425

'Because he's my brother, Patric,' Finnlay replied with half a smile. He turned back to Robert then, the smile gone. 'The council is waiting for you. They want to talk to you.'

'Good,' Robert nodded, the shadow in his eyes suddenly gone, 'I want to talk to them, too. But first, I'm going for a walk. You can tell them I'll be down soon.'

It was night. Patric hadn't said anything about it being dark outside, so by the awesome display of stars visible from the mountain top took Robert by surprise. He stopped in the middle of the field and tipped his head back as far as he could, just to see it all in one go. The sight was breathtaking. The air was so clear and crisp, so much better for thinking than that inside the caves.

It all seemed to revolve around Jenn, didn't it? The abductions, the mindspeech, the strange presence at court: everything. An odd fate for a girl who'd grown up far from here, knowing nothing of this world.

And now there was Patric. Bonding.

By the gods, no!

It was impossible that he and Jenn ... that it could happen twice. And the last time Berenice ... he'd killed her. And if he and Jenn were Bonded then would he kill her too? And all because the Key had said ... that ...

But Finnlay had said Robert had only assumed it was supposed to be Berenice. Hadn't Finn said that the Key might have meant someone else?

Damn! The Key. Those two messages, dual curses, doubly damned. And why? So he could live his life alone, for ever controlling the demon within? The demon the Key had given him?

And why did the Key hate him so much, why did it want to manipulate him amd force him to do its bidding?

Serin's blood, what did the Key want from him?

Gasping for air, Robert sank to his knees, buried his hands in the dew-covered grass. It was soft and cool, like fine-ground flour. He wanted to lie in it, like a child, to drown in that comfort just like that dream of the sea.

He shouldn't keep asking why. There was no point. He would never get any answers without asking the Key – and he refused to approach it again. It would only inflict more damage, tell him more things he didn't want to know, manipulate him again, impair his resolve to stay uninvolved . . .

And how uninvolved was he, really? The truth was, he was still in the middle of it, despite his efforts. No wonder they all refused to believe him, to leave him alone. And after what Jenn had said about needing to act?

Yes, it all came back to her, and Patric had been right about so many things. Was he right about this?

It didn't matter. The Key had started all this, but just as he had all his life, Robert would resist it with his last breath. Just as he'd resisted the demon. It was the only way forward he had. The only way to defy the future the Key had given him. He had to stay uninvolved. He had to stay away from Jenn. More to the point, he had to keep her away from the Key. It was the only way to keep her safe.

Robert closed his eyes against the beautiful sky and shut it all out. He took a deep breath, and then another. He got to his feet, but felt no desire to go back and face the council. It was obvious what they wanted, and even more obvious what they would do. He would have to brace himself, put on that public face, once again be the man they all knew. He had no appetite for it, but standing out here in the chill air wasn't going to help.

He turned for the tunnel, then paused. Perhaps this was a good time to try. Now, when there was no interruption, and where no one would see him.

He focused his mind clearly and precisely. Then, feeling new levels of energy course through his body, he sent out a single, silent word.

*Jenny?*

Nothing. It was too far. He couldn't do it – but he had to. He had to make sure everything had worked out.

Again he focused his thoughts, drew in his breath. Tightly now, he unleashed the thought, pushing it every league of the distance between them. He called her name. Again there was nothing . . . then suddenly—

*Robert? By the gods, where are you? I thought you were going to the Enclave!*

*I'm standing on top of the Goleth right now. I had a quiet moment and thought I'd try. The distance is hard to push through, but it does work. I just wanted to tell you we made it safely. I'm about to go and speak to the council, but they already know the gist of what happened from Finnlay.*

*And your injuries?*

*All healed. Have you had any trouble? Did your father believe the story?*

*Yes. He was angry that I went with you but I expected that. But, I have to warn you. We've had the Guilde here, asking questions. They've sent Osbert down to Kilphedir to investigate and . . .*

*What?*

*They're looking for a boy who was caught in the grounds of the prison.*

*Hell!*

*They don't know it was me – but, Robert, you must be careful! Once they finish in the village, they'll be on their way to Dunlorn to question you. You have to get back quickly. If they find you still haven't returned they'll assume the worst.*

*I'll leave in the morning.*

*I wrote to your mother and Micah but I hope you tell them both the truth when you get back.*

*I'll tell Micah the truth, but I can only afford to tell her Finn's alive. It's just not safe any more. Listen . . .*

*What?*

*I'm afraid I won't be coming back – not for a long time. Perhaps never.*

Silence.

*Jenny?*

*I'm here. Why?*

*I can't explain. I'm sorry.*

Silence again. *Jenny? What's wrong?*

*Nothing. You do what you have to do and don't worry about*

*me. I'll survive – I always do. Take care, Robert.* And just like that she was gone.

If this wasn't Bonding, why did he suddenly feel so empty?

A single drop of wax tipped over the brim of the candle and slithered down the side, finally hardening on the pewter holder. It joined the yellow mess along the decorated rim standing testament to the long hours of discussion. Finnlay was mesmerized by the candle, watching every tiny movement of the flame as it danced and flickered with the currents of the air. Beside him he could hear the hum of murmured conversation, but after two hours of waiting for Robert, Finnlay found his attention drifting.

The council chamber was only half full now as many of the others had gone to bed. Besides Ayn, Wilf and Henry, Arlie Baldwyn, Patric and Acelin were still there, content to wait as long as necessary. Finnlay had endured their questions, their probing for answers he could only guess at. Robert would come soon, yes. He'd speak to the council – and then he would leave and return to Dunlorn. It was a luxury Finnlay would never have again.

A pang of regret and despair ran through him and he struggled against the bitterness which threatened to consume him. If only Robert had not fallen, if only they'd not seen his ring, if only he'd never found that damned manuscript in the first place . . .

And his *ayarn*. That too was lost. Well, he could always make another one, although he'd have to recover a little energy before he did. But the ring – his family ring – was gone for ever. Irreplaceable . . . and probably now in the hands of the Guilde. The only real evidence they had with which to damn him.

He could go on and on, but in the end, what difference would it make? He'd always known the danger of being a sorcerer, always been wholly aware of what would happen if he were ever found out. Somehow, however, he'd always assumed that if anyone would be discovered, it would be

Robert, rather than himself. It was strange how life worked its way through you.

The candle flame abruptly jerked and trembled as the door behind Finnlay swung open. He turned to see Robert standing there, his white shirt billowing around his arms. From the end of the room, Ayn and Wilf stood at this sudden appearance but Robert held up his hand. 'I'm sorry I kept you waiting. I had something I had to attend to first.'

Finnlay straightened up as Robert took a seat at the end of the table, near the fire. Robert did look better, but Finnlay knew him too well to assume that meant everything was fine. Robert was too good at masking his real feelings.

'How are your injuries?' Henry asked as he stood to move further down the long table.

'They'll mend. How is it going, Wilf? Sorry you Stood the Circle yet?'

Wilf asked sardonically, 'Sorry you didn't?'

With a laugh, Robert placed his hands on the table before him. 'What? And miss all this fun? Never! So tell me, what conclusions have you come to?'

'Why do you insist on taking this all as one almighty joke, eh? Your brother comes that close to execution at the hands of the judges and now stands to spend the rest of his life a virtual prisoner here, and there is a real possibility that the Guilde Proctor may have some powers of his own. On top of that we have the first exposure of one of our number for almost a century – not to mention a confirmed Malachi at court. We have to make a decision about what to do. A decision which could endanger the entire Enclave. I don't think there is anything at all amusing about any of this.'

Robert just smiled. 'Perhaps you just don't have a sense of humour. I don't see any need for you to do anything other than warn your people to keep their heads low for a while.'

Wilf slammed his hand down on the table. 'Damn it, Robert, I'm serious!'

The smile vanished. 'So am I. Deadly serious.'

He paused to allow Henry time to find a seat and pour him some wine. Taking the cup, Robert leaned forward to rest his elbow on the table. With the wine raised in mock salute, he smiled again. 'You can't make a decision about something you know nothing about. It's foolish. And don't think I say that lightly – with my brother now a permanent resident here, I have a vested interest in keeping him safe. He is, if nothing else, my sole heir and unless I decide otherwise, he will remain so. It doesn't matter that he's officially dead. When you're secluded up here as you are, away from real life down in the valleys, it's easy for you to forget that there are other considerations to be taken into account.'

Henry leaned back in his chair and folded his arms. 'I don't see what this has to do with the matter at hand. What difference does Finnlay's status make?'

Robert shrugged. 'Quite a bit – to me. I'm merely stating my reasons for objecting to your imminent decision.'

'Oh?' Wilf's face creased in anger. 'And you know what that decision is, do you?'

'Certainly I do. You're curious about the presence Jenn felt at court. You intend to send someone to Marsay to find out who it is, what their intentions are and, assuming our mystery man is not Vaughn himself, ask them to join you. You want to find out if this Malachi Valena has any real influence on the King and whether the split in the church will herald a softening of the official stance against sorcery. Correct me if I'm wrong.'

Nobody did. Instead, looks were exchanged, glances avoided. Anything in fact, other than a response. Finnlay tried to gauge what they were thinking, but it was impossible. Fortunately, Patric was keeping quiet.

Henry leaned forward on his elbow, his voice level and sincere. 'I don't want to reopen the old argument, Robert, but you must understand our position here. For almost five hundred years the Enclave has survived against all opposition, sometimes from within, but mostly from without. We have come very close at times to actual discovery, and our current measures are a product of that constant danger. We've worked hard over the centuries to break through the morass of ignorance our heritage has left us, but still we fail. All along we believed that one day we would see a sorcerer who would be able to unlock the secrets of the Key and perhaps eventually teach us enough to release us from this prison. It is the one hope that continues to bind us all together – a hope, I might add, that would free your brother along with the rest of us.'

He paused and took a breath, folding his hands together. 'From the first day you came here, most of us believed you were that sorcerer, but you have always refused to join us. We now understand from Finnlay that the Key told you never to Stand the Circle. We are flexible, we can change direction. If there is the slightest possibility that there's a sorcerer at court who is powerful enough to shield himself from even your powers so that you were unaware of his existence, then we have a moral obligation to find him. Even if it is Vaughn.'

'Actually,' Robert murmured with a glance at Finnlay, 'to be honest, the Key said nothing about the Circle to me all those years ago. I know you all think I've been lying about it – after what my brother told you, I don't blame you. But the truth is as I have always maintained. The Key's message to me was entirely private and has nothing whatsoever to do with the Enclave. I will even go so far as to accept the possibility that I was indeed supposed to Stand the Circle – who knows? What I do know is that if you send someone to court to seek out this stranger you will place the Enclave – and everyone in it – in extreme danger. You don't know what you're dealing with, and by the time you find out it could be very much too late.'

'I don't believe this!' Wilf snapped, his patience finally at an end. 'Have you any idea how ridiculous this all sounds? If you believed you were supposed to Stand the Circle why in the name of the gods didn't you do so before? Oh, yes, I remember – it was to protect your precious independence! Well, where has that independence got you, eh? Where? And are you now just waiting for me to die so you can take my place? How dare you come here and tell us what decisions we should or should not make. You gave up the right to have a say in matters here when you refused to take Marcus's place. Oh, I know what you would have us do: we should sit here and do nothing and continue to pine after the great Earl of Dunlorn, wishing he could be persuaded to take on his destiny; to finally take his place among sorcerers. Go on, Robert, deny it!'

'Just wait a moment.' Finnlay raised both hands, not daring to look at his brother for fear of what he might see. Something had only just occurred to him. Something important. 'There is a possibility that I may have over-estimated what the Key said to me that day.'

'What?' Wilf demanded, annoyed at the way his tirade had been interrupted. 'What are you talking about now?'

'Just listen,' Finnlay replied, doing his best to emulate Henry's earlier tone of reason. 'I was angry with Robert over his refusal to Stand the Circle and when I heard those words coming from the Key I may just have applied my own meaning to them. Now that I think back on it, I may have misunderstood.'

Beside him, Robert leaned forward and held his gaze. 'What, exactly, did the Key say to you?'

Taking a deep breath, Finnlay quoted, ' "Plague not Robert of Dunlorn to Stand the Circle. His place is elsewhere and he has been forbidden to take any path other than his own. His destiny is written and that is the only salvation you will ever have from him. Leave him to that." '

With the smallest of whispers, Robert said, 'Why didn't you tell me this before?'

'Damn you!' Wilf bellowed. 'Damn both of you!'

'Please,' Ayn reached over and placed a calming hand on Wilf's arm. 'This will get us nowhere. Robert, if we don't send someone to court, we could be missing out on the one vital piece in the destiny of the Enclave. Neither of our people at Marsay are capable of such a task. It must come from here. Surely you can understand that.'

'Of course I can,' Robert looked at each of the councillors present. 'I understand your problem, but you don't understand the danger. There are factors at work here you know nothing about.'

Wilf made a rude noise and plumped back in his seat. With a sneer, he folded his arms and said, 'Well, go on. Acquaint us with them. What factors?'

In reply, Robert turned to Finnlay. 'Did you tell them everything?'

Everything except the caves and the rod – and Berenice. He would never tell anyone about that. Robert must know at least that much. 'Yes. Everything.'

'Then they have no excuse, do they?' Robert raised a jaunty eyebrow and addressed the council once more. 'Has it not occurred to you that several of these recent events may be connected? To borrow one of Patric's favourite themes, I find it difficult to believe that it is pure coincidence that Jenn was the one to sense this stranger.'

'Why shouldn't she?' Henry murmured. 'Her powers are different to ours – and she's very strong.'

'You don't know that she's that different. But even if you're right, don't you think it's strange that she was one of those children abducted – and we already know the fate of another – in the company of a Malachi.'

Finnlay blurted before he could stop himself, 'You're not suggesting that this presence at court is the man responsible for the abductions!'

Robert leaned back in his seat. 'I won't say it's the same man – he was old, remember. But who's to say they aren't connected in some way? Why would this person try to pressure Jenn? Why her and none of us? Why not me? Or Murdoch? Why is he so interested in Jenn?'

There was no immediate answer and Finnlay glanced at Patric, who raised his eyebrows in response.

'I'm sorry, Robert,' Ayn eventually replied, 'but that doesn't really change anything. For all we know, this sorcerer thinks he is isolated and sensed something from Jenn. Perhaps he tried to reach her.'

'She said the sensation was entirely evil.'

'She's untrained, Robert, how would she know what she's sensing?'

'In that case,' he replied, 'she may not have sensed anything at all. Look, I'm not suggesting for one moment that you ignore this new player – that would be pointless. I am merely suggesting you do nothing about it for the moment.'

'And do what?' Henry murmured.

'Leave it to me. Let me deal with it.'

Stunned silence filled the council chamber for several long moments. Finnlay's attention was wholly on Robert. Was it possible? Was he really going to act at last? Did he mean to . . .

Wilf slowly rose to his feet. 'Am I hearing right? Did you just say you were actually going to do something?'

'I did.' Robert replied, glancing up. 'Don't die of shock, Wilf – as yet, I still have no intentions of taking your place, so don't go rushing it. Yes, I want the Enclave to stay away from Marsay, from the King, Vaughn and whoever it is that Jenn sensed there. At least until I've had a chance to find out more. You risk all you've accomplished so far if you expose the Enclave in this manner, especially in light of Finnlay's arrest. If you are right – and this sorcerer is powerful enough to have avoided me for all the years I was at court – then that person is surely powerful enough to overcome whoever you send there. They have been shielded for a reason – and perhaps that reason is that they have no wish to be discovered by other sorcerers. There are a myriad reasons why you should do as I suggest.'

'This is ridiculous,' Wilf grumbled.

Henry, however, sat forward and said, 'You're not telling us everything, are you?'

'I never took the oath to the Enclave, Henry. I'm under no obligation to tell you anything at all.'

'No,' Henry said flatly. 'You swore an oath to the King instead. How are we to know where your allegiances lie? You refuse to tell us what we wish to know, you will not explain why – and at the same time you expect us to trust you to investigate this sorcerer at court, the same court where your old friend Selar resides. You deliberately influenced Jenn to leave the Enclave so that we could do nothing with her. You have always guarded your independence from us, refused to join us, regardless of how important it is. You cannot honestly expect us to trust you.'

'Now wait a moment,' Finnlay interjected, 'are you suggesting that my brother would betray the Enclave?'

'It's all right, Finn,' Robert shook his head briefly, 'I can see their point. I just don't understand it. After all these years of them asking me to help, when I do, they refuse to trust me.'

'Then tell us what the Key told you,' Wilf snapped. 'Then we'll trust you. For once, Robert, tell us the whole truth.'

'No.'

'Robert,' Finnlay hissed, 'are you sure you can't?'

'Absolutely,' he smiled, 'I can't do or say anything more to convince them. They must make their decision without my help.'

Henry's jaw jutted out. 'Perhaps not. Perhaps there's another way we can be sure of you. The Key.'

'The Key?' Wilf repeated in a flat voice. 'You actually want to allow him access to the Key now?'

Henry shrugged. 'It's the only way. Will you do it, Robert?'

There was a sudden increase in tension around Robert's eyes. Finnlay swallowed, but could say nothing, do nothing to help him. What was he thinking? Would he face the Key again, for the first time in twenty years? Did he dare?

'Well?' Henry insisted.

'No. I won't. I can't.'

'There it is again!' Wilf waved his arms in frustration.

'Then our decision is made,' Ayn said quietly, rising to her feet. 'We will send someone to Marsay to contact this unknown sorcerer. I will leave in two days.'

'No!' Robert sprang up, pinning Ayn with that terrible gaze of his. For long seconds they stayed like that, the air almost alive with tension. Then slowly, gradually, Robert dropped his shoulders in defeat. 'Very well, you win. I'll go to the Key. In fact, I'll do it now if you like and save you the suspense.'

The great cavern was almost empty, but the galleries above soon filled with spectators. This event was too unique to miss. Finnlay just wished they'd all go away. This was no game, no trifling occasion to be toyed with. Robert didn't need an audience.

Finnlay left the others standing to one side of the Key and followed Robert to the base of the steps. There, hanging on its ornate trapeze at the end of the hall, was the innocuous-looking bell, dull and lifeless. The moment Robert took the first of the three steps, it would awaken.

Robert came to a halt and gazed up at the bell. Finnlay came close and murmured, 'Are you sure you want to do this? After what happened last time?'

'What choice have I got, Finn?' Robert turned to face him, his gaze steady and entirely open. 'This time I've been pushed into a corner and I don't know another way out. For twenty years I've fought against doing this and now it seems I must do it by choice. No matter what the others think, I have no desire to see the Enclave destroyed. I need time – and this is the only way I can get the council to give it to me.'

'But what if . . .'

'No, Finn,' Robert smiled gently. 'Go back and take your place with them. That's where you belong.'

Finnlay held Robert's gaze for a moment, then nodded slowly. Was Robert saying goodbye? It sounded like it. But why? What had the damned Key said to him all those years ago?

He turned away and took his place with the council. His questions would be answered soon enough.

Robert lifted his foot on to the first step and in that instant, the bell began to ring, long deep peals which sang through the cavern. He raised his left hand, his *ayarn* caught between his fingertips. Abruptly the bell dissolved into the familiar black orb and hung there, shining as though wet

437

with dew. The ringing ceased but as the last echo faded away, Finnlay began to hear voices, coming directly from the Key itself. At first the words were indistinct and garbled and then with a sigh, they started to take shape and meaning. The Key was speaking to Robert again after nearly twenty years of silence but this time, Finnlay could hear what it said. Everyone could!

*You come again to us, Robert of Dunlorn. You come with questions, but you do not wish to hear the answers. She speaks to you, but you do not listen. You each have the gift of mindspeech but you communicate nothing. You are Bonded together but you walk away. She has touched the stone which binds your power and healed the wounds within it. Though you still fight us, you cannot win. Your destiny is written in your blood. You may run from it but you cannot avoid it for ever.*

Jenn! Finnlay felt a shudder of fear run down his spine. The Key must be talking about Jenn! Patric was right. But how . . .

The Key continued: *Let her live not nor be not alone. For she will be the guiding light against the Angel of Darkness. She is the light of hope and that which will break us. We strive for her life even as she for our destruction. She is the last of her line. All ends and begins with her. Cherish and rejoice in her and be Bonded with her for all eternity.*

A hushed silence filled the chamber. For a moment, Finnlay thought the Key had finished. Then, before he could move, more words came.

*Your anger will succeed where you would fail. Hasten towards your true path and come not again to these your brothers until she is among them. Always remember she is the Ally. You, Robert of Dunlorn, are the Enemy.*

With that, a searing white light shot from the Key and pinned Robert to his place. He stiffened as it held him, his face writhing in agony. For long seconds he remained frozen until briefly the light intensified, focusing its heat on the *ayarn* in his hands. Then, with a deafening explosion, the *ayarn* shattered into a thousand pieces. Robert was knocked over by the blast, landing on his back. As the last of the stone shards landed on the floor around him, the Key withdrew the light and returned to its original shape.

Finnlay rushed forward and sank to his knees beside his brother. Robert was dazed and struggled to sit up. As Finnlay helped him, the others gathered around. For a moment, Finnlay ignored them and whispered urgently, 'Was that it? What it said to you before?'

Robert frowned. 'Only the middle part. But the rest . . .'

'Well, you wanted an answer, Henry,' Wilf said firmly, unable to keep the triumph out of his voice, 'and you got it. You were right. It seems Dunlorn has been keeping quite a lot from us, and obviously for his own purposes. He and Jenn share this mindspeech talent – and he's seen fit to keep it from us! How can that be personal? All these years he lied to us. He refused to tell us this prophecy. How can he say this has nothing to do with us? As far as I'm concerned, that only seals his fate.'

Robert climbed to his feet and Finnlay turned around to Wilf. 'But you don't understand. Robert never lied. He couldn't tell you about it before. The Key literally wouldn't let him . . .'

'Do you think I give a damn? Do you think I care what plots your brother is indulging in? He has strung us along for too many years now and I'm sick of it! You can stay here if you wish, Finnlay but as soon as he is fit enough to leave, Robert will depart the Enclave and never return. From the moment he leaves here, I forbid him ever to come back. Do you understand?'

'But, Wilf . . .'

'Don't argue with me, Finnlay!' the old man thundered back. 'The Key has given its judgement. It has branded your brother as an enemy. It is the Key itself that banishes him from the Enclave. He is condemned by his own actions!'

'It's all right, Finn,' Robert murmured, placing a hand on his shoulder. 'I'll go. It's for the best.'

Robert turned to face the council, his back straight, his eyes ablaze with a fire that had been gone for too long. 'I will go, but despite what the Key has just shown you all, I have no intention of doing anything it says. There are powers at work here we do not understand and I, for one, refuse to be a part of them. Do what you wish – I cannot stop you. And now the Key has destroyed my *ayarn*, I cannot even use my powers. I'm not even sure I can make another *ayarn* now. Is this what you want? There is a warning here if you're willing to see it. This,' he pointed to the silent bell a few feet away, 'is your real enemy. It took me until now to realize that. By all means banish me from the Enclave, but whatever you do, do not trust the Key and what it tells you.'

'Save your words for someone who will trust them, Robert. I want you gone from here by tomorrow night.'

Without another word, Wilf turned on his heel and stalked away. Bewildered, confused and generally unhappy, the rest of the council followed – and Ayn with them.

A hollow breeze drifted around the cavern, chill and ominous, like an empty grave at midnight. Finnlay shivered, but his cold seemed to come from within, hastened by the truth.

'It seems you're finally on your own, brother,' Robert murmured.

Finnlay slowly turned to face him, his eyes wide in wonder. 'Is it true? Can you really mindspeak? Was it you who warned me you were on your way to rescue me?'

Robert nodded. 'I can, but only with Jenn. She was the one who warned you. I only learned the trick later. Aren't you going to ask me why I didn't tell you? Tell everyone?'

'Well, it's obvious, isn't it? They wouldn't have left her alone. As it is . . .'

'As it is, they still won't – and now I can do nothing to protect her.'

That fire was still there, in Robert's eyes. Protecting Jenn was very important to him. So important that he'd lied to them all and brought this banishment down on his own head. Was this part of the Bonding?

It was difficult to assimilate so much so quickly. Finnlay went on, 'But that wasn't all the Key told you the first time,

440

was it? There was something else – you said something dangerous. Can you talk about it now?

'No. As I said before, even if I could, I wouldn't – especially not now.'

'Why especially?'

Robert dropped his gaze to the floor and the shards of his *ayarn*. 'The Key said it, Finn. I'm the Enemy.'

'It told you that before?'

'No. That was new.'

'And the Bonding? What does it mean?'

Robert smiled. He placed an arm around Finnlay's shoulder and turned him towards the exit. 'Nothing, brother. Absolutely nothing. This Bonding thing is so old I doubt it means anything now.'

'But the Key said . . .'

'Don't trust the Key, Finn. Don't trust anyone.'

'Not even you?'

Robert paused at the entrance to the tunnel and faced his brother squarely. 'Especially not me. For whatever reason, I – and Jenn – seem to be the focus of the Key's intentions. By all means, trust her. So far the Key has said nothing to her and she is, to all intents and purposes, free from its taint. I want you to do your best to keep her away from it.'

'I will, I promise – but what are you going to do now?'

In that moment, the awesome confidence Robert had always exuded suddenly dropped away. What remained was nothing more than raw pain and dull defeat. 'I'm going home, Finn. To face the Guilde's questions about you. To face Mother. To lie. I tried to do something and failed again. I thought that if I helped just a little then I could protect you and Jenn. That I could stop this before it gets too far. But I was wrong. I can no more help the Enclave than I could help Berenice. Any attempt I make to do anything, to change anything, will end in failure. It seems the Key will only let me travel one path. I have no choice now but to continue fighting it.'

'But why?' Finnlay whispered, awed by the depth of Robert's despair. 'Why fight it?'

441

'Because I know what will happen if I don't.' He sighed and gazed along the tunnel for a moment. 'It's almost dawn now. I'd better prepare to leave. There's no point in staying and aggravating things more. I have to get home and tell Mother you're not really dead. By Serin's breath, that's going to be a fun conversation!'

With visible clarity, Finnlay saw the façade shift back into place, heard the voice resume its old tone. Once more, Robert looked the image of calm certainty, quiet confidence and easy charm, impervious to all the deep wounds life had inflicted on him. In all these years, this was the greatest piece of sorcery Finnlay had seen Robert perform.

Finnlay stopped walking and reached out a hand to Robert's shoulder. 'If you go now, Robert ... I must stay here and you can't come back ... I won't see you again, will I?'

Robert shook his head and smiled, laughter dancing in his eyes. 'Come now, Finn. You never liked having me around anyway. You were much happier when I was out of the country.'

'But that was different, Robert. That was before I understood.'

'And do you understand now?'

Finnlay met that steady gaze, but this time the fear, the anger and frustration were gone. For the first time in his life, he could look at Robert and see the truth. He nodded. 'Yes, I do.'

Robert raised his eyebrows, both cynical and vulnerable at the same time. A typical contradiction. 'You're doing well, brother. Now you also have something in common with Jenn. But please, if she comes here, keep her away from the Key. I don't know why, but I have the feeling it wants her.'

'But what do you want, Robert?'

His brother only smiled. 'Come on, Finn. I'll need some help packing.'

The End
of
EXILE'S RETURN
First Book of Elita

The story continues
in
VOICE OF THE DEMON
Second Book of Elita